To Cathy
my good, true friend.

HAWK'S GIFT

By

Mary M. Forbes

Hope you enjoy

Mary Forbes

DEDICATION

This book is dedicated to my husband George, my two sons, Shaun and Paul and my daughter, Natasha. This work couldn't have been completed without the patience and encouragement of my family.

Joan Choma, my friend, who introduced me to Beverley and believed in me. And Beverley Jones, author and mentor. Without her editing, suggestions, knowledge and help this book would still be waiting on a shelf.

My brother Pat and my sister, Nola, who helped me with my children, my lack of time and even financially over the years, always believing this day would come.

Shirley Wolford, my friend and critiquing partner through the Romance Writer's Association who wasn't afraid to tell me if 'something just wasn't working' or if 'something was especially good'.

And last, to my mother, now deceased, who said she only wished she could live long enough to see this day. I believe she can.

Copyright 2004 Mary M. Forbes
All rights reserved. No part of this book may be used or reproduced in any manner whatsoever without written permission from the publisher or author, except in the case of brief quotations embodied in critical articles and/or reviews.

Acknowledgments: Shauna Crist – ExpressMedia
Beverly Jones – Author and Friend.

Printed and Bound by: ExpressMedia – Tennessee, USA

ISBN 0-9737244-0-4

Works by Mary M. Forbes:
Hawk's Gift
Paradise on the Horizon
One Dance with a Stranger
Alberta Wild Rose
Moonbeam's Desire

FORBES
 Publications
#1 - 3 Cactus Crescent
Osoyoos, British Columbia
V0H 1V1
E-mail: marymforbes@hotmail.com

PROLOGUE

Winnipeg, Manitoba: Summer 1860

Wind spirits spoke softly through the dried grasses. Rustling reeds swayed in rhythm with a soaring hawk overhead. Sun-bleached bones were first revealed, and then concealed by the undulating prairie foliage. The smell of freshly butchered meat mingled with the warm winds. A monarch butterfly, now forgotten, fluttered away to another sweet, fresh buttercup.

Five-year-old Damien Larocque stood beside his crying *Tante* Amelia, seeing only horror in this deceivingly serene place. Silent tears slipped down his high cheekbones. Bottomless black eyes watched the sinister incident that was taking place. He felt trapped in a narrow tunnel leading him to an emptiness he couldn't bear.

Finally, his short legs moved and he scrambled towards his beautiful mother. Whimpers, like that of a puppy, started in his throat. Stumbling, unable to release the heavy lump strangling him, he forced himself to continue running. His breath came out in short, rasping gasps for air. The buffalo still looked very far away.

Snorting wildly, the buffalo relentlessly tramped Damien's mother back into Mother Earth's womb. From the corner of his wet eyes, Damien saw his father galloping towards the broken body. Both horse and rider were a brown ribbon of desperation, crossing the rolling hills. Then, with a shrill scream, the horse stumbled, tumbling head over heels like a bouncing ball. Another hoarse cry echoed across the land as the other hunters could only watch, helpless.

Damien changed course, running awkwardly toward his father. His heart pounded rapidly against his taut chest. Still he kept running. He reached his father. The dying pony moaned in anguish. Blood trickled slowly from his father's usually laughing mouth. Philippe Larocque's neck was severed nearly in half.

"*Papa... papa...*"

Dropping to his knees, Damien began to shake his father. Why was *papa* sleeping when that fearsome buffalo was hurting *maman*?

Damien lashed furiously against his father's chest. Philippe refused to move.

"*Papa, maman est mal...*"

A few yards away, there was little except torn cloth and mashed flesh to indicate his mother had ever existed.

Overhead, the hawk swooped down. Then, straight as an arrow, he darted back into the skies. His piercing voice ripped through the breezes. For a second Damien felt the brush of wings against his damp cheeks. A single feather floated gently to the earth. Reaching down, Damien picked the feather up, caressing its softness. Calmness invaded his heart. For a long moment he felt peace. How he wished he could be that hawk, flying free in the winds - feeling no pain.

CHAPTER ONE

Winnipeg, Canada: 1881

He was the son of a *Metis* hunter. She was the daughter of an aristocrat. How he knew this, Damien wasn't sure. Maybe it was the way she stood, tall and arrogant, although she wasn't much over five feet. Perhaps it was the way she was wringing her slender, white fingers or the look of utter confusion in her green, cat-like eyes. That bewitching gaze was turned in his direction, begging him to help her. And Damien, being the true gentleman he knew himself to be, raised his hand and quietly bid one thousand dollars for the little wench.

He had no idea where he was going to get that kind of money. Nor did he care. The gleaming metal pistol held ominously in his low-slung holster and his huge roan horse, tied outside the saloon, were more than sufficient to ensure he got whatever he desired. He had no use for money and a thousand dollars was a ludicrous amount to pay for a bit of fluff, virgin or not.

Still, he couldn't very well let Joseph Mills have her either. Joe was notorious for mistreating horses and women. And this *petite fille* would be fortunate to come away with her life if Joe got his hands on her. *Mon Dieu*, what ran through a female's mind to make her enter this prostitute profession?

Roberta Taylor, Bobbie to her friends, was never so petrified in her whole nineteen years. She was on a stage with a crowd of horrid looking men ogling her like dogs slavering over a tasty piece of meat. She felt icy-cold and thoroughly violated. How dare they? And how dare Gertrude ignore her pleas? She had no means of escape, all because this – stupid woman was holding her immobile and with the help of her enormous bodyguard as well.

When she heard Damien's *un mille dollars*, her mouth dropped open. Men would actually pay a thousand dollars for their selfish pleasure? Why? A thousand dollars would keep any man in this room for a year or two. Yet they would throw it all away for a moment's gratification? Aunt Hortense had always maintained men were a foolish lot, thinking only of what was below their belts, and never with their heads. Now Bobbie understood what she meant. A small shiver ran down her spine as curiosity took over. Was this particular act so pleasurable?

Her gaze darted over the smoke-clouded room, filled with bleary-eyed, leering men. In a strange way she felt gratified Damien had made a bid for her. He was seated near the stage, with a cigar clenched between strong, white teeth. He was certainly the only gentleman in this establishment. He dressed in a vested suit. His dark, waving hair looked clean. His arresting face was clean-shaven and he had a very dark tan, indicating he spent much time outdoors.

Her breath caught in her throat. Gentlemen, to her knowledge, were normally pale-skinned. So maybe he wasn't exactly a gentleman. But he was definitely her first choice in this crowd of rowdy, repulsive-looking men.

"Well girl – it looks like the breed gets you first." Gertrude, the plump, heavily rouged owner of this questionable auction, grabbed her arm, yanking it up behind her waist. She gave Bobbie a shove.

Bobbie winced as pain shot up through her shoulder blade.

Ignoring her puny struggles, Gertrude turned to grin down at Damien. "Can you afford her, Damien?"

"Breed? What on earth do you mean?" Bobbie tried to pull her arm away and groaned. Fingers biting in cruelly, the woman continued to ignore her.

Bobbie's arm was already a mass of black and blue marks from trying to escape this creature's hold. Gertrude didn't care. She was obviously out to make money and refused to listen to Bobbie's pleas. Bobbie was not the girl Gertrude thought she was. She was not Gertrude's latest virgin-prostitute.

Bobbie tilted her chin, drawing her lips together in a pout of disapproval.

"*Bien sur, Gertrude, mignon.*" Damien grinned, squinting his dark eyes disarmingly as the smoke from his cigar drifted upward.

Reaching for his billfold, he drew it out of his vest pocket and tossed some paper on the table. "*Voila – un mille dollars.*"

Gertrude pushed Bobbie aside and jumped down from the low platform. Eagerly, she scooped up the money and pushed it down her flamboyant, low cut bodice. Her ample bosom jiggled with pleasure.

"Go take her, me boy. A lot of others are gonna want her before the night's done."

"*L'amour – ce n'est pas vite.*" Damien winked broadly at the bulky woman giving her a wicked grin.

"Well then go slowly. I guess you paid enough for that." Gertrude, well past forty, giggled like a schoolgirl. "You'd charm the pants off the devil hisself."

Bobbie groaned. She stepped back, bumping into the huge man who had helped Gertrude drag her up to the stage. Her saviour was speaking clearly and fluently – in French! She hardly understood a word he said. She turned to glare at the man behind her.

Gertrude's bodyguard wore a tailored white shirt, the sleeves rolled up to his elbows, which did nothing to disguise his tremendous bulk. His nose had been broken, making him look monstrous. His cold, pale blue gaze shifted down idly to her face. His smile was as cruel as the rest of his appearance.

"What's wrong, lass?" His voice was hoarse and guttural. "You looking for a real man?"

"That man... is French! Oh my lord." Bobbie whispered to herself. Would he understand her when she demanded he set her free? Then she stared blankly at the bodyguard. "What do you mean, a real man?"

She really didn't have a clue as to what Gertrude, Damien or the bodyguard were saying. Although both Gertrude and this brute did speak English, the words were foreign to her ears. '*Breed*', '*Real man*'? She had always assumed that all men were alike when it came to this matter. Perhaps not. Aunt Hortense had never really explained this bedding matter, other than in very vague terms of a woman's duty and singing national anthems and such.

And she loathed Frenchmen, truly she did. The man her father expected her to marry was French. That was why she was in this precarious position now. She had run away from her wealthy, influential father.

"I guess he is partly French." The rude bodyguard chuckled. "Why don't you just come along with Brian here? I'll show you what a real man can do."

"Not on your life!" Bobbie blurted out, then pressed her fingers to her mouth. Aggravating these people was obviously not a solution. Perhaps Brian, unlike Gertrude, would listen to reason. "I'm really not a... I'm not this woman Gertrude was expecting. I'm a reporter. I just came to interview Mrs... Gertrude."

"Yeah? And what do you think I am? An angel sent down to protect little girls?" Brian snorted. His full lips twisted in sarcasm. "You can be whatever you want, lass. But Damien will still take you. Watch out, he's been drinking pretty heavy."

"And what is that supposed to mean to me? You all talk in riddles around here. I've had about enough. I want someone to call the police." Bobbie stamped her foot, fully frustrated. Brian wasn't about to listen either. She would have to rely on her own wits to escape this mess.

Deafening music from the tinkling piano flooded the room again, drowning out Brian's comment. Clamorous voices jarred her eardrums. She wanted to scream, but was sure no one would hear her.

Closing her stinging eyes, she stepped off the stage and began moving toward a wall. If she could make it to a wall, she could perhaps feel her way to the door. She hit against something solid. She felt hands clawing at her bodice. Then she heard her expensive silk gown tearing away from her shoulder. The grating sound caused her flesh to pucker in protest.

She let out a terrified shriek, and then stumbled, falling against Damien, who was pushing his chair back. Gently righting her, Damien kicked the chair aside and shoved his jacket back to reveal a pistol.

Jerking away, Bobbie flinched. Was he going to shoot her? Perspiration broke out across her face.

No! He was facing the man who had just torn her dress. Was she about to witness a real live gunfight? Her stomach churned. She must be dreaming.

"If you weren't so damned late getting here, girl, I could have avoided this." Gertrude hissed in her ear, grabbing her arm again. "I was afraid this would happen. They're all drunk now and it's all your fault."

"Pardon?" Bobbie asked in stunned amazement.

Fascinated, she stared at Damien. He was crouched down, looking like a cat – a sleek and dangerous cat. Shivering, she turned back to Gertrude. She didn't want to see anyone die. "Are you saying this is my fault?"

Everyone in this western town was crazy. When she wrote her report tomorrow, she would most certainly side with Reverend Silcox. And she'd had such high hopes this story would make another of her spectacular, titillating articles the people in Toronto loved to read. She had planned to take Gertrude's side against the big, oppressive church. When she's met the Reverend, she hadn't liked him at all. He was pompous and righteous. But now, she liked Gertrude even less. These Saloons were obviously run by evil people. They deserved to be shut down.

"I am not your silly prostitute." Taking a deep breath, Bobbie tried one more time to convince Gertrude. "I am a reporter. Surely, even out here, you must have heard of Taylorson Press. I'm the Taylor's son, you obnoxious woman."

"Well, girl. You're awfully skinny, that's for sure. But you ain't no son. You can say whatever you want but tonight you work for me. I have to stop that damn Damien from going Injun on me again!" Gertrude snarled. "I don't have time for your squeamish nonsense."

"Damien – No!" Gertrude turned back to the man crouched down like a panther.

A shot cracked out above the music.

"Damn it, you stupid breed – you shot me!" The other man growled his pain. He clutched his arm tightly. Blood seeped between his filthy fingers.

Bobbie noticed the man's twisted, matted beard and capacious coat straining against his bare belly and shuddered. He was twice Damien's size and would surely hurt him badly.

"I'm going to kill you..." Like an ox, the man charged Damien.

Through the smoke haze, Bobbie saw Damien, standing with his legs apart, grinning. He casually blew against the vapour escaping from his gun. She didn't see him move yet suddenly he was standing out of the path of the charging man. His foot slipped back to intercept him. The man tripped, falling heavily to the floor with a loud howl.

"*Joseph, elles c'est miner.*" Damien drawled. His voice was soft and menacing. Bobbie understood. He was saying she was his! She gasped.

"Aw Joe, let's just wait. He bought her fair and square. Gertie will let us have her next." The speaker was tall and skinny. He wore a heavy tweed coat, which covered him from his neck to his knees. He took Joe's arm and helped him up. He began to lead him back into the crowd.

"That Damien's meaner than a skunk when he's drinking. He shot me..." Joe whined.

"*Vien, mignonne.*" Damien whispered in Bobbie's ear.

His voice sounded like smooth water, rippling over a pebbled bed.

Bobbie let out a short, squeaky yelp of terror. *Vien* – come! She heard her teeth chattering against each other. She was freezing cold. Her hands moved up to rub her arms. She couldn't move.

He was dangerous. Everyone here said so. Yet, looking around this offensive room, she could see no other alternative. He must help her escape. There was no one else. Why hadn't she listened to her brother, Gilbert, when he'd ordered her to stay in her warm, safe hotel room? She was treading in very hazardous waters, heading directly towards a waterfall.

"*Je vais partir, mignon.*" Damien tossed a crooked, apologetic grin in Gertrude's direction. Turning, he took Bobbie's elbow and began steering her through the jeering crowd of men.

Slowly the men moved aside, faces twisted in excitement and anticipation. Her heart thumped wildly against her bosom. Bobbie realized they were all anticipating their turn. Moaning, she tried to focus on a solution to her dilemma. A man's arm brushed against her breast, making her realize it was nearly bare. With shaking hands, she tried desperately to pull the fabric of her gown over her chest. She leaned back against Damien. His solid frame was oddly comforting and hot! Soon, he would do... that... to her.

She was the daughter of Sir Miles Taylor, Minister of Immigration and owner of two successful enterprises, a newspaper office and a publishing company, both located in Toronto. She was a lady. How could these people treat her like a common strumpet? And how could she escape?

Her mind was churning. She was unable to think straight. Closing her eyes, she willed this whole matter to disappear. She wasn't really here. She was at home, in her father's elaborate mansion, dreaming. This was a nightmare. Soon she would wake up to the smell of hot chocolate and toast as her maid came in to start her fire and bring breakfast.

Tears burned beneath her lashes. She would never be able to go home again. Her father was demanding that she marry Etienne LaVoie. She sincerely knew Etienne was a cruel, evil man and she despised the way he treated people and animals. She could still see Tom, her beloved cat, crumbled and mangled after Etienne killed him, just because she refused to lie for him. Then she saw Gilbert's horse, beaten nearly to death, the time Gilbert had refused to go to a gaming establishment with him. She could not understand why her father expected her to marry such a man.

Her shin hit against a wooden object. She winced and her eyes flew open. They were at the stairs that would lead them to those rooms above the saloon where men and women performed those mysterious deeds no one in her social circle would talk about. Faltering, she turned to look up into Damien's compelling features.

Lord, he was beautiful.

A jolting awareness hit her like a galloping stallion. She was instantly aware of the most disconcerting gaze she'd ever encountered. He was pure, unadulterated sex appeal and she felt her own gauche innocence. She stared into his face with dazed fascination. Vaguely, she knew it wasn't fear she was feeling.

"Can you take me somewhere else?"
"*Vous voulez etre bon, mignonne.*" Damien whispered in her ear. "*Vien.*"

He smiled sweetly, an appealing gesture that enslaved her further. Had he just said she was beautiful? She moved forward. Damien still held her elbow firmly. She could feel his body heat, radiating to encompass her and she welcomed his touch. Then they were standing by a pine-slate door which would take them to privacy and...

Moaning, she shook her head, trying to pry his fingers loose.

Damien smiled, letting go immediately. He reached over her shoulder and opened the door. He stepped around her. His palms, open and warm, reached out to slide down her bare arms. He grasped her fingers and with a gentle tug, he pulled her inside and closed the door.

He was so close she could smell his musk shaving lotion and... the whiskey on his breath. He grinned as if he understood her terrified expression. Reaching into his pocket he pulled out a flat metal flask.

"*Ce va vous remede.*" His meaning was clear when he held the bottle out.

Mechanically, she took the offered container and drank quickly. Fiery liquid slid down her throat. Choking, her eyes rounded in indignity. Whiskey! She had never before tasted strong alcohol and now she knew why. It was dreadful. Then she noticed her queasy tummy begin to recede. Warmth penetrated. She took another large gulp, allowing herself no time to consider her behaviour. She coughed sharply as her eyes watered.

"You know, my father was furious the time he caught me preaching against liquor down at the Union Station. Union Station is in Toronto... civilization! If you would only take me – I'd be glad to show you. I'm sure you'd like civilization..." She stopped for a breath. Her head was spinning.

She noticed Damien was staring at her lips with a puzzled smile on his face. He didn't appear to understand a single word she was saying. "Oh for heavens sake, surely you know English. I don't like French at all. It's nothing personal, but my father wants me to marry a Frenchman. I loathe him. My aunt always did say that a Frenchman always thinks he's God's gift to women and in my experience..."

Bobbie hiccupped loudly. Giggling, she covered her lips with her fingertips. What was happening? She couldn't control her speech and Damien was watching her with such an odd expression on his face.

"You are very attractive, as I'm sure you are aware, but..." She stared back into his dark, luminous eyes with fascination. "It's obvious you are French and maybe not too intelligent. Don't you understand any English? Everyone knows English! How can I make you understand? I don't want to insult you, but..."

"*Arret!*" There was a scowl on his handsome face now, although it did nothing to distract from his compelling looks.

"Humph!" Bobbie turned her back on him. What was he getting so huffy about? He was drunk and he was French. "I did ask you to speak English and you – can't! And that's why I said maybe not too intelligent. All intelligent people know English is the only truly civilized..." She turned to face him again.

Grimacing, he turned and moved to the window, lifting it and peering outside. "*Bon, un balcon. Vien.*"

"Pardon?" Bobbie stared at him, puzzled.

Did she understand him correctly? Did he want her to crawl out the window? Was it possible? She hadn't even started to plead her case yet.

Her gaze moved to the large bed, which took up the majority of floor space in this tiny room. The covers were tousled and soiled, indicating the type of activity performed here. Her stomach began churning again.

"Please speak English. I can't understand you." She whispered, unable to move.

Impatiently, Damien came back to grab her arm and he began pulling her towards the window. He was going to leave! Excitement surged within. He was going to help her escape.

"Wait!" Suddenly she stopped short, trying to dig her heels into the hard wooden floor. "Where are we going?"

Aunt Hortense always said not to trust a man. *'If they are willing to do something for you, then surely they'll want something dreadful in return'.* Bobbie could still hear her words, although dear Aunt Hortense had passed away nearly a year ago.

A blank stare crossed Damien's features.

"Why would you help me?" Bobbie managed to croak out. Her tongue tip licked against her dry lips.

Damien's eyes were suddenly smouldering. Then he shook his head and raised his eyebrows in a mocking manner. He chuckled.

"Damien, you god-damned bastard! There ain't no thousand dollars here." The muted sound of Gertrude's rage sounded through the closed door.

Then Bobbie could hear heavy footsteps on the stairs.

"*C'pourquoi.*" Damien smiled. Picking her up, he hoisted her out the window and onto the verandah.

Grabbing her hand, he continued moving swiftly towards the outdoor stairs. "Let's get out of here, *mignonne.*"

Perplexed, Bobbie stumbled along behind him. He spoke English with an intriguing Scottish accent.

CHAPTER 2

Damien kept his face impassive as he moved swiftly away from the saloon. But his thoughts were cynical. So she hated Frenchmen did she? He wondered if she would like his native half any better. Then he scowled. Narrowing his blurry eyes, he glanced back, trying to focus on her delightful figure. She was right. He was intoxicated and not too intelligent at this moment. This woman looked very much like Anne MacLeod. If she had a similar personality than she would despise a native even more than a Frenchman. He shook his head, trying to clear his mind. This little wench didn't appear to be anything like Anne though. In one breath she made him laugh and in the next he wanted to strangle her to shut her up. Was she really so naïve – and so arrogant?

He pulled her hastily down the wooden stairs and moved into the darkness. Snatching his horse's reins, he pushed forward, winding in behind Manitoba College and walked into the dirt packed back lane.

Bobbie could no longer hear Gertrude's hysterical screams when they moved quickly away from the saloon. There were no streetlights to guide them. In the enveloping darkness she could hear buzzing night insects, croaking frogs, and Damien's large horse panting down her back. The dark buildings along the dirt road looked menacing in the purple darkness. Grotesque shadows from the warehouses danced across them, blocking out what little light the stars created.

Frightened, Bobbie wondered if she should follow Damien any further away. Where was he taking her? He made not a sound. She couldn't even hear him breathing, although she was puffing like a steam engine. Her arm felt as though it were being torn from its socket. Yet he continued to move so fast she had to run to keep up.

Unused to the eerie remoteness of empty countryside, her normal competence deserted her. She had spent her entire life in crowded modern cities, first Toronto, then London, England. A shiver of fear raced down her back. She glanced over her shoulder at the receding lights of the brothels. They were walking past shanties and run-down shacks now. They were all dark.

"Stop!" Enough was enough. They weren't being chased anymore. And it was obvious there wasn't anyone within miles of them.

"What's wrong?" He stopped, letting her arm drop. "Did you want to stay?"

"Of course!" She muttered sarcastically. She sank to the ground, hoping nothing was crawling along to bite her. His voice, now that she could actually understand him was even more potent than before. "Where are you taking me?"

"Where do you want to go, *mignonne*?" He asked. His voice was low and filled with curiosity. She felt those gravel depths caressing her to the pit of her stomach.

This man was lethal and he didn't even have to touch her. She thought uneasily, that this man, if he applied any pressure, could make her do anything he wanted. Her first priority should be to get away from him.

"If you would just take me back to my hotel room, that would be fine." Bobbie sputtered, mesmerized by his gaze that was sliding over her with a fierce gleam in their depths. "I thank you for – um – redeeming my virtue – but I really should..."

Belatedly, she thought to pull her ripped gown up to cover herself. His liquid gaze kept dropping down to that particular area of her body. Why wasn't her half-dressed state embarrassing her as it should be? His eyes were filled with blatant appreciation. Her efforts seemed to be making matters worse instead of better. The flimsy material was caught just below the swell of her bosom. Her breath stopped. A perplexing twinge inched its way to her belly.

"Allow me to help you, *mignonne*." Crouching down, Damien's long fingers efficiently grasped her sagging neckline, pulling the material up over her corset.

A startled labour for breath exploded when his thumb aimlessly brushed against one taut nipple. She whimpered her shock.

His hair was much too long, she decided, seeking faults where there were none. The silky strands fell forward, teasing her shoulder. His head was bent. Long, spiked lashes hid his hypnotic eyes from view. She wanted to touch him... touch his hair, touch his arm... Gulping, she looked downwards. Muscled thighs were taut beneath his trousers. She closed her eyes. He was beautiful – he was perfect. He was dangerous. She laughed with confusion. He was far prettier than any girl she knew.

"*Mon Dieu,* no wonder they all act like animals. You are exquisite, *mignonne.*" His voice was a low growl in his throat. "You should laugh all the time." His hand slipped inside her gown. His thumbs moved with delicate strokes along her nipples, mingled with both hands cupping the quivering mounds. Her eyes opened wide in alarm. Once again she couldn't breathe or speak. Damien was smiling, but there was a grim look in his eyes she couldn't understand. He looked angry. He leaned forward to slide his mouth along her smooth throat.

"You taste like lilacs, fresh and innocent…" His lips slipped down toward her chest.

"Stop it!" Chagrined, Bobbie pulled away, scrambling to her feet. Her legs trembled and she feared she might collapse.

In one suave motion he was looming over her. She saw the humour in his heavy-lidded eyes. He was not overly tall. She came up to his shoulders. Then she noticed the questioning expression in his luminous eyes and understood what he might be thinking.

"I am not a prostitute! Nor do I ever plan on becoming one." She swallowed deeply, dropping her gaze to the ground. "I want to go home now."

"Toronto or the hotel?" Damien smiled slightly. "Why were you in Gertrude's saloon? And what is your name *mignonne*?"

"Roberta Taylor and I was going to…" Bobbie hesitated when he stiffened.

"How interesting!" Damien's voice sounded suspicious. His eyes narrowed and looked like burning coal chips. His twisted sneer made his features look ruthless. "I met Gilbert Taylor tonight. He hired me to take Robert Taylor out to Big Bear's camp. Are you related to these men?"

"Gilbert is my brother and…" Bobbie muffled the gasp and stopped, trying to think.

Damien would be her guide for the next month or even longer. Gilbert had finally found a guide! They had been looking for one for nearly a month now. She wanted to run back to the hotel and hug Gilbert. He had indeed found her a magnificent companion. Then she sobered. This man had no intention of escorting a female into the wilds. His smooth actions and superior attitude indicated that he was yet another man who believed all women were weak creations put on this earth solely for a man's pleasure.

"And Robert?" Damien prodded.

"My brother as well. My twin brother." Bobbie answered emphatically, very pleased with herself.

Gilbert must have realized Damien, like all the others, would refuse to take her seriously. She supposed she would have to dress up like a man again. Would she be able to fool Damien? He appeared able to read her every thought. Both she and Gilbert needed this assignment desperately. Their father was supporting only one person here in Winnipeg. That was Gilbert. No one, including Sir Myles Taylor, realized that it was Bobbie, not Gilbert, who wrote the stories that helped make Taylorson Press such a success. Sir Myles also believed Bobbie was in England, not Winnipeg. He had runners searching for her there.

"Why were you in the saloon?" Damien was watching her very carefully.

"Because... I thought maybe I could work..." Bobbie shuffled her feet nervously, watching the dirt with great fascination. She wouldn't look into his face. Her mind was a jumbled mass of confusion, whirling for an explanation. "We need money and..."

"You are here with your two brothers and you have to work?" Damien shook his head, reaching over to tilt her face up to his. "Ah, *mignonne*, why are you so nervous? With two healthy brothers, why would you have to be the one supporting the family?"

He deliberately stepped closer, watching her face very closely. His eyes were narrowed in contemplation.

She could feel his breath, soft and feathery, along her cheek. His eyes were inches from hers. All coherent thoughts raced from her mind. She lowered her lashes, swallowing deeply. "I..." His touch sliced through her body. She shifted her gaze to his jaw, avoiding his eyes. "I'm feeling..."
"Now explain why you were going to work for Gertrude, please." Damien chuckled. His voice was still soft, but filled with cynical amusement. His palms moved down to caress her bare arms. His touch was hot, warming her chilled skin. "You can tell me, *mignonne*. I am not a monster, like Joseph."
"We need money." Bobbie ground out, pulling away.

He didn't believe her. He wouldn't take her to Big Bear. Then Sir Myles wouldn't get his story and wouldn't send Gilbert any more money. They would soon be starving at this rate, living on the streets and... and just maybe... she would have to work for Gertrude. A sob caught in her throat. Pity welled inside. ...And maybe she wasn't really lying after all. She tilted her chin, glaring into Damien's face.
"Don't your brothers have work? Surely Robert gets paid for his reporting job." Damien asked patiently. He wiped the tear from her cheek tenderly.
"Of course he does." Bobbie grimaced. He was softening. Did he believe her? "But he doesn't make enough to support us."
She moved back to sit on the ground. Her legs felt very wobbly. How much truth could she tell? And how many lies would she have to tell? She shivered.
"Gilbert does not have a job?" Damien squatted down beside her and tilted her chin up again.
"Not that I know of, ever." Bobbie answered in a bitter tone. Although she loved Gilbert, she had never seen two more useless people than her brother and Etienne. All they ever wanted to do was play. When she saw Damien's eyes narrow again, she thought it might be better to change the topic. "Do you have to leave right away?"
"Where?" He looked confused again.

"On your trip – Your taking my... my brother aren't you?"

"You will miss me?" Damien smiled disarmingly. "Unfortunately, I did agree to do this before I met you. I've already spent the advance Gilbert gave me. I must honour my contract, *non*?"

Still holding her chin, he tipped his head forward until their lips were nearly touching.

"You've already spent..." Bobbie gasped, leaning back.

Her mind buzzed precariously. The whiskey she'd consumed was making her bold. He was everything she believed him to be. He was extremely attractive, but just another foolish man. He would be in no position to refuse to take her, female or not, if he had already spent all his money.

"Do you have any left?" She asked cautiously.

"A little." Damien stood up. His eyes were narrowed again. "Why do you ask?"

"Just a question that's all. For no reason really." Bobbie stood as well. Slipping her arm through his, she pulled him forward. "Let's go."

Feeling no culpability whatsoever, she formulated her plan. He would spend everything he had tonight – on her virginity! Virginity was a highly overrated commodity, she decided recklessly. It was a rule invented by men in order to control women. If she were no longer a virgin, then her father would stop trying to marry her off. Etienne would not want her. Yes, it was an excellent idea. She giggled.

"Where are you taking me, *mignonne*?" Damien's eyes seemed very piercing. What was he thinking?

"Your place?" She suggested trying to act sophisticated and knowing she was failing miserably. She was petrified.

"Do you really want that?" Damien's voice was soft and sultry. He began leading her on. His horse followed.

She noticed they were moving further away from the town. The lights from the brothels were now in the distance, as was

Winnipeg's Main Street. They were still walking by a few little shacks on the outskirts of town.

"Where do you live?" She whispered, looking around anxiously.

"Nowhere! Everywhere." Damien's voice was laced with amusement. "I just thought you might like to repair your gown. My – um – cousin lives out here. Then perhaps I'll take you to a party."

Her plan was foolish. She couldn't do it. His lean fingers clung tenaciously, though they didn't actually hurt her. He would not let her go.

"I'll just go back to the hotel now." She whispered.

The night sounds of rustling grasses and noisy frogs were giving her a headache. Were there wild animals stalking about as well? She shivered apprehensively, searching the dark swaying grass.

"You are frightened by the dark, *mignonne*." Damien was laughing He jerked her against his sinuous thighs, holding her firmly by her taut, rounded bottom. She nearly swooned with embarrassment.

"Don't worry. I will protect you." Damien's lips were gliding down along her temple as his voice dropped, deep and sensual. "I see in your eyes you might like becoming my whore…"

Her breath snagged in her throat. His arms tied her securely in his grasp. Her dress was no protection against the heat of his body. Disoriented, she raised her gaze and was once more caught up in the magnetism of his alluring face. She wanted him to kiss her. Instinctively, she knew it would feel like nothing she'd ever experienced before.

"What are you asking me…? I can't seem to…" She felt extremely heated. His chest, beneath her trapped palms, felt like scalding steel, even through his silk shirt and vest. "You're so hot. Do you suppose we're ill?"

"Oh, *mignonne*." Damien burst into laughter, drawing back. He slung his arm around her shoulder and began to guide her further into the darkness. "You're just the distraction I need."

Damien took her to a one-room hut with a packed dirt floor. Bobbie's dazed eyes searched the dwarfish room. The smell of sulphur mingled with damp, cool earth as Damien lit a coal-oil lamp. The lamp was set on a timber slab attached to the wall, propped up by the hinges and two pieces of wood.

"Where does she sleep?" Bobbie asked tersely. From the few gowns hanging from wooden pegs in one corner, she assumed his cousin was female.

"On the floor."

His eyes held sardonic humour as Damien walked over to the dented and scratched metal trunk beneath the only window. He began rummaging through the contents.

He lifted his gaze to better view this strange little minx. She was the oddest combination of aggressive coquette and innocent child. She was not easily categorized. He wished he were sober. She was baffling. There must be something he was missing.

"Here it is." Standing, he stepped over to hand her a ragged cloth sewing kit. "Do you know how to sew, *mignonne?*"

"Of course I do."

He watched with amusement as Bobbie clumsily attempted to thread the needle. Moving over to straddle a bench, Damien pulled his flagon from his pocket. Seizing a battered tin cup from the dishes stacked in an unpainted crate nailed over the table, he indicated the drink was for her.

She finally managed to thread the needle and, without placing a knot at the end of the thread, she awkwardly pushed the needle through the soft material. Twisted thread hung precariously along the large tear, leaving a gaping hole. Her corset was still revealed with provocative allure.

"Perhaps a drink might help?" Dale murmured. He wondered if he should laugh or grab and ravish this enticing little wench. "I can see why you didn't choose a seamstress for your profession."

She appeared ready to decline. She looked down at the cup, then back to him. She watched him carefully as he took a swig from his tilted bottle. She seemed simultaneously fascinated and horrified. Her face revealed her every mood.

"Damned if your eyes aren't the colour of whiskey, and every bit as potent." Taking pity on her alarmed state, Damien reached out to pull her down to the bench where he sat. He knew all women responded extremely well to a compliment. And seeing her in the light, he had no reason to lie. She was a *petite ange*. Her smooth skin and golden hair matched her animated features perfectly. Her beautiful wide eyes tilted up, alluring and sexy. One moment they were green, the next they were the warm amber of aged whiskey.

Those same eyes he was admiring suddenly rounded in dawning horror. In the flickering lamplight he realized she could see him clearly as well. He watched her pupils dilate as they searched his features from his straight nose to the copper skin stretched across his high cheekbones. Their eyes met.

"Oh my Lord! You're not French. You're a heathen..." She was shivering. She looked towards the door, ready to bolt.

"Do you know your way home?" Damien grimaced, taking another drink.

"Pardon?" She gasped, standing to edge towards the opening.

"I just wonder if you really want to brave that wilderness outside – alone in the dark." Damien tried to silence the bitterness in his tone.

Most ladies soon discovered they liked his heathen blood well enough. Without exception, they expected something unusual from him. And since his aim was always to please beautiful women, he tried to give them exactly whatever they wanted.

His lips spread back over his teeth. He reached up and yanked her wrist, pulling her back to the bench. Further alarm marred her eloquent face.

"Actually, I'm *Metis*." He assured her solemnly. "I suppose I could be a Native – for you. You said you didn't care for Frenchmen."

"Louis Riel?" She blurted out. Sitting on the bench, she captured the filled cup with her free hand. Bringing it to her lips, she downed the entire contents in one nervous gulp. She coughed.

"You know Louis Riel?" Damien wanted to laugh.

"No. I have heard of him though. You look like a wolf." She looked ready to have a heart attack. "I'm sorry. I didn't mean to insult you."

"Insult me? *Non, mignonne*, you have it all wrong." Damien growled. "Or did you mean by calling me a wolf? You, *mignonne*, look like a frightened mouse. Is that an insult to you? Incidentally, are you aware that wolves eat mice?"

"Pardon?" Bobbie stiffened, glaring at him. Once again, she surprised him. "Are you threatening me?"

"Admit it. You are terrified." Damien's eyes narrowed. Like the chameleon she resembled, she shifted from frightened mouse to fierce wildcat in an instant. Who was she? "I should have realized you don't belong here. You are a genuine lady, aren't you? I would never threaten you, dear lady. I'm willing to admit – you terrify me."

"I do?" Bobbie giggled. The whiskey was obviously kicking in very nicely. "Frightened mouse, indeed! Daddy calls me his barracuda. He said Aunt Hortense put too much nonsense in my head and I act more like a man than most men do."

"You a man? I don't think so." Damien's eyes seared through her torn gown, reminding her she hadn't repaired it yet. No, she didn't know how to sew. Surely one hired someone to do such menial chores.

"Do you really know Louis Riel? Is he the troublemaker everyone claims he is? Was he really deported to the United States?" She asked eagerly. Why this man might be a fountain of information. She tried to focus on the grooves in Damien's cheeks when he smiled. Dimples! Surely a man with dimples could not be cruel. "He doesn't have to be down in Montana. I'm sure he could be anywhere out here and no one would ever know. I mean – it's so very isolated and..."

"Are you ever quiet?" Damien interrupted. But he was grinning. "Where are you from? Did you say Toronto? Do those people know anything about here?"

"Yes... Toronto." She managed to croak out as he shifted closer. "We never heard of any heathens actually being educated. But we did hear..."

"I can imagine what you heard." Damien cut her short. His voice was still laced with amusement. "Why so many questions? You look like you've spent your entire life in some fancy palace with servants catering to your every whim. When would you have time to read about Louis Riel or the heathens?"

"It wasn't a palace – it was just a very large house. And of course we have servants." She shifted nervously. Was she revealing too much?

"Why did you come to Winnipeg?" Damien's voice seemed only idle curiosity.

"I don't want to talk about this. I feel ill again." Bobbie desperately sought escape. She tried to edge back.

Once again he looked like a lean, hungry wolf, ready to devour her. She nearly toppled back off the edge of the bench. He watched her silently, making no effort to stop her.

"Please take me back to the hotel. I've never met an Indian before and I'm..."

"Not sure I'm acceptable company for a lady?" Damien interrupted her rambling. "I can't keep up with your prattle, *mignonne*. Have another drink." Damien reached for her cup and poured more whiskey into it. "Have you been anywhere except Toronto?"

"I lived with my aunt in England." Bobbie pursed her lips together, focusing on her cup. Carefully, hands weaving, she reached for it.

"Let me get this straight. You lived with daddy in Toronto. Then you lived with your aunt in England. Now you're living with your brothers in Winnipeg. Is that correct? Can you tell me why?" Damien asked with a mocking inflection.

"Brothers?" She wrinkled her nose, perplexed. Then she giggled. The secret. She must keep her secret. "We need money. You see daddy doesn't know I'm here with Gilbert and... Robert. Of course Etienne is here too."

"And who is Etienne?" Damien inserted lazily, leaning back against the wooden wall.

"Etienne is my *fiancée*."

"*Fiancée*?" Damien sat up.

"He was. Daddy wants me to marry him."

"Why?" Dale interrupted.

"For the French vote, I imagine. I can't really see any other reason." Bobbie spoke slowly, trying to enunciate carefully. Good Lord, she felt ready to go to sleep.

"French vote?" Damien whistled under his breath. "Just who the hell is your father, *mignonne*?"

"Sir Myles Taylor. I would have thought you would know that. I did tell you my name. He will be Prime Minister one day." Bobbie felt as though her tongue was sticking to the roof of her mouth. She licked her lips. "When daddy caught me preaching for a woman's right to vote, he decided to marry me off – to Etienne."

"You're married?" Damien drew his breath in sharply.

"NO! That's why I'm here. I ran away with Gilbert... and Robert." She chuckled, very proud that she had remembered.

"Then why is Etienne here?" Damien shook his head, taking another drink.

"I have no idea. I think he still plans to marry me – for my money, of course. I am very, very wealthy – or I will been soon." Bobbie wrinkled her brow, trying to concentrate. What a silly thing to say. "Gilbert is here to start up a newspaper office for daddy. And I... Robert is here as a reporter. Aren't you drinking too much?" Bobbie watched him take another swallow.

"Are you?" Damien smiled. "So Etienne is still your fiancée?"

"No!" Her face clouded. She felt like crying. "He killed my cat. I hate him. And he's French as well. Etienne is lazy. He lives off Gilbert. Gilbert just can't see it. I wish I could have my money now."

"Then you wouldn't have to go and be a whore?" Damien asked. "I'm very sorry about your cat, *mignonne*. So, your brothers have to support Etienne and don't have enough left to support you. Do they know you were going to sell yourself tonight?"

"No, of course not!" Bobbie stammered. "And you must never tell him…them. Promise?"

"I promise." Dale agreed dryly. "Why did you decide to become a prostitute?"

"I didn't. I was… Oh my good Lord!" Bobbie interrupted her own words before she told him everything. Her head was buzzing. Her eyes were bleary. "I thought it might be fun. Could you imagine me becoming a – maid?"

"Fun to be a whore?" Damien's smile was slow and easy. "How intriguing."

"Well, men seem to enjoy it!" Bobbie snapped. Men were absolutely frustrating with their superior attitudes. It made her feel quite ill. Or was that the whiskey? Men and alcohol – the two main evils in this world, according to Aunt Hortense.

"Yes. And I know there are many women who do as well. But it's much more enjoyable when you can pick your partners, *mignonne*." Dale agreed solemnly. "How old are you?"

"Nineteen." She laughed at the uncertainty written across his arresting features.

"A nineteen year old lady – looking for fun. You are certainly my type of woman." Damien edged closer.

He reached out and in one fleeting swoop Bobbie was perched on his lap, pressed to his chest. She felt the hard swell of his thighs and arousal beneath her bottom.

"To hell with it."

"What?" Shrieking her panic, her courage was forsaken. What was he going to do?

"To hell with taking you home. I like you." Damien stated shortly.

His face was so close their lips nearly touched. She could see silver lines spreading out from his pupils. One firm hand glided up to tangle in her braided hair. He resolutely cupped her head so she couldn't turn away. Squirming against his thighs only increased her confinement.

"It really is fun, *mignonne*. Let me show you." Damien's voice was husky.

Bobbie carefully licked her dry lips, watching him in hypnotic fascination.

Tugging against her braid, his fingers cleverly loosened the strands of hair. Efficiently, he combed through the boundless density. His eyes drooped, fervid with crude desire.

"Relax. I will not hurt you. I only promise you paradise and so much more..."

His breath was soft, tantalizing whispers of delight along her lips. His mouth feathered softly against hers, prodding her clenched teeth open. Her disobedient body ignored her mind's panic.

His moist tongue swirled saliently inside her mouth as soon as she opened it, twisting with hers. She sagged against his chest, feeling woozy. Her breath came out in short, gasping spurts. His aggressive fingers caressed her shoulders, then moved lower to fondle her aching nearly bare, breasts.

Pressing closer, she automatically shifted to better feel his mysterious hardness. His lips were promised pleasure. His fingers caused wanton sensations to course through her body. Twisting against him, she pressed her bosom against his fevered chest and answered his seeking tongue with her own wild exploration.

"*Mon Dieu!*" Leaning away, Damien's arresting smile was in place once again. He took a deep breath.

"I don't understand." Bewildered, Bobbie felt his even breathing, indicating he was unmoved by that devastating kiss. She felt hurt. She wanted more. "No!" She tried to pull him back. He couldn't stop now.

"You must learn patience." Damien chuckled, refusing to let her pull him close again. "We have all night, *mignonne*. First there is a favour I must ask of you."

CHAPTER 3

"Aren't you even a little curious as to why I helped you, *mignonne*?" Damien evaded her tenacious arms by leaning back, and tilting his face towards the ceiling.

"No!" Bobbie answered bluntly. Brazenly, she let the tip of her tongue stroke along his throat. Damien jerked back. She was very obvious ready to be taught those delights he loved to teach. "Why do you speak with a Scottish accent?"

Damien grabbed her shoulders, holding her back. He laughed softly at the expression on her face. She knew she was affecting him physically. But she clearly didn't know how to proceed. Then her question squelched his desire.

The vision of Reverend Ian MacLeod and his lovely wife, Anne, drove all thoughts of lovemaking away. He shook his head. Damn, he'd had too much to drink. His mother and father's deaths came into focus. Then after – living with Ian and Anne - no! He would not think of that. He never talked about those years of his life. .

He stood abruptly. Her arms reached up, clinging to his neck.

"Enough! It's the whiskey talking now. You will be embarrassed when you sober." Damien pushed her back to the bench.

Holding her wrists, he exerted just enough pressure to keep her seated. He didn't want to hurt this lady. Being hurt by ladies was more his style.

"Are you saying I'm drunk?" She slanted him a reproachful glare. "How can you even suggest such a thing? Aunt Hortense said alcohol is the root of all evil"

Then her face reddened. She yanked her hands from him, sitting back on the bench. She placed her palms, primly clasped, in her lap. Damien nearly laughed. A lady's behaviour was a fascinating sight to behold.

"I would dare suggest such a thing." Damien stated smoothly. "It's a fact – you are drunk." He looked down into her delightful, blushing features. She was undeniably enchanting. And she fit so well into his arms. She was assaulting his primitive senses, even more than his beloved Marie could.

Then his face hardened as a succinct picture of Marie infiltrated his befuddled head. He had thought Marie, a *Metis* as well, might be different. She had said she loved him. So then why did she insist she was going to marry his cousin? Damien looked away. He didn't want another lady – he wanted Marie.

"Let's have another drink." He shuffled through the contents of the trunk again, then triumphantly turned back brandishing a bottle. Moving back to sit on the opposite side of the table, he proceeded to pour her yet another drink.

"I have a proposition for you, *mignonne*. Will you help me?"

Mechanically Bobbie reached over the table and picked up the tin cup. *'I need this. It's only a small cup.'* She silently justified her deplorable actions. *'It has been an extremely trying evening.'*

"Yes."

"Such willingness – without even knowing what I'm going to ask?" Damien chuckled, taking a swig directly from the bottle, then wiping his hand across his mouth.

She should be totally repulsed, but she wasn't. What was happening? She'd never had this strange fluttering in her stomach before. No matter what he did or said, he devastated her nerves completely.

"Are you intoxicated?" Bobbie watched him in fascination.

Her married friends often discussed the effect alcohol had on their husbands. Some men were mean and obnoxious, while others went to sleep. But all the women agreed – men were impotent or terrible lovers when under the influence... She flushed. Was this why Damien was rejecting her? He didn't appear inebriated. He neither staggered nor slurred his words. His whole bearing was one of fluid charm and recklessness. Yet he'd been drinking steadily since she'd met him.

"Intoxicated?" His lopsided grin was intriguing and seductive. "No. Nothing so classy, I'm afraid. I'm just sloppy drunk. Forgive me."

Bobbie looked at him expectantly. She could willingly sit here all evening and just look at him, listening to his gravel-sultry voice.

"I want to tell you – my heart is broken." Damien looked so sad she wanted to comfort him. Then his words penetrated her fuzzy head.

"A broken – heart?" Her mouth rounded. She was a senseless idiot. Of course a man like Damien would have a woman. "Are you... married?"

"No." Damien sighed, taking another drink from the bottle. "But I was engaged to the most beautiful woman in the world."

"Surely you haven't met every woman in the world. How can you make such a ridiculous statement?" Bobbie snapped tartly, trying to ignore the pain in his luminous eyes. Her eyes dulled, moss green, in response to his cruel words.

"Forgive me, *mignonne*. But, you must understand. I love her."

"You love her? Yet you sit here all evening calling me, *mignonne*?" Bobbie tried to stop the hurt from hammering in her belly. "For goodness sake, *you bought me!* If you love someone..."

This man was a stranger to her. How could she be jealous of this woman he loved so much? It must be the alcohol. She would never touch another drop to her dying days. Jealousy was a novel, unpleasant feeling running throughout. What did she care if this savage loved a – thousand – women?

"You are so distracting, *mignonne*." Damien reached across the small table, placing a finger beneath her chin to tilt her head up. His eyes narrowed, smouldering with promise. "I'm sure *you* could make me forget Marie."

Standing to come around the table, Damien deliberately stood behind her and placed his fingers on her shoulders.

"You almost make me feel guilty." His lean fingers began kneading her shoulders and neck with tantalizing strokes. "This is a game men and women play. What you are feeling is strictly physical. I promise to help you with that, but for now I need you to come with me to a – *soiree*. It's my *fiancée's* party."

Bobbie tensed beneath his fingertips. She felt completely hostile. She shrugged her shoulders trying to stop his seductive touch.

"I'm sorry." Damien leaned down to murmur against her ear. She nearly yelped in fear. "Marie *was* my fiancée. Now she is going to marry my cousin."

"Why would she do that?" Bobbie's voice held disbelief.

If a woman had the chance to marry this exciting man, why would she choose another? *Stop this*! She knew nothing about this man except that he was devastatingly beautiful. His looks alone gave him whatever he wanted. And who could live with that? She couldn't blame Marie. No, she couldn't. Yet he was also kind... and charming...

"I left her alone too often. She turned to Pierre – for security, I suppose. She doesn't love him. He is a government supervisor. He has money." There was a bitter tone in his voice.

"She is only interested in money?" Bobbie gasped. "How awful." She really must stop feeling sorry for this man. She was fast learning money was very important. "Why did you leave her alone?"

"I had to go out into the wilderness alone – to trap furs. I didn't want her to come with me. She would suffer needlessly.

There are no friends – no shopping... There is just hard work and it is so cold." Damien stopped, sighing heavily. "But I did want her to have money. Trapping furs was the only way I knew how to give it to her. I am not skilled in any other occupation..."

"What a terrible thing to do." Bobbie turned her cheek and rubbed it soothingly against his warm hand. *'But he speaks so well. He is educated. Surely...'* Bobbie ignored her suspicions. She could well imagine his anguish. "You were alone out in the wilds and she was here with your cousin? Did you get many furs? Are you rich now? That would serve her right."

"No, I'm not rich." Damien's hands tightened on her shoulders. "There are no animals left in the wilderness."

He was trembling now. She turned and glanced at him, thinking he might be crying. Instead of sorrow, she caught the devilish gleam in his half-closed eyes. His sinuous body was shaking with silent laughter.

"You are teasing me!" She leaned forward, trying to shrug his hands away.

"No. I am telling the truth."

"Well, you certainly don't appear to be upset." Bobbie's lips puckered. She turned around again and glared at him.

"Everyone suffers in a different way." His fingers deliberately moved up her neck to cup her chin. His thumb stroked her lips. "I want you to come to Marie's party with me. Then I'll take you with me – to Big Bear's camp. We will be married."

"Married?" Bobbie gasped. She was here alone, with a demented man! "Come again?"

"If we share a lodge – then we are married in my Native world. It is simple."

"Simple?" Bobbie shook her head. Of course – he would be taking her to Big Bear's camp. But not in the capacity he intended. After saying he loved Marie, how could he propose such a ludicrous proposition?

"You don't want to marry me?" Damien's hand moved down to stroke along her bare arms. "You have such soft skin, *mignonne.* You have led a sheltered life – but you *seem* to like me. Does my being poor bother you?"

"No!" Astonished, Bobbie turned back to look into his face. It was tight with cynical amusement.

"Come now, *mignonne* – all women want rich husbands!" Damien's lips quirked. "But you also want me. I feel it when I touch you. We can have a good marriage – just with that. I will look after you. You won't have to be a prostitute."

"You are definitely crazy." Bobbie shook her head, numb with shock. He was serious? He would marry her, loving another and expect they would be happy? His colossal conceit was overwhelming. "I'm not going to become a prostitute."

"Then it's settled. We will be married." Damien slid down to sit beside her, looking very pleased.

Bobbie reached her tongue out to moisten her dry lips. Leaning forward, Damien touched her lips with his own mouth at the same time. His tongue caused a tingling sensation as it slid between her parted lips. His fingers moved up to cup her scalp. As his lips applied pressure, she willingly allowed his tantalizing assault. His tongue swirled. Shifting, he pulled her to his lap again. She was immediately on fire. She felt the heat of his damp chest against hers. She moaned.

Whimpering low in her throat, she tried to move closer. Erotic delight flared immediately as he melded his lips to hers, shifting so she could press against him. Silently, she begged him to do whatever was necessary to gratify this intense ache in her loins.

Icy reality invaded. How could he kiss her like this, loving another woman? Was it he or she who was crazy? Even when he callously discussed loving another woman, she was letting him do whatever he pleased.

"So you will marry me?" Withdrawing, he traced her moist lips with a lean finger. His eyes smouldered darkly. "I did not mean what I said earlier. It is you, not Marie, who is the most beautiful woman in the world."

Oddly, it was his impossible compliment that caused her to think again. Still feeling dazed, as though she'd just wakened from a dream, her mind cleared.

"Of course." She smiled mischievously, returning his caress with her own fluttering touch across his jaw. "How could I resist such a wonderful offer?"

Tonight she would go with him and enjoy whatever he presented. This was so much more exciting than being cooped up in her dreary hotel room alone.

Then tomorrow she would once again become Roberta Taylor, reporter. Tomorrow, she wouldn't be so susceptible to this loneliness she'd felt ever since arriving in Winnipeg three weeks ago. Tomorrow she wouldn't find this man so magnetic. Tomorrow, she would forget this tantalizing episode in her life.

Bobbie agreeably followed Damien out into the darkness. With her head spinning again, obviously from the fresh air, she let him help her mount his skittish horse. Swinging up behind her, Damien kicked the horse into motion – heading further away from Winnipeg.

"Where are we going?" Once again she felt uneasy. She did not like the dark wilderness at all. Now there were no buildings around them, not even small, dark shacks.

"St. Francis Zavier. It is a little village a few miles outside Winnipeg. That is where the party is." Damien smiled faintly. "What are you afraid of, *mignonne*?"

"It is so dark out here – isn't it?" Bobbie edged back into the hardness of his chest. She sensed he would protect her and was comforted by his flexing arms around her.

"You are afraid of the dark?" Damien's lips brushed along her ear. His arms tightened with assurance. "But you're not afraid of me?"

"It does seem silly." Bobbie laughed nervously. "I'm sure there's nothing to be afraid of, but I've never been alone in the wilds before."

"You are not alone." Damien chuckled softly. "And this isn't really the wilds at all. Big Bear lives in the wilds."

"Are you trying to frighten me more?" Bobbie asked, shifting closer. "I thought you said I would go with you to his camp. Then again, you'll be with me – to protect me won't you?"

"*Touché.*" Damien laughed, drawing her still closer. "We are riding across the *Prairie du Ceval Blanc* now. Then we will be in St. Francis Zavier."

"Why do you call it the White Horse Prairie?" Bobbie murmured She was getting sleepy.

"I thought you didn't understand French." Damien growled with amusement. "You are full of surprises."

"I did learn French in school but I didn't care for it at all." Bobbie explained in a lofty tone.

"Why?"

"Because I find the French... too..." Bobbie shrugged, stifling a yawn.

"What an intriguing comment. Finish it, *mignonne.*" Damien whispered.

"I can't really concentrate." Bobbie murmured reaching up to rub her tired eyes. "Why is this called White Horse Prairie?"

"Because there is a white phantom horse here." Damien smiled. "But, of course, he is a ghost. People have seen him for hundreds of years."

"What people?" She snuggled back into his warm arms. She rubbed her cheek along the smooth muscles of his chest, amazed at how hot he felt even in the cool dusk breezes. Her lashes fluttered periodically, ordering her to sleep. "Horses don't live to be hundreds of years old and there are no such thing as ghosts."

"You think not? The horse is a ghost. I saw him. I tried to capture him."

"Is that another fault of the French? They can't tell the truth?" Bobbie giggled, drifting into a deep sleep.

"*Non.* But it most certainly is a fault of the English, isn't it?" She didn't hear him. She was sleeping.

Bobbie mumbled irritably when Damien woke her up. She felt groggy and ill from too much alcohol and too little sleep. They were outside a two-story white house.

Inside open patio doors and large glassed windows she saw a brightly lit room. It ran the full length of the house. It was crowded with dancing, laughing people. In one corner she saw three men playing musical instruments. They were all dressed in black.

"You look surprised. Were you expecting a tipi?" Damien asked softly.

He turned to the doorway, after lifting her gently down from the horse.

"Well, I have noticed the homes are not very large out here." Bobbie snapped, certain he was displeased with her.

Damien took her arm, smiling his bewitching appeal again. He politely led her up the wooden verandah steps.

"Do you need another drink, *mignonne*? You are very pleasant, when you're drunk."

"No!" Bobbie yanked her arm away from him.

What was she doing here? Although he was dangerously attractive, he had a dominating streak she found very annoying. She was in no mood for this egotistic man. She had just wakened from too short a nap and had a nagging headache. Was this a hangover?

"Miserable little witch, aren't you?" Damien was laughing at her. "You know your eyes change to whiskey – when you are angry or – frightened."

His hands moved beneath her underarms. He lifted her up effortlessly to his hard body. Bobbie didn't care for the way she trembled so easily at his slightest touch. She was going crazy.

"I have a headache."

"Excuse number thirty-five?" Damien slid his tongue along her earlobe.

"What do you mean?" Bobbie couldn't prevent herself from leaning closer into his hard frame.

"I've heard women have three-hundred and sixty-five excuses why their husbands can't touch them." Damien laughed, placing the tip of his tongue inside her earlobe. Bobbie moaned, feeling the tingling sensations swirl throughout, sliding right to her toes.

"Please be nice to my friends, *mignonne*." Damien continued to tease her ear and neck. "And try to pretend you like me."

His sensuous lips moved over to deliberately play with hers. Like a mechanical puppet, she was immediately lost in devastating sensations. Pulling him closer, her arms slipped around his neck. She forgot where she was. Then as the sparking delight increased, she even forgot who she was.

"Damien! You came."

Bobbie turned, with bleary eyes, to see a woman standing in the doorway.

Masses of blue-black curls tumbled around tanned shoulders and a perfectly oval face. Her full lips matched a vivid scarlet, off-shoulder gown. Huge, chocolate brown eyes held a gleam of reproach in their depths. She was studying Bobbie carefully.

There was no need to ask Damien who she was. Bobbie felt his lack of warmth immediately. His arms dropped guilty to his sides.

Did Damien actually believe she could compete with this lovely vision called Marie? The idea was pathetic. Bobbie couldn't wait to meet Pierre. He must be absolutely gorgeous to be able to take Marie away from Damien.

"She's fat." Bobbie muttered, catty with hurt.

"She's not." Damien growled. His arm moved back around her slender waist cautiously.

"No, she's not." Bobbie whispered, feeling dowdy and – skinny. She could never make a woman like Marie jealous.

"Don't underestimate your charms, *mignonne*. I love *petite* blond ladies. Just ask Marie." Damien smiled. He could so easily read her every thought it was frustrating.

Then Marie was beside Damien. Taking his arm possessively, she led him into the house. Bobbie was left standing alone. She noticed, with malicious spite, that Marie was as tall as Damien, but somewhat wider as well.

CHAPTER 4

"Come along." Turning, Damien absently grabbed Bobbie's wrist to drag her along. "Marie, *mon amour*, let me introduce your to my new fiancée, Roberta Taylor. We are getting married tomorrow."

"Damien, don't be ridiculous. You know the banns have to be read in church and..." Marie's mouth tightened with disapproval.

When they entered the brightly lit room, Marie turned to study Bobbie with detailed care. Bobbie stared back, feeling gauche. She could smell Marie's elusive perfume – roses. She wrinkled her nose. Then Marie's gaze moved back to Damien. She sighed, shaking her head.

"You fool."

"But she's not Catholic, nor am I. We're going to Big Bear's camp." Damien growled belligerently.

"So what are you this week, Damien?" Marie's lips seemed to twitch, as though in amusement. They tightened again when she looked at Bobbie. "Roberta? Are you sure she's not Anne? Aren't you Methodist, my dear?"

"No. I'm Anglican." Bobbie stated slowly, truly puzzled. Who was Anne? She felt Damien's arm flinch, as though in pain. Looking up into his face she wanted to cry. He looked pale and anguished. Perhaps he did love Marie. "Who is Anne?"

Damien tossed Marie a reckless smile, then turned to grin down into Bobbie's face. "Anne is just someone I knew once. You look a little like her. She is not anyone important."

"Big Bear?" Marie couldn't hide the scorn in her voice. "Then your little... Roberta is willing to share you?"

"What do you mean – willing to share?" Bobbie's eyes wrinkled in confusion. She didn't like Marie at all.

"You really should ask Damien about that one – before you marry him, I must add." Marie smiled maliciously. "Where are you from?"

"Toronto."

"Why are you out here, dear?" Marie asked. She kept searching Damien's face with curiosity. Bobbie felt a strong urge to smack her. How could Damien possibly love such a rude person?

"She wanted to become a whore." Damien laughed devilishly. He placed his arm around Bobbie possessively. "Then she met me and decided she'd rather be with me."

"Damien!" Bobbie hissed in mortification.

"You only met tonight?" Marie's voice sounded shocked. "Roberta, are you actually going along with this?"

"No, I..." Bobbie flushed in shame. She hadn't expected this, at all. Damien had no right to humiliate her in such a raw manner. She tried to pull away from his clinging arm.

"Come along with me. I'll introduce you to my *fiancée.*" Marie's smile seemed friendly. "Ignore Damien. He can be so crude at times."

Pierre Marchand was a tall, thin man with sparse, receding hair. He was a supervisor in the Department of Indian Affairs, he told Bobbie proudly. Bobbie liked the quiet, unassuming man immediately. She looked back into Damien's beautiful face and sighed. Nice or not, how could Marie prefer Pierre to Damien?

Then Damien led her around the room, introducing her first as Gertrude's latest prostitute, then as his *fiancée.* His possessive touch along her bare arm and his strained features kept her oddly silent. She reddened whenever he mentioned Gertrude's saloon unsure of what to say.

She felt decidedly uncomfortable. Everyone here was *Metis.* Some spoke only French or a guttural language she'd never heard before. This casual *soiree* was so different from any gathering she'd ever attended either in Toronto or England. Although they all appeared to be enjoying themselves, Bobbie found their raucous voices and wild dancing alarming. The music was high-pitched and fast as the fiddles wailed out. Everyone was bouncing around. Were they doing a jig? It looked ... like something she didn't want to try.

"Have you known Damien long?" Pierre came to her side. She stood by the doorway now, contemplating leaving. But how could she get back?

Marie had finally consented to dance with Damien. Bobbie was watching the attractive couple circling the floor. They were perfectly matched. Even their hair was the same colour, mingling together in inky waves. They swayed around the room so close Bobbie doubted a piece of paper could slide between them.

She turned to Pierre when he nudged her arm. He offered her a glass of wine. She noticed his thick wire-framed glasses did not hide his sensitive, sharp eyes.

"Imported wine?" She asked with brittle carelessness. She took the glass and nearly downed its contents in one gulp. The soothing alcohol was again balm to her apprehensive stomach.

"Pardon?" Then Pierre's face broke out in amusement. "Ah, you poke fun at us – backwoods people. Out here we do not always have the luxuries they have in Toronto or Montreal. A good wine is too expensive to buy. This is our own home grown Saskatoon berry wine. It is still good, *oui?*"

"Yes." Bobbie nodded contritely. Taking a sip now, she noticed the wine had a pungent, sweet taste, almost like blueberries. "I apologize for my rudeness. Did you go to school in Montreal?"

"Yes." Pierre smiled, turning to watch Marie and Damien dancing. "Will you marry our Damien?"

"I doubt it." Bobbie muttered absently. She was again watching that lecherous oaf on the dance floor.

Damien was fondling Marie openly. The man had no shame, no morals! Turning, she couldn't help but notice the sadness in Pierre's eyes.

"All women love Damien." Even Pierre's voice was sad.

"He said it is only physical..." Bobbie's voice trailed off as she realized how crude she sounded. *'Damn you, Damien'* she muttered under her breath. She sounded just like him. She grimaced and her eyes softened. Pierre was a very nice gentleman. He was now being forced to watch his future wife with her ex-lover.

Bobbie didn't doubt for an instant that Marie had once been Damien's lover and maybe she still was. She couldn't imagine any woman being with Damien for any length of time and not succumbing to his smooth, potent charm. She snorted. She, like a simpleton, had actually considered giving him her virginity. Ha! He would never get anything from her now.

"Meeting Damien is something like getting run over by a train. I don't know him at all. In truth, I only met him tonight and all I know about him is that he is *Metis* and he speaks English with a Scottish accent. Why is that?"

"He was raised by a Scottish minister." Pierre sighed. "Damien is a good man. Everyone loves Damien."

"A *Scottish Methodist* minister?" Bobbie was trying to make sense of Marie's strange conversation earlier on. "And who is Anne?"

"The minister's wife. She still lives in Winnipeg." Pierre said cautiously. "Did Damien tell you about Anne?"

"No, your *fiancée* mentioned her." Bobbie smiled, reaching out to touch Pierre's arm. Pierre could tell her everything she wanted to know about that mysterious man. "Why was he raised by a Scottish minister?"

"His parents were killed – during a buffalo hunt – when he was only five. He went to live with Reverend Ian MacLeod in Winnipeg." Pierre looked sad again. "We didn't want him to. We wanted to keep him here. But even the courts took the Reverend's side. Damien said the reverend was jealous of the Catholic priests. I guess he told Damien that if they could make a civilized person out of a heathen, then so could he. Damien hasn't told you this?"

"Damien doesn't say much – on these matters anyway. His parents were killed in a buffalo hunt." Bobbie whispered.

"You have heard about those remarkable hunts?" Pierre's eyes lit up. "Even whites from the east and Europe came to see it. It was a sight to behold. Alas, the buffalo are nearly all gone now."

"When did Damien leave Reverend MacLeod?" Bobbie slipped in pointedly. She was, after all, a fine reporter. She knew how to manipulate a conversation when she wanted information.

"When he was nearly sixteen." Pierre answered soberly. "Reverend MacLeod was a very cruel man. He wouldn't let Damien play with us. He thought we were all no better than the animals we hunted. He was killed and then Damien left."

"Who killed him?" Bobbie asked. Her heart fluttered when she recalled the expression on Damien's face when he was holding his gun on that horrid man in Gertrude's saloon.

"Some say it was Damien. But it was never proven. I do not believe he did it." Pierre grimaced. "Anne is the one who accused him. Ian MacLeod was beaten to death. He was a big man. Damien was not. For years no one knew where Damien was. Then Gabriel found him with Big Bear."

"Who is Gabriel?"

"Gabriel Dumont is mayor of a village north of here – Batoche. He is a *Metis*."

"Do you know Big Bear?" Bobbie asked anxiously. He was the Indian she was supposed to interview.

"Damien learned all his cruel, uncivilized ways from that man!" Pierre ground out. "I don't know him personally, but I'm sure he's a *heathen*."

Bobbie couldn't discern between an Indian and a *Metis*. Yet Pierre obviously felt there was a difference. Perhaps the *Metis* felt they were superior to the natives, just as most whites did towards the *Metis*.

"What did Gabriel do when he found Damien?"

"Damien was twenty years old then. There wasn't much anyone could do with Damien. But Gabriel did convince him to come to Batoche and live with his own kind. Damien was like an uncivilized barbarian by then."

"Oh!" There it was again. The *Metis* were as arrogant and proud as any aristocrat in white societies. "Does Damien live in Batoche now?"

"Damien goes wherever he pleases. He has been down south and even to the east once. But he always returns here. I love Damien as though he were my brother." Pierre smiled.

"Truly?" Bobbie scoffed. Surely Pierre would prefer to see Damien disappear and never return to Winnipeg again.

"So you know about Marie? Do not worry, Roberta. Damien is not right for her. She needs a house, security and a settled life. Damien can't give her that. That is something you must consider as well." Pierre grinned with candour. "You appear very intelligent. I can't see you becoming his meek little squaw."

"Pardon?" Bobbie gasped. Did Pierre think she was a simpering little idiot?

"Well, you really must consider this. Damien's pride will never allow him to take Marie back, even if she wanted him back." Pierre nodded with assurance.

Bobbie turned to watch the couple, still dancing. Damien was nearly seducing Marie in front of dozens of people. Did Pierre consider that pride?

"I am very serious, Roberta. And I don't even know why I'm saying this. You look much too fragile to be hurt." Pierre insisted. "To a heathen, love means nothing. I hope you never see this side of Damien. The only man he seems to unconditionally respect is Big Bear. Damien is not a Christian, nor is he completely Heathen. Do not play games with this man. He can be very cruel when he is crossed."

"I am not playing games." Bobbie's eyes widened with alarm.

Then what was she doing? Wasn't she considering Damien could... have her in return for giving her freedom to do as she pleased? Wasn't she tricking him tonight so he would be obligated to take her into the wilderness?

She felt provocative fingers playing in her unbound hair. Damien was behind her and the world seemed to slip away in a rosy haze of unreality. Her blood surged wildly. She forgot Pierre's dire warnings. Damien was a magician, pure and simple.

"So you are going to take another woman from me?" Damien's voice was both mocking and soft.

Everyone near them immediately tensed. Marie gasped, shaking her head. She glared at Damien. Conversation stopped.

"I was only talking to Roberta." Pierre answered casually.

"While you were... Are you trying to take my woman from me?"

Bobbie's thoughts droned like a buzzing bee. She couldn't concentrate on what they were saying. She couldn't focus on anything. Her flushed cheeks and trembling limbs were visible to anyone standing near her, including Pierre. She couldn't understand the sympathy in his eyes.

"Why would I do that? I have Roberta now." Damien's quick grin was taunting. His casually, possessive fingers continued to play with Bobbie's hair.

"Will you take her to Batoche?" Pierre's voice was still calm.

"*Non.* I doubt Uncle Gabriel will like her." Damien's eyes narrowed. "We are going to Big Bear."

"Damien, you're not serious." Marie interrupted, going to stand beside Pierre. She placed her hand against his arm.

"Try me." Damien leaned into Bobbie's tense back. His fingers moved around her neck, then up to feather-stroke against her cheeks. "I do as I please." Bobbie could feel his breath stirring her hair, moving towards her ear. He bent over her. She could also feel that mystifying swell against her bottom. Panic surged. Was that for Marie or for her benefit? His words registered.

"What do you mean, Gabriel won't like me?" She cranked her neck around to see his face.

"Gabriel hates whites." Damien grinned.

She gasped at the insult. Hardening her response to Damien's beguiling smile with effort, she sputtered unable to voice her wrath. She was Sir Myles Taylor's daughter. In two years, when she turned twenty-one, she would have enough money to buy the whole west, including the *Metis*! Dear deceased Aunt Hortense had left her a fortune. She would not play Damien's silly game any longer. Her small form tightened with haughty pride.

"I really don't care what his opinion is. I have no intentions of ever meeting the dear old man."

"Are you sure, *mignonne*?" Damien voice was low and magnetic.

"This has gone on long enough. I won't become your... *meek little squaw*. I'm sorry, Pierre, Marie but this is just a silly little game. I'll just leave now."

"Let's dance." Damien stepped closer. Slipping his arm around her shoulder, he brought her against his chest.

Ignoring his mesmerizing touch, Bobbie's mind began to clear. Damien was much too conceited. He was the exact type of man she had always avoided and loathed.

"Please, *mignonne*." Damien turned her and tilted her chin up in gentle demand. He brushed his lips along the softness of her open mouth.

"I think the lady wants to go." Pierre interrupted boldly.

"Thank you, kind sir." Bobbie broke free of Damien's hold.

"But, I thought you wanted to go see Big Bear." Damien eyed her cautiously.

Confused again, Bobbie tried to focus her thoughts. Of course she was going to see Big Bear – but not as his personal love-slave! Did he know who she was? Then she smiled. She couldn't completely alienate this man. He was going to be her guide.

"Why would she want to go there?" Pierre spoke up again. "Big Bear is a fool. The old ways are gone. You are an even bigger fool, to follow him. Why won't he just settle on the reservation he was *given* instead of running off to Montana?"

"Given?" Damien asked with dangerous intensity.

His fingers cut into her flesh when he pulled Bobbie against his side. Startled, she glanced into his tense features. She was unable to believe this was the same congenial man she'd seen all night. He looked coiled and tight, like a snake ready to strike. His face was impenetrable, making him look older. Then, unexpectedly, he smiled with blunt irresistibility.

"No doubt, I'm a fool. Maybe you don't find the old ways appealing, but I do. Do you find being a white man's puppet more appealing then?"

He abruptly turned his back to Pierre and smiled at Bobbie.

"Come dance with me, *mignonne*. I will tell you all about the wild lands where we will fly as free as the hawks. I think you will like it..." Damien's voice trailed off with seductive intent.

"And she's definitely young enough to learn." Pierre snapped out. "I would not be so impulsive – *cousin*! I bet your Roberta comes from a very wealthy, powerful family."

"You just wouldn't believe who her family is, Pierre. You'd get along famously with her father, I'm sure." Damien smirked with pleasure, turning back to Pierre. "And when you figure it out – you'll realize power doesn't really impress me at all."

"Roberta Taylor. Sir Myles Taylor's daughter?" Pierre's eyes rounded in shock. He groaned. "No Damien... You fool." Pierre turned to Marie. "I don't think its Roberta we have to worry about darling."

The music started again. The tune was forlorn and sad, making her ache. It was another waltz. Damien led her out into the crowded room. But instead of holding her in a proper manner, both arms slid around her waist, caressing her back and hips.

"Please don't..." Bobbie's protest was a weak whimper of fear.

"Put your arms around my neck. Let me feel you. No one is watching." Damien whispered in her ear persuasively. "Everyone's drunk."

He manoeuvred her closer to his hard chest and slowly raised her arms to his shoulders. He kept his hypnotic gaze trained on her flushed face. Each throbbing step they took caused his abdomen and legs to brush against hers. Bobbie pressed her mouth to her arm to contain the powerful scream rising in her throat. Dancing with him was excruciating agony and she didn't even understand why.

"Just relax, *mignonne*. Tonight is ours. Don't worry about tomorrow, for it never comes..." His heated breath was delight against her ear.

"Damien, I just can't." Bobbie tried to pull away. "I feel..."

"Aroused? So do I. Let's see how far we can go before... we have to... do something..." Damien continued in that seductive tone that played havoc with her senses. She couldn't understand a word he was saying and she didn't care. She could smell erotic heat emanating from him and his words were so erotic, driving her crazy. "I may be part French, but I'm not like Etienne. Your father can't rule me. I'm willing to fight your battles with him – and win."

A surge of pleasure shot through her body. She leaned against him, wrapping her arms around his neck. It was true. Damien Larocque was not afraid of anyone – including her father. What a change from all the other men she'd ever met. She tilted her head and smiled up into his devastating face.

"You look like a cat." Damien smiled back. His eyes were a bottomless well. She felt as though she were falling... drowning. "Did I please you?"

"Not as much as you're going to, I think." She whispered boldly. She felt his hair tickle her hands and reached her fingers up to tug against the silky curls, bringing his head and mouth closer to her own.

"I think you're right." There was urgency in his voice now as it deepened. He pulled her closer. His lips breathed nearly against her mouth. "But I will, *mignonne*. I promise you I will."

CHAPTER 5

The night floated by in a sensuous haze of unreality. Damien teased Bobbie until she was wild with longings and couldn't think of anything, except him. She didn't care that Gilbert might be worried about her. She didn't care if everyone here was watching her outlandish actions. When she was in Damien's arms just the simple brush of his hips against hers created a hunger she couldn't control. She wanted this devastating man even if she didn't really know what that meant.

Then, leaving her feeling empty, he suddenly went to chase after the elusive Marie again. Bobbie slipped out to the quiet verandah. She felt nauseated and light-headed. It was time to return to her hotel room. She was alarmingly intoxicated and ashamed of her bold, unusual behaviour. This was her first experience with total freedom. Now here she was, not only falling under the spell of a pretty lecher, but succumbing to the lure of this dreadful alcohol as well. She was a fool. It was time to end this evening.

Leaning against a wooden post, she breathed in the cool air with appreciation. She fought against the queasy rumblings in her belly. Then she heard voices. All thoughts of nausea disappeared. Edging closer to the railing, she listened with unabashed curiosity. Damien and Marie were behind a lilac bush on the ground. They were directly below where she was standing on the verandah.

"You took your little whore to my place?" Marie's voice rose, shrill and loud.

Bristling, Bobbie's glazed eyes searched around the verandah. Fortunately no one was outside. Turning back to their voices, Bobbie felt anger building. How dare Marie call her a whore? At least she was still a virgin. She doubted Marie could say the same.

"Marie, everything I'm doing is your fault. Are you jealous of Roberta? You can't have us both, *mignonne*. It's either Pierre or me." Damien's voice drifted upwards, soft and seductive. "I love you."

"Why can't I have you both?" Marie's voice rose hysterically. "Why is it different for you? You had three savage wives all last winter! You don't know what love means."

"I told you why. I didn't even have to tell you. It wasn't as though I married them, really. It's our custom." Damien persisted with low urgency. "When Brown Bird died last year I had no choice. As his brother, it was my responsibility to look after his women."

"Oh, stop it!" Marie interrupted. "You are not Brown Bird's brother. *You're Metis*, just as I am. And it's our custom to have one husband or wife! Did you sleep with them?"

Damien was oddly silent. Bobbie felt her mouth drop open in astonishment. Was Marie saying Damien had... *three* wives last winter?

"I thought so." Marie laughed harshly. "I suppose it's also a custom to sleep with whomever you want, whenever you want? Oh, just forget it. I really don't care anymore, Damien. I love Pierre."

"I still love only you, Marie." Damien growled. "All those other women mean nothing. If you had come with me, like I asked..."

"Damien, just listen to yourself! All those other women! How many were there, besides your three wives?" Marie ground out. "Don't you understand – *I don't want your kind of love*? What about Roberta? Why did you bring her here? She looks like a child."

"I assure you, she's more of a woman than you, *mignonne*." Damien hissed out angrily.

Goodness! Bobbie trapped her self-derogatory laughter. Even when he was with another woman, she responded to his backhanded compliments.

"Damien. Stop this. I don't care about your other women anymore. I feel sorry for Roberta. You will hurt her time and time again, just like you hurt me." Marie's voice dropped, husky and pleading. "Pierre said Roberta is Sir Myles Taylor's daughter. Stay away from her. He could have you hung in the blink of an eye."

"Only if he caught me!" Damien stated with amusement. "She ran away from him and I caught her. I'm not afraid of him. You should know me better than that, *mignonne*."

"Just think who he is." Marie argued. "You can't fight him."

"Yes, he's going to be their next Prime Minister, according to Roberta. Do you really care, Marie?" Damien swore bitterly. "You hurt me, not Roberta or her father."

Bobbie could hear the anguish in Damien's low tone and it cut deeply into her heart. She didn't really know Damien. She shouldn't care. But she did.

"Let's go back in Damien. I'll talk to you tomorrow. No… Don't do anything you'll regret." Marie's voice sounded frightened now. "Stop it!"

Unable to see what was happening behind the brush, Bobbie stiffened, imagining Damien reaching to hold his beloved Marie. Her thoughts were painful anguish.

She nearly fell over the railing as she tried to peer around the brush. A hand encircled her waist, pulling her back to safety. With a startled gasp, she looked up into Pierre's fierce eyes. His slim hand covered her mouth to silence her short scream. Her eyes rounded, searching Pierre's pallid face. Had he heard as much as she had?

"I told you – Damien is vicious when he's drunk. Marie is terrified when he gets like this." Pierre leaned down to whisper in her ear.

"Stop it. Please…" Marie whimpered.

Was he hurting her? Bobbie struggled to get away from Pierre. Why was she here with these strange people? She had to get away or she would become as insane as they obviously were.

"I'm through talking, *mignonne*. Christ, you weren't even a virgin the first time I had you." Damien growled, low and savage.

"And you were, to expect the same from me?" Marie gasped, then her voice turned into a terrorized whimper. "Please don't..."

Damien's soft chuckle was pure evil.

Bobbie tried to peer around the brush and nearly fell when Pierre let her go. Shocked, she watched Pierre smoothly swing over the rail. Numb with alarm, she saw he was holding a small pistol in his slender hand.

"Enough! Get the hell away from my *fiancée* before I kill you," Pierre stated with a firm resolve.

"Then do it, Pierre. See if I give a damn. First you take my woman and now you may as well take my life." Damien turned back to Marie. His grin was a reckless dare.

"No!"

Bobbie flung herself over the rails, knocking Pierre to the ground. She was snarling like a wounded animal defending her young. The gun jolted from his grasp. A loud crack erupted as the pistol fired harmlessly into the air.

"Can't you see it's her fault too? She hurt him. Leave him alone." Bobbie beat frantically against Pierre's squirming form.

Pierre's eyes widened with amusement. He was making no effort to defend himself as her flailing fists pounded against his chest and face. In a long, dark tunnel of blackness, Bobbie began to realize he was not stopping her. As sanity slowly filtered in, she groaned. Behind her, she could hear Damien's loud, delighted laughter.

"Bettered by a tiny wildcat, Pierre. My, you are getting soft."

Bobbie noticed with rising shock that a number of people had come out to the verandah. They all pushed forward for a better view. Marie leaned against Damien like a limp doll.

Bobbie's eyes dropped to her exposed legs. She was straddled across Pierre's chest and her dress was pulled up nearly to her waist. The poorly mended tear in her bodice had loosened again. Her legs and chest were visible for everyone to see.

Hot with shame, she slowly raised her gaze to Damien. He was smirking above her. Even Marie was smiling. This was all a silly game to them, she realized. This was their game and she didn't understand their rules. Stiffening, she wanted only to sink into the ground. She had no desire to try and understand either,

"Marie is right. You are a bastard, Damien." Leaping to her feet, Bobbie moved to scratch his face to bits and destroy his devil-handsome features. It was those damned pretty features that made all women act like fools, she included.

Still trembling with laughter, Damien reached out and slipped his arm around her waist, just as she charged forward again. He tilted her easily against his hip. Her arms and legs flapped about in the air.

"I think it's time I took Roberta home. Come along, *mignonne*. We've about worn our welcome out."

Damien strode, with casual ease, toward his still-saddled horse. Bobbie flopped against his side, moaning. The blood rushed to her head, making her aware again of her inebriated state.

"Don't hurt her. She was protecting you, Damien." Pierre scrambled to his feet. He was laughing as hard as Damien.

Raging, Bobbie realized Pierre had no intention of actually killing Damien. She was surrounded by a group of barbarians and was acting every bit as savage as they were. Everyone was on the verandah now. Their eyes darted, some puzzled, most filled with humour, from one couple to the other.

Flipping her across his horse, Damien mounted in a single motion. He urged Attila around. Bobbie clamped her teeth together as a peculiar, spinning sensation rocketed her brain. Moaning, she prayed silently, *'Please God, don't let me be sick now.'*

"*Mon Dieu*, are you sure she's a lady, Pierre?" Marie's shrill tittering drifted out to Bobbie's red ears.

Whimpering her mortification, Bobbie slammed her hands over her ears, shutting out the mocking laughter following them. Thankfully, they immediately rode into the concealing forest.

"I – think – I'm – going – to – be – sick." She managed to mumble out. Her mouth felt as though it were filled to overflowing with putrid garbage.

"Can't you just faint with embarrassment, *mignonne*?" Damien drawled out his amusement.

But he stopped the horse. Dismounting, he helped her down as well. His body was still trembling with mirth.

"Just be quiet, please." Bobbie mumbled. "My head is killing me."

Then, scurrying behind some rocks, she was violently ill.

Contrite and silent, she let Damien help her climb back onto the stallion's back. She wished she were back in her hotel room, alone and able to hide her degradation from the world. Her behaviour was appalling.

After riding a bit, Damien stopped again. This time they halted beside a tree-lined lake. Damien dropped to the ground, smoothly carrying her with him. He set her to the ground.

Dizzy and wobbly, she staggered down to the gelid waters to rinse out her rancid mouth. She splashed it on her face.

Out in the center of the lake, silver-tipped, lacy waves undulated toward the shore. Somewhere, hidden in the swaying reeds across the lake, the poignant cry from a lonely loon sent shivers along her spine. Behind her, rustling leaves quivered in the sultry winds, sounding like exquisite music, soothing and soft.

Damien must have come to St. Francis, using a different route. She couldn't remember this lovely view of glistening water and wide, tree-lined sandy beaches. She was in a beautiful fantasyland. She couldn't believe there could be such beauty in these parched lands.

She winced as yet another aching needle jabbed inside her temple. She was filled with self-loathing. Of course, she had missed this lake. She had been sleeping on the way out – passed out in a drunken stupor. She couldn't remember anything. Damien could have murdered her – or raped her – and she wouldn't have realized anything.

Alcohol was truly the root of all that was evil. If she were sober, surely even mystifying, charming Damien would lose his appeal. He would become another dominating, conceited man. She should feel nothing but scorn for him.

Three savage wives? Weren't having three wives both illegal and impossible? Or was Damien so proficient in the art of seduction he could please three women simultaneously? How?

Then he avid curiosity dulled, giving way to the steady pounding inside her head. She didn't want to even look at that arrogant monster. She had played the simpering fool all evening and was mortified to realize how easily she played it.

"There are so very few places left where a man can be alone. That's why I despise civilization so much." Damien moved silently to where she knelt by the water's edge. She heard his voice, low with melancholy.

"Civilization – out here?" Bobbie scoffed. Imagine what he would think of London or even Toronto. She wouldn't respond to that sad note in his voice.

Again, like the chameleon he resembled, he assaulted her equilibrium with a casual ease that frightened her. A dull ache inside her belly answered the little boy sadness in his voice. She remembered Pierre saying a cruel minister who wouldn't let him play with the other children had raised Damien. Did he just pretend he liked to be alone? Where was that suave, debonair man she had vowed she could easily reject?

Slipping to his knees, Damien began to massage her tangled hair and scalp.

"I could never get used to living in a tiny box that you people call houses."

"Well the *Metis* have created villages. If you call those dirty little shacks, houses." Bobbie struggled to fight the sexual feeling he aroused with only his light touch.

"You are a snob, aren't you? The *Metis* are not my people."

"They're not?" She shrugged her shoulders as his hands slid down to caress the bareness. "Indians live in cluttered tents. I'm sure a person doesn't get much privacy in a tipi."

"Is that what you think?" Damien drawled out softly. "Privacy is a state of mind. Whenever I'm with the People, I have no trouble being alone. They understand that a person must be alone at times. But here, when I want to be alone, someone is always asking if something is wrong."

"That may be because they care?" Bobbie gasped as his lean fingers moved with subtle swiftness down beneath her torn bodice.

The rolling waters seeped up the sandy beach, stroking against her skirt, soaking the badly stained material. Basking in a delicious sense of lethargy, she couldn't move.

"Or because they're nosy?" There was a light undercurrent of amusement in his tone, as though he could sense her ineffective resistance.

His hands spread out, whispering sensuously along her chest. A thumb flicked casually across her jutting nipple. Whimpering softly, Bobbie made no effort to stop his delightful exploration. She could feel the heat from his thighs, pressed into her back.

"If you want to be alone, then perhaps you should take me back to my hotel room." Yelping, she slouched forward, shaking his tenacious fingers away.

"But, *mignonne*. I want to be alone with you." His gravel-husky voice deepened with passion. He blew gently into her ear, tickling her.

She turned. His handsome face was outlined clearly in the bright beams of the moon. She could see the demonic confidence there. Feeling gauche and petrified, she swallowed deeply.

"Don't call me *mignonne* any more. You called her that!" She bounced to her feet, flustered and annoyed.

Damien treated her, Marie, and probably hundreds of other women, without respect. He thought women were here for his pleasure and use. She couldn't let him touch her again. Pulling

Hawk's Gift

away from his magnetic gaze was so hard! She fought all the way.

"You are jealous! Interesting." Standing too, Damien began to slowly strip off his vest and ruffled white shirt.

He exposed a magnificently wide expanse of rippling shoulder and arm. With his suit on, he had looked so much more slender.

"What are you doing?" She whispered, staring at his naked chest with fascination. He had no hair there. He was sinew and sculptured bronze.

"Going for a swim, *mignonne*. You are not in the mood for the pleasure I could offer. And I'm *very* hot." Unfastening his trousers, he lithely stepped out, completely nude!

Curiosity warred with shock. Bobbie studied his magnificent frame. His chest glistened in the golden-hued moonlight. His narrow hips and legs were hard with muscle. His jutting manhood rose blatantly upwards, from a nest of dark curls, like an ominous weapon. Her breath stopped.

"Join me." He spoke softly, watching her expressive gaze glued in absolute fascination to his groin.

He wanted to laugh when he felt himself growing with just her intrigued glance touching his flesh. What would happen if she touched him... with those dainty, white hands or... He groaned.

"I'll help you undress." He drawled out, as she made no effort to move or speak. She was still staring at him. Her mouth was gaping open.

Humour building, he arched; flexing his chest and arms as he imagined the gladiators of ancient times must have posed to impress their titillated ladies.

Her eyes glistened inquisitively, a strange opaque green in the moonlight. With her silk gown falling from her small shoulders and her hair tumbling around her face and back, she looked like a lovely vision – a fantasy woman for his pleasure.

"If you'd like to touch me, *mignonne* – feel free." Damien couldn't keep the desire from his voice.

"Touch you...?" Bobbie's stridden voice tapered off as she realized she was staring at him. Her hands flew up to cover her face. Was there no end to the embarrassment she was going to suffer this evening? "I've never seen... I want to go home."

She edged back cautiously, looking at the skies.

"No, you don't. You're curious. There is nothing wrong with that, *mignonne*." Damien said soothingly. "Come swimming with me, just swimming, nothing else. I won't touch you unless you want me to."

Bobbie stiffened, and then let her breath out with relief. Once again he was the crude Damien she recognized. There was no heartbreaking sadness in his voice, only that arrogant confidence she loathed. Shrugging, he turned and nonchalantly walked into the rippling waters.

Gasping, Bobbie saw the crisscrossed welts marring his smooth back. Had he been beaten? Callously, she rejected that idea. These marks were likely some strange heathen ritual or some passionate woman's scratches.

Then felt the blood drain from her face. She needed this man to guide her to Big Bear's camp or all was lost. If Gilbert didn't get that story back to her father, he would surely send someone else out to do the job. Why didn't she take this opportunity while she had it? But it all seemed so cold and calculating now. She would bed him and it would mean nothing more than a moment of pleasure to him. She shivered. Which was worse, bedding Damien or going back to Toronto and marrying Etienne?

CHAPTER 6

"Wait, Damien."

Bobbie moved into the water, without removing her encumbering clothing. Her gown was damaged beyond repair. The water lapped at her skirts, dragging it down further off her shoulders. She didn't notice. Determination was little compensation for the empty disappointment in her heart. This calculating action she intended was not the way she had imagined this evening would end. Tilting her chin with firm resolve, she continued walking towards him.

"Why?" Damien turned cautiously, staring into her eyes.

Bobbie paled. Could he still read her thoughts again? He must know how a woman would behave if she wanted – *that*, wouldn't he? He would know if she was lying. She tried to smile. He moved closer. She felt no excitement, only dreaded fear.

"How much did Gilbert pay you?" Bobbie walked further into the water, hoping to disguise her building panic. She wanted to bite her tongue. Shouldn't she have said something – tantalizing or suggestive?

But she couldn't weaken, regardless of how his sultry eyes now showed disbelief and scorn. She had to get that story. Icy beads of apprehension trickled down her flesh. Violent shudders caused her teeth to chatter.

"How interesting – A lady who would rather be a whore, than a wife." Damien's lips drew back in a sneer.

Damien moved with graceful ease. He walked past her and out of the water. Bending down, he yanked his discarded trousers on. Digging into his pocket, he turned and grinned in her direction. There was no humour in his hard eyes.

Bobbie stood frozen knee-deep in the lake. She was frightened and bewildered. Surely if a man bought a whore, he didn't care how she behaved, did he? His face was a sneering mask of contempt. He did not look even slightly charming now. He looked cruel. He flung the money into the water.

"Of course, all you want is money. Well, *mignonne*. Here it all is. You can have it with my blessing. But it won't last long, I'm sure. It may not be enough."

Damien put on his shirt and vest. He turned and mounted his horse.

"I'm curious now – are you really a virgin? How much do you feel you are worth?"

"More than *you* could ever afford." Bobbie lashed out, closing her eyes in humiliation.

"Winnipeg is about a mile east of here, *mignonne*. Maybe I'll come to Gertrude's one day and collect what you owe me – if I ever come back this way. I'm sure that's where you'll be."

"Pardon?" Bobbie opened her eyes. Dread flooded within. "You're leaving me here – alone?"

"Sorry, but I just have no stomach for what you're offering. I don't want to look at you now." Damien was still sneering darkly. He kicked his horse into motion and disappeared into the trees.

Bobbie sank to her knees. For long moments she kneeled in the waters, numb and degraded. Powerful feelings of self-loathing surged through her body. What could she do? He, superior male that he thought he was, would refuse to take her into the wilderness. Could she really fool those deep penetrating eyes into believing she was a man – for the month or two she'd have to stay in his company? Surely, now that he'd spent all Gilbert's generous advance money, his honour would ensure he would take her?

Then it penetrated. He was gone. Damien had left her alone in the dark wilds. Honour? Truly that man didn't have an ounce of chivalry in his whole body. What made her think he would honour his agreement? Now she would have to convince him she was a man.

"Damien, please wait. Oh please! Oh God, please…"

Leaping to her feet, she tried to run in the water. It pulled her down. She floundered around, trying to stand again. He couldn't do this to her. But he had. He'd left her alone in the middle of nowhere. Petrified, she realized he was truly gone.

"What if that terrible – Joseph finds me? What if some animal comes along and eats me?" She shrieked out hysterically. There was no answer.

With a quivering fortitude she didn't really feel, she gathered up the floating, soggy money and moved out of the water. Tomorrow he would understand. When she handed him back

Hawk's Gift

his money he would thank her. He would regret leaving her here to fend for herself.

That was supposing she was even alive tomorrow and no wild beast found her first. She forced her wobbly legs to move in the direction he'd indicated. She heard stealthy footsteps behind her. She whirled. Nothing was there. Oh God, something or someone was stocking her. She closed her eyes.

"Damien, please come back." She screamed. Whimpering, she turned staring into the dark, dark trees.

The woods were ominous and silent. It was only the leaves speaking their endless song to the winds. Unless - Hadn't she read somewhere that all woodland creatures were silent when danger lurked nearby? What was out there – a bear – a cat?

She turned and began running wildly. She tripped over a loose root and fell ignobly on her stomach with a loud, painful thud. Spitting out damp leaves, she sneezed. Scrambling to her feet, she started running again. She tried to concentrate on anything except those ghostly trees closing in around her. Were there ghosts out here? Visions of floating, evil creatures swam in her mind. None resembled a white horse.

Oh, why had she done this to Damien? She had wanted only to ensure he would take her to Big Bear. Would it have been so wrong to let him give her pleasure? His touch and body had guaranteed that, all through this strange evening. But, before he rode into the forest, his beautiful eyes had been filled with loathing and disgust. Why? He had been willing to pay for – *that*, before. What was different now? *'Forget his feelings'*, she berated herself. Surely her being a reporter justified her means of getting a story. Gilbert couldn't go to Big Bear's camp. He would never survive in this wilderness. He would die.

She was a mass of shivering nerve-points when she finally reached the hotel. Beginning to doubt her own competence of surviving in the wilds, she grimaced. Damien would hate her. Without encountering even one small animal, she was behaving like a lunatic. The trek through the dark night had terrified her more than anything had in the past. Damien would surely scorn her weakness. He loved the wilderness.

Sighing, she quietly climbed the back stairs to her room. She must ensure *no one* saw her in this condition.

Damien quietly watched her petrified hike through the woods. Cynical scorn twisted his lips. He had first watched the greedy bitch take his money before leaving the lake. She couldn't be totally frightened.

But as he continued to follow her frantic trek, he realized there was one thing she hadn't lied about. She was terrified of the dark and wilderness, even this close to Winnipeg. Why did he feel guilty, and obligated to see her safely back to her hotel? What did he care if she came to harm?

A vision of her elfin, laughing features formed in his mind. She was bold, charming and wild, unlike any woman he'd ever met. To himself, Damien could admit wild creatures – and women, fascinated him. She was, after all, a virgin and he'd frightened her with his aggressive comments and uncouth words. She'd been more than honest, right from the start. She needed money to support her useless brothers and her ex-fiancée.

"Oh damn! Here I go again." He muttered to himself.

He had to get out of this insane town. He refused to fall in love with yet another lady. Tomorrow, he would take Robert Taylor to Big Bear's camp in Montana and he would stay there. Taylor could find another way back to Winnipeg.

Bobbie crawled out of bed the following morning to meet Gilbert in the hotel's small dining room. She felt terrible.

"Where on earth were you last night? Gilbert demanded. He was obviously aware she hadn't been in her room.

She had hoped he wouldn't check.

Bobbie didn't feel like having an argument with her brother. She tried to hide the dark circles under her eyes and the fact her head hurt even worse than last night. She kept her face lowered. She peeked up. His face, so similar to hers, was white and drawn. Her twin brother was furious.

"I went to a brothel. I told you I was going to interview a madam, didn't I? If I can get that written up, it will bring us some good money." She answered abruptly. She eagerly gulped down her steaming coffee, not caring it was so strong her spoon could nearly stand in it.

"I told you not to go there." Gilbert hissed in fury.

Thank God, they were the only guests registered at the dilapidated hotel called *The Prairie Goose*. There was no one else to hear their conversation. The dozen wooden tables with their mismatched chairs looked lonely and dusty as sunlight filtered through tattered grey curtains.

"You are not my father," Bobbie snapped, and then quieted as a sharp jab coursed through her head. Obviously shouting was out when one had a hangover. "We need the money desperately. I'll write it up today. Father isn't going to keep sending you money unless you start sending him stories. Did you find a building for your new office?"

"No, I didn't." Gilbert sighed sullenly. "It's just so dangerous out here. The men walk around with pistols strapped around their waists. I'm going crazy with the fighting and crude words flying around. I want to go back to Toronto."

"I agree it's none too civilized here." Bobbie smiled and leaned over to pat his hand. He looked so sad and out of his element in this crude town. Of course, Gilbert would find these people alarming. He was always meticulously dressed and such a gentleman. His timid nature brought her protective feelings to the front. He was always sickly and so meek. His nature infuriated their father. "Has father asked any questions about me?"

"Father still thinks you've gone to England." Gilbert smiled faintly. "At least out here I don't have to listen to his constant criticism all day long."

"That's true." Bobbie rubbed her forehead carefully.

Gilbert could do no right in their father's eyes. Even Bobbie had to admit Gilbert's weakness annoyed her at times. He couldn't seat a horse properly and he winced and closed his eyes whenever he shot a pistol. During their lessons, when they were younger, Gilbert had an irritating habit of either daydreaming or crying whenever their tutor raised his voice. Gilbert only seemed comfortable with Etienne or Bobbie at his side.

"Where is Etienne?" Bobbie asked. This morning she would have even appreciated Etienne's support. He always seemed to pull Gilbert out of his melancholy moods.

"Still sleeping. We have a ten o-clock appointment with your guide, Bobbie." Gilbert exclaimed obviously proud of himself. "I found you a guide."

I know, Bobbie nearly blurted out and then caught herself. Instead she smiled. "How on earth did you ever convince a man to take me to Montana?"

"Well, I – that is..." Gilbert cleared his throat. "He thinks you are a man. You've played the part before. Remember you dressed up like a man when you were investigating Hardin Steel in Hamilton? No one suspected you were a girl. I took you to work there nearly two weeks."

"I'm going to be gone more than two weeks." Bobbie inserted with dry humour. "Will I be meeting this guide with you?"

She glanced down at her dress pointedly. She would have to change. Nervously, she wondered if Damien would know. She still felt the shame of her atrocious behaviour last night. She was sure she never wanted to see Damien again.

"Yes. Of course you have to meet him." Gilbert slanted a nervous glance in her direction.

"What's wrong?" Bobbie reached out to take his hand in hers.

"I don't like this man. Damien Larocque seems to be – dangerous. He doesn't look safe." He squirmed in his seat. His face was like a ghost. "I should go with you – but I can't. I'd slow you up – I'd become ill. You won't mind, will you?"

"No Gilbert, I won't mind." Bobbie sighed, patting his hand.

It was true enough. Lately, when Gilbert was ill, there were times he'd actually coughed blood up. Bobbie was worried.

"Perhaps you should ask Father to send you to Switzerland. There are sanatoriums there that could cure you."

"Father would never agree. He wants to get this office started and he wants that story about Big Bear." Gilbert shook his head, squeezing Bobbie's fingers. "You know Father never believes I'm ill. He just thinks I'm w-weak and – and..."

"Why won't Big Bear just sign the treaty papers?" Bobbie interrupted, trying to change the topic. Gilbert looked ready to cry.

She couldn't deal with Gilbert's tantrums now. If Father asked Gilbert to come home, where would she go? Gertrude's saloon? She wanted to cry herself.

"We don't know. Everyone knows we treat our own Indians so much better in Canada than they do south of the border." Gilbert answered pompously.

Bobbie smiled cynically. "But then why is he down in Montana?"

All the politicians, including their father, insisted they dealt fairly with the Indians. Neither Bobbie, nor Gilbert, could see why their father and his associates would lie. Still, Bobbie felt it was very odd to think that if Canada treated its Indians so well, why was Big Bear hiding south of the border?

Gilbert stared at her, a blank expression in his eyes.

"Never mind. I suppose I'll find out soon enough. I have to go and change. Do you have a pair of trousers I might borrow?" Bobbie stood, shoving her plate of congealed eggs and untouched greasy bacon aside. She had no intentions of eating. Her stomach was so queasy she wondered if she might not become violently ill herself.

CHAPTER 7

Damien sauntered through the lobby of the *Prairie Goose*, behind the proprietor. He was acutely aware of the landlord's transparent aversion to him. Mr. Porter evidently didn't feel it was right to be escorting a half-breed into his own office. Damien smiled with cynical amusement. He hoped Robert

Taylor was ready to leave immediately. He wanted to end this disastrous visit to Winnipeg as soon as possible.

Gilbert, delicate and sickly looking, was seated behind Mr. Porter's dark, walnut desk. Damien smiled politely, reaching his hand across the desk. Gilbert's handshake was weak and his damp fingers trembled.

Then he noticed the other two occupants in the room. One was Etienne LaVoie, looking haughty and bored. Damien had met him the previous evening and wasn't impressed with the man's effeminate looks and puffed-up expression. Then he turned to the other man. He was a very slight, little man. Didn't they have any idea how a real man was made, back East?

He let his gaze roam over the small figure. His breath caught with mounting fury as his gazed locked with Miss *Roberta Taylor's* deceitful green orbs.

"I will not..." Damien bit his lip to stop his impulsive words. Perhaps he was being too hasty. Maybe he would let her play this little game – only this time it would be solely on his terms.

"Hello. Damien Larocque, I presume? I'm Robert Taylor." Standing, Bobbie strode across the small room, holding out her delicate hand. He wanted to laugh. She walked like she supposed a man would, but she was failing. Her gently curved hips looked absolutely provocative in the trousers.

Damien took it. He considered lifting the delicate hand and kissing it, but decided not to. Let her think he was fooled. Her handshake was decidedly firmer than her brothers. Damien continued to hold her finger, running his thumb in a circular motion on her palm. He noted the uncertainty flicker in her expressive eyes. He wanted to shake her. Did she really believe he was such a fool? She was a potent woman and those pants enhanced that particular fact. He dropped her hand.

"How's Roberta?"

"Roberta? Oh, you must mean my twin sister – Bobbie..." Bobbie stuttered. Her eyes widened in apprehension.

Bobbie flushed. She turned back to sit on the couch. He admired the provocative sway of her hips again. Yes, he definitely had to get this little urchin away from Winnipeg and teach her a much-needed lesson.

"You met Bobbie?" Gilbert interrupted. He was wringing his hands in alarm as he stood and walked around the desk. "When did you meet Bobbie? If you've harmed her..."

"Gilbert!" Bobbie snapped out urgently. Damien saw the warning glint in her eyes. Then she looked back nervously to Damien. "Bobbie told me she went out, don't worry so much Gilbert. You must know Bobbie is quite capable of managing Mr. Larocque well enough."

"Managing? Hmm!" Damien laughed softly. So she was continue to continue this charade. So be it! She must realize he knew who she was.

Now, he wanted only to concentrate on putting this sassy little brat in her place. She thought she was on top did she? Then, as he further considered the matter, he decided that was exactly where she would be. He was liberated enough to find a woman very fascinating in that particular position.

"Let's get down to business, shall we?" Bobbie sat down on the gaudy, flowered sofa.

Damien continued to smile, saying nothing. He watched her wide cat-eyes cloud with anger. Trousers suited her small frame very well. If her brother and his friend were an indication of the type of man she could so *'easily manage'*, she was in for a very unpleasant shock. Why should he fight this powerful magnetism he felt? She was so willing to oblige him. Her audacity in believing she was untouchable, superior to all mortal men, was astounding. He could taste the pleasure he was going to feel, taming this little wildcat.

"You wouldn't consider backing out, would you?" Bobbie's eyes narrowed. "Unless you can pay back the generous advance Gilbert gave you, I don't see how you can."

'Bitch!' He mouthed the word silently.

"What?" Her mouth dropped open.

"Surely, since you were talking to *Bobbie* – you must know I have already spent the advance." Damien stepped over behind the sofa. He enjoyed her apprehensive start as she shifted slightly to watch him with alarmed eyes.

"Excuse me." Gilbert's voice was a high-pitched squeak. "What does Bobbie have to do with the advance I paid you?"

"She didn't tell you? I suppose she just talked to *Robert*. Your sister promised something last night – in return for money." His insinuation was clear, even to Gilbert.

Damien turned to watch Etienne now. He was seated quietly in an armchair, watching them with an amused expression. He was silent.

"But did she deliver?" Bobbie snarled, forgetting to disguise her voice.

Damien reached down to place his hand on her shoulder. He smiled as her tiny body tensed. Her body was vibrating with frustration. He laughed, and then stood straight again, moving back to stand by Gilbert.

"There is no need to worry, Mr. Taylor. Your sister went to Gertrude's saloon and I helped her out with a little problem." Damien continued to smile. Gilbert looked utterly confused. "Now, I will help your brother as well. Don't worry. He'll learn to love the wilderness. He won't ever want to come back."

"Etienne – what do you think?" Gilbert stuttered.

"I would say he's the perfect man for the job." Etienne smiled, stifling a yawn.

Damien observed the way Etienne's small eyes, with their heavy dropping lids, couldn't hide his dislike for Bobbie. Why?

"This is really none of his concern." Bobbie made no effort to hide her disgust for Etienne either.

I am Bobbie's fiancée?" Etienne continued to smile.

"Oh no you're not." Bobbie nearly screamed out, once again forgetting to lower her tone.

"I was engaged to Bobbie. Then – ah – Robert here came up with a brilliant plan to save us all from disaster to keep us from starving. We all rely on their father for support." Etienne turned to Damien. "Robert doesn't like me and didn't want me to marry his – ah – sister."

"Does she like you?" Damien asked sardonically. His eyes filled with disgust as he turned his gaze towards the dismayed Gilbert. "How do expect to pay me the rest?"

"My father pays my salary and my expenses." Gilbert pursed his lips primly. "Our father is Sir Myles Taylor. Surely you've heard of him? He planned a marriage between Etienne and Bobbie in hopes such a merger would enhance his position."

"And secure the French vote. Bobbie told me that, last night. Where does Robert fit into all this?" Damien nodded. His gaze moved back to study Bobbie with bold contemplation. She shifted nervously. He smiled.

"He writes for Father's newspaper. That's why he needs a guide." Gilbert flushed his misery. "I run the office, of course."

"And Bobbie needs a husband – preferably French? I happen to be French myself. I wonder if your father would consider me? I'm assuming having money isn't a criteria." Damien was amused by the trio's immediate start.

"No, he wouldn't!" Etienne interrupted, looking uneasy. "You are part Indian. Sir Myles wouldn't consider that at all."

"Etienne!" Bobbie and Gilbert spoke simultaneously. Their voices were filled with fright. Damien noticed their gazes falling immediately towards his strapped on holster and pistol.

"I am *Metis*." Damien forced himself to smile politely.

Inside, his guts twisted with fury. It was always the same. These white intruders felt it was their right to come into *his* territory and insult him. Turning back to Bobbie, he unlaced his mesmerizing smile with deliberation. Nothing would stop him from making her his personal slave. It was only what they all deserved. The threat of Sir Myles and Etienne's feeble attempt to scare him only increased his determination.

"Don't worry – a real man would never be upset with a insult – would he, Robert?"

"How would I know?" Bobbie muttered, clasping her hands together in a nervous gesture. She looked absolutely disoriented.

Damien's gleaming eyes touched her intimately with caressing thoroughness.

"I suspect you are the man of this house." Damien chuckled so innocently.

Blushing, she didn't answer him.

"Well, back to business. Can you be ready to leave early tomorrow morning? I'll get whatever supplies we need today."

"I'll be ready. How will I get my reports back to Gilbert?" She asked quietly.

"We will send a messenger back – when you have anything to report, of course." Damien smiled his delight.

The little witch was falling so easily into his trap. Whenever he wanted her off-balance he need only challenge her authority.

Going to the door with Damien, Bobbie smiled with satisfaction. Damien was going to take her to Montana! She couldn't keep the excitement and relief from her voice.

Damien opened the door and grabbed her hand. He pulled her outside and closed the door. They were alone in the lobby.

"I am going to enjoy playing a wild savage to your frightened lady, *mignonne, aren't you?*" Damien leaned down, breathing sensually against her ear. "But I wouldn't mind seeing a little more fear in those whiskey eyes."

"But..." Bobbie was chagrined when her traitorous body so effortlessly answered his whisper. Every nerve tingled in her entire frame, piercing her skin. And she couldn't blame alcohol this time.

"I knew from the start." Damien smiled, but his face was grim. "Do you really think I'm such a fool, Bobbie?"

"Then why are you taking me?" Bobbie's thoughts were a mass of confusion.

"I'll take you to hell if you ask nicely, *mignonne*."

His lips were close to hers. Why was he being so pleasant? She'd tricked him into being her guide. She hadn't given him what he had paid her for, last night. She could only stare into his hypnotic eyes watching silver glints flickering in their black depths. He had such beautiful eyes. She sighed. She could stand all day and look into them. She swallowed as her stomach tightened in anticipation.

"Why are you taking me?" If she moved just one tenth of an inch closer, their lips would meet. Dare she be so bold?

"I like you, *mignonne*." Damien took the choice out of her hands. He pressed his lips to hers in a quick, hard kiss. Then he turned and moved out the lobby door. She stood and watched him, touching her tingling lips with her fingers. Her eyes drew together in puzzlement. She just didn't understand this man at all. Last night, she was sure he despised her. Today he said he *liked* her?

CHAPTER 8

Pink clouds, like bubbles in silken bath water, lined the eastern horizon. The air was cool, remnants of the lingering night. Eager to be on her way Bobbie was ready and waiting outside the hotel when Damien rode up.

Gilbert and Etienne, having spent another late night gambling and doing whatever else they did all night, were still sleeping.

After spending most of the night not sleeping herself, Bobbie finally decided her best course would be to ignore Damien. Other than follow him to Montana, she would pretend he didn't exist. He was her guide, nothing more. He was too domineering and much too aware of his appeal for her peace of mind.

"Sorry about your horse, *mignonne*. He's an Indian pony. He is not used to saddles." Damien's voice was husky with sleep.

He slid his possessive gaze over her curves, outlined so revealingly by her trousers. She swung into the saddle, scowling. For goodness sake, it was morning! Did his mind ever travel anywhere other than the dirt?

Then she concentrated on bringing a bucking, squirming mass of horseflesh under control, only just managing to pull the wild horse beside Damien's. Triumphant confidence flared up.

Had he known the horse would buck? Perhaps, he wasn't being so nice!

She tried to ignore the sultry admiration in his eyes. But the she found it impossible to ignore anything about Damien this morning. Giggles gurgled deep in her throat. She scanned the street, hoping no one else was up and about this early. To her relief it was deserted.

Damien was dressed in full Indian regalia. His chest was bare except for the elaborate porcupine quill neck choker set with vibrant turquoise stones. A single feather was encased in glass at the center. It was beautiful. Wide, intricately patterned copper bands on his upper arms drew her eyes to his smooth muscles. A leather loincloth hung low over his narrow hips. Tight, long fringed leggings encased his legs. A leather-beaded band held his thickly waved hair off his paint-streaked face.

"War paint? Were you planning on attacking Winnipeg before we left?" Bobbie laughed, purposely revealing she had done some research on Native customs.

Her belly rumbled precariously. Would he ever do anything normal? She thought that today he would be belligerent. He wouldn't like catering to the whims of a female. Instead he was acting like a clown. She looked at him as he reached up to caress the feather on his choker.

"Where did you learn to ride?" Damien grinned. Dismounting, he picked up her bag and attached it to the packhorse. "You do it beautifully."

"Did you hope I would fall off and break my neck?" Bobbie's expression hardened. Was he so cruel?

"No. I would rather break it myself, *mignonne*." Dale murmured.

Kicking her horse, she encouraged his reckless gallop away from town and that frustrating man. She had no intention of telling him that she also knew how to shoot and even do mathematics as well as any man. Then she would have to explain how Gilbert, when they were children, had refused to do anything unless his beloved twin did it as well. In order to teach Gilbert the fine art of being a gentleman, Sir Myles had also allowed Bobbie to learn those entire lessons. Bobbie was sure Damien already had enough ammunition against her. He already knew too much about her personal life. He was her guide, nothing more.

"*Mignonne...*" Damien's caressing voice floated down the street. Bobbie stopped to see what he wanted. Grinning, he wheeled his mount around, kicking him in the flanks.

"You are going in the wrong direction."

She looked back to see she was riding directly into the morning sun. Sheepishly, she turned her horse around to follow him, giving the mount free rein. He galloped by Damien with long, easy strides.

"Easy. Don't wear him out. Riding is like making love, slow and easy is much better." Damien flashed her a naughty grin as he urged his horse beside her.

That was obviously all he had on his mind! Then common sense overcame irritation. He was right. She slowed down to a mile-consuming canter.

"What's his name?"

"Your horse? Flower." Damien answered.

"Flower?" Bobbie frowned her disapproval. "Of course you would call this lovely stallion, Flower. What's his name?" She bobbed her head in his mount's direction. "Alice?"

"No – this is Attila the Hun." Damien shrugged his shoulders. "Flower deserves his name. He is too meek. My packhorse is a mare – named Willow. They are my only possessions."

"Where do you live? Don't you have a house?" Bobbie asked, forgetting she was supposed to ignore him. She found herself enjoying his congeniality.

"No. I don't need a house. I have a big backyard though." Damien's arms swept around.

"That's because no one else wants it!" Bobbie murmured with sarcasm.

"Ah, *mignonne*, I so much wanted you to like my home..." Damien was staring at her again, a sultry, possessive expression in his eyes. "How could you think *Toronto* is more beautiful?"

"Stop it!" Bobbie glared back. He was treating her like an imbecile – a weak, helpless female.

"I'm sorry for staring at you. But us poor little ol' heathens don't often see such lovely, fair hair." Damien lowered his gaze in meekness. "You should keep it hidden. I might be tempted to scalp you."

Bobbie's hands flew protectively to her hair. That was exactly what she had read – heathens often *did* scalp poor, helpless people. But Damien was civilized wasn't he? She glanced over to see Damien's shoulders shaking. He was laughing.

"Damien, I'm a good reporter. Gilbert and Etienne depend on me. I don't have time for your silly games."

"Intriguing." Damien looked into her eyes, edging Attila closer. "You are the breadwinner of the family. And it extends to your brother's friends as well? Why don't you just marry me? I would never expect you to support me."

"Don't!" Bobbie wished she could keep the wobble out of her voice. "I had no intention of marrying you. You know that."

"Then why did you say you would?" Damien's voice lowered. "What did you want from me?"

"Oh!" Reaching into her pocket, Bobbie withdrew his crumpled bills. "I believe these are yours. I was just ensuring you would take me to Big Bear."

"By teasing me all night?" Damien eyed the bills as though they were dirt, making no effort to take them. "Keep it, *mignonne*. You earned it."

"But – you have nothing." Bobbie protested. She held nearly two hundred dollars in her hand. He wouldn't just throw that kind of money away, would he?

"I told you I have everything I want." Damien's jaw clenched. "How long have you been supporting Gilbert and Etienne?"

Bobbie felt her face and neck go hot. "This is my first job. We've been here for three weeks." She started quietly, and then saw his shoulders were shaking again. "Why are you always laughing at me? This is very serious."

"I am not laughing at you." Damien's sarcastic smile made her wonder if he hadn't started drinking already. "And I expect you will soon discover just how serious a trip like this can be."

"What do you mean?"

"Aren't you even a little worried about disappearing into the wilds with a drunken Indian?" That reckless gleam was back in his beguiling eyes. "This is your last chance. Are you sure you want to do this? Why don't you just go back to Daddy and his money?"

"You'd like that, wouldn't you?" Bobbie hissed. "It would only prove to you that I'm just another helpless female. Well I'm not just another weak female and I won't go back to Daddy!"

Damien smiled grimly, reading the arrogance in her expressive eyes. Her wonderful, rich daddy would save her! If she had shown even the slightest fear, he might have reconsidered and taken her back to her brother. But her superior attitude fired his rage. He would punish this haughty little witch. He had started drinking this morning. Actually, he hadn't stopped since last night.

Abusing women was not normally his style. But if ever a woman deserved a set-down, this one did. Her father was right. She was a barracuda.

They rode steadily along rolling, gradual rises and small dips. No longer talking, pleasantly or otherwise, Damien seemed to change the further they rode from Winnipeg. Out here, he was believable in his untamed, primitive clothing. The intense heat of August sunshine, combined with endless miles of nothing but burnt grasses to the horizon and the fact he was continually taking that silver flask from his saddlebag and drinking, made Bobbie acutely edgy.

"Damien!" She gasped out from beneath dry, cracked lips. She could barely see the blurred figure, always riding slightly ahead of her. "I need to stop. I need a drink."

Silently, he wheeled his horse around. Leaning down, he scooped up the canteen attached to her saddle. His brooding, dark gaze studied her with intense interest.

Flushing at her ignorance, Bobbie took a long deep swallow of the lukewarm liquid. He looked as fresh as he had in the early dawn light. Looking up into the barren sky, she felt the sun, shining directly overhead.

"Are we going to stop for lunch soon?" She asked hopefully.

Damien's expression remained vague. Solemnly, he reached back into her saddlebag and handed her a strip of dried, tough meat.

Cantankerous with fatigue, she stared at the shrivelled, unappetizing food. This was her lunch? Weary and near tears, she searched the bald prairie for some type of shade. Couldn't he at least find a tree or boulder for her to rest and catch her breath? Turning back, she caught the flash of amusement in his eyes. He wanted her to fail and go back!

Trying to disregard the sharp, jabbing pain in her legs and the sopping wet irritation around her waist, Bobbie nudged Flower forward. Biting into the hard meat, she swallowed painfully.

"If we have to stop all the time, we'll never get anywhere." Damien stated with an innocent smile.

Glaring, Bobbie refused to speak. He would love to see her beg - and was obviously determined to make her do just that. She adamantly refused to give him that satisfaction.

Grimacing, she closed her eyes against the blistering sun. Daydreaming to stop the pain radiating throughout her body, she imagined what he would be like in Toronto. He would need *her* competent assistance then. But she would just tilt her nose and laugh. She wouldn't lift one little finger to help him.

Damien was unaware of her rising pain. The selfish little lady would be quick enough to tell him if she couldn't stand the

Hawk's Gift

pace. She was not the docile type who would stay quiet and endure discomfort willingly.

He was busy planning her downfall. It would be about a month before her father or Gilbert became suspicious because they hadn't heard from her. By that time he would have her well hidden in Big Bear's Montana camp. He would have to keep her away from Big Bear. If the Chief ever discovered that Bobbie, daughter to Sir Myles Taylor, was with them against her will, Big Bear would be livid.

Far from being a trouble-making savage, Big Bear tried very hard to co-operate with the Canadian government. He just refused to do so at the expense of his people. Damien admired Big Bear for his refusal to sign treaty papers. The reservation the Canadian government was offering him was pathetic. All the other natives who had signed those papers were now living in abject poverty.

Ominous charcoal clouds covered the darkening sky with swift penetration as night fell. Brisk winds had turned the air into freezing whips of agony before Damien stopped. Thin, white streaks of electricity tore ruthlessly through the inky skies.

Bobbie stared at those dangerous white lines, recalling she had read that lightning had caused many a deadly prairie fire out here. She shuddered. What would they do if the grass caught on fire? Where would they go? Then she whimpered. Maybe they were in hell already.

She could not dismount. She was too tender and sore. She slumped silently on Flower's back. Damien lit a fire and hastily erected a crude shelter between two large rocks. Curved aspens and low brush further screened the tiny sanctuary.

"Stubborn little witch!" He muttered when he finally came to help her off the horse.

He plopped her beside the fire, just beneath the buffalo robe he'd rigged up as a roof. Swiftly, he yanked the tucked shirt aside and opened her sweat-soaked trousers. Bobbie was too numb to resist. Moaning, she felt stinging agony as the wind slashed against her underclothing. She tried to rub against the raw flesh around her waist.

Exasperated, Damien swore. Now she was only an impetuous, silly child. She claimed to be so capable and practical. Yet she was wearing a corset! Grimacing, he reached for his hunting knife. Ripping her buttoned blouse open – with one savage swipe of his blade, that silly contraption ladies deemed so necessary, snapped free. He carefully examined the red welts of blistered flesh around her tiny waistline.

Standing, he moved back to the still saddled horses. He had intended she learn a little humility, not that she kill herself. Once again, she was not what she seemed. She had more courage and stamina than many men. She had endured this self-induced torture for how many hours now…and without making a sound?

"Don't leave me alone." Bobbie whimpered. She tried to sit up and grab him. "I don't want to be alone."

The dark clouds closed in to surround them with darkness. Damien smiled slightly remembering her fear of the dark. She thought he was going to leave her here alone.

Tears of misery trickled down her sunburned face, licking against her dried lips. Damien came back, squatting down to wipe the streaks away. Her face was dusty. Her hair was a tangled mess, falling from its pins. She was still beautiful.

Pushing her back to the blanket, he began to rub some sweet scented lotion into her waist. He knew her thighs were just as sore. He would have to put salve on them as well. Damien looked up to watch her as he slowly slid the trousers down her slender, curved legs.

"What are you using?" she murmured, not even opening her eyes. A slight smile curved her pouting lips. She was oblivious to the fact she was lying, nearly naked, letting him touch her.

He was painfully aware of what he was doing.

Studying her with a connoisseur's eye for perfection, he decided she was exquisite. Her satin, creamy skin was glazed metallic gold in the firelight. Her small firm breasts, with their teasing pink tips, rose boldly, begging to be touched. Was she sore there? Should he ask her? His gaze moved languidly down to her tiny waist and slight, flared hips. A scrap of silk covered her...there...

"Marie thought you might need this." Abruptly, his strokes against the inside of her leg changed to a firm stroke. He was losing control. His breath quickened. Brazenly, he let one finger slip down to touch the smooth flesh along her tummy. He groaned, moving his hand between her thighs, parting her legs.

"Marie?" Bobbie protested. She clamped her legs together capturing his hand between them. She winced in pain. "Poor Pierre. You saw her again... you despicable cad. He's your cousin."

"Settle down, wildcat." Damien swiftly placed one arm across her squirming chest, pressing her back. He continued to massage her soft flesh along her upper legs. "I went to tell *both* that I was taking you with me to Big Bear in case anyone was looking for me."

"What are you doing?" Her eyes widened just as his finger slid too close to that tantalizing spot he was dying to touch. The silk was hot and damp. "Damien – *what are you doing?*"

"I'm just making you feel better, *mignonne*." Damien cleared his throat. Sweat broke out on his forehead. He felt her legs trembling. Then she squirmed, trying to remove his hand. He felt the silk of her underpants and deliberately rubbed his palm over the wispy material. He could feel her heat, scalding his hand.

"Damien, please don't." There was real fright in her eyes now. "Let me go."

"I think it's time we started doing things my way, *mignonne*." He pressed his palm against her blistered skin, knowing the slightest pressure caused her pain. "This is a good example of how you mess things up when you're in charge. Why didn't you tell me?"

"And have you laugh at me again?" Bobbie shook her head. Her eyes were stormy and glazed. Beneath his hand he felt her legs tense. "I'd rather die."

"You will – if this gets infected." Damien smiled as he still massaged the softness. He moved his hand down, closer to her knees. She relaxed.

"What are you going to do with me?" she whispered.

"Now's a silly time to ask, *mignonne*," Damien's lips quirked. "You should have asked that in Winnipeg. I warned you to go back."

He could smell the fear in her trembling body and he didn't care. It was far too late.

"Don't be a fool!" Her voice rose, shrill and grating. "I'm a white lady. You can't just..."

"Wrong choice of words." Damien shook his head. His arm across her chest shifted, moving to allow his hand room to cup one lovely breast. He squeezed slightly. His fingers moved boldly upwards between her legs. One slipped beneath her underpants. "I can do as I please and even your wonderful *Daddy* can't help you now."

"You're the fool if you think that!" Bobbie cringed back on the blanket. "You can't believe that."

"You don't know when to shut-up, do you?"

Damien made no effort to be gentle as he deliberately fondled her quivering chest. His other hand was considerably softer as he stroked against the soft curls that hid her delights. Grinning with wicked intent, he leaned down to flick his tongue against her puckered nub. She screamed.

"Please don't hurt me." She tried to wiggle away.

"Surely, this doesn't hurt..." He whispered against her ear. His hand between her legs, moved to the soft folds. Looking at her face he could see the silent tears of frustration on her pale cheeks. But he felt her slight arch when he inserted a finger into her heated core. He shook his head to clear his fuzzy mind. Why was he trying to comfort this selfish lady? Why couldn't he just rape her, like he'd intended?

"I'm scared." Bobbie murmured. Then her legs loosened, parting slightly. She rotated against his palm, obviously not even aware of what she was doing.

"Damn you." Damien moved back. Standing he ran his fingers through his hair. "Go to sleep."

He didn't want her willing. He didn't want her to want him. He needed her frightened and terrified. She must learn her lessons.

"I said go to sleep. I won't hurt you." He ground out as she continued to stare up mutely into his face.

Smiling faintly, Bobbie rolled over to her side. She almost immediately slipped into a deep, exhausted slumber.

What was that smile about? She *knew* he couldn't hurt her! But why couldn't he? He didn't have a weak stomach, or any feelings of guilt. And she certainly deserved whatever he decided was fair punishment. Perspiration mingled with the heavy raindrops. Damien stood over her, just watching. She looked so appealing asleep. Once again he was astounded and fascinated by her supreme arrogance. She could actually fall asleep now. Didn't she realize what he'd almost done?

Shaking his head, he moved back to the fire. Considering she was exclusively his to do with as he pleased, you'd think she'd show a little more concern. Then he laughed. Up to this point, she had managed to control every situation.

That had to change. He would adjust his whole strategy. His heart hardened with determination. She must learn her lesson. She couldn't manipulate him without suffering the consequences.

CHAPTER 9

Swallowing rapidly, to wet her parched throat, Bobbie tried to rub her gritty eyes. Disoriented, she could not understand why her arms refused to move. What was going to happen now? Her widespread arms felt numb. She shifted, unable to roll to her side, as she wanted.

She tilted her head. She was bound at the wrists! Her blouse was open, exposing her chest and her trousers were off. Shame spread across her cheeks as she gradually recalled the events leading to this. Realization seeped in. She was tied. Why?

Terrified, she searched the surrounding darkness for Damien. She wanted to believe hostile Indians had captured them, rather than know what she feared in her heart.

Her panic grew when she saw Damien, leaning forward over the snapping fire. One bronzed arm undulated with the motion as he deftly turned meat on a spit. Tilting his flask to his mouth with the other, he swallowed deeply. He was still drinking! Dread nearly stopped her already erratic heartbeat.

Knowing she must not alert him to the fact she was awake, Bobbie scanned her surroundings, trying to rationalize her situation. She wanted to scream. She knew it would not help her. She was staked to the ground, in the middle of nowhere, with a madman. That was her situation.

She was a complete imbecile. She had no one but herself to blame for this ludicrous predicament. What made her so presumptuous and smug as to believe she could control this explosive heathen? Letting madness intrude and rule her normal sagacious mind, she had stepped blindly into his very proficient trap. She should have realized from the beginning that Damien would not play by any rules she would know or understand. She was entirely at his mercy now. He wasn't a gentleman. He was a savage heathen without honour or mercy. She had known all that, yet she'd still come along with him.

It was so terrifying in this wilderness. Crinkled lines of lightning broke through the black clouds. The wind tore at everything with determined intensity, penetrating her flimsy shelter. The icy breeze mingled with her freezing blood.

Still feigning sleep, she turned again to inspect Damien. Was there any possible way she could escape? Could she convince him to take her back? She was miles from civilization, alone and his captive. Where could she go, even if she could escape? What did he plan to do to her? Would he torture her? Her breath caught in her throat. She had read about the heathens' cruel methods of torture and degradation. She'd heard the stories of those unfortunate white women, held captive and forced to become their slaves and suffer such depraved actions they would have gladly welcomed death. Whimpering, she looked at Damien. She really didn't know anything about him.

His straight nose and high, prominent cheekbones were in stark relief against the raging skies when he lifted the bottle to his lips. With only his loincloth on, he looked as though he were a part of the striking storm. He was an evil demon, coming to enjoy the earthly furies. He was primitive and alien to all she knew or understood.

"What are you going to do to me?" Exhaling sharply, she was unaware she had voiced the question aloud.

Like an animal scenting his prey, Damien turned. Bobbie gasped. He looked dangerous and wild with the grotesque shadows and light from the fire playing along his harsh features. He stood with fluent grace. He moved over to squat down beside her. He traced one finger along her soft bottom lip.

"I'll do whatever I want." He supplied as a fact. "You're mine."

Panic streaked through her. She tried, unsuccessfully, to avoid his smouldering eyes. They were heavy-lidded and so terrifying. His breath reeked of whiskey. He leaned nearer. She stiffened, petrified. Her mind buzzed with confusion. Everyone's dire warning echoed in her mind. *'Damien is dangerous when he's drunk... Damien is unpredictable when he's drunk...'* Damien was drunk.

"What will you do to me?" She whispered, trying to sound firm and knowing she sounded terrified instead.

"That all depends on you." His voice sounded reasonable enough. But she heard no compassion.

"I want to go back to Winnipeg. Take me back – Now!" Fright didn't stop her from fighting the ropes binding her to the ground. Some animals responded to a firm voice. "Untie me."

"It's much too late for that now. I did warn you – several times. Why didn't you listen?" Damien's voice was flat and emotionless. "Besides, I'm betting that within a few days you won't want to go back." Then suddenly his voice lightened, cajoling and husky.

Bobbie closed her eyes. She loved the sound of his voice. She snorted. She couldn't believe what she was thinking. He was lethal and he meant to harm her.

"Untie me. I demand it!" She uttered her command through clenched teeth.

"Such a haughty attitude for someone in your position, *mignonne*. Are you sure you wouldn't like to reword that request?"

He seemed to take delight in her arrogant words. Bobbie knew it was the wrong approach, but knowing didn't stop her. She still couldn't believe this was happening. She took a deep breath, trying to calm her building rage.

"Why would you do this?" Bobbie asked. Her stomach growled with hunger and fear. "Damien, you can't be such a fool."

"Who's the fool now?" His sensual lips twisted, feral and predatory.

With ease, he grasped her cheeks between one palm, squeezing lightly. He forced her to open her eyes and look into his. She blinked rapidly, trying to focus.

"You must have *some* idea what's going to happen to you," he continued softly.

"You are kidnapping me?" Bobbie laboured for breath, unable to believe what she was hearing. "You want Daddy's money? I hate you." It was the only thing that made sense.

Twisting her head to the side only increased the pressure of his biting fingers. He obligatory turned her back to look into his fiery eyes.

"How easily you use words. Love, hate. Well, I love the way you hate me. You've wanted me from the moment you saw me. Don't deny it." Damien stilled her shaking head with ease. "I'll tell you what, Wildcat. If you give me what we both want tonight, I'll take you back to Winnipeg tomorrow. Just ask me nicely."

Bobbie gulped back her own rage. She wasn't sure whether his bitter laughter was mockery or confidence. She was sure he had no intention of ever returning her to Winnipeg, tomorrow or ever.

After what he was doing tonight, he couldn't take her back. Bobbie knew enough about the law to realize that a native wouldn't stand a chance in any white man's court. Once he'd done whatever horrible things he intended to do, he would have to murder her. Her queasy stomach rumbled, increasing to alarmed panic.

"You can't do this Damien. Be reasonable. I'm a white lady. Do you have any idea what will happen if you harm me? You can't just..." Her voice tapered off. His face darkened with every word she uttered.

Moaning, she wanted to crawl in a hole and die. "What about my reports? I have to send back reports."

"There will be no reports." Damien spat out venomously. "Did your actually think I would let *you* write about my people?"

She knew she was going about this all wrong. Her autocratic manner would drive him crazy.

"You are drunk and not thinking straight." She tried to soften her voice.

"And you are?" Damien smiled, squeezing her cheek again. "Who's the captive here?"

Bobbie cringed, terrified by the condemnation in his blazing voice. Yes, he definitely meant to kill her. She could read that in his glittering eyes. Then a triumphant flush caused her to regain some composure.

"You better kill me – fast. They will be looking for me soon."

"Who are they, *mignonne*?" His grip on her cheeks increased painfully.

In horrified fascination she watched his wide lips, drawn back over his sharp teeth. She could imagine those teeth sinking into her flesh to devour her.

"Do you eat people?" She could not remember anything now about these strange people. Were they cannibals, like certain African tribes?

She had no doubt she was going to die tonight. She only hoped she could die with some dignity and pride. Instead she felt like crying and begging this cruel man for mercy.

"Pardon?" Damien's eyes widened in confusion. "What are you saying?"

Stubbornly, she remained silent. Then the agony of his fingers cutting into her cheek penetrated, drowning out her determination.

"Please stop." Whimpering, she realized it was not going to be easy to accept death courageously.

She blinked furiously, trying to stop the tears from pouring out. He was going to kill her tonight and no one would ever know, let alone help her. Daddy thought she was in England. Gratefully, she realized he'd loosened his fingers. His thumb grazed softly along her cheek. He didn't look at all menacing now.

"Yes, *mignonne*." Did she hear laughter in his voice? "I'm definitely going to eat you."

She drew her breath in. He sounded – erotically depraved. What was he saying?

"Gilbert will come when I don't send a report back. He knows I'm with you." She pleaded, still trying to assimilate what he'd just said.

"You can't possibly believe he can do anything?" Damien laughed. "And stop looking so terrified. I wouldn't literally eat you, *mignonne*..."

"Daddy will save me." Bobbie frowned. He was talking in riddles.

She spoke with confidence now as she thought about Sir Myles. Her father had always solved her problems in the past. This time would be no different. Then her heart sank ominously. What could Daddy do about this? He didn't even know she was here. But surely, suspecting she was in danger, Gilbert would tell him. But not before she was murdered! She bit into her lip to keep from crying out. Who could ever prove Damien had murdered her? He had never been charged with Reverend MacLeod's murder, even after his wife had insisted he had done it. Reverend MacLeod had been white and an important man.

"My father is more powerful than Reverend MacLeod. He will hire anyone and do whatever it takes to find you. Then I pity you. You may be able to k-kill me tonight. But you'll be sorry..." God, she didn't want to die. Her voice broke.

"Kill you? *Non, mignonne*, I have no intention of killing you." Damien peered down into her strained face, stroking his fingers along her damp cheeks. "I want you alive. I don't want your pity either. Where I'm taking you even your *Daddy* won't be able to save you. Do you really think the American Army is going to ride into an armed Indian camp on some Canadian politician's say so? And do you think Gilbert will even tell him where you are? Just think – what does Gilbert have to lose – if your father finds out you do all his work?"

"But Gilbert loves me..." Bobbie hiccupped.

Damien was right. After nineteen years of doing whatever she pleased, her good fortune had run out. First her father, and now this barbarian, were both intent on ruining her life. Suddenly marrying self-centered, uncaring Etienne looked appealing. He, at least, was only interested in his own pleasure. He wouldn't care what she did. All her hopes shattered into hundreds of pieces. Dejected, she sagged back on the blanket. Her eyes closed and she willed herself to die quickly.

"Not very intelligent – but damned attractive..." Damien's voice deepened with malicious humour.

She moaned as yet another indiscretion returned to haunt her. Those were the very words she'd uttered only two nights ago, when she had believed Damien didn't understand English.

"Don't fret, *mignonne*." Damien leaned down close to her face. She felt his tongue feather along her lips. "I've never heard a single complaint from any lady yet."

Horrified, Bobbie wondered if it were true that there were fates worse than death. Her independent nature would never allow her to become this man's – whore. Yet, if he succeeded in getting her to Big Bear's camp, no one would help her. She must escape before they left Canada. But how?

"I'm getting money – lots of money. In two years..." She blurted out desperately.

She flinched as his knowing hands began roaming freely along her naked bosom. Deftly, he stroked the peaked buds, ignoring her puny whimpers of protest. Embarrassed, she felt her nipples harden.

"I'll give it all to you. Only, please let me go. I'm sorry if I've offended you. I have a fortune. Truly I do. Please Damien."

A piercing white flash lit the heavens, illuminating his face clearly. She saw his sculptured features stiffen with resolve. One hand continued to caress her chest. He turned his face to the skies. His laughter was as horrid as the booming thunder overhead.

Another ribbon of lightning lit the ground, making her feel the whole world had gone insane. She knew her words were futile. She had been tossed into an alien world where normal rules and behaviour did not apply. He had taken her to hell and she was now sole playmate for the grand demon himself.

"Will your money keep me warm this winter?" Damien asked, his voice hoarse with a need she didn't understand.

Gliding his hands up her sides with a smooth motion, Damien leaned over to touch her face. Placing tiny, rapid kisses along her rigid jaw and cheeks, he slowly moved back to capture her lips.

With teasing strokes, he quickly warmed her flesh. His tongue licked against her lips until she moaned, parting them for his exploration.

Bobbie felt his tongue inside her mouth, twining with her own, willing her to respond. She was burning. She wanted her arms free to draw him nearer. His warmth was paradise. Although he wasn't touching her she could feel the heat radiating from his chest.

"*Sorciere.*" He groaned, moving back. For long moments he sat on his heels, staring into her eyes.

Then crawling on his hands and knees, he savagely cut the bonds holding her to the ground.

"Go! Get the hell away from me." He snarled with furious intensity.

Not waiting for him to change his mind, Bobbie scrambled to her feet. Her heart pounded loudly against her naked chest. How could she possibly respond to this cruel heartless barbarian? How could her own body betray her like this? She stopped. Where were her clothes? Where would she go? She looked into the darkness and knew she was thousands of miles from anywhere.

Frightened again, Bobbie looked first at her tethered pony, then back to Damien. Like a bird, ready to fly, she stood quivering, wanting to run. But where? How far were they from Winnipeg? Were there any other towns near here? Would she still be alive tomorrow if she ran off into the wilderness tonight? Groaning, she chewed on her bottom lip and looked back to Damien.

"Where shall I go?" Her husky, perplexed voice reminded him of a confused child.

With her tangled, gilded hair, plastered heavily around her smooth white shoulders and her heaving bare chest, she looked pagan and magnificent. Her exquisite legs were perfectly outlined as she moved to clutch the sopping wet trousers and pulled them up to fasten them.

"Stay here."

Damien growled. He couldn't believe he would actually suggest such a thing. But what else could he do? He wasn't about to go chasing after her in this storm. He had one hell of a headache.

"You best come back inside before you catch pneumonia. I won't hurt you."

"Well..." Dubiously, she crawled back into the shelter. "What else can I do? I don't know how to get back to Winnipeg."

"Are you asking me?" Damien was suddenly laughing.

He reached across and dragged her against his body. Giving her a soft hug, he ran his lips across her hair.

"What am I going to do with you, Wildcat?" He murmured against the silky tangles. She was the oddest combination of woman and child. She placed rape, kidnapping and even murder in the same category with the terrors of darkness.

Not with Anne, nor Marie or any other woman he'd ever had did he feel this need to possess and – protect this woman. She was in his system like a nagging sore he couldn't get rid of. Yet he abhorred everything she was and everything she believed in.

He was much too intoxicated to make any sense of his feelings.

"I often discuss situations with myself." She began and then smiled. "I do sound silly."

She lay back against the blanket, pulling another cover over her shivering form.

"Maybe not so silly. Maybe we all should discuss our situations with the person you always know will give you the best answer. Take your pants off. They're sopping wet." Chuckling, Damien settled down beside her.

Surprising him, she obeyed. Then he watched the little witch seek the comfort of his body heat. Nestling down against his warm body, she looked at him with trusting credence. Then she slept.

Again he was reminded of how easily she played havoc with his mind. It was ages before he slept.

CHAPTER 10

Damien woke to a pounding headache. He noticed Bobbie was sprawled across his chest, still sleeping. He groaned. Once again, she had bettered him. Why couldn't he just use her – abuse her and then throw her away like she deserved? It was obvious the lovely Anne and Bobbie were cut from the same cloth. Both were self-centered, spoiled ladies. Both would sell him out without blinking an eye.

Yet he had to admire Bobbie's audacity and courage. That way, Bobbie was very different than Anne. He couldn't imagine Anne riding through this harsh countryside without complaining. Actually, he couldn't imagine Anne riding a horse and Bobbie did that very well.

He decided to get up and have a bath. He couldn't lie here and let her stay sleeping, nearly naked. Already he felt that familiar stirring in his loins.

Morning mist floated around the saturated trees and grass. It would be another hot day. He grimaced. His actions last night were not very admirable and he was ashamed. She was so tiny and fragile in his arms. She shifted to press closer. He jerked when he felt her taut breasts press into his chest. Her sweet mouth was slightly open. Her feathered touch plagued his shoulder. Maybe now he could take her by force. His jaw clenched. Woman always came to him. He didn't have to force them.

Yet, last night he'd nearly raped this teasing wildcat, tempted as never before to make her co-operate and do what he wanted. He could easily read the desire in her amber-green eyes. Eventually her curiosity would make her succumb…but was he willing to wait? He stiffened. Of course he was. Damien carefully rearranged the dainty form and slipped quietly outside their crude shelter. Bobbie only murmured, not wakening.

A meadowlark's artistic trill broke the early morning silence. Butter-hazed beams shot down through the small cluster of Aspen. The sun caught dewdrops on the leaves creating a shimmering sea of gem-like sparkles. The fresh fragrance of damp earth and the meadowlark's demand she wake up and share this divine morning gradually forced Bobbie to open her eyes.

Damien was standing over her, grinning his bewitching smile. He had obviously just returned from a swim. Today he was wearing a pair of buckskin breeches with no shirt to cover his top. Droplets of water spangled his smooth flesh. Bobbie felt grubby. Would he stay long enough to let her have a swim or would he insist they begin traveling immediately? She was fast learning Damien's changing moods dominated his actions. One moment he was an exciting, accommodating companion and the next he was a cruel, obnoxious boor.

"So, you're finally awake. Are you ready to start riding again?" His tone was mild enough.

"Can I go for a bath first?" She asked cautiously.

She looked like a little girl again. Her hair was a tangled labyrinth of sparkling gold. Her chest, still bare with her gaping blouse and cut corset was small but the exquisite perfection caused him to react immediately. Her wanton and curious nature peeked through, making him realize she was no child. He wanted her. If ever there was a woman primed for loving, it as this one.

"Damien, we should talk." Bobbie tried to pull the ends of her shirt together.

There were no buttons left. He'd torn them off, last night. He was a vile monster.

"I was drunk last night, *mignonne*." Damien tried to smile casually. Stepping over to her baggage, he pulled out a clean shirt and another pair of soft, woollen trousers.

He didn't want her to go back to Winnipeg. He wanted her to stay with him. But he knew he would take her back if she asked.

"Yes, that's another problem. Are you an alcoholic?" Bobbie's tone was laced with disapproval. "I heard out here – people have a problem with drinking."

"That might be your fault." Damien stated gruffly. He turned to stare at her. Only Bobbie would be bold enough to discuss alcohol, all alone in the wilderness, with an Indian. He grinned.

"Go have your swim." He commanded softly.
"You won't watch?" Bobbie scrambled to her feet, still holding her blouse together. Tentatively, she leaned over to scoop her fresh clothing from his arms. His eyes dropped to her shapely bare legs and that little piece of tantalizing silk, hiding her.
"No, I will make breakfast." Damien growled. His eyes moved back up to devour her partially bared bosom. He wanted to tell her that her being half-undressed was as erotic as seeing her fully unclothed. "I don't cook too well though."
"But I thought that was what Gilbert was paying you for as well. I don't cook – at all."
Damien stiffened. Then he shrugged. To prove his honourable intentions, he casually gathered together a few supplies and began mixing some flour and water near the fire. He looked up at her again. "Somehow, that doesn't surprise me, *mignonne*. I can't see you being capable of doing many things."

Bobbie moved away. The morning was lovely with brilliant sunshine and the pleasing twitter of birds. She didn't feel like arguing. She had slept very well and wasn't even sore from yesterday's ride. Marie's lotion was a working miracle.
Slipping out of her torn clothing, she winced as the chilled waters washed over her rash. It stung. Hopefully Damien had some left. Sinking beneath the surface, she washed away the grime.
She felt her cheeks go hot as she thought about the previous night again. Then she sighed. Should she go back to Winnipeg – and do what? What could she do – besides work for Gertrude? Even two years was too long to do that... She sighed. No, she would have to go and get some articles to send back to Myles.
Damien hadn't really hurt her, although she knew he wanted to. He had frightened her but from the time she'd first met him she'd instinctively felt safe with him. He would never force her to do anything like that... She shivered with curiosity, wondering what his torrid looks promised. Should she find out?

She wondered what Aunt Hortense would say to her ridiculous thoughts. *'It was a woman, not a man who suffered the consequences of this type of indiscretion.'*

Bobbie held a very high regard for her deceased aunt. Aunt Hortense, instead of teaching her the behaviour of a lady, had taught her that any woman was capable of standing on her own two feet. They didn't need a man's support. She used herself as an example. Aunt Hortense had never married or even went out with a man. She was wealthy. She had owned and operated a chain of quality schools for young ladies across England. Now, she'd left her wealth to her only niece. Unfortunately, Bobbie couldn't touch the money until she turned twenty-one.

Lured by the enticing smell of coffee, Bobbie returned to the campfire. She settled down on a log and took the plate of bacon and biscuits Damien offered her.

"Have you decided what you want to do?" Damien asked. His eyes were nearly shut.

"I want to interview Big Bear." Bobbie looked up, startled.

"Bobbie, this may well be a waste of time. Big Bear won't take you seriously." Damien frowned, looking at her.

"I've come up against his type before." Bobbie smiled with confidence. "He'll change his mind. They all do."

"Who are they?" Damien asked, smiling.

"All the men I've ever interviewed, of course." Bobbie laughed. "I've been interviewing people for the past year – and mainly men. Do you think there is *any* man who takes a woman seriously?"

"Once she's trapped him into marriage, he does." Damien pitched her a teasing look.

"Trapped him?" Bobbie arched a brow. "You don't even know me and you've asked me to marry me three times? Or were you just teasing?"

"Would you marry a man like me?" Damien asked lightly, but she thought she heard the underlying seriousness in his voice. Was Damien, with his looks and personality, insecure? Then she shook her head, grimacing when she saw the gleam in his eye.

"Seriously, I need this story. Daddy will just send Gilbert back to Toronto and send someone else out. Then what will I do?"

"The way I see it – you have two choices. Marry Etienne or marry me," Damien suggested.

"What if I don't want to marry either? What if I just want to be a reporter and continue doing Gilbert's articles?" Could he possibly be serious? "You don't know me."

"In the biblical sense – not yet." Damien gave a short laugh, setting his plate down. "But I know what I want."

"I'm beginning to know that myself. You want any woman within a few feet proximity of you." Bobbie felt her face turn red again. She dropped her gaze to study the grass beneath her feet. "This conversation is ridiculous."

"Is it? Why don't you marry me, *mignonne*? It would solve all your problems." Damien moved smoothly over to her side, kneeling in front of her.

"How many women have you asked in just this past week?" Bobbie could picture Marie and God only knew how many other women who had heard these exact same words. Why did he look so sincere and lie so smoothly?

"I've never meant it before." Damien brought both hands up to grasp her upper arms. Tugging gently, he brought her down to her knees, facing him.

"Don't!" Bobbie murmured, lost in the luminous cadence of his seductive eyes and voice. She closed her eyes.

Would it always be like this? Regardless of what he did or said, would he only need to look at her or touch her and she would behave like a mindless idiot? *'Remember how sad he sounded, only a few nights ago, when he was talking to Marie? – Remember?'* She tried to straighten her chaotic thoughts.

"Why not follow your heart, *mignonne*. You could go to Big Bear as a reporter or as my wife. As a reporter – you have to worry about your father and everyone else. As my wife you can do as you please and never worry about anyone again. I will protect you, even from your father." Still holding her by her arms, Damien slowly tilted forward, until his lean chest rubbed against hers and rotated against her abdomen as well. It was a feathery, excruciating feeling. She felt her nipples harden immediately. She felt an ache in her belly and lower.

"There are no ministers out here." Bobbie murmured in confusion. She had no will to draw back. She was fast losing all thoughts of resisting him.

"We will be married when we share a lodge and... a bed, *mignonne*. That is my people's way." Damien continued to tease her with light touches of delight.

"How simple is that." Bobbie wanted to laugh. She couldn't believe she was kneeling so complacently listening to his ludicrous words. He was incredibly beautiful and she did want to go to bed with him. Perhaps she should. Bedding him wouldn't make them actually be married, would it?

"Open your eyes."

She slowly raised her lashes. His eyes, narrowed and gleaming captivated hers with a delightful promise in an impact so hard, she couldn't breathe. Her body loosened, responding to the pit of her aching stomach. A lump in her throat clogged her voice. She could not answer.

"*No... No...*" Her mind screamed even as her body screamed "*Oh yes!*"

Her nipples were rigid and sensitive. They nearly tore from her body as they brushed eagerly against his taut muscles under his tender manipulation. She could feel the intense heat from his loins right through their clothing.

A faint yelp of surprise erupted to the excruciating jolts beginning to throb between her legs. Her eyes rounded in frustration. Damien continued to hold away, not letting her press any closer.

"Please..." She begged, opening her eyes.

A thin sheen of perspiration made his golden skin glisten. Bending forward, he moved his tongue tip across her open lips. Her whole body twitched when his mouth moved up towards her ear.

"Please what, *mignonne*?"

He breathed inaudibly against her ear, and then placed his tongue inside. With practiced, twisting motions of delight he teased her.

She must stop him. He was playing with her so skilfully it hurt. Yet, she couldn't summon the power. Her fierce curiosity and longing was too strong. She could feel his throbbing arousal lightly touching against her thighs.

Then he moved back. She felt so cold and empty. His laughter was soft – and triumphant. He was completely in control and playing that game she didn't understand.

"Don't hurt me – anymore..." She reached out to draw him back.

She threw her head back, trying to repudiate what was happening. She was frightened by the knowledge in his eyes. He was rejecting her?

Her hair brushed against his fingers. She felt completely wanton and reckless. Angrily, she moved back to touch him. His loins were like hot coals. She would make him obey! She tried to free her confined arms. He licked along the smooth arch of her neck. She could feel the small whimpers in her throat. Then his tongue moved up to play in her ear again.

"Sweet. So damned sweet..." Then he leaned back again, so close, but not touching anything but her arms.

"How would you like to go to Montana, *mignonne*? Do you want to be my wife or a reporter?" His voice was hoarse with desire. But still he did not move back.

"A reporter." Bobbie gasped out. She clenched her eyes tightly together. She wouldn't look into his eyes now without falling into their deep bottomless depths.

"You lie so easily." There was humour in his voice as well. "I don't believe you mean that."

"Well, I don't believe you either." Bobbie stiffened, managing to pull from his arms. Taking deep gulps of air, she sank back to sit on her heels. "Is this another form of torture? Well, it's much more pleasant than last night, but it's still only torture – isn't it?"

"It's only a form of torture until we make love." Damien's eyes sparkled. He made no effort to bring her back. "Then it's paradise."

"If that's so, why not just do it!" Bobbie ground out. She didn't stop to consider her words. "I *know* you want to punish me, so just do it!"

"You think paradise is punishment?" Damien mocked. "We're finished for now. You are angry and we both know how – masculine – you are when you're angry."

"Can't you ever be serious?"

"Maybe, I am." Damien laughed softly. "But no. I have found it's never fun to be serious. Do you always have to make everything so complicated?"

He could see the confusion in her luminous eyes. She was so frustrated. He would never give her paradise while he punished her. He had told her that and as stubborn as she was, she wouldn't listen. After all the headaches and trouble she had caused him, he was determined she would want him and him exclusively.

He wanted only to enjoy life, nothing more. It was not complicated at all. With Reverend MacLeod, even the smallest of life's details was to be questioned and endured. Ian did not believe in fun either. Damien had made a vow many years ago to contradict every lesson Ian MacLeod had taught him.

"Life is just fun?" She spoke up quietly.

He could read the fascination and annoyance in her eyes. She stiffened. Scrambling to her feet, her flushed expression was disturbed. She moved to Flower.

"Let's go."

"What's wrong?" Damien smiled with mock innocence.

"You are just too frustrating for words..." Bobbie shook her head. "Let's go. I have a story to write."

"Anything your little heart desires, dear lady." Gracefully, Damien stood and gave her a deep bow.

He saddled the two horses and hitched the pack pony's rope to his saddle. From the corner of his eyes, he watched her frantic, agitated movements as she paced back and forth, wringing her hands.

Suddenly she stepped to his side and placed her tiny hand on his arm. He glanced down to study her intriguing expression.

"I think we should – move ahead and put our relationship on a professional level now," she started brightly, not looking into his face. "I tricked you and you t-tortured – me. We're even, wouldn't you say?"

"But *mignonne* – speaking of professions, mine's seduction. What are we going to do about that?" He watched her eyes move up to his face, shock in their depths. "I'm very good at it."

"Oh for God's sake!" With a small shriek of annoyance, she turned to mount her horse. "Don't *ever* touch me again!"

Damien grinned with satisfaction. His lady was definitely off-balance. He intended keeping her that way.

CHAPTER 11

Damien had no intention of letting Bobbie regain her equilibrium. Over the following two weeks of traveling, he showered her with absorbing attention and affection. He took every opportunity to touch or caress her without ever allowing her the opportunity to experience the culmination of what they both wanted. His groin ached and his nerves were stretched tight. Still, he would wait for her unconditional submission. He wanted his revenge for her spiteful little tricks and her autocratic superiority, which said she was better than others.

But he found he was fascinated with her as well. Bobbie adapted to carefree freedom as though she were made for it. She showed enthusiasm and pleasure for the wonders and sights available in the wilderness that made him uneasy. He didn't want to fall in love with her. He wanted her to fall in love with him. From the moment he'd met her, she'd been nothing but a lying little flirt, promising everything and delivering nothing. She was a liar, a cheat and a spoiled brat. She was haughty and a lady. He wouldn't fall in love with such a creature. Anne MacLeod had fooled him once and he wouldn't ever be fooled again. The pain of Anne's betrayal and rejection would live in his heart forever.

Bobbie found it took little more than Damien's devastating smile or his light touch to ignite a yearning she couldn't believe she possessed. As they rode through the prairies and hills, stopping to admire the animals, the birds, and the lakes and rivers along the way, she found she was forgetting everything even her family or her previous life. For the first time ever someone else's opinion and needs came before hers. She tried desperately to get him to make love. Her need was a continual ache in her stomach. Even knowing he was her superior in this matter, with jealousy for all his other women eating at her mind, she couldn't resist the magnetic hold he had on her senses. Then she didn't care what he'd done in the past. She was concerned only with the present.

Their pace was leisurely. Damien would stop whenever she asked. She felt like a child freed of all restrictions. She loved living so uninhibited here in the wilderness. She never wanted to go back.

"We used to play cowboys and Indians when I was a little girl." She kicked Flower to catch up with Damien. They were riding in grass nearly up to their horse's bellies. "It's all the way I imagined it would be – so free, so wonderful. Is it always like this?"

"The winters can be tough if you don't have a roof over your head, *mignonne*." Damien smiled lazily. "Look – a hawk. That's my name with the People."

Her attention was turned to the bird soaring overhead. He was beautiful, gliding in the winds.

"Because he's free and wild?" Bobbie murmured. The hawk did remind her of Damien.

"You know me too well." Damien grinned nonchalantly.

Each day the landscape changed as they passed through nearly flat grasslands into sandy dunes and then further into cool, tree-covered crags, called the Cypress Hills. Then he showed her some very odd shaped rock formations he assured her were made by the Gods of the past. He told her delightful stories about the birds and animals, saying they too, were Gods and explaining that each of their individual abilities were something superior to all others.

Vivid sunsets brought the easy glide of a soaring eagle. Purple clouds touched golden grass at nightfall. Sparkling blue waters rippled in the winds. She tried to describe the sights on paper. Damien watched her with an amused expression on his face.

"Could anyone ever capture the truth, even painting this?" She sighed.

"It's been tried. Some artists come close. Have you ever seen Charles Russell's work?" Damien rolled over to his stomach and reached out to play with her unbound hair.

"You always surprise me." Bobbie murmured, reaching out to run her lips along his palm. "Tell me – how would you know about Charles Russell."

"Maybe some day, I'll tell you." Damien stated, and then jumped to his feet. "I'll race you to the lake."

The lakes and rivers had become an exquisite turquoise as they neared the hazy, white-capped mountains. The lakes were her bathtubs now, more appreciated than ever before. She didn't need an elegantly set table to enjoy food. She didn't want fashionable clothing. Damien told her how wonderful she looked in a hundred different ways every day.

Oddly, it was she who felt trepidation the day he mentioned they were near Big Bear's camp. She didn't want this glorious dream to end.

"Do we have to go there?" She asked with apprehension. She didn't want to ever stop. She wanted to stay with Damien – here and forever.

"A few weeks of freedom and you will forget *everything*?" Damien smiled with affection.

"Except you." Bobbie nodded solemnly.

They were now lying on a small rise, faces nearly touching. As Damien softly kissed the freckles across the bridge of her nose, she could hear droning dragonflies in the nearby pond. Hazy heat mingled with the rustling aspen leaves overhead.

"Can't we just stay forever – alone?" Bobbie looked deep into his hypnotizing eyes.

"Forever?" Damien smiled lazily. He continued to softly stroke her face with his lips.

"Yes. I could live like this forever – with you." Elated, Bobbie swept her arm around before reaching her hand out to caress his beautiful jaw. He was handsome and kind and gentle and so exciting to be with that it was a delight. He was everything she wanted.

Turning slightly, Damien ran his tongue playfully along her palm, and then firmly held her wrists to the ground.

"Potent as whiskey." His voice dropped, low and deep. "I can almost believe you. Think – *mignonne*. I threatened to rape you. I tied you up. I left you in the dark – *by yourself.* Sometimes I drink too much. Do you still want to be with me?"

Was that a cynical twinge of self-condemnation she heard in his tone? That stormy first night with its complex innuendo still haunted her dreams sometimes. This particular dangerous aspect in his inscrutable nature and his heavy drinking that night did cause an uneasy feeling in the pit of her stomach. Hostile and intoxicated, Damien seemed very capable of cruel, calculated violence. But the two extraordinary weeks following that night made her believe he would never hurt her – even angry and drunk.

"You never hurt me." Bobbie whispered slowly. "Nothing matters now. It's in the past. I love you."

She felt nervous suddenly. Why was he bringing up that particular night? It *was* in the past. He'd taught her to think this way.

"You love me?"

She felt the slight tensing in his lissom form. She nodded slowly. Bewildered, she watched in stunned pain as he threw back his head, laughing in triumphant glee. Her stomach tensed, queasy with misgiving.

Not once had Damien ever actually said he loved her. Dawning awareness made her realize loving and in love were two very different things. Did he only want to bed her? She grimaced. No – he would have, if that were his intention. Her eyes widened. Or did he intentionally set out to make *her* fall in love with *him*? Could he actually carry a small grudge so far?

Alarmed, Bobbie considered all those other poor women. Just over two weeks ago, he wanted to marry Marie. He loved her. Then Marie's reason for rejecting him penetrated. He had lived with three women last winter. Were they, even now, patiently waiting in Big Bear's camp for his return? Then there was some woman called Anne, who made his face darken – with passion?

"Did you really mean it when you said you wanted to marry me?" She fought the tears welling in her eyes. Dropping her gaze, she concentrated on the abundant grass beneath her fingers.

Damien was still holding her wrists to the ground. Like a gauche, moonstruck schoolgirl, she had blurted out her deepest feelings. How could she, normally so logical and realistic, fall in love with this sleek, dangerous rake? She was only his new toy to play with. Eventually she would be discarded when a new, more fascinating playmate surfaced. Why hadn't she seen this coming?

"Yes."

Damien watched the emotions crushing her expressive features. Shamed pride won and her face settled into rigid determination. With instinctive ease, he understood her thoughts.

"Was I going to be wife numbered four?" She raised her stormy eyes to his.

"You can't judge me by your own narrow-minded standards, *mignonne*." Damien whispered, soft and low. His hands tightened on her wrists.

She wasn't his yet. What could he say to appease her prim mind? He could tell her he wanted her more than any other woman he'd ever met, including Marie or Anne. Her acceptance of this wild freedom pleased him more than he could say. How could he explain that love was a mirrored illusion, never real? Love was here today, then gone tomorrow. He had seen that happen too many times to count. Would she understand and how could she, when he, having fallen in love many times, didn't understand it himself?

"Do you love me?" Bobbie asked bluntly.

"I can love you, *oui*." Damien smiled, trying to soothe her rage.

"Is that a yes or no?" Her voice was sweet with sarcasm now.

"What does *oui* mean?" Damien teased. "I can't believe your French is that limited."

"Did you love Marie?" Bobbie continued, a determined set to her chin.

"No."

"You said you did. I heard you tell her." Bobbie muttered. "Were you lying?"

"I..." Damien cleared his throat. "I thought I did. She is a very beautiful, warm woman. She is my close friend. When she chose Pierre I found it was only my pride hurt, nothing more."

"Why did she choose Pierre over you?" Bobbie's voice rose hysterically. He watched her swallow deeply, and then continue in a shocked whisper of reproach. "Did you really spend last winter with *three* wives?"

"*Mignonne*..." Damien ran agitated fingers along her bare arms. Then moving back to her hands, he held her trembling fingers. "I had to take them. I gave them to other men. All three have new husbands now."

"When did you give them away?" She hissed, trying to pull free. "After enjoying them all winter, then leaving camp in the spring?"

"Yes." Damien stared into her wet eyes. Hurting Bobbie was not as enjoyable as he had thought. "A man has certain needs. Marie refused to come with me last winter. How can I begin to explain century old customs that you'd never understand anyway? I would have been wrong to refuse to take Brown Bird's wives. It would have been an insult to them and my people. Women need a man to take care of them."

"I don't!" Bobbie spat out. The disgust in her eyes cut through him like a knife. "Was I going to be sharing you with them?"

"No! You and I are perfect together." Damien protested, amazed that he meant every word.

"Do you love me?" Bobbie interrupted with a blank expression on her face. It was as though she wasn't listening to a word he said.

"I said yes." Damien really tried to stay calm. Inside, rage was building rapidly. She was being totally unreasonable. He couldn't say anything more than yes. What did she want?

"I don't believe you."

"I won't let you go." Damien flung back belligerently. After swearing he would never fall in love again, here he was admitting to be doing just that and she called him a liar? "I'm being as honest as I can. I didn't have to tell you this. I won't let you go!"

"But you will. Can't you see – down the road you will…?" Bobbie's voice broke.

"Damn!" Damien swore, trying to take her into his arms. She struggled. "Why didn't I just make love to you? Then you wouldn't be so frustrated…"

Bobbie tried earnestly to pull away. He was so sure of himself, so sure he could make her do whatever he asked. Her struggles turned frantic. What would she do if he exerted that devastating pressure on her? He was a master of seduction. She knew that. She managed to break free and edge backwards.

"Is that what I am, Damien, - frustrated?" She was crying now and she didn't care. "Of course, you would know. It's your professional duty to know that."

"Bobbie, I was teasing when I said that." He pulled her back into his arms.

"I doubt that. LET ME GO!"

His words meant nothing. This complex barbarian had managed to manipulate and control her every thought with a demonic ease that terrified her. But he had refused to give anything in return. She was a self-assured, capable adult, not his submissive little doll. Eventually she would have realized that. She should be grateful he was revealing his true self now. It was not too late. Why hadn't she listened to Aunt Hortense's cynical, but lucid advice? *'A man will say or do anything to get you into his bed.'*

"Don't, *mignonne*." Damien growled, low in his throat. His fingers bit into her arms as he made her turn and face him.

"More bruises?" She eyed his hands, condemnation in her gaze.

"What do you want?" His eyes were pleading with her. It gave her no satisfaction. It was just another trick.

"I was a blind, stupid fool! I worshipped you. I loved you. I loved you even though I knew what you were like..." She cried with hostility, berating herself.

She still couldn't stop the silly tears from flowing. They tickled her cheeks, as mocking as this horrid savage holding her. She wanted to die.

"This is silly." Damien's eyes held sympathy. He could look so sincere it was frightening. "I don't want to fight. I don't want to lose you. Already you say – I *loved* you – in the past tense. Can your heart change so fast?"

"You are smooth, Damien." Bobbie wiped her eyes. "What about you? Two weeks ago you said you loved Marie. Am I your second choice? If Marie wanted you back, would you go? God, I wish she had taken you. Then I wouldn't be like this now..." She screamed her agony.

"Why doesn't your strange behaviour surprise me?" Damien snarled. His eyes darkened with rage. "You're exactly like every other *lady* I've ever met. When your hot little body wants something – you'll say anything. Why would I think you'd be any different?"

"Maybe I said I loved you in order to justify my behaviour." Bobbie muttered vindictively, wanting to hurt him like he'd hurt her.

How dare he mock her love, insinuating it wasn't real?

"Just consider what I would be, if I hadn't convinced myself I loved you," she continued when Damien remained silent. "Than I'd be no better than you. A male whore – that's what you are! You and your stupid profession..." Her voice broke. She couldn't talk anymore. Aloud, her words sounded cruel and evil. But they sounded so true. Humiliated beyond repair, her shoulders sagged.

"You're saying we're both whores?" As though she'd physically slapped him, a shutter dropped down over his eyes. Cold rancour slid over his arresting features making him look savage and alien again. He released her wrists as though they were smouldering coals. Standing, smooth and graceful, he turned his back on her.

Bobbie shivered, wishing she could take back her cutting words. Did it really matter if he didn't love her? Wasn't it enough he wanted her? Was she selfish to expect more? Pride and honour or love – which was more important? Sadly, she realized pride and honour might be very lonely companions.

"I'll take you to Big Bear's camp now Miss Taylor." His voice was icy with contempt. He made no attempt to look at her.

"As my guide?"

Bobbie stood slowly. She tried to still the hope within, begging him to dispute her words and take her into his arms again. Why wasn't she happy? Hadn't she managed to convince him she was a person, not his personal toy?

"Did you want more?" He finally turned, smiling that so calculating grin she hadn't seen in over two weeks. "Should I perform for you – as well? You are so obvious. I can see the disappointment in your eyes. And yes, my beautiful lady, a man can please three women together. Isn't that what you were too scared to ask?"

"I... I... didn't..." Her breath swished out in a short gasp. She moved to her waiting mount, covering her ears. Oh my God – how?

Suddenly, she sympathized with Marie. He was an uncouth animal - and proud of it!

"One more little thing, Miss Taylor." Damien drawled out slowly. "Unless you want to become fair game for any man in camp, you should share my lodge."

Catching her in two easy strides, he took her wrist again. His thumb began to stroke seductively along the inner softness of her hand.

Yanking her arm away, Bobbie kept moving. Were all the native men like him? Agony meshed with tight pride. Did she really want this independence? Again, Damien was changed. Already he was teasing her, no longer hostile and cruel. Maybe she should just turn around and go back into his arms.

"You don't have to worry, my little whore."

Her head jerked around in total disbelief at his crude insult. No one had ever dared talk to her in such a rough manner – except Damien.

His thumbs were hooked into the loops of his waistband. His legs were spread apart, pulling his buckskin trousers taut across his groin. With unconscious ease, her heavy-lidded gaze glided along his arresting body. Then moving to his face, she blushed.

"A whore *never* blushes! I just thought you should stay in my tent because unlike the others, I won't play your stud when you get those uncontrollable urges..."

"Uncontrollable urges..." Bobbie interrupted, shrieking at his vulgar words. She felt the burning fire lick throughout her veins. War was declared.

"You will regret that remark, my stud." She hissed, sticking her tongue out in anger. "I think I'd rather have any other man in the village – so long as it's not you!"

He made no reply. Further infuriated by his casual indifference, she turned in time to see him grin, smug with satisfaction.

"You will never win with words either, *mignonne*. And might I now suggest perhaps I could teach you how to use that tongue in a much better way? All the men in the village will love you!"

She swung awkwardly into her saddle, unable to respond. She was thankful she didn't understand him now. His suggestion sounded positively wicked and depraved.

She tried to analyze this complex man as they rode. Silent and brooding, she wondered what he had expected of her. He reacted like a wild, injured animal every time she contradicted or questioned him. She never knew if he would sit quietly and let her speak her mind or leap forward and tear her apart. But how could she ignore his contagious laughter and delightful teasing?

CHAPTER 12

Bobbie was further infuriated when Damien left her outside a shabby-skinned lodge after they arrived in the camp near the Little Rockies in Montana Territory.

"Bye, Miss Taylor."

Saying nothing more, he whirled Attila around and immediately joined a group of men leaving the village. She couldn't understand their words, spoken in guttural Cree. But they appeared to be very happy to see Damien. She noticed a few women seated up behind some of the men and her resentment grew. Why didn't Damien take her along? Why was he leaving here alone to fend for herself in these strange surroundings?

Scowling at her cowardly weakness, Bobbie dismounted. She was here to interview Big Bear. Once that was done, she could surely hire another guide to take her back to Winnipeg. She ducked into the opened doorway. This must be Damien's lodge. She would never let him know he'd hurt her again by leaving her like this.

Thankfully, she saw an old, emaciated woman huddled by a central fire. At least she wouldn't be alone.

"Lone Woman." The seamed, leathery face broke into a nearly toothless grin as the old lady beckoned her inside.

Bobbie obeyed, sitting cross-legged near the fire. Although Bobbie immediately started perspiring from the suffocating heat, she noticed Lone Woman was bundled up in a very heavy fur robe.

"Sit! Woman sit..." Lone Woman ordered fiercely, shaking her head. "Not like man! Sit... like woman... Sit." She flung her arms up in disapproval.

Finally comprehension penetrated. Smiling, Bobbie unfolded her legs and sat on the hard packed earthen floor. Her legs were now folded neatly beside her. Obviously only the men were allowed to cross their legs. Bobbie filed that interesting piece of information in the back of her mind. Hopefully, she could one day enjoy watching Damien's annoyance when she crossed her legs and mocked one of *his* silly customs.

"Eat."

Warily, Bobbie eyed the metal pot bubbling over the fire. It was as though the old woman knew they were coming. There was entirely too much for one old lady to eat. She shivered when she recalled Damien telling her that his people had developed senses the whites couldn't possibly comprehend. Had Lone Woman instinctively known they would arrive today?

Bobbie searched the shadowed tent, wondering where she could find a plate. She hoped the cooking meat was of a known variety. What if she were being offered snake, or even rats?

In exasperation, Lone Woman grabbed her hand impatiently and pushed it into the steaming pot.

"Ouch!" She immediately sucked on her burnt fingertips. Her shock produced hilarious cackles as the old woman rocked back and forth in amusement.

"I can see where Damien gets his perverted sense of humour." Bobbie snapped out. Reaching carefully into the pot, she pulled out a piece of meat. Gravy dripped down her fingers. Did these people have no manners?

"Eat."

Thankfully Lone Woman didn't appear to understand her. She sighed. Damien was turning her into a rude shrew. She began to nibble on her meat. It tasted fine, if somewhat hot. And if Lone Woman ate this meat, it would surely not kill her. Lone Woman was positively ancient. Still, she decided it might be better not to ask.

"Dress. Woman use dress." Now the old woman was pointing at Bobbie's trousers, and then towards a creamy white-fringed dress hanging on a post. Perplexed, Bobbie nodded. She would have no peace until she agreed. Lone Woman's demands were very persistent.

Trying to ignore Lone Woman's piercing, curious eyes, Bobbie disrobed. She would not have her own bedroom here.

Black button eyes studied her naked curves, and then Lone Woman nodded. "Pretty. Good enough for my man."

"Surely not!" Bobbie exclaimed, eyeing the old lady with trepidation.

What exactly was Lone Woman trying to say? Had Damien just *given* her to some old decrepit man? Closing her eyes, Bobbie shuddered. She could well imagine what Lone Woman's man would look like. Damien's attractive features focused so intensely she wanted to cry. *But isn't it equality and respect you want?* Her inner voice mocked.

She slipped the soft, velvet-like leather over her head, enjoying its luxurious caress against her bare skin. Perhaps Lone Woman's husband would at least be polite. She would learn to love and cherish him and show Damien... She giggled at the idea. She was going insane.

"Pretty Robin for Hawk!" The old woman chuckled along with her.

Bobbie's heart leapt, pounding furiously. Hawk was Damien's name here. Then she eyed Lone Woman with disbelief. Was Lone Woman one of his three wives?

"Hawk your man?"

Good heavens, she was even adopting Lone Woman's manner of speech. Fresh, pealing laughter erupted in her throat as she tried to imagine Damien with Lone Woman – and two other women, both as old as this one. There was nothing erotic about her thoughts now!

"Hawk my son. I loose odder son to dem damn Blackfoot. Hawk here, den I have son again."

Bobbie flushed, hearing the pride and love in Lone Woman's voice. She took the offered copper belt and clasped it around her waist. Goodness, her thoughts were every bit as depraved as Damien's.

The elk-skin gown fell in graceful folds almost to her ankles. The wide neckline was a circular scoop with fringed ribbons falling almost to her waist. Eyes glittering with pleasure, Bobbie twirled around. The skirt lifted in a wide flare. She liked it.

"Sit."

Bobbie obeyed. Everything was going rather smoothly. Now if only she could find Big Bear it would all be fine. Perhaps she could leave this camp by morning!

"Big Bear." She asked slowly. "Do you know Big Bear?"

"Don' unnerstand." Lone Woman frowned.

"Your chief. Big Bear – the chief." Bobbie persisted. "I must see him."

"Don' unnerstand." Lone Woman growled. "Head hurt. Need quiet. You unnerstand?"

And in the baffling days that followed, Lone Woman continued to pretend she didn't understand whenever Bobbie asked about Big Bear.

Bobbie was confused. Damien wasn't here. He couldn't have warned Lone Woman. Then how did she know? Lone

Woman appeared to be a very shrewd lady and seemed to understand most other questions.

As the days dragged into a week, Bobbie grew steadily angrier. Damien was an inconsiderate boor. How dare he neglect her this way? Whenever she tried to approach anyone else, that person would shake their head as well with a pat "don' unnerstand."

It was a conspiracy against her, all started by Damien. She searched the camp, but he didn't appear to be anywhere around.

Lone Woman was determined to teach Bobbie the proper decorum and rules of the village. Whenever she made a mistake, everyone except Lone Woman laughed at her. To Bobbie their laughter seemed malicious rather then friendly. Why? She felt worthless. First Damien, now these people, mocked her civilized ways. They had more silly rules here in this so-called free world than she'd ever encountered before. This seemed especially true when it came to a woman's rights. Women were expected to cook, wash, clean and look after the children. They were expected to keep their tongue silent and show only respect for any man.

Grudgingly, Bobbie admitted it wasn't so different anywhere else. Women were treated like second-class citizens wherever they lived. She vowed to learn the Cree language and teach these women differently. Then, when Damien finally returned, wouldn't he be furious? She spent many pleasant nights imagining all the women in this village revolting.

She eventually learned the seemingly casual atmosphere was a deceptive front. Beneath the relaxed attitudes various societies or 'policemen' enforced a rigid code of laws and ethics. All obstacles too difficult for these men to deal with were turned over to their 'council of elders' and a man called 'Peace Chief.' These chiefs and their assistants were like a white man's judge and jury. It was more democratic than she expected.

Sometimes she wondered if she hadn't already met Big Bear and he, like the others, *'don' unnerstand'*. No one would tell her if she had. Her anger increased toward Damien. He had been paid to deliver her to Big Bear! She was here to interview Big Bear, not learn the ways of these poor, abused Indian women.

  She wasn't blind. These people all lived in appalling poverty. They wouldn't listen when she tried to tell them to move back and take a reservation. The government would supply food, shelter and clothing. They would provide hospitals and schools. Whenever she tried to talk to them, they would just shake their head with a *'Don' unnerstand'* following. She further damned Damien. He, at least, was educated and familiar with white society. Couldn't he explain to these people?

  Her avid curiosity grew daily. What was Big Bear like? Why was he one of the few chiefs who refused to help his own people? In her mind, Big Bear became an absolute, autocratic dictator. Why would everyone follow such a man? Did they have a choice?

  Then there were those men, women and even children who stumbled around the village, belligerent and drunk. Bobbie tried to avoid these people and learned to appreciate Lone Woman's efficient protection. Even the most inebriated drunk seemed to respect Lone Woman, whose contempt for alcohol was well known.

  "Gonna kill us all," she would mutter whenever she saw a man staggering past her lodge.

  Bobbie agreed. As she watched the evil looking white whiskey traders making their rounds, she wondered if any of the people could stop drinking, even if they wanted. For that dreaded liquid many would trade or sell anything, even their wives. And the vile whiskey traders would take whatever was offered, especially the young women.

  Then she noticed that one particular warrior seemed to watch her continuously. She could read mistrust and suspicion in his dark eyes. His arrogant strut indicated power. Was he Big Bear? Finally she dared approach him.

"I'm looking for Big Bear." She enunciated slowly. "I'm Roberta Taylor – from the Taylorson Press. I wondered if you could answer a few questions."

The man's eyes, icy and remote, roamed up and down her body. He folded his arms across his chest. He didn't say a word.

"Please. Will you help me?" She continued bravely. "I'm looking for Big Bear."

The man gave no indication he heard her, let alone understood her.

"I know – you *don' unnerstand*!" Bobbie snapped impatiently. "Why don't you just *say so*?"

Startled, she watched his lips twist. Was he smiling? He still wouldn't speak.

Then Lone Women crawled out of her tent. With a shriek, she beckoned to Bobbie.

"Robin –get here – right now!"

"Is that Big Bear?" Bobbie asked eagerly, coming to Lone Woman's side.

"No!" Lone Woman scowled. "Wandering Spirit. Pretty man too – eh Robin?"

She squatted down and began her painstaking scraping of a hide pegged out in front of the tent. Sighing, Bobbie followed suit.

From beneath her lowered lashes, she studied the man who was still watching her. His wide mouth was drawn back in a perpetual scowl. His nose was long and straight. His rigid chin jutted out boldly. If he didn't radiate such intense dislike, she might consider him attractive. But never pretty!

"Wandering Spirit don' like whites." Lone Woman shook her head. "But maybe woman he like. He watch you all du time."

"Who is he?" Bobbie turned back to her duties.

"War Chief."

"What's a War Chief?" Bobbie sighed. They appeared to have a chief around for every occasion. If she never got her interview with Big Bear, maybe she could write an article on the structure of Native society. Or if – Wandering Spirit liked white *women* – maybe she could get an interview from him!

"We go to war. Wandering Spirit our chief." Lone Woman shrugged her shoulders. Grey, thin strands of hair loosened from her tightly braided hair. She leaned over the animal skin. Amazingly strong, bony fingers pushed down, cutting away the unwanted hair.

A War Chief! Surely he was more important than Big Bear. She looked up. Wandering Spirit was still watching her.

"Don' go looking at him! You Hawk's woman." Lone Woman looked up and indicated Bobbie should start working and stop gossiping.

And if Bobbie hadn't liked Lone Woman so much, she would have got up and flirted so outrageously with Wandering Spirit he wouldn't have been able to ignore her. Hawk's woman indeed! Then why wasn't *Hawk* here?

"Does he speak English?"

"Yeah!" Then Lone Woman clamped her hand to her mouth. She would speak no more.

A long, lonely month passed. Bobbie no longer had difficulty sleeping. She was familiar now with the noise and confusion of the village. Even during the hot nights when wild laughter and other barbaric activities were taking place until dawn she could sleep, feeling safe. There was no routine here, especially with the drinkers. Their children were left to fend for themselves. Was Damien amongst that rowdy group? Sometimes she wanted to get up and spy on these parties. Maybe both Damien and Big Bear attended them. But she could never summon up the nerve to venture outside at night. She was safe here inside the lodge with Lone Woman.

Instead, she lay, night after night, fuming about Damien's arrogance and inconsideration. Couldn't he see this debauchery and pleasure to the exclusion of everything else would destroy his beloved people? He couldn't blame the whites for this. This was their own problem and surely the majority of whites wanted only to help.

Then one sunny morning he was back.

"It's too hot to be cooking inside, *mignonne*."

Seething, Bobbie nearly spilled the heavy metal pot she was carrying inside. It always turned balmy hot during the daylight hours and she would have enjoyed cooking outside. But Lone Woman preferred the tipi and that was where they cooked. An elder was always right.

"How would you know?" Bobbie tried to stop her heart from beating so erratically. She couldn't have missed him. She despised him.

Damien sat on Attila, who pawed restlessly against the ground, ready to run. His eyes were heavy-lidded and lazy, hiding his bloodshot agony. His head was pounding fiendishly and he needed a nice soothing dip in the river to bring him back to life.

"Aren't you going to welcome me home?"

He had been watching her for a good five minutes before she had realized he was sitting there. He knew he still wanted this little wench and badly. Perhaps he shouldn't have satiated himself in wine, women and song so avariciously last night.

Nothing, from the usually exciting horse-raid against the Blackfoot, to the copious amounts of alcohol, nor the various eager women who wanted to please him, had made him forget this haughty, little lady. He was astonished to learn how well she was adjusting. Lone Woman had told him last night how easily she mastered even the most menial, difficult task. Even Wandering Spirit had contributed a grudging compliment. *She was good – for a white woman.*

Last night he'd wanted her so badly he nearly crawled beneath the robe cradling her. He abhorred his maudlin weakness, considering she despised everything about him. He'd left and joined the party on the other end of the camp. Pride demanded that she beg him for any help now.

"Where were you?" Still on her knees, she placed the pot inside the lodge and turned to Damien.

He could see she hadn't wanted to ask. He stiffened at the scorn in her tone, and then relaxed. If she didn't care – why would she be asking?

"You sound like a wife. Did you miss me?" He arched his brow in a mocking salute, grinning. "I sure missed you."

"I just asked a civilized question!" Bobbie snapped. She leaned back on her heels, glaring up at him. There was a longing in her sweet features, he couldn't mistake.

"I was out, my sweet." Damien smiled, enjoying her very obvious agitation. Nothing had changed. She wanted him as badly as he wanted her. But she was fighting just as hard to deny it. "Is that what a *civilized* husband would say? Did you miss me?"

"No." Her gazed shifted to the ground. Her voice sounded bitter. "No, of course I didn't. I was having so much fun here. I learned to cook and clean and cure hides and..."

Damien couldn't help himself. He interrupted with a hoot of laughter. "Oh *mignonne*, you are entertaining. A man would never get bored with you."

"You'll never find out. I want my interview with Big Bear, like you were paid to do – then I'm leaving." Bobbie stood up. "Damien, don't you realize how much time has passed? Gilbert will be frantic."

"You don't like it here?" Damien voice turned to mocking innocence. He felt guilty. "Why? Lone Woman told me you were doing *'jest mighty fine'* – I think her words were. Before you know it, you'll be ready to be my docile, little..."

"Don't you dare!" Bobbie interrupted. Her shoulders bent over wearily. "I don't want to fight. I just want my interview."

Damien felt like a heel. Why was he being so cruel, tormenting her so? Then he shook his head. She was every bit as hard, always throwing her wonderful money and Daddy in his face. Daddy could do everything. While he, Damien, was just a shiftless, no account drunk. She always made it so very obvious how superior she was.

"You took our money." Her voice was firm. She looked at him with scorn. "You will help me!"

"I was paid to bring you here. I did that – with a few added bonuses for you, I might add. I earned my money." Damien's voice dropped to a husky warning. "Surely a resourceful woman like you could find Big Bear."

He was well aware of the suspicion and hostility this little termagant was causing in camp. Almost everyone, and especially Wandering Spirit, wondered what she was doing here. He would take her home, before winter set in. But first he still wanted her to know what it was like – to be an outcast and never good enough to belong.

"You know I can't." Bobbie whispered. Then taking a deep gulp she continued quietly. "How long have you been back?"

"Three days." Damien admitted, and then lowered his lashes.

She looked so fragile and hurt. Why? What did she want? She'd made it more than obvious it wasn't him.

"I see." Keeping her face averted, she bent over to go inside the tent. "I would appreciate it if you would take me to see Big Bear. Please?"

Damien heard the tears in her voice. They cut deeply into his soul. He groaned in frustration. What could he do? Take her into his arms and chase her misery away? She didn't want that. She wanted to interview Big Bear, than leave.

"I'll take you tomorrow." Feeling exactly like the sinister cad she believed he was, Damien's voice was throaty with shame.

Damn her! This whole ludicrous arrangement was her decision. She didn't want to share his lodge. She didn't want to be in his arms. She wanted her interview and then to return to her wonderful world of wealth and power.

"I'm going for a swim. Would you like to come along?" Damien asked with a grimace. He sounded like he was begging!

"No... No! I..." Her voice broke. She ducked into the tipi with a muffled sob.

Shrugging helplessly, Damien turned his horse and headed down to the river, alone.

CHAPTER 13

The following dawn was frosty and cold, a portent of winter. True to his word, Damien came early to get Bobbie. He took her to Big Bear's lodge. He decided he would have to take Bobbie back tomorrow. The weather was decidedly turning cold and it would soon snow. Besides, having her so close, yet not touching her was much too hard on his libido. He was more and more inclined to just take her and to hell with the consequences. She wanted to be in his bed. When had it become so important to have her love him as well? It had never mattered before. He was very well aware of what most *ladies* thought of him – outside their bed. Why did he care that Bobbie felt the same way? He smiled grimly, wondering if she had any idea of the consequences *in her world* if she followed through on what her eyes revealed she wanted. Or did she think *daddy* could help her there as well? Daddy would disown her.

"Why is he in the middle?" Bobbie asked curiously as they walked through the oddly hushed camp to get to Big Bear's lodge.

"The chiefs are always in the center. They are always well-protected and hard to reach, in case of an attack." Damien answered.

"Too bad I didn't know that before." Bobbie murmured.

She peeked up at him. She wanted to ask him where he slept. Was he sharing a lodge with his three wives again? She squelched the instant jealousy that thought brought. But she really didn't want Damien to go to other women.

She noticed the brooding, distant look in his eyes. His long strides and set jaw indicated he wanted no conversation. He would only take her questions as an invitation to be obnoxious. She was too weary and depressed to spar with him this morning.

Big Bear was a small, wrinkled old man. He was even shorter than Bobbie. He couldn't possibly be the aggressive troublemaker the Canadian government claimed he was.

Perplexed, Bobbie let the man lead her inside his smoke-sated tent with its standard heavy buffalo robes scattered about for sleeping and sitting on. Big Bear's smile was reserved and polite. She noticed his openly affectionate grin when he looked at Damien. Was he another native who '*hated*' whites? Belligerently, she crossed her legs, not caring that both men immediately showed their disapproval with slight frowns. After formal introductions, Damien leaned back watching in silence.

Apprehensive and tongue-tied without knowing why, Bobbie tried to remember she had not been treated with any respect by anyone other than Lone Woman. She owed these uncultivated people none in return.

"Why won't you sign our Treaty?" She began abruptly.

"My people do not wish I do so." Big Bear answered in flawless English. "I am surprised by your question. Usually the white man skirts around the issues and never makes a point."

"Will you fight if you are forced to take a reservation?" Bobbie peered up at the old man suspiciously. His words sounded as though he were complimenting her.

At her side, Damien grunted, but made no comment.

"Robin – I understand you are Hawk's woman. Whose side will you be on, if we fight?" Big Bear had the audacity to grin and wink at Damien.

"I am not Damien's woman!" Bobbie made an effort to control her building rage. Talking to this hideous old man was just like talking to Damien. And why not? This crude barbarian had taught Damien his way. This was the man Damien respected so much.

"Hawk said you don't like Gabriel Dumont. Why?" Bobbie was determined to make this elusive man answer her questions.

She nearly turned and stuck her tongue out at Damien when he shifted beside her. She smiled when she saw the slight frown Big Bear directed at Damien. Then he turned back.

"I like you, Robin. You are direct. Gabriel and I have our differences. Just like you and Hawk do. Does this mean you do not like Hawk?"

"It's not at all the same! Besides, Damien and I have nothing in common. Surely you and Gabriel do."

"Dumont and I have something in common? How interesting! What do we have in common?" Innocent eyes rounded in amusement, nearly disappearing into his dried folds of flesh.

He was the ugliest man she'd ever encountered and his mockery was fast making her believe his personality was no better.

"Everyone in the west has complaints, except the white settlers! Both the *Metis* and Indians are always complaining." Bobbie snapped out her exasperation.

"Have you interviewed the white settlers?" Big Bear leaned over and peered carefully into her eyes. Then he nodded. "I thought not. They have the same complaints the *Metis* do. And we – *The People* – do not have *anything* in common with their complaints!"

"What's the difference?" Bobbie asked desperately. He was efficiently twisting all her words around. He told her nothing.

"I would think as a reporter, you would know." Big Bear's voice was hard.

"I'm *asking* – because I am a reporter!" Bobbie nearly screamed, fighting tears. What could she expect? They all hated her, including Big Bear.

Big Bear stiffened. Damien intervened lazily, with a few words in Cree. She really should learn that damn language.

Then Big Bear relaxed. His face broke out into a wide grin. Shrivelled, aging flesh jiggled. He nodded.

"I will tell you a story, Robin. Then maybe you'll understand. It is a story about Dumont and myself." He held up a hand to silence her when she opened her mouth.

She was sufficiently intimidated, by Damien's commanding eyes, to remain silent.

"A few years ago Mother Earth had swallowed up nearly all the buffalo in our lands. But one summer the buffalo came back – near Batoche. Gabriel is a *Metis* captain and he decided the buffalo were his. He wanted everyone who hunted the buffalo to follow his rules. I would not follow his rules."

"Why not? Pierre Marchand told me that the *Metis* are extremely efficient at organizing these hunts." Bobbie didn't mean to sound rude. She was just curious.

"I am Chief! I do not follow *Metis* rules."

Bobbie's opinion changed when she saw the arrogant power in his simple statement. Then Big Bear's eyes began to shimmer with a mysterious glint.

"Now I will tell you another story. I will tell you why I will not sign your government Treaty."

Bobbie remained silent. Perhaps if she did so, he would answer all her questions in his roundabout way.

"Many long years ago, your people stole something of great importance to my people. In your language it is called the Iron Stone. *Nanebozo* has great powers for my people. One of our Gods gave us this stone so we could all prosper and be happy. When your Christian men came out here, they stole the stone and took it far away. Perhaps they even destroyed it."

"Why?" Bobbie's eyes widened by Big Bear's fascinating story.

"They say our beliefs and our Gods are wrong. Do you think we are wrong – and you, a Christian is right? How do they know?" Big Bear's small eyes were fierce, burning orbs of sorcery.

"I'm not sure." Uneasily, Bobbie shifted, moving closer to Damien. Her flesh tingled eerily. She was unable to control a shiver. Was Big Bear a magician? Did he have his people under – *a spell*? But how did anyone know? No one had ever seen God, had they?

"Now many people follow the Christian teachings. The Iron Stone is gone. Since it no longer protects us we have trouble. And in my visions I see more coming."

Bobbie turned to Damien. Did he actually believe that some minister or priest taking away their silly stone caused all their troubles? Damien frowned.

"Today we have your spotted sickness. We have no food and your people are taking away all our land as well. They will dig and use Mother Earth until she becomes angry. I think you will be sorry. One day – soon, all my people will be gone. Then who will be here to look after Mother Earth?" Bobbie blinked back tears at the sadness she heard in Big Bear's voice.

"Can't we share? There is so much land in this new country." Bobbie tried to repudiate the ominous foreboding in Big Bear's words. Did he really believe the whites wanted to kill all the Indians?

"For how long?" Big Bear's face filled with painful scorn. "Until the People starve to death, like those ones who have already signed your treaties? No child, it is better to die – fighting for freedom, than to starve to death like a coward."

"So you will fight!" Bobbie whispered, pouncing on his comment immediately.

"That decision is not mine to make. I am Peace Chief. I only fight to keep the peace. I am too old and weary to become a warrior now." Big Bear shook his head.

"I don't understand." Bobbie turned to Damien in bewilderment.

"I am an old man and I do not understand. How can you expect to understand?" Big Bear looked as though the burdens of the world were resting squarely upon his shoulders.

Bobbie felt a strong compassion for the tired, old leader. She had her answer. Big Bear was not a troublemaker. If the Cree Nation went to war against Canada, he would not be leading them.

"Who decides if you will fight?" She asked softly.

"Our War Chief and the warriors will vote. No single person can make such an important decision." Big Bear smiled, sad and distant.

Leaning over, Damien touched her arm, and then stood to leave. The interview was over.

Wandering Spirit and the warriors would make that decision! And she knew Wandering Spirit wouldn't talk to her.

"You said he was such a great man. But I only saw a sad, broken man – living in the past." Bobbie whispered as they moved past the lodges now alight with breakfast fires.

Aromas of cooking meat wafted into the cool mountain air. With a sudden yearning, Bobbie wondered if Gilbert and her father were searching for her. Would Gilbert tell Myles or would he try to write some story to appease him? Now, she could almost understand Big Bear. It was difficult to forget and have nothing to do with all that was familiar and safe.

"Big Bear *is* a great man."

"I expected someone more like you."

Damien grinned and surprised her when he threw his arm across her shoulder. His ephemeral moods were driving her wild. Would she ever understand him?

"You think I should be Peace Chief? You don't understand much do you, *mignonne*? I have neither the desire, nor the wisdom to lead these people. Don't underestimate Big Bear like so many of your kind do. He just refused to take you seriously. I warned you."

"He told me a lot, in his roundabout way." Bobbie stopped abruptly.

She flung Damien's hand from her shoulder. No man ever took a woman seriously.

"Why are you upset now, *mignonne*?" Damien smiled with his usual magic. "Big Bear refused to negotiate with Dewdney when he found out your Lieutenant had no authority to change the laws. Why should he talk to you? What can you do for him?"

"You imbecile! The press can do plenty for people – or against them."

Damien laughed, ducking when she took a swing at him. Leaning over to grasp some water from a pot simmering by an outside fire, he flung it playfully in her face, dodging her immediate charge with ease.

"Stop being so childish!" She ground out, dropping her raised fist and brushing water from her face. "Why do you always treat me like an idiot? What does Big Bear want?"

"He wants to talk to the Queen or even the MacDonald – your Prime Minister. He finds the concept of governments and countries very confusing." Damien shrugged, keeping his features solemn. "I guess you could say he wants to talk to your Peace Chief. Do you have one – or don't you need one? You have enough people to just take what you want, don't you?"

How many times would she reject him before he understood she didn't want him? He was *Metis*. She was a white lady. She hadn't adapted to his ways to please him, but to further her own ambitions and get her story for Daddy's newspaper.

"You think he's such a great man?" Bobbie interrupted his thoughts, sniffing her scorn. "You would let some simple old man rule you yet dare criticize me? He believes in stones that give you power and…"

"Don't continue!" Damien's voice dropped with icy menace. She had gone too far with her bold, arrogant words.

He dug his fingers into her upper arm, grabbing the soft flesh. Yanking upward, he began to drag her, forcing her to walk on her toes.

"Stop it, you animal!" Bobbie hissed.

Ignoring her, Damien flung her callously inside the lodge. She stumbled, looking shocked. He didn't care. Lone Woman looked startled as well. She immediately scrambled to her feet and moved outside.

"I should beat some sense into that foolish head of yours! You have no manners. You are a guest here only because Big Bear lets you stay. Yet you dare call him a simple old fool?"

"A guest? I thought I was a prisoner." Her voice tapered off when he whirled on her, evidently seeing the violence in his eyes.

His chest rose and fell with long, deep shudders. He felt his mind buzz with uncontrolled rage and all because she had a very bad habit of saying whatever she was thinking!

"A prisoner! Do you want me to show you how a prisoner is treated?" Damien took a deep breath, trying to calm himself. It wasn't working. "I can't reason with you. You won't even try to understand." He leaned down hissing into her face. "Why? Why are you always right and everyone else wrong?"

"Damien, I'm sorry." She started cautiously, looking very frightened. He was glad. "But surely, you must realize he's senile..."

"You honestly don't know when you've gone to far, do you?" Damien pushed her back to the robes, and then squatted down, tilting her face between his palms. His dark eyes were slits of dangerous fury. "That is what is saving you now, *mignonne*. You are a rude, ignorant woman."

"Your opinion doesn't matter to me." Bobbie refused to back down now. The man was calling her a rude, ignorant idiot! How dare he? "You are a vain – ignorant barbarian!"

"I am a barbarian. I never denied it." His wide lips opened in a sensual sneer, displaying his wolf-like white teeth. "I see no fear in your eyes. Have I misled you? Have I been too kind?"

Snarling, Damien flung her back. Leaping to his feet he viciously kicked a burning log. Protesting sparks scattered into the air. Hot embers showered down.

Bobbie quickly ducked to avoid their scorching heat, and then watched them die out on the packed earth floor. He was deranged and he was certainly scaring her now. She searched around the tent, gauging the distance to the door. But even if she escaped, who would help her? Damien was right. She was stupid to forget one simple fact – She needed him to survive.

"Do you think kindness is a form of weakness, *mignonne*? Many women do."

Damien asked the question so softly she almost didn't hear him. Her gaze probed his uncompromising face warily. She could still feel a brutal intensity radiating from his rigid body, although he was standing a few feet from her.

"No." She swallowed with difficulty. Her throat felt tight and sore.

"I am not kind, my sweet. Nor am I weak. It would be foolish to think I am."

Bobbie's eyes widened. She recalled the times he had been kind – and considerate – and gentle. He grunted, watching her closely. She lowered her lashes. Could he read her every thought?

"Have you heard about the war down here? Did you read about General Custer?"

"Yes."

Nausea built within. The barbaric torture the heathens had inflicted on honourable soldiers was known throughout the civilized world. To needlessly slaughter innocent men had showed everyone exactly what type of degenerate animals they were dealing with.

"I was there."

Her head jerked up in disbelief. Her mouth dropped open in protest. No sound could emerge.

"The Sioux welcomed anyone – there were Blackfoot, Cheyenne and even the Cree. I *enjoyed* watching those sanctimonious bastards suffer and die. I could tell you things about your kind soldiers that would make your skin crawl. But I won't. You might believe I have a reason to feel this way. I'm not apologizing." His voice was hoarse. "I love fighting. I don't want to work for your government and be grateful to have a life of all work and no play. I agree with Big Bear. I don't want to see all this land destroyed. Your way is unnatural. The land provides all we need – not your damned government – not your damned people."

"But Damien, you're educated. You've seen..." Bobbie protested weakly. He despised her and everything she believed in.

He had willingly taken part in butchering her kind. And still she loved him.

"What have I seen?" He interrupted bitterly, glaring down at her until she cowered back on the robe. "All I've ever seen is your people destroying what is mine!"

"You have schools and medicine and food now..."

"We had all that before you came." Damien stiffened.

"Not proper schools or hospitals..." Bobbie disagreed, watching his swift changes with immense fascination. He appeared calm now. "Why even the horses you love – we brought over!"
"And so we just keep going around in circles." Damien sighed. Turning he smiled tentatively. "We both are sure we are right. Well, since you've had your interview I will take you back tomorrow. I'm sorry I don't know how to control my temper and I'm sorry if I hurt you."
For long moments, Bobbie couldn't speak. There was a clogging in her throat, threatening to choke her. Now that he was so willing to let her go, she didn't want to leave him. Even with his temper raging violently he wouldn't hurt her. Turning white, she watched him walk towards the door.
"I *hate* arguing with you, Damien. Please... I..." Finally she managed to speak.

He heard the pleading in her tone. She had the power to make him agree to anything. He would never let her know that. She wanted the exact same thing he did. That want was so excruciating it was tearing him apart, and maybe she too. But then what? After they enjoyed each other physically, what was left? He knew there could be no future for two such completely opposite people.
He walked out.

CHAPTER 14

The following morning, Damien couldn't be found.
By mid-morning, Bobbie's heart felt strangely lighter. She'd spent a sleepless night wondering whether she should find him and explain. Now she knew her principles and beliefs weren't as important as being with him. Was he too, avoiding their separation? Did he want her to stay? Did it matter what the world was like? It would go on regardless of two insignificant opinions. Why did they fight so much? Bobbie easily admitted she loved Damien's carefree, wild nature. He was fascinating

and not really wrong. Did she really need to hold onto her own stuffy values? Were they important?

A violet shaded arch hung over the mountains, bringing powerful winds and creating summer warmth. Lone Woman called this strange phenomenon a Chinook, saying they waited every winter for this unique respite from the cold.

A full week passed in a warm haze. There was still no sign of Damien. Bobbie thought deeply about herself and her situation. She'd spent two glorious weeks alone with Damien. She had to admit there weren't as many silly restrictions in his world, even as a woman. She wanted to stay. So long as one didn't hurt another, she could do as she pleased. If she felt like taking a walk or exploring, rather than cooking, she could. Even if she wanted to join in the nightly parties, she could. No one would reprimand her. These people, living so close together, had a great respect for individuality, even hers.

Once again Bobbie was unable to sleep. She listened to Lone Woman's soft snores. She didn't want to imagine life without Damien. Why did she argue about things she didn't understand? He was right. How would she or her people like it if someone took them over and told them what they could or couldn't do? Damien wanted only to play and have fun, nothing more. Was that so wrong? Did she really want more than sharing his hot caresses and teasing laughter?

In her mind she could hear his delightful laughter and she could almost feel his unique touch. He still had to teach her that pleasure his eyes promised. Groaning her frustration, she flung her robe aside. It was too hot to sleep. Lone Woman needed an abnormal amount of warmth to ease the ache in her bones.

The discarded blanket pressed against her side, reminding her of Damien's touch. For fourteen beautiful days he'd lain beside her, cuddling and caressing her. It had felt so wonderful, so right.

Chagrined by her growing weakness and fantasies, she tried to push the robe further away. If she knew where he was sleeping this night, she would go to him so intense was her need. Her sensitive flesh twitched. Moaning, she tentatively slid her palms down her torrid sides. It just didn't feel the same.

Her head jerked around and her eyes flew open. Was that a little chuckle she heard? Disjointed thoughts scrambled together. Damien was here. He was lying right beside her. No! He couldn't see her in this wretched condition.

"I'm so glad you're here." She whispered, forgetting all about that last encounter. Her pupils dilated, trying to adjust to the smouldering campfire light. He was a dark shadow beside her.

"I'm sorry I forgot to show you how to please yourself, *mignonne*." His soft breath tickled her sensitive ear.

"Show me."

Pressed against him, she could feel the whole glorious length of his body. His flesh, even through his clothing, was burning. As he rubbed against her side, his resourceful hand nudged her dress up her thigh. He daringly smoothed the curled hair between her legs.

"You do this – and this – and..." His fingers began to fondle her tender flesh with expert finesse.

His lips swooping down smothered her shocked exclamation in a scorching kiss. His tongue grazed her lips. She parted them allowing him entry.

Then one lean finger slipped inside her wetness to follow the delightful rhythm of his darting tongue. The touch was excruciating exhilaration. Beams of delicious bliss consumed her whole body. She clenched her legs around his searching hand. He'd never touched her like this before. Arching up, she pressed him deeper.

Suddenly she realized they weren't alone. Lone Woman was sleeping a few feet away. She tried to move his powerful chest back when he rolled over to lie on top her.

He murmured against her ear, first kissing the outer lobe, and then letting his tongue glide inside to explore valorously.

"Lone Woman will wake up."

"If you don't keep quiet, she will." Damien laughed softly.

His lips moved down to play with a taut nipple. Her legs flopped apart as he continued to search along her swollen, slick opening with ingenious fingers. His tongue moved back to play along the contours of her panting lips, then shifted back to her ear, licking with fleeting tenderness. He was touching her everywhere and it was so delightful she couldn't stop him.

Intense pleasure lapped against his sliding finger. Shimmering signals tore throughout, making her forget everything except his obliging touch.

He moved back to her lips when she began to whimper, squirming with need.

"Damien... Oh..." Her hands moved across his taunt back to caress the intriguing flesh. She could feel the hot hardness, pressed against her thigh and instinctively she moved her leg up to rub against the bulge.

She nearly screamed aloud when his thumb began massaging her aching mound. What was he doing? Her body reacted with a will of its own. God, he was touching her so intimately – so delightfully. Wrong or not, his seeking fingers felt so right.

"*Oui, mignonne* – let it come," Damien breathed deeply, moving back slightly.

"Come back!" She whimpered, trying to draw him to her. She had nearly reached – was climbing an aching cliff toward something mysterious and beautiful. Her body ached, twitching with a promise of paradise.

"I'm here with you," His voice was playful and soothing. He continued to manipulate her torrid flesh. She opened her eyes. He was watching her.

"Please..." she groaned, arching up to press his hand closer.

A thin sheen of perspiration covered his face. She exploded. Her legs clamped around his fingers. Her body quivered. She felt the scream building in her throat. Tilting her head back, her lips parted.

Damien muffled her erratic scream with aggressive lips.

"Hush. We will wake her..." he murmured against her mouth.

Bobbie moaned, still squirming. Pinpoints of electric shocks coursed through her body to center in that spot between her thighs. She was unaware of his muffled caution.

"Let's go outside," he continued with a groan. He shifted away from her.

Languidly, Bobbie reached her arms up to draw him back, focusing with difficulty. She turned her head and looked at the old woman sleeping. She gasped.

"I could use a swim, couldn't you? She's still sleeping," Damien whispered seductively against her ear. His eyes glittered in the darkness. "Although not for long, she won't be."

"Why not?" Anxiously, Bobbie sat up, pulling her dress down.

"You are very vocal, wildcat." Damien laughed softly. "Come on, let's go for a swim."

Crackling, dried leaves of the dying aspens mingled with honking geese, flying south, infusing the looming rocks and crags with echoing sound. Across the camp from Lone Woman's lodge, a blazing fire spit crimson showers into the violet-black skies. Another debauched orgy was in progress. Loud shrieking laughter and boisterous quarrelling became muted, receding as they descended the sloping ridge leading down to the river.

"Lone Woman hates those people." Shivering, Bobbie clung to Damien's arm, pressing against his muscled comfort. She could not rid herself of this fear of being alone in the dark.

"She said that?" Damien's voice sounded almost sarcastic.

Sliding down a well-used dirt slope, he turned and gracefully swept her into his arms. He let her slide, languid and provocatively, along his full length. His shimmering eyes were suggestive with promise.

"I feel so tall, when I'm with you. You are perfect for me, *mignonne*." He laughed. "Your God made you specially for me."

"Only my God?" Her eyes dropped to the pebbled ground. She felt herself going hot again. His eyes were so intense and mystifying, he frightened her again.

"It's not my God." His jaw tightened, making him look foreign to her. She groaned. Why, oh why couldn't she just be silent and...

"Damien, maybe we should just slow down." Her voice tapered off when she saw the fierce look in his eyes.

"It's easy for you to say now, *mignonne*." His eyes narrowed with insult. "You – at least got a little pleasure."

Flushing with mortification, she looked back to the ground. He'd pleasured her body and now she should feel obligated? All was forgiven and forgotten – for a few moments of pleasure?

"Why do you always avoid talking to me?" Her own jaw tensed with agitation. "I've had a lot of time to study your people – thanks to your neglect, incidentally. They would be so much better on a reservation. At least it would stop this atrocious abuse of alcohol."

"You have studied us. Sort of like studying an insect under a microscope, I suppose." She tried to ignore the baleful glint in his beautiful eyes. "You figured all that out in your own pretty little head? Amazing." His breath was a delicate breeze against her cheek and – smelled suspiciously like whiskey! Goodness, was Damien like those others? She shivered. She had fallen in love with a drunken Indian.

"Alcohol has ruined better men than you. It frightens me to think you are like those..." Bobbie started to blurt out, then stopped. She could vividly recall Damien's temper when he was intoxicated. She shouldn't aggravate him now.

Letting her go, Damien tilted his head, staring into the star glimmering heavens.

He was clenching and unclenching his fists. Taking a long, shuddering breath, he turned back to her. Kneeling in front of her, he grasped the hem of her fringed frock, slowing gliding it upwards. His lips, like liquid fire, followed his masterful progress.

"I missed you. Each moment away from you is a living hell. I need you. But it sure as hell isn't this, I'm needing..." Like a smooth panther, he was standing again. His palm brushed against her head. Violently, he grabbed her arms, slamming her body to him. "Your head is empty. You always spout such nonsense. You sound like a prune-faced old lady. Yet your body is like a goddess."

"These are meant for this," His predatory lips moved with grinding energy against hers. "Not talking."

"Damien." Squeaking, she struggled against the magnetic pull of his plundering lips. Again he would ignore what he didn't want to hear and used his skilled touch to master her protests with frightening ease.

"Fine!" Damien's deep voice sounded grim as he stopped his tantalizing assault. Taking her hand, he led her to a flat boulder and pushed her down. "We'll never settle anything until you have your way. Let's talk then. This just isn't going to work."

Damien began pacing back and forth in front of her. He shoved his hands through his silken hair and stopped to glare at her. Jerking his eyes way, he shuddered. A distant, crooked smile crossed his features. Then he was calm again.

"Sorry. I'm not much for serious talking. Especially when I have a beautiful, willing woman – not even wearing underpants."

"Lone Woman said we don't..." She jumped up, darting a look of reproach in his direction.

"Easy, wildcat." Damien lifted her back into his arms, her legs dangling helplessly off the ground. He nibbled with lavish attention, along her neck. "Didn't I say the first time I met you, that you have a very bad habit of changing subjects?"

"You were drunk that night." She tried to ignore his practiced caress, unsuccessfully. Whenever he touched her, her body quivered in anticipation.

"No worse than you, my bitchy little prude. Do you want to talk or make love? In case you haven't noticed this lovemaking has been a one-way street – all in your favour."

"That's your fault..." she murmured, and then stopped. "Let's talk."

Tossing her a sardonic smile, Damien placed her back on the rock. Turning away, he walked to the edge of the glittering silver water, lapping against the white-pebbled shore.

"Let's pretend we are alone in the whole universe. Right here – where everything is perfect. It's just you and me – all alone." Damien spun around as she rose in response to his hypnotic words. "I told you to sit!"

"I definitely see a resemblance between you and Lone Woman." Bobbie sat down.

Leaning back on the boulder, she realized she was nearly naked, wearing only a dress. A short giggle escaped. Only a month ago she wasn't even aware people actually bared themselves for anything other than bathing. Now she felt so comfortable, wearing only this soft, short gown.

"Roberta Taylor – such an aggressive, annoying lady." His wicked grin indicated satisfaction when her head shot up. He did however, now have her full attention.

"So you actually believe we would all be so much better off on a reservation? After all – the buffalo are nearly gone and the Americans sure don't want us here. Their ranchers and farmers are begging the army to remove us."

"Exactly. So why are you still here?" Bobbie smiled with smug satisfaction.

Then she cowered back, terrified at the desolate bleakness in his eyes. He had started out, speaking so reasonably.

"Please allow me to finish." He growled with exaggerated politeness. Taking heavy gulps of refreshing mountain air, he continued. "In the very near future you will have your wish. It does not matter that for countless centuries this was all ours, does it? We didn't have borders. We weren't told where we could go and where we have to live. We went wherever we pleased. It is our country."

"You're half white." Bobbie inserted, not caring for the condemnation in his tone. Or were the French actually white? God, she was confused. How could she possibly love a man who hated everything she represented?

"My white ancestors were *voyageurs*. The *voyageurs*, like the People, hunt and trap furs. They are nothing like the whites who are coming now." Damien's voice was bitter.

"And so what happens now? Will your hatred and bitterness help put everything back the way it was?"

He shook his head, glaring at her sullenly.

"Then what's left, except to go forward and adapt? You have to accept the way things are now." She couldn't stop the niggling guilt inside.

"Don't patronize me!" He stepped forward to yank her to her feet, digging his lean fingers into her soft upper arms.

Then, as though realizing he was hurting her, he stopped. He rubbed the bruised flesh with tenderness. "So will you allow us heathens into your elite world? Where will you place us - a step above your cattle, hopefully? But a hundred steps below you no?"

"That's hardly fair." Bobbie gasped, cringing at his scornful wrath. "When have I ever behaved as though I'm superior to you?"

"Every time you open your mouth. And the sad part is that you don't even realize it."

"Just because I refuse to accept your every word," she sputtered, as hesitant doubt crept in. Did she consider Damien inferior? Of course she didn't. She loved him.

"You are getting better." Damien smiled his teasing, chameleon smile. "By this time next year we should be equal."

"Damien – is this by chance another of your depraved lessons?" Bobbie asked. Was he teasing her or was he serious?

It didn't matter what society she was in men were always the same. They expected absolute obedience from a female. Wasn't that the true issue – even here? This didn't have anything to do with who they were. He was distorting the whole issue. What did it matter to her, one way or another, how these people chose to live? It was how Damien chose to live that mattered to her.

"No lesson. I was trying to explain about your wonderful reservations. I can't. You can't understand. Our culture, like yours, took years to evolve. Now it is disappearing in a few short decades. Someone – somewhere – is ruthlessly destroying it and that someone has decided our way is evil and wrong. Do you really expect me to smile and say thank you?"

"I'm sorry." And she meant it. She could understand what he was saying. Put this way, it was her people who sounded evil and wrong.

"You didn't do this did you?" Damien's laugh was short acceptance of the way things were. "No one person has. It just happens. It's progress, isn't it?"

"You are intelligent and educated. Surely you could help. You could be something other than a – vagrant." Bobbie sighed. "You were raised by a Christian minister."

"Stop!"

Suddenly he was hostile again. His smouldering eyes pierced her pallid face with blazing assault. Bobbie felt tears beneath her lashes.

"Yes, *mignonne,* I was raised by the wonderful Reverend MacLeod and his so lovely wife. They were pillars of society in Winnipeg. I was so very fortunate. I was five years old when both my parents were killed. I can't remember much about them except – sunshine and laughter and – happiness. I can't ever remember that with the good Reverend... They were only *Metis,* not important to anyone. I had such a better life with Reverend MacLeod. And I had an even better time with his lovely wife."

His laughter was cruel and bitter.

"Why did he take you if he didn't like the *Metis*?"

"Because he could?" Damien grunted, shaking his head. "Maybe it was because the Catholics were supposedly having such great success with the orphans? The Catholics raised Louis Riel. He even went to university in Montreal. Riel is smarter than most white men."

"Reverend MacLeod was jealous of the Catholic Church?"

"Reverend MacLeod hated the Catholics. He taught me so well. I learned it is wrong to play – to dance – to smoke and drink – or swear. It is wrong to enjoy anything including riding and food even. He wanted me to bring him the highest grades in every subject. But even when I gave him that it wasn't good enough. He made me sit and listen while he lectured and prayed for my soul. While the others were out playing I was learning – progress. Would you like to know how he made me listen?"

Grabbing her hand, he pressed it along the raised ridges on his back, then across his taut waistline. Beneath his shirt, she could feel the puckered, raised scar tissue. Reverend MacLeod had beaten him brutally. She was barely able to keep her icy numb fingers against those elevated welts. Tears ran down her cheeks. She felt the guilt penetrate. She felt awful. She had believed possibly some woman had... Oh my God. A minister had abused and tortured a small, defenceless boy.

"I don't want your pity." Damien's short laugh was ruthless. "I got so much of that from his lovely, pious wife. She soothed my pain very well. She even looks a little like you do."

"You were only a boy." Bobbie gasped out in shock.

"I was fifteen – and very much a man. Anne thought so. She noticed I needed other things besides my cuts being attended to. Stop crying. I learned so much from Reverend MacLeod and his lovely wife about white man's ways..."

"Then Anne taught me another thing – so well, I will always carry it with me and I can never change it. I am *Metis*. And because I am, you lovely white ladies only want me in your beds. In your public I will never be good enough."

"You're wrong." Bobbie sobbed angrily. "I love you." Inside, his words whirled around in her head. Could she introduce Damien as her husband in Toronto society? Would she be able to introduce him proudly to her parents? Yes, she would. She did love him.

She didn't feel him move until he gathered her into his strong arms. Now it was he, comforting her as he stroked her wet, streaked face. Amazed, Bobbie could only stare mutely into his beautiful eyes. How could there be any gentleness left inside this man?

"Don't cry. I ran away from him. I didn't kill him. Anne killed him. She hit him with a poker after he caught us together. She didn't do it because he was beating me. She did it to save her reputation. I begged her to come with me and she laughed in my face. Then I met Big Bear. Lone Woman had just lost her son. She adopted me. Big Bear and Lone Woman taught me everything I consider important. I belong here."

"I understand." Bobbie whispered forlornly. "But Damien – I do love you. I would never be ashamed of you."

"And I think I love a stubborn little wildcat who doesn't have a clue what she's getting herself into." Damien pulled her closer, nuzzling her slender neck. "Is this enough serious talk for now, *mignonne*? Can we play in the river now before the sun comes up? Unless you'd like an audience again?"

"Damien!" She was amazed at how easily he could shock her – and arouse her curiosity. Did people actually watch other people – make love?

Damien grinned a knowing grin as though he understood her thoughts. "One day Big Bear will have to sign a Treaty. When he does, I'll take you for a visit. Then you'll understand. Until then – let's enjoy now."

In one fluid leap, he flung his arms around her waist. Then one powerful lunge and they both tumbled into freezing mountain water.

"Let's get married tomorrow." Damien's lips were very close to hers as they surfaced.

"Sure, if I don't freeze to death first..." Bobbie agreed through chattering teeth.

"I'm sorry I pushed you in the water," Damien didn't look cold at all.

He kept his arms around her as he led her back to the tent, but shook his head when she asked if he would come in with her.

"Tomorrow night I will give you a wedding night you will never forget."

He laughed softly, placing a lingering, sensual kiss against her lips. He disappeared into the darkness.

CHAPTER 15

Bobbie woke to the sound of birds singing in the sunshine. Filtered beams edged into the tent, creating designs on the walls. Flickering and weaving, the shadows looked like dancing figures against the tanned hides.

It was going to be a beautiful day. Her wedding day! Bobbie smiled with excitement. She shuffled to her side. The furs were warm and soft against her body. Was it really going to happen? Would Damien actually marry her? Looking across the tipi, she saw Lone Woman, grinning madly. She sat before the fire, stirring something as she hummed.

"Gotta eat Robin. You gonna need to be mighty strong tonight." The old lady cackled indistinctly.

"Good morning to you too, Mother." Bobbie rubbed her eyes.

"I needa talk, Robin." Lone Woman's round gaze darted over to her. She smiled with fondness.

"Where's Damien... um, Hawk?" Bobbie sat up and pushed the furs aside.

"Hawk here and gone a hundred times. He ain't gonna go this time." Lone Woman's voice was gentle as though she understood Bobbie's fear. "I didn't mean to scare you Robin. I was jest gonna talk about tonight."

"Oh!" Bobbie's mouth rounded. A mother/daughter type of conversation about... she flushed. Maybe she knew too much already. Damien was an excellent teacher.

"No. Not that." Lone Woman laughed. "I leave that to Hawk. I mean about living with Hawk. It gonna be tough."

"Tough? Why?" Bewildered, Bobbie crawled over to the fire beside Lone Woman.

"You different. You don't like our ways." Lone Woman shrugged, dropping her eyes. "It gonna be tough."

"I don't care." Bobbie sighed, and then smiled. Today, she didn't care. She was going to marry Damien. She loved him.

"Well, you gonna stick to yore silly ways or you gonna love him?" Lone Woman demanded in her blunt way.

"My silly ways?" Bobbie bristled, and then dropped her shoulders with another sigh. Lone Woman was right. What chance did their marriage have, if all they did was fight? Damien wouldn't change. He believed this life of poverty and chaos was so much better than her ordered society. She would have to swallow her pride and try to adjust. Besides, she was beginning to believe he was right. Who needed material possessions when they had love? "I know what you're trying to say, Mother. I will try very, very hard to make Damien an – obedient wife."

Lone Woman raised her eyebrow, snorting.

An exquisite young woman coming in interrupted them. The lady smiled shyly, but kept her head bowed as she handed Bobbie a package. A white, suede dress was inside. Her wedding dress.

"Thank you."

"I wish you happy," The girl giggled softly. "Hawk, good man. He look after me good."

"He look after you good?" Bobbie repeated, throwing Lone Woman a puzzled glance.

Oh, good heavens. What was she getting into? Then a light dawned in her eyes. This was one of Damien's three ex-wives. She wanted to jump up and scratch this lovely creature's eyes out and simultaneously ask her a thousand questions.

"Gotta get ready, Robin." Lone Woman grabbed her hand to open her clenched fist. "You go now Dove. See if everything ready for us."

After Dove left, Lone Woman looked at Bobbie carefully, then shook her head.

"Obedient wife? You gotta understan the rules. Hawk gotta take his brother's wife. Big insult if he don't."

"I'm trying," Bobbie muttered weakly. *"But he will not have any other wife but me – and he better understand that!"*

Damien's teasing eyes with their promised pleasure, emerged. He had explained, making no apologies. He had done the honourable thing. She must accept that or leave. And God only knew, she didn't want to leave.

"Go to river, get you dressed." Lone Woman smiled grimly. "You think love gonna be enough?"

"Yes." Bobbie whispered. She leaned over to give Lone Woman a hug. This old woman, although often harsh and abrupt, had accepted Bobbie without question.

The grey bonfire smoke wafted into the violet-black skies as dusk settled in with sultry slowness. Bobbie squinted as it stung her eyes. The pungent smell of burning logs penetrated her nostrils. The sound of heavy beating drums echoed in the valley, mingling with laughter and loud voices.

Lowering her eyes, Bobbie followed Lone Woman to the fire. Looking up, she saw Damien dressed in full raiment with a long sleeved fringed shirt and matching white-fringed trousers. He looked exotic and dangerous. Again that intriguing-quill choker was around his neck. The glass surrounding the single feather glinted in the light.

When he reached out his hand, she swallowed and stepped forward to take it. The crowd grew silent. Big Bear raised his arms. She felt a slow churning start in the pit of her stomach. Damien squeezed her hand.

Big Bear began a low, husky chant. She weaved precariously. She felt weak. Suddenly, Damien took her by the shoulders and turned her around. Carefully, he placed something around her neck. It was his necklace! Startled, she turned and looked into his eyes.

"My most prized possession – It's yours now, wildcat. I've never given this to anyone else – ever." His voice was low and husky, cracking as he spoke. She continued searching his face. Then she nodded and smiled.

Everyone started cheering and moved forward to congratulate them.

"That's all?" Bobbie yanked at Damien's taut arm. "Don't we say *'I do'* or anything?"

"Notice you didn't have to say obeys either." Damien leaned down to whisper in her ear. "We're married. Don't ever forget that."

Shivering, Bobbie stepped back. She felt his breath slide along her bare neck and shoulders.

"And there's another thing. Why am I the only naked person here?" Her arms swept around the milling crowd. Flushing, she dropped her eyes to the ground again. "I thought brides were supposed to be modest."

"You aren't naked, *mignonne*." With deliberate ease, Damien let his gaze drift along her body, making her tingle with awareness. "You're exquisite. You are meant to enflame your husband with desire. And you do! No one is playing tricks on you. It's a traditional wedding dress."

"It's not a dress." Bobbie shook her head, her hair flying around her bare shoulders. "It's just two panels, tied together. Lone Woman said I couldn't wear any undergarments, either."

"Don't tell me that!"

She flushed again. Damien's eyes were burning passion as he continued to search her body intently. He reached out, pulling her against his body. His hand rested on her bare hips. Boldly, he inserted a finger beneath the crepe soft material.

"It's for me. Bridegrooms are too awkward. We couldn't possibly be expected to remove a normal gown." He laughed against her hair. "This is easy. I undo the belt and pull these strings at your shoulders and *voila*, you are naked."

"Don't you dare!" Bobbie hissed, checking to make sure her shoulder straps were still fastened. She looked around. Thankfully, everyone was dancing now. No one was paying any attention. She looked down at this traditional wedding gown and grimaced. Surely, if she moved it would gape open and show everything.

"Would you like to dance?" Damien's voice sounded strained.

"Yes."

Everything appeared different now that they were married. She thought about the night he'd turned savage and tied her up. A shiver ran down her back. Would he turn violent again? Would he ever hurt her?

"No, *mignonne*. I'll never hurt you – although you didn't mind being tied, did you? So long as I touched you – gently – in certain spots…" Damien reached one hand down to tilt her chin up. His other arm remained around her waist, binding her close to his body. There was laughter in his eyes.

Her eyes widened. He could read her thoughts so easily.

They joined the horde of shuffling couples already moving to the beat of the hollow drums. They sounded strange and – erotic. Some couples were dancing together while others were lined up, males on one side, and females on the other, swaying sensually to the music.

Feeling very self-conscious in her wedding dress, Bobbie watched Damien when he placed his hands on her hips and began to rotate his torso in a very suggestive manner. She felt the heat from his body burning into her flesh.

"I'm hot." She whispered absently, feeling stiff and awkward. This was like no dancing she'd ever seen before. It was so suggestive and so seductive. Anxiously, she peered over his shoulder. No one was watching.

"So am I, *mignonne*. Should we get – naked?" Damien suggested smoothly.

"Damien!"

"Relax. No one cares," Damien urged softly moving her hips in motion with his. "Feel the beat. Let yourself go. How about I let you tie me up, *mignonne*? Then you can touch me wherever you please – I can't stop you."

I – don't..." Bobbie gulped as a vision of his erotic suggestion surged through her mind. She felt like a stranger was in her body.

"Here. It helped before." Damien let go and reached down to grasp a jug. Smiling, he passed the bottle to her. "What's wrong?"

"I'm scared." Bobbie choked on the liquor but took another gulp anyway. Slowly the warmth stilled her pounding heart.

"You are?" Damien grinned. Taking the jug from her trembling fingers, he set it down. He pulled her against his burning body again.

"Are we doing the right thing?" She murmured in disoriented confusion. She felt the length of his legs against her own. His hand was pressed into her back, just above her waist. Each rotation of his hips caused a twitching ache in her abdomen.

"Don't talk now.' Damien's voice was a husky demand. Swaying against her, his lips moved along her hair. "Please don't."

"What's wrong?" She asked. He sounded upset. She still felt his warmth against her and was comforted. She loved to touch Damien. She slipped her arms around his neck and swayed with him in rhythm with the beating drums and his seductive movement. It felt so good.

"Let's go." Damien didn't answer her. Instead he moved his lips down to glide with silky ease along her quivering neck and shoulders.

Feeling a familiar quivering in her abdomen, Bobbie closed her eyes. Was anyone watching? She didn't want to know. He was fast making her feel like they were the only two people in the whole universe.

They were still swaying together, taking small shuffling steps as Damien guided her slowly backwards. It felt cooler now. Bobbie sighed as his lips continued to search along her bare flesh. His skilled motions were making it impossible to think. Then he stopped moving. His lips moved to hers and he kissed her deeply. She felt her body sag against his and was thankful he was still holding her. She couldn't stand alone. As his lips and tongue began a thorough search of entry and retreat, his hands moved to hold her bottom tight against his loins. She felt his hardness and moaned against his lips.

Still holding her with one arm, still kissing her, Damien reached down to lift the door flap away. Bewildered, Bobbie opened her eyes. They were away from the crowd now. They were by his tent.

"No more interruptions, *mignonne*." He pulled her inside.

A small fire burned in the center. Buffalo robes were tossed nearby. The smell of sweet grass filled the air. Bobbie felt lethargic.

"That's better, wildcat." Damien took her hand and drew her down to the robes. Kneeling, facing her, he held her arms against her sides, looking deep into her wide eyes.

She was silent, trembling slightly. They were alone. They were going to make love. She tried to remember anything she'd heard and couldn't recall a single word.

"Aren't you curious anymore?" His eyes were brimming with humour.

"Why are you always laughing at me?" She whispered.

"I wasn't laughing at you. I'm happy. Remember last night? You weren't at all shy."

"I'm embarrassed." He leaned down, putting his mouth to her ear. She smelled the faint scent of his hair and nuzzled her face into it. He was beautiful.

"Why?" There was still laughter in his voice as Damien shifted closer. He began a slow tantalizing massage along her arms, up to her shoulders. He leaned forward to touch her lips lightly. "Your lips are delightful, *mignonne*. Your body is paradise. You have nothing to be embarrassed about. You're perfect."

Bobbie's lips parted. Her tongue, reaching out to wet the dryness, instead touched his. Familiar longings were beginning to stir in her belly. Damien sat back, tracing his finger along the soft contours. Instinctively Bobbie reached out to pull his finger into her mouth. He groaned as his eyes darkened with desire. His hand trembled. She smiled with satisfaction.

"Are you happy now?" Damien's voice was husky with need. Still, he let her make the moves. "We have all night."

"Yes." Still on her knees, Bobbie reached forward to kiss him. He tasted like the winds, a flavour that was uniquely Damien, impetuous, lustful and free. Moaning, she brought her arms around his neck, putting more pressure against his lips.

Growling low in his throat, Damien pushed her back to the robes and jabbed his tongue into her parted mouth.

"Honey. Pure sweet honey. I've waited long enough." He murmured.

His mouth slanted possessively against hers as he moved his lips against hers with demanding eagerness. She was aware of his pulsating hardness, throbbing against her abdomen, and matched his sensuous rotation. Hips locked together, swaying in the soft firelight. He continued his skilled, delightful exploration.

Frantic with a need she still didn't understand, Bobbie's fingers bit into his neck. Instinctively, she pushed his leather shirt up to his shoulders. His bare flesh was torrid silk over hard steel. His arms flexed, bringing her closer.

"Easy, wildcat. We have all night." Panting softly, Damien moved down to graze along the tender flesh on her neck and shoulders. With his teeth, he unfastened the strings holding her dress together, baring her to the waist.

He leaned back on his heels to look at her. Bobbie looked down to see her nipples were hard. He leaned down to take one nub between his lips.

His contact made her plunge against him. Threading her fingers into his glossy hair, she pressed him to her chest. Reckless sensations splashed inside her. For an endless time he played with her, creating delightful sensations through her body. His lips parted to allow her tongue time to taste the savoury treat he offered.

"Damien, you must..." She gasped. There was an intense pain below that only his pressure seemed to assist. She tried to move nearer.

"I must what, wildcat...?" Damien drew back, sliding his arms down to unfasten her belt and strip the panels away.

She watched the firelight playing on those fascinating arms.

She lay, naked against the robes. His heavy arousal enlarged drastically. Breathing deeply, he managed to untangle her clinging arms. Getting to his knees, he stripped the offending shirt away in one swift motion.

With avid curiosity, Bobbie watched him undress. He unfastened the laces on his trousers. Slowly, he manoeuvred the cloth down his hips to his firm thighs. His distended shaft sprang forward. Her eyes widened. Unconsciously, her tongue darted out to lick her suddenly dry lips.

"That... that is what..." Blinking rapidly, she tried to turn her gaze only to be drawn back to that terrifying, fascinating object before her.

His pants slipped past his ankles. He was now as naked as she.

"That." Damien leaned down and smoothed her wild hair from her face. "You've seen *that* before. Do you want to touch *that*?"

Breathing erratically, Bobbie arched her body up to enjoy the feel of his palms brushing her sensitive nipples. Her hands reached down to tentatively touch him. Damien groaned as her fingers slid experimentally along the shaft.

"Yes. Oh yes." Her fingers encircled the hard flesh, squeezing lightly. It was amazingly silky and so smooth, like velvet.

"It's big," she murmured, watching his face consort with pleasure.

"I hope not too big. I want to be inside you with *that* all the time." Damien grinned.

"I don't think I'll ever look at the word *that* quite the same again." Bobbie giggled softly, but made no protest when his hand slid down to probe between her thighs. Those same feelings she'd had last night penetrated her quivering body as his fingers, with subtle manipulation, played with her.

"Look at me." Damien said softly. Obediently, she opened her eyes to stare up at his taut, beautiful features.

He slid a finger inside her, rotating with devastating thoroughness. She felt her whole body floating upwards towards the heavenly pleasure his touch brought. Heavy jolts of delight cut through her body. She arched into his hand. He lowered his head. Tiny drops of his perspiration touched her face as he kissed her deeply.

"I waited so long. I can't..."

Stretching out over her, Damien held his weight away with his stiff arms as he lowered his torso against hers. She felt his heavy, pulsating shaft between her parted legs and instinctively she moved up to accommodate him. One violent thrust and he'd penetrated her barrier. He shifted back to hold himself away.

"Did I hurt you?" His breath was short gasps of anticipation. He stayed still.

"How long do you stay in there?" She whispered in disappointment. She liked the play that led to this, but it wasn't what she expected. "Is that all?"

"Not yet." Laughing, husky with amusement, Damien lowered himself again and proceeded to show her otherwise.

As he continued to take smooth controlled strokes into her, his gifted lips and hands left no part of hr body untouched. She was burning with a need satisfied by his gyrating strokes of delight. Arching up, she couldn't prevent the scream that tore from her as his motion led to an explosion within. She couldn't control her pulsating, throbbing body. She didn't want to. Only then did she feel his release, hot and wild, flooding her. Limp with exhaustion, she could only lie there, letting the pleasure jolts surge throughout her body.

All through the night she felt those same pleasures. It was not until dawn broke across the eastern horizon that Bobbie pleaded for rest. Her body ached with a pleasure so profound she was breathless.

"It's about time. I was getting worried." Damien chuckled, sinking back on the robe. He flung his arms out. His body was slick with perspiration.
"About what?" Bobbie murmured, ready to sleep.
"I thought I'd never be able to satisfy you, wildcat."
"Are you ever serious?" She asked wistfully, and then felt guilty. With a childhood like his, it was more a wonder that he could be as playful and loving as he was. But she still felt as though something was missing.
He made her laugh, and he made her scream with wanton pleasure, but he rarely mentioned his own feelings.
"I'm not sure what love means, *mignonne*." Once again he was reading her mind so easily. He leaned over to nuzzle her ear softly. "But what I'm feeling for you is stronger than any feelings I've ever had for a woman before. It was teenage infatuation with Anne. It was friendship with Marie. I still like her. But with you... I think its love."
Smiling, Bobbie's lashes fluttered, closing. His smooth words were a start.

CHAPTER 16

Bobbie squeezed the sponge, letting the glorious warm water trickle down. Outside, she heard the howling winds. But here inside, she was cozy and warm thanks to Damien. Damien's second gift to his new bride was a large metal bathtub. Anxiously, she looked to make sure her necklace was nearby. Damien didn't seem to like it when she wasn't wearing it. Yet, he wouldn't tell her the significance. There were many aspects of his mysterious life he refused to discuss and she wanted to know everything. She closed her eyes. She was so in love with this man, it was terrifying. She smiled.
"The bathtub is for me as well as you, wildcat." He whispered wickedly against her ear – the first time they'd used it together.
Now, four wonderful months after their strange marriage, she was still enjoying the luxury of bathing comfortably in the

winter. Only tonight she was alone. Damien was at a council meeting. There was a problem in paradise.

The Montana ranchers and farmers were both adamant and loud in their demand that the Canadian Indians be sent back to their own country. It didn't matter that the treaties for both countries specifically stated the natives had free rein in either country. The Indians were jeopardizing the well being of all civilized people. The Cree were not American Indians.

"Our own country?" Bobbie recalled Damien's burst of anger. "This is *all* our country."

Sighing, Bobbie knew enough not to comment. Damien had been born in Canada and that made him a citizen. Would they go back or would they fight? That was going to be the decision at the council meeting tonight. She shuddered. It would be certain death to fight the American army.

As the water started to cool, Bobbie reached out to grasp the towel beside the tub. This was the part she didn't like. The air inside the tent wasn't warm. It was just a little warmer than the outdoors. Shivering, she hastily stepped out and wrapped the warm flannel around herself. With one swift jump, she crawled beneath the welcoming warm fur robes.

Her eyes widened. What would happen to her if they decided to go back to Canada? With a guilty start, she realized she hadn't really thought about Gilbert or any of her family in months. My God, they must be frantic with worry. Were they now searching for her, worrying that she was dead? A dull ache stabbed at her abdomen. Why hadn't she insisted Damien send a message back? Somehow, Damien managed to cleverly change the subject whenever she mentioned getting in touch with Gilbert. It was always in a very erotic, distracting manner.

"What's wrong?"

Startled Bobbie looked up to see Damien at the door, watching her carefully. Snow clung to the robe he had around his shoulders. In a smooth motion, he flung off the heavy garment and came to kneel by her side.

"I was thinking about Gilbert and Daddy." Bobbie murmured.

"Umm..." Damien leaned down to nuzzle against her neck. "You smell good." He searched beneath the robe, his fingers skimming along her flesh. "Do you want me to warm you up...?"

"Damien, we have to talk about this." Bobbie slapped his playful hands and pushed them away. "They will be worried. They probably think I'm dead. My God, they don't deserve this."

"That's why I'd rather do it to you – not them." Damien whispered seductively, nibbling at her ear lobe. His fingers moved beneath the blanket again. "How have you enjoyed our honeymoon so far? It hasn't been easy, keeping such a demanding woman happy."

"Stop it!" Bobbie shouted, once again trying to remove his searching fingers. She was determined he would not distract her this time. "I feel awful. I've been so cruel."

"Yes, you have..." Damien tried to kiss her lips. She jerked back.

Damien rolled over and turned to stare into the low burning coals. "I thought you ran away. I thought *Daddy* wasn't so perfect – trying to make you marry Etienne."

"He wouldn't have. He was trying to scare me. Daddy didn't like Etienne." Fond memories of Sir Myles seeped inside. He'd never been cruel to her. How could she describe her beloved father to Damien? "He put up with a lot of nonsense. Damien, I know you would like Daddy. He only wanted me to be happy."

"And you would have been happy – married to Etienne?" Damien growled. He turned his head to watch her. There was a scowl on his face. "If he wanted you happy, why did he want you to marry Etienne. And don't give me that crap about the French vote."

"I belonged to a woman's advocate group in Toronto. Daddy didn't mind – too much. Normally we concerned ourselves with problems such as the damage alcohol incurs, things like that." She flushed and dropped her eyes as Damien's lips twitched.

"But the election was coming up. We want to vote too. I was speaking at the Union station when Daddy drove by."

"About the damage – alcohol incurs?" Damien reached over to stroke her bare arm. As she sat up, the robe dropped, revealing her bare chest. His eyes narrowed, smouldering.

"No. I was demanding we have the right to vote." Bobbie muttered darkly. "It's only fair. But Daddy was livid. He said I would marry Etienne and settle down to raise a family. That would keep me out of trouble. He said I was – jeopardizing his career."

"For Prime Minister or MP?" Damien snorted. "Why Etienne? Wasn't there anyone else available to marry?"

"Not any that would agree to marry *me*." Bobbie whispered slowly, looking at Damien with a puzzled expression. "Men seem to like me well enough – until they get to know me."

"I really can't imagine why." Damien had humour in his gaze now as his gaze drifted down to her chest. Was he laughing at her again? It hurt to know she wasn't desirable. "They're fools, *mignonne*. You're the most perfect little creature I've ever met. When we are kissing – it's paradise. Maybe you talk a little too much – but I love you. So continue. *Daddy* would have only kept you engaged until after the election, you think? I remember he needed the French vote."

"When?" Bobbie gasped.

"The day I offered to marry you. Weren't you listening? Or were you too busy trying to trick me into believing you were a man?" He asked lazily. Rolling over, he leaned heavily into her naked body, pushing her back. His eyes darkened, mesmerizing and sultry. Damien's mouth quirked with humour. "You are such a contradiction."

"Why don't men like me?" Her voice tapered off. Why did she care? Damien liked her obviously.

"I think most the men you've met are weak." He leaned down to nuzzle her neck. "Do you think *Daddy* will like his half-breed son? Maybe he'll be happy to get the French *and* the Native vote, you think?"

"Don't sound so – sarcastic! Daddy's isn't like that. He will be happy – if I am. But when I ran off and didn't tell anyone where I am – that wasn't the smartest thing to do. Think of his position."

"I'm thinking about the exalted Minister of Immigration having an Indian son-in-law – and enjoying that! It's not that I really *care* who he is." Damien's laugh was bitter. He moved over to his back and flung his arm across his face. "So he caught you preaching. And that made him so angry he was going to make you marry Etienne? He sounds pretty narrow-minded to me."

"No, not right then. It was after I – mocked – him that he said I was going to marry Etienne." Bobbie murmured reliving that horrible scene with Sir Myles being so livid his face had turned a blotchy red. She'd never seen him like that before.

"You – mocked him?" Damien asked with sardonic horror. "How?"

"I told him – right on the steps with everyone watching – that if he gave women the right to vote, he'd win his damned election."

"Was he angry because you wanted to vote or because you swore, *mignonne*?" Damien's lips twisted. He still kept his eyes covered.

"Stop it!" Guilt welled up in her. She was ruining her father's career. Damien just didn't understand the subtle intricacies of politics. There were many silly rules to follow, but it was still true. A man's reputation – and his family's – had to be unblemished. Why was she so impulsive, not thinking of the consequences of her actions? Now Damien only mocked her concerns. "I've spent months listening to your every word. I've followed *all* your silly, stupid rules. And for what? You won't even try to understand."

"Oh, I understand just fine." Damien sighed, feeling he was caught in that dark, narrow tunnel again – going nowhere. She was right. What she was doing, as Sir Myles Taylor's daughter, was contemptible. It would destroy her father's career. "But what hurts me, *mignonne*, is that you care so much. I know I'm being selfish – but..."

Moving like a panther, Damien shifted and was leaning over her in a swift motion. His head bent to capture her trembling lips with fierce longing. "I was hoping I could make you forget – everything – but me."

He brushed her lips with soft strokes. The pain he was feeling was a tangible ache. He was a cad, expecting her to be different from the others. She couldn't help what she was. Nor could she stop loving her father, just because he wanted her to. He leaned back to watch her expressive eyes. Like cat eyes, they stared unblinkingly into his face. He smiled. Already her face was openly revealing her desperate need for him and the way he could make her forget everything, except him.

"I do love you." She reached up to rub her palm along his taut cheekbones. "I do! And I will stay with you – even if my family doesn't approve. But I want Daddy to know I'm happy and – not hurt. Can't I do that?"

"He'll take you away from me," Damien whispered with anguish. He brought his arms around her exquisite little body. He squeezed tightly. Sir Myles would never let his daughter stay with a breed.

"No, he won't." Bobbie insisted, pressing her arms tightly around his neck. "He wants me to be happy."

Damien smiled with knowing sadness. She was too naïve. She believed Etienne would give her a family. She couldn't see he hated women. She couldn't see her father loved power more than anything else either.

"If we stay here, Daddy can't very well take me away." Bobbie insisted, arching her back up to press her breasts against his chest. "Please Damien, let me tell him. At least he'll know I'm not dead."

"Sure, wildcat." Damien felt the blood surge through his body, into his groin. He knew it was wrong to give in to her on this matter. But like she claimed her father wanted - he too only wanted her to be happy. "I'll send someone to Winnipeg tomorrow."

Bobbie heard no more on the subject. Then spring came with imminent disaster, striking their lives with menacing reality. A warrior came from Little Pine's camp nearby, and warned them that the United States government was sending their army in to remove the Canadian Indians from the country. The farmers and ranchers had won their battle.

Within minutes, Big Bear's camp was ready to move out. Bobbie was amazed at how little time it took to dismantle the whole village. She was still seated, in dazed fascination, at their smouldering campfire, when Damien came to her.
"Come on." He pulled her to her feet. "We do have to hurry."
Already the camp was nearly vacant as everyone rode out.
"Does it matter if they catch us or not?" Bobbie asked, wondering what all the rush was about. "You said we weren't going to fight."
"Don't be naïve about this, *mignonne*." Damien's face was strained. "They may slaughter us anyway. No one cares."
"But we're not Indians." A niggling premonition of their danger filtered into her mind.
She felt the blood drain from her face. It didn't make a difference whether she was a Native or not. No one would bother to check. If they intended to slaughter them, everyone would be slaughtered. She turned to Damien again, searching his features.
There was no humour in his expression. She could read the dark, desperation in his face and shivered. It was no joke.
"Will they really slaughter us?" Her voice trembled.
"Yes!" His voice was harsh. "If they want to. Now get on your horse and catch up with Lone Woman."
Turning to Flower, Bobbie's elbow connected with hard flesh, directly behind her. Jabbing pain stiffened her whole arm.
"You hit me, White Woman?" Wandering Spirit's thin curled lips barely moved. She didn't have to look up into his eyes to know hatred vibrated there.
"*Then get out of my way, Dogface.*"

She spoke in Cree. Throughout the cold winter Damien had taught her many words in the Cree language. Her accent was atrocious, yet he seemed pleased with her efforts.

Now his head jerked up warily. He watched Wandering Spirit. Bobbie gulped. Maybe Wandering Spirit was not the man to be insulting. He was the Chief now.

"Your pale hair would look good on my lance." Slowly, Wandering Spirit picked up a curl from her shoulder, running it through his lean fingers. He turned to Damien and winked. "You should keep her quiet, Hawk. Or maybe you want me to instead? Let's go."

"Damn it, Bobbie, don't go offending him now." Damien swung her easily up onto the back of Flower. "He's our leader."

"Your ways are so strange." Bobbie watched Damien vault to his own mount in a graceful motion. The horses twisted and tensed, as though sensing the urgency.

"We are in trouble. Our War Chief automatically assumes full authority. What's so strange about that?" Damien's handsome features were alight with rising excitement. "Stay with Lone Woman. I'll be with the warriors."

"'Damien, no!" Bobbie screamed at his receding back. "Please come with me. I'm terrified."

"No one will harm you, *mignonne*, so long as I have breath in my body." Damien turned around. His face changed as his beautiful smile spread across it. She drank in the sight with fear. "I love you, Bobbie. I mean that."

"I love you – Hawk." Stunned, she felt faint with reaction. He'd said it! He'd said he loved her with a sincerity she had to believe.

"Come back soon. I'll never forgive you if you leave me alone now. Damien, I need you."

It was too late. He was gone.

The frightening premonition that she would never see him again crossed her panicked mind. She thought of the many massacres she'd read about. She knew, with building terror, that being a white woman would not help her now. No one would even notice if they intended to slaughter her. She sighed. But surely the army had only gentlemen? They would only battle the warriors. They wouldn't harm the women and children would they?

"Come!" Lone Woman's abrupt command filtered into her mind.

Unwillingly, Bobbie trailed along, feeling as though she was loosing something, never to be recaptured again. Freedom.

Not even one child made a sound in the moving mass of human flesh and horses. Not one baby whimpered. Silently, steadily, they moved north.

They were now into their second day of riding. Over and over again these startling facts rolled throughout Bobbie's numb mind. She could hear the plopping slurp of hundreds of hooves, cutting through soft, melting sod. Small rivulets trickled through snow banks and slushy, thawing earth. A faint, hazy mist mingled with blasting winds. It was snowing again. Still, she knew they would suffer through another night without fire. It would be a bitter night and more of the old and feeble would die.

No one would help them. No one could help them. All during the horrible trek back to Canada Bobbie knew that. Damien was right. God, how she missed Damien. Everything was so silent – so serious – so terrifying. She needed his comforting touch to reassure her she would survive.

She turned her stiff neck, looking for Lone Woman. She was riding right behind. The old woman's slight smile indicated she was better equipped to handle this miserable situation than Bobbie was.

"Where's Hawk?" She murmured, her lips almost frozen together. It felt as though a bee was buzzing between them whenever she spoke.

"Jest behind a bit, Robin." Lone Woman made a vast sweep of the disappearing landscape closing in around them. "They watch our back. He gonna be fine."

"Are you going to be fine?" Bobbie asked apprehensively. Lone Woman looked so frail, atop her mangy pony.

"I jest good, little one." Lone Woman chuckled. "Don't worry. Nothing happens behind. We would hear."

Bobbie was not sure where behind was, or ahead for that matter. The grey skies thickened, heavy and silent with snow. She could barely see the figures ahead of her. Behind. Damien was behind, leaving her to die an excruciating death of freezing pain – all alone. Just so she need not suffer the sudden death of a soldier's bullet. She smiled grimly. Right about now a soldier's bullet sounded very inviting. Then she couldn't stop the fear licking through her veins. She prayed nothing would happen to Damien. He would be the one stopping that bullet, not her.

Nearly a month later, Bobbie was amazed she was still alive. Every bone in her body ached with painful intensity. Lone Woman appeared to have no ill effects. Ancient and wizened, she puttered around the fire, stirring her stew as though everything was the same.

Misgivings clouded her eyes as Bobbie searched around Piapot's pathetic little village. They were in Canada. The gaunt people who greeted them, with torn clothing hanging on skeletal frames, all looked like they were starving. They looked like refugees from a war-torn country, not residents of Canada. In contrast, Big Bear's people looked healthy and even well dressed. Their ponies were loaded with buffalo meat. A large herd of horses followed the group into the village.

A large central fire boomed, echoing into the hills and night skis. They were near Fort Walsh. A travel weary Bobbie listened absently to the conversations around the fire. Some spoke English. Some spoke Cree and she could understand a little of their words now. These people were telling such horror stories. She didn't want to believe what she was hearing. *'Oh Damien, I'm sorry. I'm sorry.'*

God, it was a wonder Damien hadn't murdered her for her presumptuous attitude. She knew nothing. Everything he said was true. The Natives were starving here. She wanted Damien back so desperately. She wanted to apologize for ever thinking she was right and he knew nothing. Did her father, a part of this government, know what was happening? She felt guilty and cringed into the shadows.

"I spend five days in jail. I don't say *sir* fast enough..."

"He wouldn't give my wife up. He said give him money and he'd see..."

"They all fat enough. They don' starve."

"They eat our food..."

"They sell our food..."

"Brown Arrow beat bad. Teach him for stealing bacon..."

"Who wants bacon? Give him buffalo. He don' need bacon..."

Bobbie wanted to scream out in protest. She clamped her hands over her ears. But then she could still see... Silent, clogging tears burned inside her throat. Here was the proof. The people who had signed their Treaty were much worse off than the people who followed Big Bear. And even the alcohol that she had insisted was forbidden on the reservations was in abundant supply.

"Where did you get that?" Bobbie leaned over to whisper in one very young girl's ear.

"Want some? Sojer give it to me. You young. He buys you too." The girl grinned precociously.

Watching the maiden tilt the bottle like a master, Bobbie felt nausea fetter inside. She did not fit in. She did not want to become one of these pathetic creatures, selling her body for wine. She needed Damien. Where was he? He must take her away – right now – tonight!

CHAPTER 17

The sky crackled with sparks. Grotesque, weaving shadows danced on the tents. Wild figures pranced around the fire, yelling and laughing as the thick spirits penetrated to numb their minds. Bobbie's mind was consumed with hideous visions of torture and mutilation. Everyone here accepted her now as Damien's wife. But she knew very well, after spending a winter with these people, they were liable to do anything when drinking their wonderful *'firewater'*. Tonight, it appeared as though everyone except her and Lone Water were drinking. Her mounting terror caused her to seek out Wandering Spirit. He was standing quietly and obviously sober, back from the fire. Their eyes met. Was he still their Chief? Would he let them – kill her? Where was Damien? Wasn't he with Wandering Spirit?

She jumped to her feet when she heard the dull thud of hooves against the ground. Damien was back! Eagerly, she ran out from behind the tipi's dark screen. Then she stopped short. Two scarlet-coated mounted men sat on their horses directly in front of her.

For long moments they were silent in gaping shock. Their horses shuffled impatiently as they both stared at her like she was some apparition floating by. Bobbie stood, trembling.

"It's her – Roberta Taylor. It's gotta be Tom." The red-haired, younger man finally spoke. "Inspector Crozier told us to watch for her. She was with Big Bear. And sure enough, here she is."

"Good evening, ma'am." The older man was stockier and looked worn out beside the enthusiastic youth. His cap, as he doffed it, revealed a smooth, baldhead shining beet-red in the firelight. "Constable Robson, ma'am. Guess you're mighty glad to see us."

"Pardon?"

Bobbie sputtered in stupefaction. What was he saying? Did they think she was here against her will? It wasn't possible. Her father knew. As he'd promised, Damien had sent a messenger to Winnipeg over two months ago.

"Pictures of you in all the forts, Miss Taylor. But we couldn't go down to Montana to get you. That would have been suicide."

"I didn't need to be rescued," Bobbie whispered, her voice cracking. "Daddy knew that."

"Don't look like you were too badly mistreated. These heathens can make a mess pretty damned – excuse my language, ma'am. Come along. You're safe now."

"Safe? Mistreated? No you don't understand." Bobbie couldn't make her voice any louder. The words seemed to stick to the sides of her throat.

"We'll take you back. We'll come back later for that breed what captured you," Constable Robson continued, ignoring her. "He won't get far. He can't just go running off to the States now."

"No – he didn't. You don't understand." Bobbie protested frantically.

Tom Robson dismounted and went to lift her up onto his horse.

"No. I wasn't captured. I'm Damien's wife. Please, you must listen..." She tried to struggle. His arms were like a vice.

"Cracked right up, I'd say." The red-haired man's face was a mixture of fascination and repulsion. "Damn breed. Damien's been playing around with our women too long. I can't wait to get my hands on him."

"He's my husband, not a criminal." Bobbie screamed out, still trying to get out of Tom's arms. "If you touch one hair on his head, you'll be sorry."

"Ma'am, you're hysterical. Everything is fine now." Tom began softly, and then growled his rage as Bobbie's foot lashed out, connecting with his jaw. His pale eyes gleamed. He nodded slightly to his partner. "Go ahead Brian."

Drawing his gun from its holster, Brian reached over and tapped sharply behind her ear. His arms swooped out, bringing her across to his saddle. She slumped slightly forward, seeing stars, and then darkness.

"Reckon if she enjoys a dirty redskin..." Brian's hands moved upward to fondle her taut breasts.

"Don't even think about it lad. She is still Sir Myles Taylor's daughter and I'm sure he'd hang us as easily as he's going to hang Damien." Tom shook his head, mounting. "Let's get her back to the fort."

He hoped they would ship Roberta Taylor out immediately. She was a looker, but no respectable gentleman would have her now. Sir Myles would soon find that out.

The Indians were unnaturally silent, all standing or seated around the fire. No one made any effort to stop the two policemen. Then Lone Woman struggled to her feet. Tottering towards the two men, her piercing shrieks cut through the quiet air.

"You can't take Robin. No!" Like the claws of a bird, Lone Woman's fingers grappled with Brian's leg, raking at his trousers. "Hawk's woman. Put her down."

"Shut up, you stupid old crone."

Lifting his rifle, Brian bashed it into the old woman's distorted, haggard face. The sound of crunching bones echoed around the camp. Wandering Spirit tensed, then relaxed. Lone Woman crumbled to the ground, blood seeping from her gaping mouth. There were murmurs of protest and a few of the men started forward. They stopped. No one challenged the men as they rode away.

Tom Robson had his request fulfilled. Inspector Crozier had her escorted to Winnipeg immediately. His fort was not equipped for ladies. She was put on the first train going to Toronto.

To still her fanatical ravings, they sedated her heavily. Whenever she woke, she demanded they return her to Big Bear's camp. But they had their orders and they would obey them. Sir Myles wanted his daughter back. Every soldier at Fort Walsh was relieved to see the last of Miss Roberta Taylor. Regardless of how pretty the lady was she was obviously deranged.

CHAPTER 18
Toronto, Summer – 1884
"You wanted to see me, Daddy?" Smiling cordially, Bobbie entered her father's prestigious newspaper office. Myles was standing by an opened window, looking out over Lake Ontario.

He looked weary as he turned to smile. "Is something wrong? You look ill. It's not Etienne again, I hope."

"No. He's still in Paris as far as I know. And Gilbert's in Switzerland." Myles smiled, swinging around to sit behind his huge, cherry-wood desk. "There's really nothing more Etienne can do to us. Sit down."

He looks so tired; Bobbie sighed and obeyed his quiet command. *I hope he's not sick.* A few years ago she wouldn't have paid any attention to her father's discomfort, feeling he brought all misfortune on himself. A few years ago, she had been a very selfish, self-centered spoiled brat.

But now, she felt more mature and – compassionate. She knew life was not all fun and games. Sometimes a person had to face consequences. There were no white knights. There was no one who could spend a life of unadulterated pleasure with no cares or concerns. Damien was just another lie from her past, just as his words and promises were.

Bobbie was determined to keep herself so busy she had no time to think about that rotten man who had abandoned her three long years ago.

"Nothing is wrong, sweetheart." Myles cleared his throat and began playing with his pen. He didn't look directly at his daughter. "I have a proposition for you. But first I'd like to ask a few personal questions – and Bobbie, I'd like an honest answer."

"We have a different relationship now, wouldn't you say?" Myles smiled, looking up. "Do you still hate me?"

"I never really hated you, Daddy." Bobbie flushed, and then turned silent.

For comfortless months Bobbie had foolishly waited for Damien to come for her. In her mind and words she knew her father was keeping her a prisoner. She believed that Damien had come for her and her evil father had sent him away – or had him killed. Whenever she saw her father she could only plead with him, begging him to let her go back to Winnipeg. Myles flat out refused. It was enough he had dropped all charges against the man. He would do no more for the philanderer who had ruined his daughter.

"Well, I've reconsidered your arguments. I've decided you can go back to Winnipeg." Myles smiled.

"Pardon?" Bobbie gasped, staring at her father as though he'd sprouted two heads. "Did you hear from Damien...?" Angrily she squelched the eagerness from her voice. She didn't care. It was too late.

"Daddy, you know I don't want to go back to Winnipeg." Bobbie continued more calmly. "I love my job and I'm happy here."

"Happy?" Myles shook his head. "Content perhaps, but not happy. What about Lisa?"

"What about Lisa?" Bobbie tilted her chin defiantly. "Surely, you aren't going to suggest she needs a father? She's nearly two years old. Besides, I thought mother handled that department, years ago."

Now Bobbie knew, shortly after her return, that Amelia discreetly passed around the word that Bobbie had married a man in the west. None disputed the fact Bobbie had known a man. Her baby was born a scant seven months after her return. But everyone seemed to know the heathens had captured her. When did she meet this fine policeman Amelia talked about?

Bobbie didn't hear or care about the insulting sniggers and ambiguous words flying around. She was in a gloomy depression. She was still waiting for Damien to come for her.

But looking back, she could well imagine her parents' embarrassment and shame. She reached across her father's desk and took his hands, stilling their agitated motion.

"Thank you for staying with me." She smiled with grim reluctance, swallowing. "It must have been very hard. Did anyone believe mother?"

"Probably not." Myles admitted gruffly, lowering his gaze again. "I tried to keep it hushed but everyone knew you'd been captured. I had reward posters plastered everywhere."

"He never captured me." Bobbie whispered her mortification. She would be honest though. "I went – willingly.

I was such a spoiled hooligan. I wanted to believe him. And that's why you retired from politics, isn't it?"

She had to know and she had never dared voice her question aloud before. She was too afraid of the answer.

"Good heaven, no child. I could have lived that down. It was Etienne – and the fact I wanted to retire. You must know that!"

Bobbie could still remember the conversation she'd heard between her father and Etienne. Etienne was blackmailing Sir Myles. Either Myles gave him money and supported his licentious habits or Etienne would reveal Gilbert's unnatural obsession. Gilbert was in love with Etienne! Finally, faced with poverty and bankruptcy, Myles had no choice. He refused to support Etienne any longer. Etienne, in a fit of rage, did what he'd threatened to do. He exposed Gilbert's peculiar tastes to Toronto society.

"But no one seemed that shocked." Bobbie stated gently, reading her father's discomfort. "They all knew. That must have surprised you."

"It surely surprised Etienne." Myles smiled. His face was pale and strained. "But that didn't matter. There is a difference between gossip and knowing something for sure."

"And that is why a politician must evade the truth?" Bobbie lightened her tone. She patted his hand as though she were comforting her daughter. "Etienne's not bothering you now, is he?"

"Not since Gilbert turned on him." Myles held her hands, smiling with affection. "I didn't call you in to talk about Etienne. I want to talk about Winnipeg."

"What about Winnipeg?" Bobbie asked with a wary glance at him.

"You know I've always wanted an office in Winnipeg. I'm offering you the chance to run it, sweetheart." Myles plunged in quickly. "There's trouble brewing out there and no one here seems to know or care."

"Me?" Bobbie asked. Her mouth dropped open. She didn't know whether to feel elated or sad. "Daddy, it's a wonderful offer. I would have my own office."

"Yes. But I'd have to monitor your activities a bit until I was sure you could do it." Myles inserted smoothly. "I have complete faith in your abilities but..."

"I've been working for you for the past year. I have no complaints – you being my boss, Daddy." Bobbie smiled.

Her father was not a domineering, arrogant man, as she had believed he was. Once he found out that a person could do their job, he left them alone to do just that. Bobbie was sure that was one of his best assets for the successful man he'd become.

"I was also thinking of your welfare, sweetheart. You and Lisa could have a good life – without a man if you want. You don't still – umm – care for Damien do you? What would happen if he were around?"

"N-no..." Even someone speaking his name evoked anguished memories. "He won't be around Daddy. He'll be off in the wilderness, playing Indian. He does it so well."

"Was that the attraction? Did you like playing Indians too?" Myles shook his head. Obviously he didn't want an answer. "Then you'll go?"

"Yes, I'll go." Bobbie sighed. She was at the crossroads now. She could move ahead and become a powerful, independent woman or she could let her memories destroy her. She tilted her chin with determination. She knew what she would do.

"Good." Myles stood and went back to stare out the huge window. "Your mother said you should continue passing yourself off as a widow."

"I really don't know anyone there. I left before I got into their society circles." Bobbie grinned a winsome smile.

"Did he teach you that?" Myles turned to look at her. "I'm sure Hortense didn't."

"Teach me what?" Bobbie stiffened. All Damien had ever taught her was mistrust and licentious behaviour.

"Being able to laugh at yourself in tough situations." Myles nodded his head. "It's a good asset to have in the business world, sweetheart."

"So is having the man in my life – dead." Bobbie grimaced. Hopefully Damien was still running around playing with his Indian friends in the wilderness. Hopefully, she'd never have to see him again.

"Some day I'd like to meet your Damien Larocque." Myles laughed. "He changed you."

"You wouldn't like him, Daddy. He's very..." Bobbie's voice broke as she tried to smile. "Irresponsible."

"So it seems." Myles came around to hug her. "Chin up, sweetheart. People do change."

"I don't care!" Bobbie let the tears flow, unable to keep up the teasing any longer. She'd been every bit as irresponsible as Damien. "I thought he was – different. He said all the men I'd met – were weak. He said that was why they didn't like me. He said..."

"He was right." Myles muttered softly, patting her back.

"It's the last time, Daddy." Bobbie took a deep gulp of air and stood up, rubbing her eyes. "I'll never cry for that man again, I promise."

A few weeks later, she and her daughter were on the train, heading for Winnipeg. She was no more prepared to meet Damien now than she had been the day she realized he had no intention of ever coming for her.

A woman's gurgling laughter caught in Pierre Marchand's mind. His head jerked around, a puzzled expression crossing his strained, haggard face. He knew that sound. Where had he heard it before? Marie was staring at him as though he had just sprouted vampire teeth.

Ignoring her, he edged closer to the white painted house and peered across the hedge surrounding the yard. The lady in question, a vision of lovely elegance in sprigged chiffon over yellow satin, was pushing a giggling cherub on a tree-swing. Sunlight filtered through the lacy leaves of a blooming maple tree. Golden glints from both the woman's and the child's hair flashed, blindingly beautiful.

"Pierre!" Marie hissed, tugging at his thin arm. "Have you gone mad?"

"Roberta!" Pierre gasped loudly. "Roberta Taylor."

Flickering jolts of agony crossed her features. Bobbie turned. She had been in Winnipeg nearly two months now. She knew eventually she would meet someone she would recognize. At least it was not Damien. Panic gave way to bland, haughty ice. She scooped up her doll-like baby from her perch on the swing and moved towards the gaping couple standing in the street.

Time and time again, she had coached herself, preparing for this very situation. What would happen to her newfound poise should she ever see Damien again? Surely, she was mature enough now to accept her supposedly deep love had only been a schoolgirl's infatuation for a charming man, nothing more.

"Pierre and Marie Marchand. How delightful to see you again." She extended her hand calmly.

Gallantly, Pierre took it, running his lips lightly along the smooth flesh.

"Have you come to see Damien, Miss Taylor?" Marie smiled.

Bobbie's expression immediately hardened.

"Of course not!" Nervously, Bobbie shifted her daughter back on her hip. Marie was staring at Lisa. Was that suspicion in her eyes?

"You're married?" Marie asked. Now, Bobbie could hear gentle reproach.

"I was. He died in a tragic accident – at sea." She murmured, trying to inflict a sad note to her voice. Marie thought Lisa was another man's child? Thank God.

The past few years had not been kind to Marie, Bobbie noted, spitefully. Her voluptuous figure had spread out. Even the sombre black gown could not disguise the rolls around her waist. Her face, with those large, limpid eyes and her glorious blue-black curls, were was lovely as ever though.

"When did you get married?"

"Two years ago." Bobbie muttered, trying to suppress her defensive attitude. Two years ago – she meant to say three! Or could she? Was it three years ago, she'd been taken from Damien? Lisa was two years old.

"You must not have been married long... When did it happen?" Marie sounded hostile.

"He passed away within a week..." Bobbie's voice hardened. She wished they would just disappear and leave her alone. Did Marie still hold a grudge after all these years? And why? She was still with Pierre.

"What a darling little girl. And so bright! What's her name?" Marie giggled, looking at the toddler in Bobbie's arms.

She was instantly rewarded with an answering grin. Bobbie gasped. Anyone knowing Damien would recognize that magnetic, lopsided smile. Marie made no comment as she turned back to Bobbie, but there was a speculative glint in her eyes.

"You and Damien seemed so well suited. Didn't they Pierre?" Marie smiled with seemingly friendly candour "He's not married."

"Marie – this is really none of our business." Pierre reprimanded, looking very uncomfortable. His large eyes, behind the wire glasses, looked appealingly at Bobbie. "Please forgive Marie. She doesn't mean any harm. She just loves children."

Bobbie tilted her chin. She had no intentions of getting into a squabble with Marie.

"Do you live in Winnipeg, Mrs...?"

"Watson. Mrs. Watson." Bobbie sighed. At least she got that right. "I'm editor for Winnipeg's newest newspaper – the Taylorson Winnipeg Press." She supplied with caution.

"Ah, yes. I find your paper has a very unique insight concerning western problems. I did think it was strange, an eastern paper and all. Now I understand. Your living with the natives for a few months must have helped. Oh dear!" Flustered, Pierre smiled wanly.

"Yes it did." Bobbie smiled as well. Poor Pierre was trying so hard to be polite. He was a very dear man. "Thank you for your kind words."

"You must come out for dinner. I would love to have some conversations with you. Perhaps I could help you…"

"Of course." Bobbie murmured noncommittally. She wondered what Marie's thoughts might be on this unorthodox invitation. "Perhaps you could. You must be aware of what's happening and maybe even know some of the people I need to interview."

"I most likely do!" Pierre chuckled eagerly.

"Yes. Please come. Come tomorrow. Pierre can tell you… things and you can bring your darling daughter." Amazed, Bobbie saw Marie was genuinely eager and sincere. She was making funny faces, causing Lisa to giggle with glee.

"Lisa. Her name's Lisa." Bobbie felt her heart soften. It wasn't their fault Damien was who he was.

"Yes. Bring Lisa too. Tomorrow. Unfortunately, Pierre and I… don't have any children…" Marie's voice broke with tears.

"I'm not sure…" Bobbie stated, feeling sorry for the perceptible sadness in Marie's eyes. She couldn't have children? But still…

She turned to Pierre for help. Her eyes pleaded for his understanding. She never wanted to see Damien again. Damien and Pierre were cousins.

"Damien now lives near Batoche. He doesn't visit us often. He thinks Winnipeg is much too crowded." Pierre intervened.

"He lives in Batoche?" Bobbie abhorred the way her heart leapt up in excitement at the mere mention of his name.

She couldn't quite picture Damien away from Big Bear and his Indian friends. He fit in so well with them. So, he was still alive? Often, in the past, she'd wondered if Myles hadn't been lying when he assured her that no charges were brought against Damien. She tried to convince herself that had been the reason he had never come. But he was alive and had made no effort to find her.

Injured, she tried to blank out her pain. She had known this would happen. Winnipeg was a fairly small place, regardless of what Damien thought.

"Does he live with Gabriel Dumont?" Bobbie asked. Gabriel was one man her father wanted her to interview.

"Actually, he has his own ranch. His horses are in great demand. He is a very wealthy man." Marie answered smugly.

"Damien?" Bobbie floundered, not believing a word Marie said. It was not possible. Damien settled down? Damien ranching?

"She would have found out eventually," Marie hissed at Pierre's reproachful gaze. "It's no secret. You will come for dinner tomorrow, won't you? I promise I won't mention his name again, if you don't want."

With glum reluctance, Bobbie nodded. Pierre was a connection she couldn't pass by. "Yes, I'll come."

"We really must be going." Marie slipped her arm through Pierre's. "My fitting is for two. Roberta, we will expect you for dinner around six – no excuses."

Bobbie wanted to say no but recognized she didn't have the strength to argue.

Painful, distressing images floated in her mind. All she could see was a laughing, carefree Damien saying he loved her. Tears welled in her eyes and she turned from the prying eyes watching her.

"I must put Lisa down for her nap." She wouldn't look up. Marie would most likely laugh if she broke down.

She carried Lisa into the tiny cottage. After placing her protesting daughter into her bed, she wandered aimlessly back into the parlour.

Her new home in Winnipeg was small but temporary. She would have a mansion built – Her lips twisted. Who was she trying to impress? A ranch? He had a ranch? Why? Was he lying about that too? She was so sure he didn't care for material possessions – so very sure. Her thoughts moved to that mysterious choker, hidden now in the bottom of her drawer. She wanted to throw it away. It wasn't valuable... '*My most prized possession – for you...*' Angrily, she pushed her maudlin thoughts away.

Yes, she would build a large...elaborate mansion! And what was wrong with that? Why shouldn't she have a beautiful home? She looked around her small cottage.

She would have to ship more furniture out. Here, she only had two small bedrooms and a kitchen and front parlour. The furniture was cramped and crowded. She had shipped it out via the new Canadian Pacific Railroad, Prime Minister Macdonald's pride and joy.

Bobbie grimaced. Macdonald's railroad was one of the problems out here. Canada's newest province – British Columbia, wanted a railroad. Ontario and the other eastern provinces were happy. Only the people on the prairies didn't want the railroad.

The Indians didn't want the railroad at all. The tracks were destroying the land and their spitting stacks were also causing numerous prairie fires and killing off the wildlife. The *Metis*, on the other hand, wanted a train to run along the Northern Saskatchewan River – where they lived.

But Macdonald had built his railroad through the southern territories instead. It was much cheaper. He thought the *Metis* should move south, if they wanted a railroad.

Sighing, Bobbie sank into her large pearl-gray sofa. She pushed the lace embroidered curtains aside, staring out into the quiet, dusty street, seeing nothing.

Like a crumbling dam, the walls in her mind slipped away. What would happen if she ever met Damien again? Would he be the same carefree barbarian she'd known before or would he too be changed? Would he take her into his arms and kiss all her problems away? What reason would he give for not coming for her? And most important of all, would she be strong enough to reject him?

CHAPTER 19

Bobbie noticed, with feelings akin to nostalgia, that the brothels had been moved out of Winnipeg's city limits. Reverend Silcox had won his battle. Now they sat, about a mile outside of the town, surrounded by vacant prairie. Still, business must be good. She could hear loud voices and screeching music coming from the new shabby buildings.

Smiling derisively, she could still recall her terror that one night she'd nearly become Gertrude's *virgin-whore*. Then all humour fled as she also remembered her saviour, he white knight in shining Armour. Her wonderful knight had turned out to be a scoundrel in tarnished flesh. She had been so naïve. Now she carried a small handgun tucked into her handbag and she knew how to use it. She didn't need any man's help.

When she rode into the small village of St. Francis Xavier, she saw a carriage was parked in front of the Marchand house. Trying to imagine Damien driving a carriage was impossible. Her fears were ridiculous.

Lisa was asleep in her arms. Instead of taking her horse into the stable in the backyard, she tied the reins to the verandah rail. She had no intention of staying very long.

Her feet lifted, dreadfully slow, as she mounted the wooden steps leading to the front door. She wanted to disappear into the shadows. Why had she agreed to come? She was sure she didn't like Marie. She liked Pierre well enough and he could probably get her interviews with Louis Riel, Gabriel Dumont and maybe even with Poundmaker, another Cree Chief, Myles seemed to think might know something. Besides, Pierre had said Damien was in Batoche. No! Pierre had only said he lived in Batoche. Terrified, Bobbie turned to leave just as the door opened.

"Roberta. How nice. You're a bit early. Come in." Was there a malicious tone beneath Marie's cheerful greeting?

"You must join us for a drink before dinner." Marie led her into the large parlour. "Would you like some wine?"

From the moment Bobbie stepped into the house, she was aware of him. She could smell an elusive, wild scent. She could feel him in the excited air as though he was touching her. No! How could they be so cruel? She tried to calm herself as she stepped into the room. After three long years, Bobbie felt as though she were starving. Her hungry gaze turned to him. He was standing by the window. Sunlight filtered in on his lean frame. His face was shadowed.

He wore tight jeans, as though denim had been invented specifically for him. A black shirt was unbuttoned halfway down his chest. He was as tantalizing and primitive exciting as ever. She felt the jolts wracking her body.

Fighting her tortured equilibrium valiantly, she refused to look into his eyes – his bewitching, devil eyes. Instead she studied the heavy gold chain around his neck. A golden cross dangled from the chain.

Sacrilegious heretic! He was not a Christian. He had made that perfectly clear – three years ago. Damien loathed the white man's churches.

A raw, futile moan clogged her throat. She fought for composure. She didn't want to see him. Closing her eyes, she tried to ignore the longings washing throughout her body.

"Here's your wine, *mignonne*." His voice was that same husky sound, like water running over pebbles, gravel and soft simultaneously.

There was nowhere to hide.

"Did you know?" Bobbie whispered. She looked up helplessly into his eyes. She could feel his magnetic heat immediately.

"Did I know what?" Damien smiled. He didn't look surprised to see her.

"That I was coming?"

"Of course, *mignonne*. I always knew when you were coming." His voice was smooth rapture. He moved with catlike grace, closer.

Not even glancing at the sleeping baby in her arms, he touched her shoulder. "Marie, take the baby."

Startled, Bobbie blinked rapidly. The baby? Of course, Lisa was still sleeping in her arms. Her hands tightened defensively around the little body. Lisa would be a reminder... a reminder of how evil this man was. Yet, she let Marie take the child with no protest.

"I'll just lay her on our bed for now." Marie gushed, reaching down to stroke Lisa's soft cheek. "What a little darling, Mrs. Watson. You are so fortunate."

"Mrs. Watson?" Damien's voice turned hard.

"Yes, I was married." Bobbie's voice trailed off as she noticed Damien watching her lips with special interest. *Oh my God... Please help me.* "He was killed... tragically... by savage Indians..."

"Didn't you say he died at sea?" Marie turned from the hall, looking startled.

"Perhaps she's had two more husbands!" Damien's sensual mouth quirked, revealing his dimples. Bobbie wanted only to touch those lovely creases – with her lips. "That makes – three, doesn't it? Take your wine, *mignonne*."

"I don't drink." With stiff reserve, Bobbie forced her shaking legs to move over to the chair. She needed to sit down. *What game is he playing now?*

"I know you don't drink." Damien moved over to the chair. He leaned down, his breath tickling her ear with erotic skill. She winced.

He carefully placed the wine glass into her hand and Bobbie automatically downed the contents.

"Where's Pierre?" Bobbie whispered. The wine sank, thankfully soothing, into her belly.

"In the kitchen." Damien shrugged his shoulders, still holding her gaze with his mesmerizing eyes.

"Is that your carriage in the driveway?" Bobbie laughed softly, as the warmth of the wine penetrated.

"Yes. My horse was brutally murdered by savage Indians." Damien grinned, raising an eyebrow. He walked over to the sideboard, bringing a bottle back to her chair. Holding her hand, he carefully poured some red liquid into her empty glass. "No, it's Madeline's."

"Madeline?" Bobbie's eyes narrowed vehemently. Was she his current wife? She wanted to fling herself up and scratch his eyes out, then go away and die. "Where is she?"

"In the kitchen – probably trying to impress me with her culinary skills." Damien shrugged his shoulders with unconcern. "We both know I don't care if a woman can cook, don't we? You look beautiful, *mignonne.*"

"So do you." Again Bobbie was unaware of what she was saying. Her hand was shaking when she raised her glass to take a large gulp of the wine.

"Slow down, wildcat. You shouldn't guzzle wine." Damien laughed softly, using his eyes to caress her body with skilled ease. She could feel every touch, deep inside her stomach. "You know you look beautiful. You surely didn't get such a provocative gown here."

Bobbie laughed with delight. Her gown fit perfectly, showing off her slender curves in a subtle way that only a gown designed in Paris could. "I got it in Paris."

"You went to Paris? Was that the ship where your husband – tragically died? Did he tire you, *mignonne*? Did you push him overboard?"

Startled, Bobbie looked up into his satanic features. He was hiding his eyes now. His lashes lay against his high cheekbones. She wanted to touch him. Then she saw the twitch in his taut cheek. He was angry. Why? It was his entire fault they had spent three miserable years apart. She stiffened. This obnoxious man had abandoned her. Now, here she was again behaving like a simpering idiot.

"Dinner is served." Pierre interrupted softly.

Bobbie stood abruptly, and moved to take Pierre's arm. She had to get away from here as soon as possible.

Marie was placing plates on the table. And obviously Madeline was already seated there.

"Roberta, Lisa is still sleeping." Marie's smile was friendly and warm. "I'd like you to meet Madeline Caron."

Casually, Damien sauntered around the table and placed his hands on Madeline's shoulders.

Bobbie blinked, knowing her eyes were filling with tears. She looked at Marie. She was surprised to read the sympathy in Marie's eyes.

"Madeline is Eileen's daughter." Marie continued brightly. "Eileen is Damien's cook – and Madeline does the cleaning. Madeline, this is our dear friend, Roberta."

"Call me Bobbie." Bobbie murmured.

"Have some trout. It's fresh." After seating her, Pierre reached for the fish platter and handed it to Bobbie.

"Thank you." Bobbie looked at Marie and smiled. She took the offered plate and turned to Madeline. A maid? Madeline was a coltish looking girl. Bobbie wondered if it was her jealousy making her see no beauty in that plain, vacant face.

"Do you want some wine, *mignonne*?"

Bobbie's heart cracked precariously. Damien was not talking to her in that exquisite voice, but to that dull creature sitting beside him. He leaned forward and gave that drab child the full consequence of his seductive smile. Only Damien could call every woman *mignonne* and make them always believe it was specifically theirs.

"Bobbie, I wanted to ask you something." On her right, Marie leaned forward to touch her arm. Thankfully, Bobbie turned to her.

"Since you are working in the office, I thought I could look after Lisa for you. I could come into town in the morning with Pierre. Do you take her to work with you every day?" Marie's eyes were pleading. "She needs to play."

"Lisa is always with me." Bobbie whispered. How could she explain the security and pleasure Lisa offered to her bleak world?

"But it would only be a few hours a day." Marie begged. "I so desperately wanted a baby and I can't..."

Pierre jumped up to come around to Marie's side. Marie was sobbing quietly.

"For God's sake, Bobbie, let her look after the child. Don't be so damned selfish." Damien interrupted. His voice was harsh.

Startled, Bobbie looked at him. His eyes were glazed with old memories. And of course, he wasn't thinking about her either. He'd never been allowed to play when he was little. Her eyes darkened with sympathy. He scowled and his face hardened.

"Yes, you can look after Lisa." Bobbie smiled warmly, looking into Marie's tear-stained eyes. Then she understood. Marie was a kind, generous woman – without a baby. Lisa would be fortunate to have such loving care.

"Thank you, Roberta." Pierre whispered, squeezing Marie's shoulder.

"You will never regret it!" Marie jumped up, bubbling with energy once again. "I have some chocolate cake for dessert. Let's celebrate."

"I can't stay." Bobbie muttered frantically. She couldn't watch Damien pay such attention to Madeline any longer. She felt sick. She had to get away. "I have more work to do and I should put Lisa to bed."

"You can't think of taking her out tonight." Marie pleaded again. "It's freezing out there. She hasn't had her dinner yet. She can stay the night and I'll bring her in with Pierre."

"No." Bobbie moaned feeling abandoned.

"Then you stay here." Marie offered triumphantly.

"I can't stay here." Bobbie mouthed frantically, hoping Marie would understand.

"I know. You have work at home." Marie obviously picked up on Bobbie's desperate cry for help. "But you must leave Lisa. It will be easier to – work alone."

"Yes." Bobbie smiled through her tears. She kept her face averted from Damien's stare.

Standing, then nearly running toward the door and freedom, Bobbie was barely able to say good night. Grabbing her shawl, she wrapped it tightly around her shoulders. She turned to face Marie.

"Thank you for a lovely evening. I'm usually finished work around five o'clock." Her voice broke when Damien came to the door. "Give Lisa a kiss for me…"

"So *Daddy* finally realized who was writing his articles?" Damien sneered. "Was he angry with his little darling?"

"Yes and no." Bobbie lowered her eyes to the floor. She would never let him see her tears.

"Do you want me to ride back to Winnipeg with you?" Damien's voice dropped to that seductive drawl again. "It's dark outside."

"Absolutely not." Bobbie snapped, raising her eyes to his face. "Miss Caron might not like that."

Damien's eyes held a reckless, speculative gleam she traced to the amount of alcohol he had consumed during dinner. Nothing had changed.

"She's my maid, not my wife." Damien drawled out with insolence.

"Yes, I understand." Bobbie said in a small dignified tone. She turned and walked out of the house. "We all mean nothing to you. Good night."

"But you're wrong, *mignonne*." Damien walked over to grab her arm as she began to mount. "You mean everything to me."

"Liar. If you ever call me that again – I'll kill you." She jerked her arm away and covered her ears.

Self-condemnation against her weakness was uppermost in her mind. She managed to pull her eyes away from his. Madeline came to the door. The worship in her face as she stared at Damien was sickening. Bobbie felt ill.

"She can have you. I don't want you." She leaned down and spat out the words.

"Who's the liar now, *mignonne*?"

Yanking the reins sharply, Bobbie lashed out with her foot. He jerked back before she kicked him. She spun her mare around. She urged the horse to gallop faster as she directed her towards Winnipeg. The wind loosened her coiled coiffure. Long strands streamed out behind her, whipping locks around her moist, tear-stained cheeks. She made no effort to check her mare's wild, uncontrolled pace.

She felt remorse only when she dismounted, leading the frothing horse into the small barn. The mare's heaving sides revealed a heartbeat throbbing as frantically as her own.

"I'm so sorry, Annabelle." Bobbie flung her arms around the sweating mare's neck, unmindful of her gown. "I had to get away from him. I'll make it up to you."

She quickly removed the saddle. Gently, she rubbed down the panting, quivering Annabelle. How could she do such a cruel thing? Damien would not follow her. He hadn't bothered before, so why would he bother tonight?

"I didn't even say goodnight to Lisa." She felt Annabelle nuzzle her shoulder as she poured oats into her trough. Bobbie jumped, startled, searching the darkness.

Moonbeams slid through the cracks in the plank walls, giving the stable an eerie, almost hazy light. She heard faint rustling hay as a small animal crossed the vacant stall next to Annabelle's. Outside leaves shivered in the breeze. All else was silent.

"He has me as frightened as that poor little mouse." Bobbie laughed unsteadily.

Her ears picked up the hushed cadence of shuffling straw. It could only be a small rodent, walking so softly. She patted Annabelle affectionately.

"Rest now. I won't ride you for a few days to make up for my cruelty."

She opened the stall gate and moved toward the door. A large chunk of luminous moon penetrated the interior, lighting the enclosure clearly.

"And I won't ever ride you again – after tonight, my little barracuda."

Terror held her immobile. She saw his dark shadow through a sparking blur of panic. He pushed himself from the wall and moved with slow determination toward her.

Shaking her head, Bobbie was unable to speak. Perspiration broke out across her throbbing forehead.

His dangerous, evil expression reminded her of that stormy night so long ago. He was drunk and he was furious.

"Only *you* would be so careless with a Paris gown. Which is just as well." He stopped in front of her. "Now you can't blame me."

Like a striking panther, his fingers twisted around the shimmering satin, yanking savagely. Only her corset and silk stockings were immune to his punishing destruction. Her panic-stricken limbs refused to obey her command to move.

"Why?" She managed to find her voice.

His heavy lashes hid his eyes. His fingers stroked lightly up her sides, stopping to grasp, then squeeze ruthlessly when he reached her breasts.

"I need to hurt you." His voice was husky with pain. "Then I can forget…"

His versed hands remained fixed on her aching chest. Leaning forward his teeth began a pleasure-pained search along her face and neck, nipping subtly, then as she relaxed with more pressure.

"Don't. Please don't…"

He smothered her stifled pleas with his crushing lips. Grinding callously, he forced her lips open and pushed his tongue inside to scrape against her contours with deliberate abuse.

Gagging, she tried to yank her face back as she sagged towards him. Her legs were too weak to hold her up any longer. His hands vanquished her puny efforts as he held her head still with his palms.

She bit his tongue.

"Bitch!" He yanked her head back. "Pretend you like it – like you did before…"

Snarling, his lips softened, persuasive and masterful. Her panicked thoughts cried out against this calculated indignity. He wanted to hurt her. Her lips felt like frost. Her limbs trembled. She was terrified of this horrible savage and even his highly skilled touch could not assuage her denial. This was not the man she loved.

"Damn it, wildcat. You feel like a block of ice. Respond. I'm going to take you with or without your consent."

"Why?"

She managed to squirm back, but couldn't completely escape his merciless torment.

"Because I want to. I feel like I've died and gone to heaven, every time I'm inside you." With an enterprising manoeuvre, his legs shifted behind her knees and she was toppling backwards. Holding her head and waist, he eased her fall.

Prickling, dried straw tickled her back and legs. He loomed above her, dangerous and evil. A wicked grin brought forth his exquisite dimples. His ardent gaze trapped hers with easy intensity. Leaning forward, his hips rotated pleasure along her abdomen. His lips and tongue sought to soothe her anguish with delightful promise now.

Whimpering, her arms moved up to come around his neck. Their kiss was everlasting bliss. His lips moved with fervid passion, encouraging her to follow.

She made no further protest when he moved down to explore every curve along her writhing body. His lithe fingers parted her trembling thighs as his other hand reached below her bottom to arch her up. Clear, unobstructed moonbeams bathed them. Plunging through the gilded curls, his finger stroked the already swollen flesh with magical skill.

"I don't care..." He moaned, watching his fingers play. His eyes were wild with desire.

"Damien – what do you mean?"

Moving down, his searing torrid mouth connected with her quivering mound. His tongue feathered lightly along the jolting nub, then changed to a jabbing thrust inside. Bobbie screamed as she felt the exquisite penetration inside.

Forgetting why she shouldn't let him do this, her head spun with pleasure. This decadent lovemaking - it was all so long ago and seemed only a minute ago.

"Now you want me..." Smiling grimly, Damien lifted his head.

"I don't – understand..."

"You never did and you never will..." Damien snarled. He stood up abruptly. "It's always you."

"Damien, don't leave me like this..." Her command was a shrill demand. She could read the uncertainty in his expression. Was he going to walk away now?

"To hell with it." Yanking he violently opened his pants.

In a swift, vicious motion, he leaned down to haul her to her feet. Placing his arm around her bottom, he hoisted her upward as though she weighed no more than a feather. In one smooth motion his rigid, flexing sword impaled her completely. Shifting her slightly, he pushed her back against the stable wallboards.

And she, bewitched lunatic that she was, welcomed his maniacal, diabolical thrusts. Eyes open, she hungrily studied his distorted features. His mesmerizing eyes were clenched shut.

Then nothing mattered as he quickly brought her to that distinctive pleasure-paradise where she wanted most to be. He raised his lashes, revealing a liquid, searing gaze. A gradual gleam entered, bringing reminiscent, hypnotic humour.

His lips spread out, outlined in his familiar, lovable grin. Overwhelming flutters affected her breathing. She wound her arms tightly around his neck, bringing him closer. Smiling, she moaned with happiness. Her very own Damien was back.

Her legs were wrapped tightly around his straining waist. His lean palms held her hips steady, guiding her frantic movement to a rhythmic delight. Lifting her up with lingering anticipation, he again brought her down, filling her completely. All the while he continued too watch the glazed rapture in her features.

She could feel the rough material of his jeans rubbing against her tender flesh. Such a blatant insult should be humiliating, but wasn't. The peculiar feeling of cloth only intensified the erotic sensations building inside.

Excruciating pulsation erupted into desired satisfaction. Damien took one more languid, penetrating stroke, deep and strong. She felt his scalding release mingle with her own torrid juices.

He immediately took his hands away from her. Her legs dropped heavily to the ground. She slid against him, her feet touching the straw. For long seconds she felt nothing except ecstasy throughout her quivering body.

"I forgot how quick you could come. I intended it to be otherwise. But it was delightful, wildcat. If I'm ever in Winnipeg again, I might come back."

"Damien! Wait!" She screamed at his receding back as he turned and walked to the barn door. He was casually fastening his trousers. "Damien, at least tell me why."

"You said you loved me. Then you left." The icy scorn in those words pierced her already smashed heart.

He kept his back turned towards her. She couldn't see his face. Suddenly he lifted his shirt. "Then there was this. See the new welts, wildcat? Thanks to *Daddy*."

"No! He promised. He let you go." Tears clogged her throat. His back was a mash of cuts and welts. There were more than... No. Her father wouldn't do that.

"After a few weeks of torture, he did." Damien dropped his shirt. He didn't turn around. "I wouldn't even care – except you just left me."

"I didn't. Ask Lone Woman. I did not leave you."

"Lone Woman is dead."

Now he turned. There was only bitter abhorrence in his blazing eyes. "Your friends killed her."

"No, it can't be true." She struggled blindly toward him.

Grabbing his shirt, the wretched misery made it impossible to see his features clearly. "I'm sorry. I'm so sorry. I didn't know. But ask the others. They saw the police take me away. They knocked me out. Please Damien, you must believe me."

"They *all* said you went willingly."

"No! They're lying." She screamed out. "I swear on my baby's head. They're lying."

Jerking his shirt in desperation, she tried to bring feeling back into his stony, unyielding body.

"Yes, you're baby. Who's the father, wildcat? It sure didn't take you long to forget me, did it?" Damien snarled with fury.

"You're wrong. You can't believe that I would forget..." Panting, as though she'd just run a marathon at top speed, Bobbie fought the restricting clench invading her chest. Her breath was cut off.

Shuddering jolts wracked her body. Even lifting her lead-filled arms was a supreme effort. Her balled fist smashed weakly against his taut chest. He never so much as flinched. It was useless to say Lisa was his child. He would call her a liar.

"For God's sake, wildcat. Settle down. What will your good neighbours think – you entertaining a heathen in your barn?"

He walked away from her then, with frozen resolve. He only paused a second when he heard her self-destructive moans. Then he moved again. She was too selfish to hurt herself. Her tears were only dramatics to get her own way.

Still, he had to fight the desire inside that made him want to believe she was telling the truth. There was a dull ache in his chest, hurting him nearly as much as his obsessive need to take her back, lying bitch or not. She was like an evil narcotic flowing in his blood, begging him to come back.

Fortunately, he had learned one lesson very well. He could and would deny himself, regardless of how much he needed her victimizing love.

CHAPTER 20

Bobbie was devastated. The only thing that kept her from running out into the lonely empty prairies screaming like the madwoman she felt was Lisa and her work. She didn't want to accept Damien's cruel rejection. She couldn't let her father down. He was in Winnipeg again. She'd asked him again about his punishment.

"I saw the marks, Daddy. He wasn't lying. He was beaten."

"I never condoned that. I promise you I didn't, sweetheart." Myles assured her with absolute, solemn seriousness. "I'll check into the matter."

And true to his word, Myles had investigated. He found out that Damien had been beaten. He'd been in jail in Fort Walsh for a week before they received Myles telegram, ordering Damien be left alone. Constables Tom Robson and Brian Wilson were the main culprits. They were being duly and harshly punished for taking matters into their own hands. Bobbie believed him. She knew her father had no reason to lie. Unlike Damien, Myles sincerely wanted her to be happy.

If her editorials suffered, Bobbie blamed Damien and those heathens who had destroyed her life. She knew she was being childish. If Damien had truly loved her, he would have believed her or at least given her a chance to explain. She was not ready yet to deal with the fact Damien had never loved her – not even in Big Bear's camp. For the past month, by keeping her mind carefully blank, she had managed to get on with her life.

Now, Pierre was making that impossible again. He stood by the door of her office, frowning with concern. Behind him, she could see her assistant, Jimmy Dawson, puttering with the presses.

"Why do we even need a guide?" She glared at Pierre. "Surely you know how to get to Piapot's village."

"Bobbie, the natives are furious. They are talking seriously about leaving the reservations. They could harm us." Pierre stiffened. "I'll go with you, of course. But I can't guarantee your safety. They all know I work for the Canadian government."

"But why Damien?" She was nearly in tears now. The idea of Damien being her guide – again – was excruciating bringing forth memories she couldn't think about. "Can't you find someone else?"

"No one that I would trust." Pierre shook his head. "Do you have any idea what a valuable hostage you would be? Besides, the Natives all like and trust Damien."

"You trust him?" Bobbie's eyes narrowed in hostility. "He'll hurt me worse than any heathen."

"Bobbie, please..." Pierre lowered his gaze, and carefully studied the papers on her desk. His knuckles were white as he clenched the side of the desk. "You have to understand. Damien in a temper is vicious and cruel. But he gets over it –

very quickly. He probably can't even remember what you fought about."

"Get real, Pierre. He remembered for three years!" Bobbie snarled, and then took a deep breath to calm herself. This wasn't Pierre's fault. He didn't even know what their *problem* was. "I know he's your cousin and I know you don't want to hear what we fought about. I'm sorry. Are you sure the Natives are planning on leaving the reservations?"

"I'm sure." Pierre nodded slowly. "God, I wish it weren't so."

"Why doesn't anyone else seem to know? Daddy said no one is even talking about it in the east." She sighed.

People were so blind. It was frustrating. Canada was heading, very fast, into a major war with their natives and no one cared. They smugly sat in their drawing rooms, burying their heads in the sand, and believed it wasn't possible – here in Canada.

"They don't even know we exist in the east." Pierre answered with bitter intensity. "But, I know war isn't the answer either."

"And does Damien agree with you?" Bobbie asked wistfully, and then could have bitten her tongue out. Damien loved fighting – and battles. She hoped Damien went to war with his heathen friends and was killed!

"Yes, he does as a matter of fact. He's been to the east. He knows what we'd be up against." Pierre answered, a sad note in his voice. "Are schools and hospitals too much to be asking for? Are agents who might distribute food properly too much to ask for? Is a railroad running through our communities too much?" Pierre grimaced and looked up, smiling. "Are your parents coming out to look after Lisa?"

"Of course. They'll be out tomorrow." Bobbie returned his smile. "Marie can come with me."

"She wouldn't let you go without her." Pierre grinned, obviously pleased with that particular turn of events.

Marie's practical, bubbling nature was restorative medicine to Bobbie's wounded mind. With Damien as their guide, she would need Marie. She smiled. It was amazing how genuinely she and Marie had developed a firm, deep friendship. They both had a common love – Lisa. Without Marie's support, she would have gone back to Toronto, a broken, devastated woman. Instead with Marie's help, she was gradually losing that tortured pain numbing her. Now, she even felt as much anger against Damien's cruelty as she did hurt. Anger was a good thing. Surely, it would help her hate that man.

"Well, I must get back to work." Pierre nodded his farewell. "For what it's worth, Roberta, I think Damien is a fool."

"Does he still hate me?" Bobbie asked, almost to herself. It was amazing how Pierre and Marie supported her without hearing the full story. Bobbie couldn't talk about the shame Damien had inflicted on her, not even to her good friends.

"He doesn't hate you – quite the opposite, I'm thinking." Pierre turned back, smiling grimly. "I think the question you should be asking is whether you really care. Can you forgive him? I don't know what happened. He won't talk about it and if you told Marie, she hasn't said anything."

"I don't talk about it." Bobbie steeled her heart, feeling the tears clogging her eyes.

"Don't cry." Pierre was obviously embarrassed. But he didn't turn away. He was a true friend. "All I'm saying is that it's obvious he's hurt you badly. Can you forgive him?"

"No, I can't." Bobbie sat up, drying her eyes. Oddly, Pierre's words comforted her. Of course, she could never forgive him. But...

"Then it doesn't matter what he feels, does it?" Pierre stated in a no-nonsense tone.

"Thank you." Bobbie smiled with determination. There were no buts to consider.

On the way to the village, Damien didn't speak to her directly, even once. Occasionally, he spoke to Marie or Pierre, but mostly he rode somewhat ahead of them and didn't even share their meals. Riding across the rolling prairie hills again, she only saw his back.

"He still hates me." Bobbie wanted to cry.
"He doesn't." Marie disagreed. "Look at his eyes."
"He never lets me get close enough. It doesn't matter – Pierre's right. I can never forgive him for what he's done?"
"And what's he done?" Marie arched her brow in a question.
"Good try." Bobbie laughed. Marie was always trying to probe. But to this point, Bobbie just couldn't talk about. She did notice Damien turned quickly. Then just as quickly, he turned back. She decided to change the subject. "I wonder how Lisa is getting along with her grandmother."
And that simple comment effectively quelled Marie's curiosity.
When they arrived in Piapot's reservation, Bobbie looked around curiously. Would anyone recognize her as the lovestuck, silly girl who had once lived with Hawk? After speaking to Pierre for a moment, Damien disappeared immediately. For three long days, Bobbie didn't see him at all.
"Do you think he's found a new wife?" Bobbie asked pettishly.
"How well you know our Damien." Marie's wide brown eyes were twinkling. "I thought you didn't care."
"I don't." Bobbie stated firmly. Then she impatiently concentrated on the problem at hand.
And there were problems in abundance. Conditions had deteriorated drastically in just three years. The people were wandering around like skeletons in rags. Although they didn't refuse to talk to her this time, there was a despondent hopelessness in their voices that was heart-wrenching.
Albert Hobart, the Indian Agent in Piapot's village, was even less helpful. He was defensive and surly. He regarded Bobbie with open disgust that declared he doubted her credentials to report anything.
"Why would they send *you*?" He asked, reluctantly opening the storage sheds for her perusal.
"I sent myself." Bobbie answered firmly.
She nearly had to push him aside to enter the shed. There was very little inside. There were a few flour bags and some

rancid bacon. She could see the bugs crawling around on the meat. Her stomach heaved. They didn't even bother hiding when she stepped inside the compartment.

"I've seen enough." Turning, she stepped into the bright sunlight, gulping the fresh air gratefully.

"The new supplies should be coming in soon." Albert blustered, locking the door.

"Why don't you farm your own crops?" Bobbie demanded in a harsh whisper.

"Ever try to get an Injun to farm, lady?" He muttered in defence.

Bobbie sighed. Obviously insulting them was Mr. Hobart's solution to the problem.

"Of course, they don't just know. They're a nomadic people, Mr. Hobart. They didn't need to farm – before we came."

"Can you see any horse or oxen around?" He snickered. "Are you guarding your own horses? They eat them as fast as Ottawa sends us anything."

"They have to eat something." Bobbie murmured. Her eyes roamed around the village street. She'd had enough of Albert Hobart. "I'll go back to my tent. Thank you for your co-operation."

The Natives were willing to answer her questions, but she was very well aware of their staring at her fine gown and healthy skin. Did they think she could help? She sincerely hoped she could. Her father was still a friend to Macdonald. Maybe he could talk to him. But she knew politicians moved so slowly. And something had to happen – very quickly – or there would be war. There would be no other choice.

"Are you going to fight?" She whispered to one young man who stared with moody intensity – towards the Agent's cabin.

"I was in jail all winter." Little Knife shrugged his shoulders evasively. His eyes shifted around, always returning to the young girl seated outside Mr. Hobart's house. She was shelling peas with solemn intensity.

"That's my wife." Little Knife shuddered violently, clenching his fist. "Hobart say I steal a cow. I didn't."

"Why did you go to jail then?" She turned to study the young maiden. Was she working for Albert Hobart?

"Hobart want Arrow Woman. I say no. He can keep his damned *firewater*." Kicking the dirt with angry gestures, Little Knife whirled and sprinted towards a clump of trees at the edge of the village.

Bobbie wanted to go back to Winnipeg. She had more information than she could possibly get into a few articles. She'd seen more than she could ever explain. There was nothing good to report here. She wouldn't blame one single native if he decided to fight.

She went back to her tent, set a ways from the village. Sitting down, she stared into the fire.

"You've had enough?" Surprising her, Damien approached her.

She kept her eyes glued to the sparking flames, feeling weak and ill. Even Damien could not make these pathetic conditions disappear. Visions of absolute disparity with no hope danced in her mind.

"How will they fight?" She shook her head. There was no hope.

"Pardon?" Damien squatted down beside her. Taking a stick, he began to draw circles in the dirt. "Pierre told you they would fight? He's worse than an old lady."

"Maybe they told me! Does that surprise you?" Bobbie whispered, with hopeless despair. "It doesn't matter. Anything I say won't help."

"That's the first time I've ever heard you admit defeat." Damien's voice lightened to a teasing tone. "Maybe you'll see things better when you're back in *civilization, mignonne*."

"But war? These people don't even look like they can walk, let alone hold a rifle. If they even have any." Bobbie peered at him from beneath lowered lashes.

She could feel the heat from his body, a scant foot away, more intensely than she could feel the heat from the campfire. Would it always be like this? Would she ever be able to ignore this man?

"They can't fight. It's not the answer." She could feel him staring at her. "It'll only make matters worse – if that's possible. Imagine the consequence?"

"They? Aren't you going to fight?" Bobbie finally lifted her gaze to his. She felt the pull immediately, like a magnet drawing her to him. She tilted forward. He leaned back. Dropping his gaze, he continued with his etchings on the ground.

"Well, wildcat, at least I'm healthy enough to fight." Lifting his head again, she could see the reckless humour in his face. She nearly cried as memories washed throughout. "But I'm one man – against thousands of soldiers? I'm good, wildcat, but am I that good? Will I fight – is that what you're asking? Maybe."

"No!' Desperately, she clenched her eyes together, unable to bear the thoughts he evoked. Damien, dead or dying, somewhere out in the lonely prairie – all alone.

"No what, wildcat?" She could feel his movement as he shifted closer. She couldn't open her eyes.

"No – don't call me wildcat. It's a silly name and I don't like it." She answered, not looking at him. She could feel his gaze on her face, searing and hot. "*Mignonne* is good. You call all women, *mignonne*..." She stopped, realizing she was voicing her thoughts aloud. Damien despised her. And she couldn't forgive him – she just couldn't.

"Wildcat is special? Is that it? Or is it – don't fight, Damien? I don't want to see you die." He asked. His smooth voice penetrated her blood like potent wine.

"I don't care if you die. I hope you fight. But..." Bobbie felt him move terrifying closer. How could he possibly be doing this – when he despised her and everything she stood for? More cruelty? More torture? Hadn't she suffered enough?

"But...?" She felt his breath on her cheek.

Her eyes flew open. She could just lean forward and touch him. Humiliation washed inside. She raised her gaze. They were bleak and frozen, like ice. She could never let Damien inside again.

"I could care less. Whatever you do is your concern. I just find Wildcat a very silly name. You can call me Roberta or even Mrs. Watson." Her voice was a flat monotone to match the numbness inside.

"Fine, Mrs. Watson. Be ready to leave about five in the morning, Mrs. Watson. Good night, Mrs. Watson."

Damien stood, in that graceful motion he had, and turned away.

Again, she spent the whole night crying for him. Again, she cursed herself for her obsessive weakness.

When they returned, she didn't see him for two months. Her life resumed a calm routine of working and playing with Lisa. She sent two articles to Toronto regarding the conditions on the reservation. Myles said there was no reaction whatsoever in the east. He would try talking to Macdonald. Pierre was right. The east didn't even know the west existed.

Big Bear: Native Messiah?

Her gaze dropped down to the words she'd written. She really must get this article done tonight.

Pity stirred in her heart. Big Bear, stubborn and haughty, was right. The Indians should not have signed the Treaties. Big Bear knew that. Now, he, just like the others, had settled for a horrible reservation. He would never die a warrior's death now... unless they went to war. Her breath caught when her thoughts turned to Damien. Would he fight? She did care – so much!

Carefully numbing her thoughts, she resumed staring down at her paper. She must get this article written. Myles, who was once again in Winnipeg, wanted to take it back with him.

Myles had just taken Marie and Lisa for lunch. She heard them removing their coats, amidst murmurs and chuckles. It was November and bitterly cold. Bobbie was astounded at how easily her father had taken to Pierre and Marie.

She heard Lisa's screams and giggles. Weary, she pressed her fingers into her eyes. Lisa was a spoiled, aggressive little devil. Bobbie wasn't sure what she was going to do about that.

No one, meeting that carefree, vivacious bundle of energy, could resist her charm. Consequently, Bobbie had a cosseted, *enfant gate* on her hands and she knew she had to do something,

When Marie brought Lisa into the office, Bobbie didn't bother looking up. She really had to finish this story before four o'clock. Doodling tiny, sad faces around the edges of the sheet, she gave a short laugh.

"Goodness, Marie. I can't seem to get the words down. My mind is blank."

"I always told you not to use your mind, wildcat."

Stiff with hostility, Bobbie looked up. Damien was standing directly in front of her desk. Lisa was in his arms, noisily sucking her thumb. Her impish, dark eyes brimmed with excitement.

"*Papa.*" She explained with a muffled sound, not bothering to remove her thumb when she spoke.

Bobbie's overtaxed nerves snapped. She toppled her chair over as she vaulted to her feet.

"Get away from me!" She ran toward the door. "And don't ever touch *my* daughter again. Marie – get her away from him!"

Going into the front, she saw Marie standing by the door. She grabbed her arm.

"You get Lisa away from that monster right now!"

Without bothering with her coat, she yanked the office door open and moved outside into the swirling snow.

Running toward her house, she sank into deep snow banks. The snow clung tenaciously to her stocking feet and delicate slippers. But she felt nothing except boiling rage.

It was nearly an hour later, before Myles and Marie came into the house with Lisa.

"Where's Damien?" She sniffled loudly.

Her slender ankles were exposed and her feet were immersed in steaming water to thaw them out. They still felt like icicles and it was his entire fault! This time she would kill him.

"He's still writing – your article." Myles came into the parlour. His voice was gruff with caution. "You will have to talk to him eventually. He is Lisa's father."

Bobbie stared down at her blue and white Persian carpet, not speaking. Even her beloved father was deserting her.

"He explained everything. I think you're being childish..."

"Surely not everything!" Bobbie interrupted, muttering with anger. "Somehow I doubt that."

"He even apologized for his own – childish behaviour. He's sorry he – ruined your reputation and..."

"He's a liar!" Bobbie felt wretched. Her eyes were watering and her nose was red. She had a cold. Now, it appeared as though her father was really siding with Damien. Numbly, she looked up.

"Marie? Where is that traitorous bitch?"

"Roberta! Your manners are atrocious!" Myles gasped out. "You will not use such foul language."

"Your darling Damien taught me that – and many more – foul words. Do you want to hear them?" Bobbie smiled with childish sweetness.

"Here I am." Marie entered the parlour with casual disregard for Bobbie's churlish behaviour.

"You told him about Lisa! How could you?" Bobbie glared at her friend.

"No, I didn't." Marie protested softly. "He saw her. He walked into the café when we were having lunch."

"And he just suddenly knew he was Lisa's father?" Bobbie snorted.

"Well, it's so obvious." Marie smiled. "Other than that blond hair..."

Myles looked at the two women. Grabbing Lisa from Marie's arms, he took her to her bedroom for a nap. A few minutes later, he returned, looking very awkward.

"I'll go make some coffee," he announced, making a hasty escape into the kitchen.

"Maybe you should go help him. He doesn't know how to make coffee." Bobbie's mouth rounded in amusement. She turned to Marie. "Daddy hates it when women get emotional. I'm in for a big lecture now."

"Why?" Marie's smiled with humour.

"I'm not behaving like a – man." Bobbie's voice deepened as she tried to emulate her father.

"Does he think you're a man?" Giggling, Marie knelt before Bobbie's chair.

"He knows I'm a woman." Bobbie leaned forward, mockery in her voice "But – I don't think he likes it. Marie, I'm sorry I swore at you. But Damien saw her before and didn't react like this."

"Yes. He's something else, isn't he?" Marie patted her shoulder. "I'd say forget him - but it's much too late for that. Don't you realize – he never looked at her – before today?"

"It's not too late!" Bobbie stated, clearly and distinctly. "I don't need his help – raising my daughter. Did he say what he plans?"

"He's writing your article right now." Marie prevaricated. Bobbie just knew she was hiding something.

Myles walked back into the room. Marie's face revealed gratitude. Myles had three steaming mugs balanced on a tray.

"I read some before I left. He writes an amazing story. I'd love to hire him. But he just laughed when I suggested it."

"Damien doesn't even like the word work." Sipping her coffee gingerly, she was amazed to see it actually tasted like coffee. "He isn't very ambitious, Daddy."

"Bobbie, that's beneath you." Marie interrupted. "His ranch is doing very well."

"By whose standards?" Bobbie asked sweetly.

"Bobbie!" Myles roared. "I never taught you to be so rude."

"I can't recall you teaching me anything." Bobbie looked up, not hiding the pain in her eyes. "Aunt Hortense taught me everything – and she was right! Men are bastards."

"That woman!" Myles snarled. "I swear if she wasn't dead, I'd strangle her. She took a perfectly accomplished lady and..."

"Mommy didn't think I was," Bobbie interrupted. But she smiled. Sir Myles and Aunt Hortense were so much alike, but he couldn't see that, because Aunt Hortense was a female.

"Yes, well..." Myles grinned. Moving to sit down on the sofa, he brought his cup to his lips. "You were a perfectly accomplished gentleman. I am proud the way you handle yourself – like a man when you have to."

"What are you planning?" Bobbie groaned. Whenever her father paid her such an elaborate compliment, he was going to ask her to do something she didn't want to do.

"I thought you should go to Batoche. Louis Riel is there." Myles began slowly. "Damien insists he may be the solution to this whole damn problem. He's writing Macdonald and he did a very efficient job in Winnipeg, settling things."

"And?" Bobbie knew there must be more. She couldn't see a problem here.

"Damien has offered his assistance. Considering his connections and – insight, we would be foolish not to accept his offer."

"What did he offer?" Bobbie asked with her teeth clenched.

"He said the *Metis* hostility is just as potent as the Natives'. So far, Riel's letters are being ignored in Ottawa. It looks like it may not just be the natives going to war." Myles explained, looking out the window. "Damien has offered to let you use his ranch as your base during the investigations." He stated quickly.

"No!" Bobbie shrieked, splashing water onto the hardwood floor when she stood. "I'll go to Batoche and talk to Louis Riel. I don't have to stay there."

"And you can evaluate the situation in just one day?" Myles snapped, setting his cup down with heavy emphasis. "Besides, these plains are dangerous in the winter. You can't go roaming around alone in this kind of weather."

"Make up your mind, Father!" Bobbie suggested coldly. "Either I'm as strong as a man or as weak as a woman."

"Bobbie, be reasonable."

"Be reasonable when you suggest I go live with a man?" Bobbie shrieked. She couldn't do this. It was unfair for her father to expect her to.

"I'm suggesting no such thing." Myles roared back. "Damien has servants. You will be sufficiently chaperoned."

"Yes, I'm sure we'll be one big happy family, all together in one tiny tipi. How nice." She laughed, hysteria edging her voice. "No. I won't go."

"Damien has a large house now." Marie interrupted quietly. "Joshua and Eileen Caron do live there. They have two children, Julian and Madeline. You met Madeline, Bobbie."

"Yes, isn't she wife number five?" Bobbie snarled with pain. "How foolish of me. It was nearly four years ago when I was wife number four. His wives surely number in the teens by now." She would have expected Marie to understand. "I don't imagine he told you that, did he Daddy?" She whirled back to face Myles. "I was his fourth wife."

"Yes, he did. I understand it's a custom in his society." Myles stated calmly. "You are his only wife – in a manner of speaking. If you have the marriage blessed..."

"You approve?" Her eyes rounded in shock. The whole situation was ludicrous. Yet what else could she expect? Men always stuck together. It was the way of the world.

Myles blue eyes darkened. "I will not judge him – if he was honouring a custom with his people either. If you intend working for me, you will go to Batoche and stay with Damien."

She could see that Myles had lost all patience now. She could see the red blotches in his face. He was breathing heavily.

"If you can't separate business from your personal life then you have no business being in a man's world. You can go back to Toronto. I'll finish this story."

"You're my daughter." Myles jaw clenched as he continued. "You are always welcome to live in my house. But it is becoming very apparent you're something other than what I thought."

"When do we leave?" Bobbie ground out. She tried to accept that Myles was only saying these cruel things in order to have his own way.

"Damien is leaving tomorrow. I'll let him know you're coming with him." Myles smiled graciously.

Standing, he calmly wandered around gathering up the coffee cups. He walked into the hall and down to the kitchen. The two women stared at each other. Both their eyes were rounded in amazement.

"He's cleaning up now? But he sounded so…" Marie whispered.

"Like a man?" Bobbie nodded. "They *are* bastards, you know."

CHAPTER 21

Damien's home was a surprisingly large dwelling of stone and mortar, not the logs Bobbie had expected. The two-story structure had a pillared verandah running along the front bottom level. Turret rounded corners made it look like a miniature castle. Frosted trees, taller than the house, gave the grey stones an enchanting bacchante-like appearance. It lay, sturdy and welcoming in a valley in the Eagle Hills.

The hills were rugged groves and slopes, nearer Battleford than Batoche. Their shape, jagged dips and cliffs were more like foothills, than plains. It was nothing like the southern flat prairie she'd pictured. Recalling her comment about sharing a tipi, she smiled.

"Look Lisa, your *papa* has just gone up considerably in your mother's eyes. It's because of my castle. I built this castle for my very own little princess," Damien stated conversationally.

"You didn't even know she existed." Bobbie broke her promise not to talk to him.

Lisa yawned then gurgled her response. She snuggled deep into her warm furs. She was ecstatic to be with Damien, and like her mother, she loved the sound of his sultry voice.

"Not this little princess." Damien reached below the robe, tickling his little daughter. "Once I had another princess. But alas, even when I fought dragons for her it wasn't good enough. She left me."

"Dragon? We fight dragons?" Lisa sat up, staring up with awe in her darling features. She looked around anxiously. "Where?"

"They're all gone, baby." Damien soothed, pulling her into his arms. "Daddy saved you."

A small twinge of guilt pierced Bobbie's numb heart. She watched Lisa, clinging to Damien. Lisa should have a father. Then she sniffled. Damien would never make a proper father. The time Lisa needed him the most, he would be out gallivanting across the prairies with his friends.

"So you still use buffalo robes for your bed." Bobbie stated with mock sweetness as Lisa nuzzled down into the furs, closing her eyes.

"No. I gave them to some people – who needed them." Damien growled softly. He manoeuvred the team with easy skill, down a steep, slippery slope.

"And your clothes as well?" Bobbie eyed his sheepskin jacket and denim jeans. "I see you like the civilized world well enough now."

"I didn't give them away." Damien turned to face her, giving her the full impact of his so seductive smile. "I keep them for my lady friends. When they want a wild savage – I oblige them. Remember?"

Bobbie flushed, looking away. Oh yes, she remembered a time when he was her very own – wild savage.

"We can't go on like this, wildcat. We have to talk." Damien sighed his frustration.

"We have nothing to talk about. I think you said everything succinctly – in my stable." Bobbie stiffened. Why was he so charming again? Hadn't he punished her enough yet?

"I was mad. Just seeing you again… I apologize for my furious temper." Damien stated flatly. "I'm sorry."

"And with that apologue I'm supposed to forgive you?" Bobbie winced. "No."

"I can forgive and forget everything – for Lisa." His beautiful voice was soft with enticement.

"How benevolent of you. Did you ever consider you have nothing to forgive?" Her voice rose, then she swallowed. "I don't care."

He had hurt her – beyond repair. The pain of his violent brutality cut much too deeply for her to respond to his flippant attitude. Damien was the last man she would ever want.

"Let's put that to a test, wildcat. Shall we?" Damien grinned.

Angrily, she turned to look into his exotic eyes again. Damn him! Surely he couldn't still read her mind so easily.

"*It is amazing how complete is the delusion that beauty is goodness.*" She quoted Leo Tolstoy, feeling that phrase so appropriately suited Damien.

"Pardon?" Damien held a puzzled expression on his face now.

"It was something Tolstoy said." Bobbie shrugged her shoulders, looking away to search the snow covering the slopes.

"Who? Who the hell is Tolstoy?" Damien asked suspiciously.

"Leo Tolstoy. He is a famous author. He wrote *War and Peace*." Bobbie laughed softly. It wasn't often she confused Damien.

"I don't read much now." Damien mumbled, dropping his gaze to the reins in his hands. "I don't much like it."

"I'm not surprised." The pain filtering in his eyes surprised her. She sighed. "I'm sorry."

"She looks like you when she's sleeping." He looked down to his sleeping daughter. There was affection in his eyes.

"I don't want to talk about this." It hurt too much. Damien could speak, using such flowery compliments so easily. Every word he uttered sounded like another lie. "Will you really get me an interview with Riel and Dumont? Why are you helping me now?"

"I've always helped you, wildcat. Sometimes you even begged me to – help you." Damien flashed her his charming – fake smile.

Her face darkened with rage. He would still take nothing seriously. How could she have ever loved such a man?

"I want Lisa." Damien seemed to read her thoughts again. At least that comment sounded honest enough.

"You can't have her!" Bobbie's hostile hiss was laced with smug confidence. She wanted to pierce that elusive, teasing veneer he adopted so easily. "Regardless of how successful your quaint little ranch becomes, you'll never compare to my wealth – or my fathers'"

"I always hated you being *'Daddy's'* little girl. But, I remember when you forgot all about *Daddy*. I wonder how long it would take to change your selfish mind again?" His true feelings surfaced, like crackling fire, out of control.

She winced at the savagery in his face. Now, at least, he was being honest.

"Do I give you the impression I might be easy, Damien?" She asked in a calm, icy tone. Inside her stomach was churning. *Please God don't let him try.* "I'm not. I will raise Lisa to be a young, *civilized* lady – not a wild little heathen. And I'll do it without your help."

"You're hard, wildcat." Damien whistled under his breath, giving a mock shiver. "I can't forget how much you loved this *wild heathen*. You did anything I asked. And don't for one moment think – *you won't do it again.*"

"God, you're conceited!" Bobbie lashed out in fear. "All you have is your looks – and they don't last forever!"

He stopped the horses in front of the house. Jumping down from the sleigh, he swept Lisa into his arms. Stomping up the verandah steps, he ignored Bobbie's struggles to get out of the sled.

She caught her foot in her billowing petticoats and fell into the soft, fluffy snow. Lisa giggled, rubbing her sleepy eyes. She struggled to get out of her father's arms.

"Momma play!"

"I'll help you up – if you beg." Damien's laughter was loud and rude.

Bobbie swore in a vehement scream of rage.

"Remember – our daughter will be no wild heathen." Damien clamped his hands over Lisa's ears. "Watch your mouth – *lady*."

Still laughing, he turned and opened the door.

Joshua and Eileen chattered throughout the long evening meal, ignoring the guest seated there so awkwardly. They both spoke French.

Bobbie was seated on Damien's right at the large oak table in the huge dining room. She was amazed that his servants ate with him. Then she became apprehensive at the pure, venomous hatred in Madeline's eyes.

Shifting, her eyes drifted to Julian, the Caron's teenaged son. Julian was watching her with an admiration he couldn't hide. She found his stares amusing. He kept looking with such longing – at her loose blond hair. She smiled, fluttering her lashes in his direction. He, at least, was friendly. She was sure; he would some day be as handsome and appealing as Damien was.

From the corner of her eye she caught Damien's dark scowl. She smiled at Julian again, feeling better.

"We don't speak too good English." Eileen interrupted. She was looking at Bobbie with a perplexed expression on her plump, rounded face. Then she looked at Damien and at Julian. Bobbie flushed, looking at her plate. "Do you want more to eat?"

"No, thank you." Bobbie looked up to smile politely at the woman.

"Stay away from her son, baby. She'll kill you." Damien leaned forward to whisper in her ear. She felt his breath tickle her ear with erotic pleasure. She closed her eyes.

She opened them, knowing they were glazed with longing. Ignoring Damien, she smiled at Julian again. He grinned and winked! She gasped, dropping her eyes. Perhaps he wasn't as inexperienced as she thought. She groaned, softly. Damn, she didn't want this. She had no interest in Julian.

After the uncomfortable meal, Bobbie decided to retire. Lisa was already sleeping. She was exhausted from the long sleigh ride from Winnipeg in the freezing air.

Entering her assigned upstairs room, Bobbie locked her door.

The room was beautiful. A luxurious spread of silky, red fox furs covered the four-poster bed. The windows were set in a rounded corner, covering the complete alcove from floor to ceiling with glass. She could see the looming hills and crags, covered with snow. The moon shone in, causing a sheen of silver to spread over the land.

Her fear Damien might seek her out went unrealized. She spent her first night in Damien's house – alone. Of course, Damien didn't want her. He had sweet, docile Madeline to satisfy his carnal appetite now. She hoped Madeline's obvious lack of enthusiasm extended to her bed! She grimaced. She didn't want Damien.

She had breakfast in the kitchen with only Eileen for company. She wandered over to stare out into the bleak outdoors.

"Where's everyone?"

"Joshua and Damien out for chores. Lisa playing with her dolls. Madeline sleeping. You want more coffee, madam?"

Nervously, Eileen flitted over to the cast-iron stove, ready to pour her another cup of coffee.

"No, thank you." Bobbie smiled tentatively. "Please call me Bobbie. Would you like some help, cleaning up the kitchen?"

"No!' Eileen looked shocked. "No, that lazy Madeline's job. I get her up…"

She looked ready to cry.

"What's wrong?" Bobbie frowned. Eileen did not look happy at all.

"I am good Catholic. I don't like this – going around here… This…" Astounding Bobbie, Eileen broke into blubbering tears of misery. Her corpulent frame was jiggling with distress.

"Please don't." Bobbie moved to the stove and placed her hand on Eileen's shoulder. "It isn't like that! I'm not here to – for Damien. I'm here to interview Louis Riel. I run a newspaper office in Winnipeg."

"Lisa is his daughter!" Eileen cautiously lifted her face, wiping her eyes on her apron.

"Unfortunately…" Bobbie's eyes hardened. "I was his wife – many years ago. We were married in Big Bear's camp – not by a priest. It was a mistake. But it won't happen again."

She caught the frantic look in Eileen's wide brown eyes. Bobbie turned to the doorway.

Damien, looking as violent as the winds outside, stood there.

"Get some trousers on, wildcat." He ordered autocratically, stomping wet snow deliberately onto Eileen's clean floor. "We're going to Batoche today. You can interview Riel instead of gossiping with my servants."

"I was not gossiping."

His chameleon smile was in place again. He turned to Eileen.

"I sympathize with your concerns – but no one is forcing you to stay. There are a number of people looking for work around here. What Bobbie is to me is no business of yours. Do you understand?"

"Damien, how dare you talk to Eileen like that?" Bobbie snapped furiously. Her arm went around Eileen's plump shoulders.

Damien leaned against the door, grinning with mock innocence. His sultry eyes slid down her body.

"I figured out what that Tolstoy guy was saying. But do you know what I was thinking wildcat? That guy was talking about you, not me." He continued to smile, perusing her body with interest. "Now go up and change. We'll leave for Batoche right away."

"Not until you apologize to Eileen." Bobbie ground out, a puzzled expression crossed her features. What on earth was he talking about? Why would he think Tolstoy was writing about her?

"Please go. I will look after Lisa careful. Damien is right. It is not my business. I like my work. I am sorry Damien." Eileen whispered frantically.

"No, Eileen, I'm sorry. Forgive my rotten temper?" Damien flashed his irresistible smile at her now. "Don't worry. She's still my wife. We'll get married in church when we get to Batoche. I promise."

"*We will what?*" Bobbie shrieked, unable to believe she was hearing correctly. "You promise..."

"Go get changed wildcat, or I'll change you myself." Damien threatened in a low voice.

"A bad storm comes out there." Joshua came through the back door. "I think you should stay, Damien."

"What the hell is going on?" Damien growled. "Why is everyone suddenly questioning *my* decisions?"

He glared at Bobbie, as though blaming her.

"Go get dressed or so help me God, I will come with you."

"I come too, *Papa*." Lisa ran into the kitchen. She pulled at Damien's leather breeches. Large, crocodile tears rolled down her plump cheeks.

"*Non*, you will stay with *Tante* Eileen. I will buy you something. What do you want?" Damien scooped her into his arms, grinning.

"Pony?"

"That's my girl. Yes, *papa* will get you a pony. But only if you are a good girl for *Tante* Eileen."

"I be good." Lisa nodded solemnly.

Damien looked up to stare into Bobbie's stormy eyes. He had a dangerous threat on his face she couldn't ignore. He would take her up and change her. She turned, running up the stairs. Locking the door, she could hear him chuckling in the hall. He had followed her!

When Bobbie came down, she couldn't help but see the blatant lust entering his smouldering gaze as it ran down her figure.

"Let's go." He sauntered into the front hall to get her cloak. His fingers brushed along her flushed cheeks as he helped her into the garment. Smiling, he leaned down to place a light kiss on the tip of her nose.

"Don't touch me again or I'm going home." Bobbie jerked away, stomping outside.

She was quivering with rage and fear. He had every intention of following through on his threat. He was going to marry her. Her heart beat madly in her chest as she prayed wildly for help. Damien, when he applied it, had a charm few people could resist – least of all her.

"Whoa." Damien grabbed her arm, laughing. "Your horse is over here."

He helped her mount, keeping his hand on her leg even after she was seated on the horse.

"So you think I'm beautiful." He smiled up into her blazing eyes. "Now, let me show you how good I am."

Looking down into his sultry, persuasive eyes, Bobbie winced. Groaning, she closed her eyes, thinking it might be a very puny defence against him.

CHAPTER 22

Bobbie and Damien wound their way through crystallized hills and snow piled gullies. Their progress was slow. Their horses sank, sometimes to their bellies, into deep banks. Damien's meandering and turning soon had Bobbie completely lost. She wasn't even sure what direction they were moving in. The skies were covered in grey clouds and a fine mist of sleet obscured her vision.

They reached an ice-solid river near noon.

"The North Saskatchewan." Damien dismounted, indicating she should do the same. She obeyed. Her joints ached their protest.

The smoky mist of her pony's breath dampened her fur-coated shoulders. Instantly the moisture froze into crystal icicles. She could barely lift her numb legs. She bent her knee and thrust forward. Immediately she was sliding along the smooth, wind-swept surface. Her face lightened. This was so much easier.

"Does this go into Batoche?" She asked. Why didn't they just skate to Batoche?

"No!" Damien turned to watch her. "Look out."

Her horse objected to her movement. He jerked and the reins slid through her fingers. Trying to grasp at the trailing ribbons, she managed instead to land on her bottom with a solid thump.

Bobbie sat in paralysed fear. She was positive the ice was cracking dangerously around her. She clenched her eyes shut, preparing for the icy waters to engulf her.

"Do you really think you could make a dent in this?" Damien reached down to help her up. He was laughing.

Their hazy breath mingled as he leaned closer to straighten her loosened hood. She could see the striking silver edging his black eyes.

"I'm frozen." She whined. When he touched her she felt so much warmer.

"A minute ago you were ready to play. And before that you threatened to go home if I touched you." Damien's lips twisted. "I'd like to oblige you, wildcat. But we have to get moving."

His hands, when they dropped from her shoulders, seemed to be reluctant. It was uncanny how easily he could read her thoughts.

"You are such odd contradictions, wildcat. I can't keep up with you." Damien moved over to his horse. "We'll have a quick lunch, then go as far as we can today."

"We can't get there in a day?" Bobbie followed, leading her horse up a steep, pine-covered slope. She was ashamed of her weakness, but it was so cold. Would one day in her long, lonely future matter? She could... Viciously she pushed those thoughts aside.

"No." Damien turned back when he answered. An uneasy frown marred his features. "Joshua's storm is coming in. Today we'll have to stop and ride the storm out."

"How long will that take?" Bobbie shrieked in panic.

She couldn't stay overnight – alone – with Damien. Was he lying again? He appeared more than willing to play his games again.

"Sometimes they last until spring." Damien chuckled, his dark eyes gleaming mischievously. "Would you like to spend another winter with me?"

"I'm going back." Bobbie shook her head. Terrified and cold, she turned around to stare at their trail. Could she follow it?

"Coward." Damien ridiculed. "Was your winter with me so bad? Normally I can make Batoche in a day."

"I'm slowing you down?" She muttered in frustration.

She couldn't ride back. She didn't know where they were and already the fine, filmed snow had covered their tracks.

"No. Not you, wildcat. As always, your stamina amazes me. Even your delicate appearance is a lie." Damien reached into his saddlebag and handed her some bread and left over roast-beef.

"Why did you have to add that…?" She murmured. She bit into her sandwich hungrily. Surprisingly, it wasn't frozen. "If we have to stop, why not here?" She didn't feel like traveling any further.

"Can't you make it any further?" There was no concern in his fleeting smile. He was challenging her.

"Of course I can."

By the time they stopped again, there was no light in the charcoal skies. Bobbie groaned in agony. She'd spent the last hour or so in frozen impotence. She just couldn't help him set up camp.

Using willow branches, he quickly assembled a small enclosure, covering the tree limbs with robes. Inside he piled pine foliage and covered that with a large fur. His fire, encircled by stones, immediately filled the small structure with heavy smoke. To Bobbie it was a palace.

She dozed as he began to make coffee and something to eat.

"Wake up lazybones." Damien nudged her and handed her a cup of steaming liquid.

"I'd rather sleep." She moaned, propping herself up on her elbow. Sipping the fiery brew she nearly choked. Of course it was laced with whiskey.

"Do you still have to drink all the time?"

Feeling much warmer now, she removed her heavy cloak, no easy task in a dwelling where one person could barely turn around. She was so aware of Damien, close enough to touch.

"Why did we have to go to Batoche today? Why not wait?" She continued when he didn't answer. She leaned over to take her plate of stew.

"I wanted to get you alone – today." He stated, his voice even and calm.

Flinching, her head shot up. Her appetite disappeared immediately. So long ago, she had fallen into his evil trap. He'd shown her paradise – then hell! She was terrified she was heading for hell again. Was she a masochist?

"I swear, I'd rather die than ever let you touch me again." She searched the confined enclosure. She decided to die in the icy winds outside rather than submit to him. He was closer to the door.

"You are so melodramatic, *mignonne*." Damien laughed, looking at his plate. "Eat. You'll need your energy."

"You sound like Lone Woman." Bobbie muttered bitterly. "Are we still married?"

"We haven't been married since the day you moved your bedroll from my lodge." Damien's face was dark and taut.

"How convenient! Of all the irresponsible, stupid..." Her voice rose. Why had she mentioned Lone Woman?

"Shut-up, wildcat," he requested quietly. "You have called me every rotten name you could think of, but we both know it doesn't mean a thing. If I ask you to spread your legs – you will."

"You conceited, vulgar bastard." Bobbie turned blood red with shamed anger. "How can you do this? You hate me and that's fine by me. Just leave me alone."

"Surely, I've never said I hate you." Damien extended a brow, grinning again. "I don't hate. Hate means as much as love does. Are they even words? No, I feel like getting even. I guess you'd call it revenge."

"Oh! I give up." She flopped back, staring up at the low ceiling overhead. Hot liquid filmed her eyes. Without ever hearing her side of the story, she was condemned. He was being honest enough, she had to give him that. "Your methods of seduction astound me."

"You're giving me lesson on how seduce you?" he asked with insolence. "I'm not going to seduce you."

Stretching out beside her, Damien casually leaned into her side. Mutinously, she turned her back on him.

"Do you want me to?" He whispered softly in her ear. "Relax. If you stay this tight, you'll never be able to ride – tomorrow."

Damien began a soft caress along her shoulders, massaging with gentle strokes. Tensing further, she felt his proficient fingers move around, touching her intimately.

"I didn't plan to seduce you last time either.' His breath fluttered against her ear, causing pinpoints of pleasure to tingle along her body.

"Last time?" Her eyes jarred open. She rolled away from him.

Thank you, God. If she kept that horrible night foremost in her mind, she could reject his skilled seduction. She knocked against the side of the flimsy enclosure. Even moving away from him, she could feel his blatant arousal against her bottom.

"You call *rape* – seducing me?" she mumbled against the robes.

He was still rubbing her tight back. His hands moved down to loosen her shirt from her trousers. His fingers touched her bare flesh.

"I never raped you, *mignonne*. Or do you always come – even when you're raped? I wanted to rape you…"

His lips feathered along her neck like a fleeting breeze. Slipping her blouse down, he nuzzled the silky flesh along her shoulder. She rolled around to face him. She stared into his breathtakingly beautiful face that hid his ugly brutality so efficiently.

"Why are you doing this?" She whispered sadly. "I would have thought if you wanted Lisa, you would have tried to kidnap her."

"I thought of that." Damien's thick lashes covered his sultry eyes. A small pulse flickered in his cheek. "But for some perverse reason, I need you too. Maybe after what you did to Lone Woman, I need to see you suffer - and suffer..."

"Damn you! I suppose next you'll believe I strangled her with my own bare hands. Why are you so stubborn?" She demanded, hostility building within. She was so tired of paying for something she hadn't done. She drew in a sharp breath. "I will only tell you this once more. The police knocked me out. I didn't see what they did to Lone Woman."

"Why did *everyone* say you weren't unconscious? Why did some say you laughed and everyone say you left willingly?"

"They hate me." Bobbie stated flatly. It was no use. She wanted to cry. Why did they say that?

"Well, they certainly didn't like you." Damien drew his breath in sharply. "You thought you were superior. You were right and they were wrong. All you ever cared about was wealth and prestige. Hell, I knew that."

"How can you believe I'd laugh – when they..." Bobbie cried out.

"Bashed her face in with a rifle?" Damien finished her sentence. His eyes blazed with fury. "There wasn't even an investigation."

Damien was breathing harshly. His mouth twisted with pain. He looked down into her tear-filled eyes.

'The sad part is, *mignonne*, I want to forgive you. I nearly convinced myself it wasn't your fault." He whispered, running his fingers lightly along her neck.

"I didn't just watch. They knocked me out." Bobbie gulped heavily. "I didn't go willingly. Damien – what if I *am* telling the truth? How does that make me feel about you?"

"What if?" Damien's eyes were still hard and distant.

She was too weary to fight anymore. She could never convince him of her innocence.

"We're not getting married." She wouldn't marry a man who believed she was capable of everything he said she'd done.

"Yes we are." Damien said with quiet determination. "Stop being so selfish, Bobbie. Think of Lisa. We'll go the *padre* when we get to Batoche."

"No."

"Go to sleep before I strangle you."

The hands roaming along her body were gentle, not violent like his words. Then, as though aware of what he was doing, his eyes darkened with self-loathing. Rolling over, he presented his back to her.

That was the worst insult of all. He could lie there beside her and go to sleep. While she lay, emotionally stripped bare, exposed to every wonderful memory from the past. She wept. Muffling her sobs against the fur, she finally dozed. If Damien heard her, he remained silent. She could hear his slow, heavy breathing long before she dropped off into a restless slumber.

Frigid ice pressed against her chest, twining with her legs. Shrieking her agony, Bobbie was held still by glacial hands of steel. Terrified, bleary-eyed, she woke. She wondered if Damien had tossed her outside into the raging storm.

"I had to check the horses." His teeth chattered. "It's blowing so hard, I built them a shelter. We won't get too far if they freeze to death."

Rubbing his frozen feet along her legs, he ingeniously unfastened her trousers and placed his palms between her thighs. She tried to squirm away, hitting against the side of the hovel, nearly knocking it over.

"Don't break it." Damien ordered. "I'm not building another one tonight."

"You're hurting me." She hissed as prickling jolts of agony shot along her legs.

"Imagine how I feel." He growled, nuzzling his icy nose into her warm shoulder. "Sorry, wildcat. It's the best way to warm up."

"I don't think this is a good idea," she whimpered as his flesh started warming. His hand moved suggestively. "Think of the consequences."

"I can live with them if you can, *mignonne*." He brushed his mouth along her earlobe.

His tongue started a tantalizing search along her ear and teased inside. Shifting slightly, his lips immediately heated when they slid across her cheek to meet with hers.

"No!" Her protest was smothered against his demanding mouth.

His lips traced patterns of delight along hers, urging her to open and accept his plunder. His skilled fingers spread out to flutter teasingly between her tightly clenched legs.

"Love me wildcat. Please."

His hands roamed possessively and deliberately, along her quivering flesh to find the anticipated spot to touch that drove her wild. Her breath caught in her chest, heart pounding furiously. "*God give me the strength to resist him.*" But he was using that irresistible magic he knew she couldn't resist.

"How much more – should I suffer – before you're satisfied?" She whimpered in fear. His touch was fatal. "Just kill me... please?"

"*Mignonne...*"

He took her hand, guiding it downwards until she made contact with his hard arousal. Unable to halt now, she placed her fingers around him, using that lingering motion he'd taught her to further excite him. A luscious purring in her throat erupted. All though escaped, replaced by excruciating need. He groaned his own pleasure. Now she was floating in exquisite delight. An overpowering throb in her abdomen spread outward.

"I can't wait any longer."

Rolling over to mount her, his eyes blazed with passion. He smiled down into her glazed eyes. His lingering, erotic strokes brought them both to the peak they most needed immediately. He rolled off, flinging his arm over his face.

Reality slowly seeped back in. What was she doing? Opening her eyes, she saw the perspiration along his lean body. He shuddered, and then sighed heavily.

"I'm sorry, *mignonne*."

"*For what?*" she wanted to scream out. "*This time it's as much my fault as yours*." She remained silent.

As he sat up she saw his false grin was back in place. His chest was still heaving as he took deep breaths to control himself.

"I'm warm now."

Tears streamed silently down her cheeks. Bobbie wanted to bring him back inside her. She wanted to forget everything except his touch. She felt so lost – so alone. It was a dull agony throughout.

"Don't..." Leaning over, Damien brought her chin around until she was facing him.

Like a trapped animal, she gazed up into his pain-filled eyes. Her mind was a whirling ball of confusion.

"You make it so hard." Damien sighed, looking away from her. "I need you. Tonight, I will say whatever you want to hear. Ask me anything."

"Do you love me?"

"Yes. Yes, I do."

"And tomorrow? What happens tomorrow...?"

He shrugged, saying nothing. Still, he wouldn't look at her. His shoulders were tight and corded.

"I remember a time when you didn't even believe in tomorrow..." Anguish sliced through her chest. "Remember – tomorrow never comes..."

"Tonight, it doesn't have to..."

A jagged sob erupted. She moaned, turning away.

"Hell!" Damien leaned down to face her. His finger moved to wipe the tears from her cheeks. He licked against the flushed softness. Grimacing he sat up again. "I grew up, *mignonne*. The truth is – I didn't want to be a *Treaty* Indian."

"Where did you get the money to buy a ranch?" Bobbie asked feeling as though she'd just lost something so beautiful it was unbearable.

"The government gives land to anyone willing to homestead it. The materials for the buildings are all here – on Mother Earth. I built the house myself. I trapped for two winters – and I had two stallions and a beautiful mare to start my herd."

"Why do something so out of character?" Bobbie whispered.

"I had this insane idea to match your father's wealth. Then I'd show you what you threw away. It was an impossible dream." Damien laughed grimly, shaking his head.

"Why would you think I'd want that?" Bobbie felt her heart lighten. Surely, that one winter she'd spent in his arms proved otherwise.

Like the chameleon he resembled, he was suddenly sardonic. Amusement blazed in his eyes. His fingers gently stroked along her moist cheek.

"I don't care even if you do." He smiled. His eyes filled with anguish. "I'll give you anything you want – if you give me what I want."

"No. You can't." It was her turn to avoid his seeking eyes.

"Yes, I can. You want love – I give you love, *mignonne*. I don't lie." He whispered softly on her cheek. "I'll love you to eternity, I swear."

'And'... She screamed silently. He said no more. Her heart ached. The days and nights she had waited for him to come were tortured memories surfacing with stark pain. And all that time he was out here – seeking revenge. He believed she'd left him willingly. He believed she'd *laughed* when the soldiers murdered Lone Woman. How could there be love without *trust?* Without trust there was only lust. It wasn't enough.

"It is enough!" Damien's voice was sullen. He sighed. "We will be married."

"No." Her heart was breaking.

Neither spoke again. Throughout the remainder of the night as the winds howled around their crude shelter, she lay stiff and wide-awake. Bobbie knew any further conversation would only cause further pain. It would solve nothing. The chasm between them was too wide to cross. She could even understand why he wouldn't believe her. If everyone said otherwise, why should he?

"You could – if you really love me!" she muttered inaudibly. Then she was silent. She couldn't beg again.

Beside her, Damien stiffened. He sighed heavily.

"What did you do with my necklace?" His voice was low and urgent.

Bobbie's breath caught. What a strange question – now. Did it make a difference – knowing that she was a complete idiot? What did it matter that she kept it, hidden and cherished? She was still unable to discard his *prized possession*, clinging to it as though it were her lifeline. How often she'd held it, stared at it, caressed it – hoping he would come to get her.

"What do you think?" She asked bitterly.

He shuddered. Then there was silence again.

CHAPTER 23

Bobbie was exhausted by the time they reached Batoche. She refused to talk to Damien again. He wouldn't listen, regardless.

Louis Riel was in Prince Albert, not Batoche. Bobbie hoped Damien wouldn't suggest they go there. She was bitterly cold. And she was in no mood to interview anyone now. They all resembled the people who had lied and ruined her life. Right now, she was beginning to believe they deserved whatever they got.

"*God, he's driving me crazy.*" She felt guilty even thinking that way. She could see Piapot's reservation clearly in her mind. No one deserved that. But why did they lie? Fine, she was packing a very superior attitude while she was with them. But to ruin her life? She snorted. It was as much Damien's fault. He refused to believe her.

Looking around the village, she was surprised to see wooden homes and stores. It looked like any white man's village. Aspens and poplars, now bare and frost-covered, surrounded log cabins and wooden shops.

"Expecting tipi's? You're amazing, wildcat." Damien looked at her and laughed. "How often have you been out to St. Francis? There is no difference between the *Metis* and white people – except the whites seem to have all the money."

She tilted her face away, reading the derisive scorn in his face. She didn't know what to expect, wherever he took her. He wandered around different societies with such frightening ease.

"We'll stay with Louise Carriere for a few days until Riel returns." Damien laughed with no humour. "She's another of my – adoptive mothers. Be nice to her, please? For now you can interview Gabriel Dumont. He owns a saloon here. We'll go there first."

"How convenient!" Bobbie gasped out, tears clogging her throat. Was he insinuating that she might hurt this woman – like she'd hurt Lone Woman? Which she hadn't! She had been so fond of Lone Woman. Surely he knew that. "And you can have a drink! Is that your solution to everything?"

"Yes. Why do you care?" Damien's tone was belligerent. He was itching for a fight and she wouldn't give him the satisfaction.

They entered a large, smoke-filled room. She could see only men standing around a large billiard table on one side of the room. Behind a longer counter, a burly, middle-aged man stood. He looked none too pleased to seeing a female enter his domain.

The gigantic black stove spewed out thick puffs of smoke, making it nearly impossible to see. The stale smell of ale mingled with burning wood and cigars.

"*Bonjour, mon fils.*" The man standing behind the bar hailed Damien with affectionate enthusiasm.

Gabriel Dumont's husky frame was intimidating. His dark eyes moved toward her with a stern, piercing expression in their depths. His cheekbones were high and covered with swarthy skin.

Damien, after talking for a few moments so rapidly in French to Gabriel, turned and belatedly pulled her up to the counter.

"This is your wife?" Gabriel growled his disapproval.

His eyes shifted back to study her thoroughly. She suffered his examination silently. Damien's lengthy reply was again too swift for her to understand. Gabriel shook his head slowly, and then grinned.

Padre Andre won't let you marry her if she doesn't agree."

Astonished, Bobbie saw Damien flush and nod. She smiled.

"Congratulations Mr. Dumont." She said to Gabriel. "I've never seen Damien agree to anything, unless he wanted to. I understand you are the self-appointed judge and jury of this community."

"Judge and jury?" Damien growled a strangled swear word. "Sorry. She's a reporter as well."

"Ah. That explains the manners, *non*?" Gabriel nodded, still smiling as though she were an insubordinate child, speaking out of turn.

She shifted, disconcerted by Gabriel's patient, kindly smile. She turned to frown at Damien. Gabriel was supposed to hate her. She was obviously white, wasn't she?

"You must forgive him, Roberta. He has led a very confusing life. He has been raised in three very different societies. It can't be good." Gabriel's voice was thick, with a heavy French accent. "But he is a good boy and will do what is right."

"Boy?" Bobbie's eyes sparkled. Damien looked stiff and embarrassed. "But really, I have no interest in Damien. I am here as a reporter. Can I ask you a few questions, *Monsieur* Dumont?"

"Ask away." Gabriel's expression hardened. He busied himself pouring some amber liquid into two glasses.

"Why have you brought Louis Riel here?" She plunged in.

"I wanted him here." Gabriel answered simply. "If you are a reporter..." and his tone sounded doubtful, "then you know what we want."
She nodded stiffly, once again feeling like an unruly youth. She could almost understand Damien's subservient manner. This man was just too intimidating.
"You understand Macdonald's *'National Policy'*?" Gabriel snorted his scepticism again. "Then do you feel this policy is fair? We must buy everything from Ontario and Quebec, instead of the States? Even when the US has cheaper products and they are closer?"
"It's not fair." Bobbie agreed. Now they were being heavily taxed if they bought American products. "But if you are patient, I'm sure..."
"Patient?" Gabriel interrupted. His eyes were blazing. "Let me assure you, madam, I've been more than patient. I only ask for what every other Canadian has. For years we've asked for schools and hospitals – but still we have none. There is nothing more to discuss."
He turned back to Damien, smiling fondly. Pouring another whiskey, he passed it across the counter. Damien downed it, grinning his familiar, audacious smile. The attractive dimple on the side of his cheek deepened.
Bobbie looked at the ceiling, fuming. She was condemned again before she could even finish a sentence. She was sick and tired of this male attitude.
"Why has Louis Riel come back to Canada?" Her voice rose with determination. "Will there be more trouble, like there was in Winnipeg fifteen years ago?"
"I hope she has some fine hidden qualities." Gabriel leaned over the counter to Damien. "A beautiful face won't last nearly so long as the ugliness inside."
Damien choked on his whiskey, laughing. "She said almost the same thing. Have you been reading Tolstoy by any chance?"
"Tolstoy?" Gabriel chuckled, looking bewildered. "Read?"
He turned to Bobbie. His voice was polite and low as he continued patiently.

"Louis Riel is not a violent man. But he can read and write – I can't. I can, however, use my rifle better than anyone else in these territories. If there is trouble brewing, be assured it will be me, not Riel causing it. Is that patient enough, my child?"

Gasping nervously, she nodded. She moved instinctively closer to Damien. Gabriel looked completely hostile and very frightening. Then his expression softened as he looked at her hands. She realized she was clutching Damien's arm so harshly her knuckles were white.

"She knows she could not survive ten minutes alone out here!' Gabriel chuckled with glee. "She is not stupid. That is a good quality, *non*?"

"I'm sorry." Bobbie murmured, keeping her eyes downcast. She kept holding Damien's arm though. His warm flesh was comforting. "I didn't mean to offend you."

"Don't worry, *petite,* I would never hurt a woman." Gabriel's eyes were twinkling when she dared look at him again. He was teasing her! "*You* didn't offend me. The situation offends me."

"Does she drink?" He turned to Damien, pouring her a drink. Gratefully, she swallowed the fiery liquid just as Damien shook his head. "She's a lady – she doesn't drink."

The two men laughed.

"Will you fight?" Bobbie asked as confidence grew.

Gabriel raised an eyebrow. His lips quirked with humour.

"She's very persistent." Damien stated solemnly.

"She is a good reporter then." Gabriel shrugged his shoulders. "If I have to, I will fight. I would ask you not to say that, but you will anyway. But when you do – please add that I will only do so – if your government makes me."

They stayed with Louise Carriere for three days, waiting for Louis Riel to return.

Although Louise made Bobbie feel somewhat welcome, her pious, religious attitude soon grated on Bobbie's already strung-out nerves. There were only two small rooms in her house. Damien slept on the floor in the main room and Bobbie shared Louise's wide bed in the bedroom.

Bobbie woke up often during the nights, feeling uncomfortable. She wanted to go and crawl beside Damien. Louise seemed to know that. It seemed as though every time Bobbie woke, Louise was staring at her, eyes wide open. Louise fluttered around, offering Damien coffee and food but continually reprimanded him for living in sin. Finally, unable to bear the stifling atmosphere, Bobbie agreed to go with Damien to see Father Andre at the *Mission of St. Antoine de Padue*. She just wanted out – she wasn't agreeing to marry him.

"I liked Lone Woman so much better." Her voice trailed off. Why did she always bring Lone Woman's name up?

"Why? Her attitude towards the joys of sex?" Surprising her, Damien grinned.

The air outside was still freezing but if felt much better than the cloistering air inside Louise's house.

"You don't see the way she watches me." Bobbie agreed, suddenly feeling breathless. It was only because he walked so fast. She grabbed his arm to slow him down. "I feel like a harlot."

"How often do you wake up and want to…" Damien leaned down, whispering in her ear. Straightening, he sighed, sounding weary. "She does seem to take *'Thou shalt not commit adultery'* very seriously. Aren't you religious at all, wildcat."

"Of course, but…" Bobbie shook her head. "We always went to church on Sunday, and we always gave to those less fortunate. But it always seemed society rules were more important. I suppose there isn't much difference when you think about it. But Louise – she's fanatical. Didn't it bother you when you live with her?"

"I wasn't a woman." Damien smiled.

"Oh yes, those double-standards again." Bobbie murmured. "I think I should lead this fight – you know Joan of Arc type fighting. I should gather the women together and…"

"That would be interesting." Damien agreed. "I'm getting so good at fighting women…"

"Damien is Father Andre involved?" Bobbie asked as the large church and rectory loomed near.

"You want to interview him?" Damien stopped. His face darkened. "He's going to marry us."

"I never agreed to that." Bobbie's mouth rounded in panic. "I just wanted out of the house."

"We can't live in sin around here." Damien's eyes narrowed. "Not here. I have to live here now."

"I say – to hell with them all." Releasing his arm, Bobbie whirled, running to the riverbank.

Slipping and sliding down the slope, she landed at the bottom on a hard bank of snow. She just couldn't marry this mercurial man. Without trust there was nothing expect their consuming lust. Living with him, knowing what he thought of her would be unparallel anguish. But, oh she wanted that lust he offered so willingly. Sobbing her frustration, she flopped down to the snow and wept bitterly.

"Let's go home." Damien spoke quietly. He was a dark shadow above her. Bobbie didn't look up. "I'll bring you back when Riel gets here."

She ignored him. She didn't want to talk to him. His erratic, hot and cold attitude was driving her crazy.

"For Lisa's sake, we have to get married." Damien repeated slowly. "It's the only way the people will accept us. We have to live here."

"Who are your people, Damien?" Bobbie finally lifted her head to peer up at him. "I never realized you were such a devote Catholic. When you were with Big Bear, you were so..."

"Is that what you want?" Dropping to his knees, Damien grabbed her shoulders, dragging her up. His burning eyes, searing her strained face, revealed only building rage now. "There you are my wife. Do you want to go live in Big Bear's village?"

"Yes." She answered recklessly.

His heavy lashes dropped over his suddenly smouldering eyes. A muscle jolted in his taut cheek.

"Let's go." He snarled, lips drawn back across his sharp teeth. "Let's forget about Lisa – and about your parents. Hell, let's forget everyone. Let's do what *you* want, wildcat."

"You make me sound so selfish." Bobbie interrupted with a guilty whimper of protest. "It's not that... it's just... The way we were..."

"Ah, yes. The way we were." Damien's exotic eyes glittered. His fingers tightened. "If it were possible – it would be so, *mignonne*. But do you really want to live on a reservation? Be thankful you have a choice. They don't!"

"Stop making everything so complicated. I only wish..." Bobbie's voice trailed off, leaving the sentence incomplete *"I only wished you really loved me."* She would never say that aloud again.

"I do." Damien's fingers dug into her arms as he leaned down to brush against her lips. His mouth was hot with longing. "Believe me, I do. But I *wish* I didn't."

Bobbie didn't care any more. If she could live with him, having him love – only her body, then she would do it.

"Don't you understand?" She reached up to stroke his jaw. "I'm ready to crawl into your arms and never think again. You have me – on any terms you want. I'm so tired of fighting."

"How long would that last?" His hands moved from her shoulders to lift her tear-stained face. "I only do what I must. It's not necessarily what I want."

"And what *must* you do?" Bobbie asked bitterly.

"I must marry you. For Lisa's sake, yes, but also because we can't seem to stop... this..."

His hands slid beneath her fur cloak. He caressed her flesh with expert skill. Bobbie moaned, sagging against him.

"Let's just go live somewhere else. I have money..." Bobbie whispered against his lips as they hardened with need.

"And live more lies wildcat?" Damien withdrew slightly. His fingers stopped their provocative search. "Coming from you, why doesn't that surprise me?"

"Damn you!" She moaned weakly. Large tears dropped to his quivering hands as he moved up to hold her cheeks.

Rubbing his thumb along the cold flesh, Damien moved closer, peering down into her wide eyes with intensity.

"I want to believe you." Damien brushed her trembling lips with his callused finger. There was an arrogant, reckless glint in his beautiful eyes. 'It doesn't matter. It's all in the past, *mignonne*. I don't care. Why will you live with me and not marry me?"

"Marriage is so – final. We're always fighting. And you don't really love me..." She blurted out her doubts, knowing her words couldn't change things.

"I love you too much." Damien interrupted, his face darkening. "Do you think you're saying I don't – doesn't hurt?"

"Why do you think its love... you feel?" Bobbie's eyes opened, glazed with bewilderment.

"Because, even knowing everything I do – I still want you." Damien whispered against her lips. "Will you please marry me?"

"Yes."

She answered his kiss with eagerness. She was so tired of fighting. She would take him on any terms he offered. She just wanted to feel him, touch him...

"Let's go to the church." He murmured against her lips. "It's damn cold kneeling in the snow."

Father Andre was very happy to see the young couple. Of course he would marry them – tomorrow morning. He'd heard all about Roberta and Lisa. They would really have to bring Lisa in to be baptized as soon as possible.

CHAPTER 24

Bobbie was married in a borrowed dress once again. When Bobbie woke up, for the first time in three days, Louise was smiling. She pointed at the dress lying on the bed.

"I asked Juanita if we could use her dress. She about your size." Louise stood by the bed, wringing her hands.

"Thank you." Bobbie murmured politely. Inside butterflies started in her stomach. She wanted to giggle. Maybe, for her third wedding – to Damien – she would have her own dress.

It wouldn't surprise her if there would be a third wedding. She knew their precarious relationship was on very shaky ground. But now Damien was right. It was selfish of her to expect or want any more than Lisa's respectability. Inside her heart longed for so much more. She couldn't stop that, regardless of how hard she tried.

The ivory lace and satin gown was beautiful. The wide skirt draped down in elegant folds. It had no crinoline underneath. The waist had a wide satin sash, and heavy crocheted lace trimmed the scooped collar and draping, loose sleeves. It fit her very well. The lace veil was held together with dried white flowers and a satin band. It fell behind, nearly to the floor.

Father Andre married them in the vestibule, not at the alter. He couldn't do otherwise, he explained hesitantly. Bobbie was not Catholic. She would have to come to Batoche for lessons before they could have another, proper ceremony.

"Our third wedding?" Bobbie did giggle then. She was so nervous.

Then the service began. The church was full of onlookers.

"Perhaps you can come with your little daughter for instructions." Father Andre offered after the service. Bobbie knew he was determined for her to make a commitment. It seemed very important.

"We'll come when the weather warms up." She promised solemnly.

She looked around Gabriel's saloon where their reception was being held. The whole village had turned out and once again she didn't know any of the guests. Everyone was cheerful, toasting the bride and groom with glasses of wine – supplied by Gabriel.

"What lessons do I have to take?" Bobbie grabbed Damien's arm. Yanking him aside, she pulled his head down to whisper in his ear.

"You'll have to be baptized." Damien grinned his endearing smile, keeping his head tilted close to hers. "Then there's Holy Communion – then Confirmation to go through."

"All that?" She glared up into his sparkling eyes. "Did you do all that?"

"Yes, I did." Damien laughed, seeming to enjoy her discomfort.

"And confession?" Bobbie shook her head. It was a wonder these people had any time left after attending to their church duties. "How many days does that take? How often to we have to…"

"Well, you don't have to go into detail, *mignonne*." Damien's face was filled with humour. "Usually it only takes a few minutes."

"Even with all your sins?" He must be joking. "Then what happens?"

"Penance." Damien chuckled. "After a while you don't want anymore of that, so you just don't sin. Least ways that's my theory."

"What sort of penance? Walking on hot coals?" Bobbie asked suspiciously. She didn't think she would bother taking lessons. "I don't want to be Catholic."

"No. You have to say prayers."

"Oh!" Her eyes widened and shifted to Louise, talking animatedly to the Padre. "Then Louise is very, very bad? She's praying all the time. What do you think she's doing all the time that could be that terrible?"

"Maybe she takes men – in the carnal way?" Damien whispered. He leaned closer to kiss the tip of her nose. "Maybe that's why she didn't like you being in her bed…"

Louis Riel was expected to return the following day. Both Bobbie and Damien agreed to forego their wedding night until they returned to the ranch. Although Louise offered her bed, neither felt very comfortable accepting that offer. Would Louise sleep on the floor?

Louis Riel was nothing like she expected. He reminded her of an agitated Father Andre. Dark and thin, he was dressed in a priest's robe. Gabriel stood protectively by his side. Why did Gabriel feel he had to protect Louis Riel?

Then, as she interviewed him, she had to admit he was a fascinating man. He was very well educated and she watched his jerky, oddly graceful motions with awe. He could talk rings around any politician she'd ever met.

"Is he a priest?" She whispered to Damien.

"He thinks he is a Prophet." Damien's voice was sardonic.

"Why are you here, Mr. Riel?" she asked tentatively. There was a strange gleam in his face she found quite disconcerting. A Prophet? Did he hear her?

"Gabriel wants me to write his letters." Louis answered swiftly. Then, bending his head, he began pacing around the room, muttering beneath his breath. He stopped to stare out the window.

"And if the letters go unanswered – will you fight?" Bobbie continued.

"I have never fired a gun in my life, my child. Isn't the gun another tool of the devil? It solves nothing." He turned back to Bobbie.

Bobbie smiled with a gentleness that surprised her. She couldn't understand why anyone could possibly fear Louis Riel. He was a kind man, more interested in religion than politics.

She continued to chat about the various problems facing the Western Territories. She kept her tone light. Gabriel relaxed his stiff stance and turned to talk to Damien.

"Well, what do you think of Louis Riel?" Damien asked, looking at her with respect as they left Gabriel's saloon.

"I think..." she smiled with pleasure. Damien approved of her interview! But she didn't want to insult Louis Riel either. "That no one should fear Louis Riel. He is kind and gentle."

"So you don't believe there will be war." Damien smiled back, sadly.

"I don't think he will start it." She replied.

"Again you underestimate people, *mignonne*." Damien opened the door to Louise's cottage. "Haven't you read about – religious fanatics – in your history books? A lot of wars are fought in the name of God. Let's go home today? It's only noon. We'll be back sometime during the night – if you can ride all night."

"Yes." Bobbie felt her heart lighten. Although Louise was somewhat nicer now, she was still irritating. She couldn't get used to being watched and judged by such critical eyes. "I'll ride all night. And Damien, I'm not underestimating him. He's almost too intelligent isn't he? I've also heard of geniuses crossing that line and going crazy. I think Riel may be a genius. Damien, do you think there will be a war?"

"Yes, definitely." It was a simple statement.

"Will you fight?" She continued with caution.

"No." He flashed her a grin. "Will you let me?"

Her heart lightened even more. She didn't want him to fight. And although she honestly believed Riel was no threat, she couldn't say the same about Gabriel. And she couldn't say Gabriel was wrong. Why didn't Macdonald answer at least one of their letters? She would talk to her father again. Maybe he could convince Macdonald to reply.

Louise fluttered around, gathering together enough food to last a week. She insisted they take it all.

"Dat Eileen she don't always cook good." Louise's smile was smug.

"But..." Bobbie closed her mouth. She'd only eaten a few meals there, but the food was excellent.

"I think I come out to cook Damien." Louise looked at him with reproach in her eyes. "Unless Roberta cook good."

"Oh yes, she's a fabulous cook." Damien and Bobbie's eyes met. Bobbie's were filled with thanks and Damien's twinkled with humour. "Besides, I didn't want you to work so hard anymore. You've done your share."

It had warmed up somewhat. They rode across the hard snow in the sunshine. Bobbie enjoyed the freedom, away from the oppressive atmosphere in Batoche. She looked at Damien. She was amazed he would follow such strict rules. Then she smiled. Damien would fit in wherever he was. It didn't mean he liked it.

Their horses' hooves crunched. A rabbit, white as the snow, leapt up as they rounded some small shrubs. His white ears flopped as he hopped across the snow. Her thoughts drifted to Winnipeg. Her breath caught in her throat. Where were they going to live? She rode up beside Damien. He smiled down at her absently. His eyes, half closed, were hazy and obscure.

"Damien, what am I going to do about my newspaper office?" She asked softly.

"Quit." Damien's brief comment was simple and immediate. Her blood ran cold.

"Just like that?" She really did try to keep her voice even. But she felt the rage boil inside.

"Just like that." Damien agreed with an arrogant assumption that was frustrating. He turned to her. "Would you like to stop for something to eat?"

"No, I don't." Bobbie muttered through her clenched teeth. "I want to talk – about my newspaper office."

"What am I supposed to do? Should I sell my ranch and go live in Winnipeg with you?" Damien swore. He looked sullen and hard now. "You're my wife now."

"Regrettably." Bobbie snapped. "What about Daddy? I can't just quit on him."

Her eyes blurred. What could they do? She didn't expect him to sell the ranch.

"Your Daddy won't mind at all, *mignonne*. I happen to know he'll be happy we're married." Damien's voice was flat, devoid of emotion. He stared straight ahead, guiding his horse with his knees with graceful skill. His shoulders were stiff and erect.

"And after meeting him – just once, wasn't it – you know that?" Bobbie cried in protest. She knew he was right. Her father would be happy that Lisa had a father. But she didn't know how he would react to her quitting. Besides – she wasn't sure she wanted to quit. She loved her job. "My father placed a lot of faith in me when he offered me the Winnipeg office. I won't let him down."

"He'll find someone else."

"Who?" Bobbie snapped her own arrogance. "Do you think I'll be that easy to replace?"

"How am I supposed to answer that, *mignonne*?" Damien shrugged. His lips quirked in a helpless gesture. "Let's stop."

He pulled his mount to a halt. Bobbie kept riding, her chin tilted in the air.

"No." She disagreed as she passed him. "I won't let you – *talk* – me out of this one, my darling Damien. I'm not giving up my office and that's final. I've given up enough."

"What have you given up?" Damien kicked his horse into motion again. "Is it so hard living with me?"

"Yes. You'll never know how hard." Bobbie cried out, trying to ignore the magnetic seduction in his tone.

"Tell me." Damien's jaw clenched tight. The tiny tick was back in his cheek. Bobbie swallowed, still not knowing what he was apt to do when he was like this.

"Do you really want to know?" She plunged forward, edging her horse away from him. She didn't want any sudden movements on his part. "We are married now. We have – insurmountable – problems, wouldn't you say? Now this comes up and just like everything else – *I'm the one who must give in.* Wouldn't you agree that might be hard?"

"I think we always manage to solve our differences – in a very pleasant way," Damien disagreed, smiling grimly.

"That's just it! You think because you can control – my body that you can control my mind. You can't!" Bobbie lashed out with fury.

Damien's jaw clenched again. He glared straight ahead, saying nothing.

"I want more than just sex. I want..." She stopped. She wouldn't mention trust or love to him yet again. "Why did you marry me?"

He did look at her then. His eyes were smouldering. Their eyes met and still he remained silent. She felt herself slipping into the depths of his hypnotic power. Shaking her head, with a little moan, she managed to pull away and stare out into the endless banks of snow ahead of them.

"Fine! Lisa now has a daddy." She muttered darkly. "So now, we'll just go back to Winnipeg and you can stay here on your damned ranch."

"No, *I want*..." Damien bit off his words. Looking back at him, she saw him shudder. Then he was calm and remote. "Well, wildcat – that's what you say you want. Do it! Go back to Winnipeg. I don't care. But will you stay for Christmas? It's only a month away and I'd like to spend at least one Christmas with Lisa."

"Is this another of your tricks?" Bobbie asked, and then realized what he had just said. He wanted her to go back to Winnipeg.

"No more tricks, wildcat." Damien's features were harsh and bitter. He was angry again. "I'm sick to death of all this bickering all the time. You can do as you please. I have no intention of ever – *talking* – you out of it again. You don't know what you want."

"Oh yes, I do," she moaned silently. "*I want you to say you love me – and mean it. I want you to say you believe me – and mean it. With those words I'll give up everything for you. I just want you to love me like I love you.*"

But he said he didn't know what love meant. He'd shown her in a very crude manner that he didn't trust or believe her. But he still insisted he loved her – and sounded so sincere when he said it, she thought wistfully.

"I'll stay until Christmas – and then I'll go back to Winnipeg." She whispered. "But you have to – not touch me again. Please?"

"I agree to everything." Damien smiled with sardonic humour. "You should be very happy – again you get your way."

They silently agreed to ride through the night. It was well past midnight before they arrived at the ranch. Bobbie was so weary, she wanted to crawl into bed and stay there the rest of her living days. She forced herself to dismount.

"I'll take the horses to the barn." Damien offered laconically.

She nodded stiffly, not seeing the underlying concern in his eyes.

For the next month she tried to avoid him as much as she possibly could. There was nothing more to be said. He obviously felt the same way. He no longer teased her. He no longer even talked to her other than any polite words he might say to a stranger.

Lisa adored him. He managed to steer her in a firm direction with patience and affection. Damien was a wonderful father. Bobbie felt guilty, knowing she was going to deprive both him and Lisa. But there was no way she could breach the gulf separating them now.

Eileen was happy. Bobbie and Damien were no longer living in sin. She chattered on about Bobbie and Lisa taking religious instructions soon. Bobbie didn't have the energy to explain that she was leaving, right after Christmas.

CHAPTER 25

Even Madeline was somewhat friendlier now if Bobbie could consider those smug, pleased smiles as a sign of friendliness. When she watched Damien's easy affection towards Madeline she wondered if Madeline didn't have a reason to feel so confident. Jealousy ate at her insides. She felt like she wanted only to go to him and beg him to touch her again. She felt empty and miserable.

Christmas Eve finally came with poignant sadness. She felt a complete outsider in this cozy family gathering. She wanted to cry. Everyone was gathered together in front of the fireplace in the front parlour. Lisa was cuddled in Damien's lap, sleeping. Madeline was curled on the floor – leaning against Damien's knees. Joshua read the Christmas story from the bible. It was all too morose for Bobbie to bear.

When Damien reached down, fingering Madeline's brown locks she nearly died. He poured himself yet another drink from the nearly empty whiskey bottle at his elbow.

"Up, *mignonne*." He murmured. "I must put Lisa to bed."

Mignonne! How could he be so cruel? When he returned, Madeline returned to her position and he didn't stop her. Unwillingly, Bobbie watched the sinuous smirk on his face. He was reckless and intoxicated. He was dangerous and deliberate. His fingers caressed Madeline's hair with blatant seductiveness. His eyes were half-closed and – looking directly at her. Bobbie looked away, hoping he couldn't read the pain in her face.

She looked at Joshua and Eileen. Neither would condone nor approve of a licentious relationship between Damien and their daughter. But neither was looking at Damien and Madeline either. She wanted to scream and make them see – and stop this torture.

Fugitively, she looked back to Damien. His dark eyes were still directed at her. His smile broadened, ruthless with satisfaction.

"I'm going to check on Lisa." Bobbie was pasty-white and trembling when she got up to leave. She waited until she got into the hall and started up the spiral staircase before she let the scalding tears fall.

There was a heavy pounding on the front door. She completely disregarded her wet-stained face or the fact that Damien had come out to open the door. She squealed in delight.

Running back down the stairs, she flung herself into Marie's arms.

"Oh thank God, you're here! I nearly forgot. I'm so, so happy you're here..." she blubbered against Marie's comforting shoulder.

"It's all right, dear." Marie patted her shoulders, trying to push her back slightly. "My God, what's wrong?"

Bobbie lifted her face to see Marie looking at Damien very sternly. Then sighing, Marie pulled Bobbie close again.

"What's he doing to you?" Marie whispered in her ear. "You're wasting away to nothing. I feel positively gigantic."

Sniffling, partly with happiness, but mainly because of Damien's cruel actions, Bobbie smiled. She moved to Pierre's comforting hug, unable to speak.

"What's she doing to *me*?" Damien's tone was husky with

belligerence.

"You're drunk!" Marie hissed. Taking Bobbie's arm, she steered her towards the stairs. "I thought you had grown up by now, Damien. Come show me our room, Bobbie. Is Lisa sleeping?"

"You have the same room you always have, Marie." Damien leered, fuzzy-eyed, in Marie and Bobbie's general direction. "I'm sleeping in the study. My *wife* has the bedroom – all to herself. Just like she wants."

He grimaced, berating his mood. Marie was right. He was being a lout. He also knew that if he'd been even remotely kind to Bobbie, in this past month, he'd take her. But regardless of how honourable his intentions were – he couldn't help her make up her mind. This time she would have to decide for herself. It was the only way they would ever find happiness.

"Now you should take pity on me, *mignonne*. Share my bed?" He asked seductively, unable to stop taunting her. She'd made the rules. He only followed them.

"Damien, you can be such an insensitive bastard!" Protectively, Marie put her arms around Bobbie. "Ignore him, darling."

"I'll be damned!" Damien's demonic expression changed to pondering contemplation. "Can they really be such good friends? Bobbie always despised Marie. Damned if Marie isn't still one attractive woman, Pierre."

"I know. She's my wife. Stop being so crude," Pierre supplied with dry humour. "If you're trying to hurt Bobbie, forget it. She'll break you long before you make a dent in her. She's one tough lady, isn't she, *cousin*? Your jealousy is obvious."

"She can't break me." Damien scowled darkly.

Then his unconcerned grin slipped back into place, effectively covering his feelings. He was jealous of anyone Bobbie talked to – male or female. He wanted her all to himself. She was doing an excellent job in confusing him. What did she want? She said she wanted to go back to Winnipeg. Yet, when he agreed she should, she still wasn't happy. Did she want him to go to Winnipeg too? Did she want him to live off her? Did she think he was – Etienne or any of those other men she knew?

"You think you know her, Damien? I understand her better than you do. I know she'll take whatever abuse you want to give her and she'll survive." Pierre laughed.

"Is that a challenge, Pierre? Because, you'll lose. She's going back to Winnipeg with you and Marie. Shall I try to change her mind?"

"No." Pierre shook his head. "You've already decided not to do that, haven't you? Let her decide. Don't do anything you might regret."

"I'll be an old man before she decides.' Damien grimaced.

Again Pierre was right. But he wasn't sure he had the patience to stay away from her much longer. Patience hadn't ever been one of his virtues and he believed it was highly overrated. *Live for the moment* was his motto and it had served him very well in the past. Until he met Bobbie, that was. Now he wanted more than just a moment with her. He wanted forever.

When the two women eventually returned, Bobbie's bright energy made Damien very uneasy suddenly. He didn't recognize the gold, sparkling dress that clung so seductively to her small, firm bosom and very tiny waistline. She had lost weight. But the bold shimmer in her golden-green eyes and peach flush in her cheeks made her into that enticing woman he so desperately needed.

He tilted his glass in a mocking salute, draining it when she so casually turned to gaze in his direction. His eyes flashed dangerously. Only minutes before Pierre and Marie had arrived, he'd managed to crack through that calm exterior she wrapped around herself so effectively. Now she was acting as though nothing he did or said would ever bother her.

Julian stumbled in his haste to bring her a glass of wine. She beamed at him. Damien scowled. Eileen and Joshua watched her with apprehension. Damien groaned as he heard her musical laughter and husky voice. He should be amused by Julian's obvious infatuation – but instead he felt the surge of rage washing over his body.

Pierre placed his hand on Damien's flexing arm when Damien began to move toward Julian.

"She's trying to seduce him! He's only eighteen..." Damien snarled softly, so only Pierre could here him.

His gaze dropped to Pierre's confining hand, suggesting without words, that he'd better remove it and fast. Pierre grinned.

"Julian's not much younger than she is. He isn't a boy either. Marie said all the women just love him. You'd know what *that* means, wouldn't you?"

"Get your hands off me, cousin." Damien growled, shaking Pierre's hand away.

"If you don't want her, set her free." Pierre refused to be intimidated.

"I did." Damien's eyes were smouldering with rage. "But not so she could go to another man. I'm her husband. God, she's like a bitch in heat. I can smell her from here."

"Damien, don't be so crude." Marie came gliding to his side. "Men can be so stupid. First, you teach a woman to – enjoy – then you act like fools when she does just that. Damien, she doesn't want Julian. Is it her fault Julian is infatuated?"

"She's doing a damn good job of pretending she does." Damien snapped, pouring out another glass of whiskey.

Madeline came to his side. He barely glanced at her. He was in no mood to play games tonight. Instead, he continued to glare at Bobbie. Her pixie-beautiful face was alive with brightness. She was listening to every word Julian said – and it was all in French! She hated Frenchmen!

"Merry Christmas, Damien. I hope you get everything you deserve." Marie's tinkling laughter grated on his nerves.

"Is she doing this for spite?" Damien groaned, puzzled. "Why? I only did what she asked. She wants to go back to Winnipeg. I agreed, and now she's acting as though I kicked her out."

"Are you so blind?" Marie squealed with glee. "You're so

good at courting women – you figure it out. Are you losing your charm?"

Damien glared at her, saying nothing.

"You could at least talk to her. She thinks you hate her." Marie relented.

"She knows I love her." Damien stated absently.

He was watching Julian's arm as it slid hesitantly along the back of the sofa. Julian's fingers were nearly touching Bobbie's bare flesh. The lecher! He'd kill him. He'd fire him now!

"If you love her then why are you having an affair with Madeline?"

Startled, Damien turned back to Marie. She was studying his features very carefully.

"An affair with Madeline? Don't be ridiculous. I would *never* do that. What would Joshua and Eileen say? It's Bobbie I want, not Madeline."

He didn't even see Madeline walk away. He was still watching Bobbie and Julian very carefully.

"Is that why she's doing this? Is she going to have an affair with Julian – to get even?"

"She's only talking to him." Marie smiled with satisfaction. "And Joshua and Eileen are very well aware that their precious daughter is no virgin. Isn't that why they were in such a hurry to leave Batoche?"

"You women and your damned gossip." Damien stated furiously, and then checked himself. He desperately wanted to hit someone or something. He thought Julian's face might do the trick. Violent fury licked inside.

"Would you like to go outside for some fresh air?" Pierre suggested softly.

Damien nodded, barely able to drag his gaze away from Bobbie. At least with Joshua and Eileen here, nothing would happen.

Once Damien left, Bobbie's forced gaiety vanished. She bid everyone a hasty good night and escaped to her bedroom.

Slipping her warm flannel nightgown over her head, she

crawled beneath the soothing furs. As she drifted into a light slumber, her thoughts were centred on that perplexing man downstairs. He had been livid and so jealous. Did he really love her? She dozed off, a smile on her lips.

She woke to some obscure sound. She searched the eerie darkness. No moonlight penetrated the thick clouds outside. Even the fire had burned out. Shaking her woolly head, Bobbie searched the room, seeing nothing. She sat up, moving to the edge of the bed. What has wakened her?

She listened carefully. Maybe Lisa was up. No, when Lisa woke during the night, she always came into Bobbie's room and was very vocal about whatever disturbed her. Flopping back to her bed – Damien's bed... She muffled a foul oath. She must forget about him. He would never move to Winnipeg and she would never leave her job. But very clearly, his arresting features formed in her mind. Slipping beneath the silky fur again, she thought about his mesmerizing caresses. Her body heated, tingling with stark desire. Exasperated, she rolled over to her back, trying to get comfortable again. That was impossible as well. So long as visions of Damien's beautiful face emerged, she could only squirm about with building need.

"Does it hurt, *mignonne*?" Damien's hand pressed against her lips, preventing her startled screech. "I sure hope so. It's *killing* me."

He couldn't be here now! This was too humiliating. She needed him too much. He would know. He would see.

Shame tingled her features. She'd sooner face a firing squad than see that devilish, knowing smirk in his eyes. Slowly she opened her eyes. She saw he had lit the lamp at the bedside. The covers, much too hot a moment ago, were crumpled up around her feet. He could see everything. That look was in his eyes. She groaned.

"Who were you thinking about – me – or Julian?" He whispered, staring into her eyes. Hypnotized, she could only stare back, unable to stop the happiness from flooding her features.

The lamp by the bedside cast eerie shadows along his taut, beloved face.

"Damien, shut out the light. Please?" She mumbled against his still restraining hand.

His other hand moved with deliberate motions to caress her aching breast. It slid dangerously down her abdomen and further... The feverish heat increased her desperate need. She arched up.

"Answer me," He ordered softly.

He was primitive, fierce drunk, and he looked ready to explode with violence. She wasn't afraid.

"Only you. Always you." Her head rolled back against the pillow as she licked against his hand. Excitement licked within.

Then his lips crushed against hers with savage possession. He moved ruthlessly against the softness. His tongue pushed inside her trembling mouth to circle hers, licking the contours with delicious skill.

His deep rumbling growl of passion terrified her. He was like a rabid animal out of control now. Fighting against the weight holding her down, Bobbie managed to free her swollen mouth. His fingers moved down to grope around her waist, trying to strip her nightgown aside. He tore the fabric with ease. When his lips moved back, ready to claim hers again, she opened her mouth and bit viciously into his bottom lip.

Startled, Damien drew back. His eyes cleared. Groaning, he slipped off. Rolling to his back, he threw an arm across his eyes.

"I'm sorry, wildcat. I'd sooner kill myself than hurt you."

"We can't go on like this." Bobbie's voice was bleak. "We're both sick!"

With disgust, she knew she would have feasted on his ravishment. They were both sick and depraved... She wanted him and she could never deny him, when he touched her.

"I'm sorry. I'm drunk and I know that's no excuse. I just want you."

"Do you know how many nights I wanted to come to you?" She turned away from his hypnotic eyes, trying to rub the shame from hers. She couldn't pretend anymore. "Do you know how many nights I've lain awake – needing you? Then one night – after you get drunk – you sneak in and try to rape me – like it's something sinful. And I wanted you to! If you hadn't – hurt me – I would have…"

"It wasn't like that." Damien whispered his denial. "You were ready before I even got here. I just needed you… and it's been so long… I wasn't – myself. I would never consider this – sinful."

"I was beginning to wonder if these people's opinions weren't rubbing off on you." Bobbie laughed, then sobered. "You're right. I am a weak idiot. I wanted you to ravish me… not so cruelly, but still…"

Unwillingly, she felt the tears roll down her cheeks. She caught back a sob. She was crying all the time now. What was happening?

His lean fingers clasped over her trembling mouth again. He pulled himself up, until his mouth was against her ear.

"Please don't cry. You're not the idiot. I am." He whispered softly. "You're right – we have to do something. Be honest for once – we both want each other too much to deny it."

"If you ever mention my lack of honesty again, I swear I'll kill you." Bobbie's eyes narrowed. "What do you want me to do? You ignored me for a month. Then you sneak in here and expect me to just…" She bit vehemently into his finger.

Muttering, he pulled back.

"It's your choice that we don't live together as husband and wife." He swallowed harshly. "You *begged* me not to touch you. What the hell do you want? Then you come downstairs tonight like some aggressive little slut. I noticed you left your door unlocked - for Julian, I presume."

"You couldn't trust me if your life depended on it." Bobbie sighed. It always came around to the same thing. "I leave the door unlocked because Lisa comes in when she wakes up and she screams if the door is locked. But you'd rather believe I'm up here entertaining men, wouldn't you? I've never let any other man touch me. Can you say the same? I don't *want* any other man to touch me. You can believe that or not. I don't care." Glaring up, she seriously considered slapping his accusing face.

His sultry eyes narrowed, daring her to do just that. The reckless, violence revealed he was not satisfied. He obviously needed an outlet for his burning rage and he'd chosen her.

"What's the matter? Are you getting tired of Madeline and want a *real* woman in your bed? I knew she'd just lie there like a lump of coal. I prayed she would." She wondered at the wild thoughts searing her mind. She wanted him angry. She wanted him violent. Then he would just take her and satisfy this horrible lust driving her mad.

"And you call *me* conceited?" He was grinning now. She felt his body relax. "Where did you ever get the idea I wanted Madeline? Don't you think I'd know she would just lie there like a – lump of coal?"

"Then why were you mauling her all month?" Bobbie hissed her jealousy.

"I wasn't." Damien continued to grin. He seemed very pleased about something. Placing his arm around her shoulder, he drew her tightly against his chest.

"Damien, can I ask you something without you getting angry?" She whispered.

She just couldn't keep up with his strange moods. One moment he was violent, ready to abuse her and the next he was so gentle her heart ached.

"I told you, I'd never hurt you." Damien turned his sultry gaze to her face. "You know that."

"Well, your temper is awfully intimidating and you expect me to believe you, don't you?" Bobbie murmured, looking out the window. "Can't I ask the same of you? I would never willingly leave you. Please believe me."

Damien stiffened. Bobbie winced. He would never believe her. Without trust, she couldn't stay with him.

"I said it doesn't matter." Damien tilted her chin around to stare into her pained eyes. "I want you too much to care."

"Want me?" Bobbie smiled faintly. Want – not love? God, she was pathetic.

"And I love you – too much." Damien growled, keeping her face to his. "I don't know why I'd put up with what I do, if I didn't."

He was grinning. Was he ever serious? And he didn't believe her. Why couldn't she accept that?

"You're wet, wildcat." With an enterprising manoeuvre, Damien had his hand up beneath her twisted nightgown.

"Ssh..." He murmured against her lips when she opened them to protest. His fingers increased the pressure, doing a delightful dance along her torrid flesh. She turned fully into his arms. She could no more stop what was happening, than she could stop the sun from rising every morning.

"Mommy."

She didn't hear.

"No." Damien rolled off her.

"Go back to sleep, Lisa. Go back to bed." Bobbie saw him speaking. Her eyes were passion-glazed. She could only feel – cold?

"Want a drink." She heard Lisa's voice coming from a long tunnel. Lisa?

"Yes, I'll get you a drink." Damien slipped off the bed.

Jerking up, Bobbie stared at Lisa, a blank expression on her face. Lisa's wavering face began to focus. Moaning her disgust, she flung herself back to the bed. She hadn't even heard her own daughter!

Damien was casually tucking his shirt back inside his trousers. His grin was wicked when her turned to Bobbie. Then he turned back to Lisa.

"It's nearly daylight. Let's go see what Santa brought you." Damien suggested. "Go get *Tante* Marie."

"Santa. Santa." Lisa ran out into the hall, screaming loudly.

Damien's features hardened. He sat on the edge of the bed, not touching her.

"You're still going to Winnipeg." It was a question and a statement. His jaw was tight and that muscle was twitching in his cheek.

"Yes."

God, it hurt. But not nearly so much as if she stayed here without his complete love and trust.

CHAPTER 26

Over three months later, Bobbie stood in front of her mirror and patted her undisciplined hair to ensure it would stay up in its neat braids. Already strands were escaping in an unruly mess. She sighed. Why couldn't she have lovely, curly hair like Marie?

Outside her bedroom window she could smell the blooming lilacs. She breathed their elegant scent with enjoyment. She looked into the mirror again and decided she would pass. Her eyes saddened as she reached up to finger the choker around her neck. Damien's unique, but beautiful necklace didn't really go with her black gown – another daring French creation – but she couldn't resist wearing it. She missed him. As spring swept over the lands she was finding her feelings going more and more to – loneliness. She didn't want to be alone. Then she grimaced. She may as well go out and get this chore done.

Damien's prediction had come true. The *Metis* had separated from the Dominion of Canada. They had declared their own country. Macdonald had immediately immobilized thousands of men and sent them to the west. It was treason.

Tonight those soldiers were in Winnipeg. The Winnipeg Social Club was having a dinner and dance in their honour. Bobbie didn't want to go. If Macdonald had answered Riel's letters, none of this would be happening.

Her father disagreed with her. She must go. She was a successful businesswoman in the community. These people she scorned were her bread and butter.

Marie came to her bedroom door, tapping lightly.

"Are you ready to go?" She came in at Bobbie's invitation. "It's nearly starting."

"I don't want to go." Bobbie whispered. "I know some of the people in Batoche and now I'm supposed to go cheer the men who are going to kill them off?"

"I know exactly how you feel. Pierre says we are Canadian citizens. The *Metis* in Winnipeg are not rebelling, thank God. And since we received this invitation it would look suspicious if we refused." Marie shrugged her shoulders. She moved over beside Bobbie. Her mouth rounded, going to Bobbie's neck.

"Is Damien going to fight?" Bobbie whispered, reaching up to gain comfort from the mysterious necklace. "He said he wouldn't."

"Where did you get that?" Marie whispered. "He gave it to you? My God, Bobbie do you know what that means?"

"This?" Bobbie looked down at the intricately twined quills, painted aqua, white and black. Then she saw the feather, lying calmly between the crystals. "No – what does it mean?"

"It means he really must love you – so much!" Marie was excited now. "He gave that to you? My God, do you know what it means to him?"

"This?" Bobbie frowned. "It's not valuable, you know." She winced at the accusing look of reproach in Marie's eyes. "Yes, it's valuable. It's the most important thing I own. What does it mean to him?" She remembered him saying – it was his most valuable possession.

"When his parents died – were killed, he said a hawk came down and brushed his cheek. He was only five at the time. He said the hawk left him a feather. He said that feather is what kept him alive. He knew one day he'd fly as free as that hawk, regardless of what he had to endure." Marie whispered. "He's here you know. He came to see Lisa again."

"Did he ask about me?" Bobbie asked with forlorn hope. She hadn't seen Damien, even once, since she'd come back. She knew he came to see Lisa numerous times. He'd made no effort to contact Bobbie.

"Don't be so stubborn. Why don't you just go to him?" Marie snapped, losing patience. "This is ridiculous."

"We never seem to be able to just – talk." Bobbie smiled. Every time they tried to talk, they ended up making love. Was that really bad?

"Let's go." Myles bellowed from the parlour.

The two women looked at each other and smiled. When Myles issued an order, they found it much easier to listen.

"You look so lovely, Roberta."

Bobbie's mother took her hand and squeezed as they entered the large Community Center gaily decorated with ribbons and bows. Long tables with white linen and sparkling crystal were set up on one side of the huge room. The other end was open for the dancing that was to take place after their meal. On a small platform in one corner, five musicians played their instruments softly. The flickering candles made the room look dreamy and elegant.

"Thank you, mommy." Bobbie smiled in surprise. Did Amelia understand that she was nervous and didn't want to be here?

"Did your father tell you his surprise?" Amelia asked as they seated themselves at the table their hostess indicated.

"Now, Amelia." Myles interrupted, patting his wife's hand. "She'll enjoy it so much more tomorrow."

"Enjoy what?" Bobbie was looking at all the strange men around. Her eyes turned sullen and apprehensive. She had never fit in very well in this type of social gathering. Surely her father knew that. "Do I actually have to dance with any of them?"

"Would you rather spend some time in jail?" Pierre interrupted. His eyes, behind his wire glasses, searched the room carefully. "There are many people here who know you're married to Damien. And Damien is from Batoche."

"And I know there's a least one person who might wish you harm, dear." Marie, seated beside Bobbie, stiffened. She was looking at the next table.

"I don't even know anyone." Bobbie protested lightly. Marie sounded so ominous. She turned to Pierre. "But Damien said he wouldn't fight!"

"No one here knows that." Pierre smiled. "Don't worry, Roberta. He's not going to fight."

Then the soldiers began filing into the room amidst explosive clapping and shouts of joy. A number of them were seated at their table. Bobbie's heart sank. There were so many! *Oh, Gabriel, you poor, poor man.*

She tried to smile as the men made their introductions. They all eyed her with eagerness, even after Sir Myles introduced her as Mrs. Roberta Larocque.

"Where's your husband, Mrs. Larocque?" Edward Barnes, the soldier seated near her, asked boldly. He didn't look any more than twenty years old and his eyes flared with open admiration.

"He's at our ranch near Battleford." Bobbie murmured politely, looking down at her plate.

"He let you come here alone?" Paul Bradford, seated across from her, leaned over the table.

"No! He left her with her father." Sir Myles inserted with dry humour. The men sat back to eat their meal.

"What's wrong?" Bobbie leaned toward Marie, who was once again glaring at the table next to them.

"That's Anne MacLeod." Marie whispered back, bringing her napkin to her mouth to muffle her voice.

Bobbie spent the next few minutes studying the woman who had hurt Damien so badly. Her heart sank. Anne MacLeod was beautiful. She couldn't understand why Damien would ever compare her to that gorgeous woman. Her blond hair was piled in careful disarray, atop her head. Her cheekbones were high. Tilted green eyes sparkled with life. Her mouth was luscious and full. And her figure was breathtaking in a royal blue silk gown. Her manners and bearing were impeccable.

"Don't look at her like that." Marie hissed. "That's all she does. She studies etiquette books – if she even knows how to read. She just mimics the gentry. She's really a slut."

"Marie." Bobbie giggled. Marie had a way with words. But she did feel much better.

Then the dancing began. Bobbie had more than her share of partners as the long night dragged on. She felt tired and only wanted to go home. Her parents were on the dance floor. She decided to ask her father if it would be all right to leave. When she noticed a number of men heading in her direction, she decided a breath of fresh air was in order. She couldn't stand the idea of having her feet massacred one more time by these awkward soldiers.

Slipping outside, she breathed in the fresh scent of lilacs again and sighed with pleasure. Above her, the stars and moon were as bright as daylight. The night was cool, but not cold. She wandered down the path leading around the Community Center. The scent of freshly turned earth from the flowerbeds assaulted her nostrils. She smiled. Maybe she would just wait out here until her parents came out.

Then she saw the two figures standing beside the corner. She recognized Damien immediately. She ducked behind a bush and felt a fit of giggles coming on. This reminded her just too much of the first night she'd met him. And again, he was with a woman. But who? It certainly wasn't Marie. She edged closer to hear their voices.

"I've missed you, Damien." The woman's husky voice was dripping with sexual tension. "No one can make me feel like you did."

"I don't care, Anne." Damien's voice was taut. "Get away from me before I strangle you."

Anne MacLeod. Bobbie felt like running out and scratching her evil eyes out. She didn't. But she did edge closer.

"Your wife looks like an insipid little child! She can't possibly make you happy. I know how you like it – savage and..."

"Shut-up!" Damien ground out. "She keeps me more than happy."

"Damien, be reasonable." Anne's voice hardened. "I can make things difficult for you."

"How?" Damien laughed rudely. "You didn't succeed before. No one believed I killed your husband."

"Things are different now. I know Judge Fairbanks and the Mayor." Anne's voice rose. "I know..."

"I don't care whom you know, Anne," Damien snarled, grabbing her wrist. He pressed down ominously. "Can't you understand – *I don't want you*? I'd rather die than touch you."

"What if I tell them you are here spying for your friends?" Anne hissed.

"You bitch!" Damien roared. His eyes were wild with fury. His hands moved up to encircle her neck. "Leave me alone."

"Damien – no!" Bobbie couldn't let him do what she wanted him to do. She stumbled from behind the bush.

"Wildcat?" Damien turned, glaring. Then his eyes cleared and he started to laugh. His hands dropped to his sides. Anne began edging back, towards the door.

"You – just wait." He grabbed Anne's wrist, yanking her back.

"What are you doing here?"

"I could ask you the same question. Are you a spy?" Bobbie felt foolish. He'd caught her, blatantly eavesdropping. But she couldn't just let him murder Anne, could she?

"What do you think?" Damien's eyes were alight with amusement. His gaze moved to her neck.

"Well, maybe I'll just go back in." Bobbie murmured, wringing her hands. "I'll let you finish your conversation, now that you're in a better mood. What are you going to do with her?"

"Don't you dare leave me alone with her. Any suggestions, wildcat?" Damien grinned, still holding Anne's wrist in a tight grip.

"Well, she did call me an insipid child and I wouldn't want to disillusion her too badly." Bobbie chuckled. Damien seemed very happy to see her. "Strangling her did seem right, but we're too close to all these soldiers. Why don't we just take her out into the wilds where we'll have all the time in the world to decide?"

"Good idea, wildcat." Damien agreed eagerly. "Let's go." He began pulling Anne toward the horses.

"Let me go." Anne found her voice. Her mouth rounded and in an instant Damien clamped his hand over it, muffling her screams. Anne's eyes rounded further, moving to Bobbie.

Bobbie could read the horror in their depths.

"Let's stake her out, until we decide. Please Damien." Bobbie continued. This was the most fun she'd had all evening. "It's been ages since I tortured anyone. Can I, please Damien..." Her lips curved in a mischievous smile. "Can I poke her with a hot poker again? That was so much fun."

Anne sagged in Damien's arms. Her eyes rolled in horror.

"I don't know, wildcat." Damien was obviously more than willing to play her game. "If we torture her too badly – do you think someone will come looking for us?"

"No, darling." Bobbie inserted smoothly, smiling at Anne. "Daddy will help us. He did before. He doesn't want me in jail."

"But she knows Judge Fairbanks." Damien protested.

"Yes, well..." Bobbie leaned up her tiptoes to whisper loudly in Damien's ear. "When he was over at our place playing cards the Judge did mention her – in that way. Rather intimately, he said. Daddy just laughed. He said all men need a mistress. Do you have a mistress, Damien?"

"Enough!" Damien let go of Anne as he clutched his stomach, bending over with laughter. Anne sagged to the ground, whimpering. "Was your mother there when – you played cards?"

"Of course not. She had retired for the evening." Bobbie moved to stand over Anne. She looked down with disgust at the sobbing woman. "Aren't you even going to try to run?"

"P-please let me go. I p-promise I won't tell anyone." Anne cried out.

"Tell them what?" Bobbie's voice hardened. She despised this pathetic woman.

"That you were going to t-torture me and..." Anne flung her hands to her face, weeping bitterly.

"Can you really imagine they'd believe you?" Bobbie's eyes narrowed. "I think it might be best if you just went home. Can you imagine the soldiers' reaction if you went in there and told them *I* threatened to torture you?"

"Yes. I'll go home..." Anne whimpered, slowly getting to

her feet. "I'll go home…"

They didn't try to stop her when Anne moved to her carriage.

"Do you think she'll say anything?" Bobbie turned to Damien.

Moonlight bathed his lean form with light. His beautiful face was etched clearly. She wanted to leap into his arms. It had been over three months since he'd kissed her.

"Do you think she's crazy, *mignonne*?" Damien studied her face carefully, not moving.

"Yes." Bobbie's eyes glazed with a need too powerful to deny. Kiss me!

"But not crazy enough to jeopardize her position in society, I think." Damien groaned. He reached out and pulled her against his chest. One hand moved up to tilt her chin. "*Mignonne*, when you have thoughts like this, how can I resist."

He kissed her then, deeply, erotically. His lips spread over hers with an eagerness that was almost violent. The pressure was paradise. Sticking the tip of her tongue out, it was Bobbie who made him open his mouth for her search. Like a man starved, he responded, pressing her small form to his. He held her and rotated his hips seductively.

Then he pushed her back, still holding her arms.

"Lets go in and dance." Damien took a deep breath.

"Yes." Bobbie's eyes sparkled with delight. The evening took on a whole new meaning. "The soldiers don't even believe you exist."

"Or more likely that I'm a fool." Damien grinned, taking her hand to lead her back inside. "They weren't too forward were they?"

"No. Have you been drinking, Damien?" She stopped and peered up at him suspiciously. Maybe she shouldn't take him inside.

"No. Are you ashamed of me, *mignonne*?" Damien stopped. Then he shook his head. He tugged on her hand, making her walk again.

"Never that, Damien. But will you be safe?" Bobbie panted,

nearly running to keep up with him.

"Because I'm *Metis*?" He asked softly. "Or because you think I might be a spy?"

"I don't believe that you're a spy." Bobbie stated emphatically.

The night passed like a fairy-tale come true. Damien was so charming and so beautiful, she refused to leave his arms. She loved dancing with him. His seductive teasing was impossible to resist. So she didn't try. For one night everything would be perfect.

He let her father take her home.

CHAPTER 27

Bobbie's surprise that her father and mother had talked about the evening before, arrived on the train the following afternoon. Gilbert arrived at her doorstep. She and her parents were just sitting down for tea in the front parlour.

Squealing her delight, Bobbie rushed into her brother's arms. Her father looked on, grinning. Her mother had tears in her eyes.

"Gilbert, you look fabulous." And she meant it. Gilbert looked the healthiest she'd ever seen him. "Come in and have some tea and cookies. I made them myself."

"You didn't?" Gilbert laughed. Taking a cookie, he bit into it gingerly. "Oatmeal. What else have you learned, dear sister?"

"I learned how to cook over an open campfire." Bobbie giggled. "Let me tell you a stove is much easier."

"Did he hurt you?" Gilbert's face paled. His gaze darted to his father, filled with apprehension.

"Oh no." Bobbie reassured him, taking his slender hand into hers. "Sit down Gilbert. Make yourself at home. I've married him twice already."

"Yes, but will you do it a third time?" Gilbert smiled, still looking at Myles as though waiting for him to say something.

"*And a forth and fifth into forever*" She wanted to say, but didn't. She couldn't understand her obsessive need for Damien and she was quite sure her family wouldn't either.

"Gilbert, are you back for good?" Bobbie asked instead.

"Well, yes." Myles finally interrupted. He stepped behind the sofa, placing his hands on Bobbie's shoulders. "That's part of the surprise. Gilbert would like to stay in Winnipeg."

Startled, Bobbie looked at Gilbert. He looked strangely uncomfortable.

"I've changed." Gilbert cleared his throat. "I was such a fool. I followed Etienne around like a dog – I'm ashamed to admit. Believe me, I had no idea what he was doing to father. I didn't know he was telling all those lies... about me."

"I know." Myles reached over to squeeze Gilbert's shoulder. "Now about Winnipeg..."

"Let me ask." Gilbert interrupted. "I think I hear Lisa. Perhaps you and mother could bring her in here. I've never even seen her."

"What's that all about?" Bobbie asked in amazement when she saw her father nod. There was a worried expression in his eyes. He left the room with Amelia.

"Bobbie." Gilbert leaned over to take her hands in his. He looked into her face. "Let's start at the beginning. You love Damien very much, don't you?"

"I..." Bobbie started, but she couldn't lie to her twin. "Yes, I do."

"He has a ranch in the middle of nowhere and you feel obligated to father and want to stay in Winnipeg to run the office." Gilbert continued, still not looking into her eyes. "Now, that could be quite a problem, couldn't it?"

"Partly." Bobbie sighed. What had her father told Gilbert? "That's only a part of our problems, Gilbert."

"That's the part Father knows." Gilbert shifted uncomfortably. "Father believes that if you didn't have the newspaper office, you'd be with your husband."

"I wish it were that simple." Bobbie murmured.

"Do you want to talk about it?" Gilbert asked. Finally he looked up into her face. "You look so sad, Bobbie. Can I help you?"

"Just tell me what Daddy plans to do." She whispered, instinctively knowing what Gilbert was going to say.

"Father has suggested that I run the office and you can go back to Damien." Gilbert blurted out.

"He would suggest that!" Bobbie scowled, not knowing whether to feel happy or sad. "So now he'll push me out in favour of you."

"Bobbie, it's not like that." Gilbert put his arm around her trembling shoulder. "If you don't want to go to Damien, that's fine. I would never push you out. You've done an excellent job here – much better than I could ever do. And Bobbie, I know Father's not the evil man, I always thought he was."

"Don't you think I know that Gilbert?" Bobbie groaned. Her mind was whirling with confusion. "I have to let this soak in for a bit. To be honest, I'm not sure I should be happy or sad."

"But Bobbie, surely you want to be with Damien."

"Yes, I do." Bobbie laughed softly. "But do you think you can run the office? Who will do the reporting? Things aren't much changed out there. It's primitive."

"David Ryerson is coming out." Gilbert explained. "I'd just manage the office here. But that's only if you want, Bobbie."

"I'm not sure." Bobbie shook her head. "Can I go out for a walk and think this through before I make a decision?"

Bobbie wandered the side streets of Winnipeg, trying to understand what she was feeling. She knew her father only wanted to see her happy. She was married to Damien and he was Lisa's father. Her place was with him at the ranch.

Her eyes turned dreamy. After last night... She winced. Had her father already talked to Damien? Then why would he leave? Last night she'd felt completely loved. Not since that wonderful winter they'd spent together in Montana had she felt so wonderful. But then with a chaste kiss, he'd left her. Was he truly letting her make this decision?

Her heart lightened. Damien couldn't forgive Marie. He couldn't forgive Anne. Yet going against everything he said, everything others said about him and even his own principles he was willing to forgive her. He must love her. And now, going against the very grain of his impulsive nature, he was not putting any pressure on her – letting her decide.

Her face lit with joy. She'd made up her mind. She would go to Damien and forget he believed she was capable of hurting Lone Woman or deserting him. He seemed more than capable of forgiving her – could she do any less?

Bobbie flung her satchel out the window after she was sure everyone was asleep. Lifting the glass higher, she crawled out and dropped to the ground. She stood waiting to see if anyone had heard her.

"You will wait until Damien comes to get you." Her father had advised just this evening. "Big Bear and Poundmaker have left their reservations. Poundmaker took over the fort at Battleford and Big Bear killed some people at Frog Lake. I hear they're on their way to Batoche."

Sir Myles painted a dire picture, but she didn't care. She wanted to see Damien! Her heart ached.

Damien would be proud. She was leaving – in the dark – by herself. She giggled. She knew April days could be hot, but also knew the nights were always cold. So she brought her warm cloak. Annabelle began a slow canter as soon as they left the stable. For hours she rode, in a north-westerly direction. She knew where she was going! The hills shone silver in the moonlight as frost settled onto the woolly grass. After hours of riding, she became weary. She held tightly to the saddle horn, knowing it wouldn't save her from falling if she went to sleep. Her nodding head moved in rhythmic unison with each jarring hoof beat. It would be well after midnight by now. Her aching fingers loosened. Eyes bulging, glassy with fatigue, she bit her lip in vexation.

After nearly falling from the saddle, she decided to stop. If she broke her neck, she'd never see Damien. She stopped by a clump of aspen near a slough. Annabelle's puffing breath coated the crisp air with a fine mist. Bobbie decided to start a fire. She ignored her father's warnings. Everyone knew she was Damien's wife. They wouldn't harm her.

She managed to get a small blaze started. She sank back against the ground, huddling into her warm cloak. Oddly, she wasn't in the least frightened.

Something prodded her side with soft intensity. Bobbie fought the waves of sleep engulfing her. Groaning, she rolled over to her side. It was daylight. Pink-streaked clouds cluttered together on the eastern horizon. Her eyes opened... and she looked directly at buckskin-clad legs. Slowly her gaze rose as her heart fell. Wandering Spirit! She sat up, shaking. Would he harm her or let her go? Behind him, a large number of braves gathered, all staring at her.

"Imagine meeting you here." Bobbie stated brightly.

"Robin." Wandering Spirit grinned his appreciation. Reaching down, he pulled her to her feet – by her hair.

"I was just going to Hawk's ranch." She whispered, rubbing her scalp. She watched him warily. What would he do?

"Ah!" Wandering Spirit's eyes darkened. "That coward. He will not fight."

"Let's go." He turned to his men.

Yanking Bobbie's arm, he dragged her to her horse. Throwing her into the saddle, he whirled and jumped to his own horse. Annabelle skittered sideways, nearly unseating her.

"Where are we going?" Bobbie asked hopefully. Her eyes darted around the prairie hills. Would he take her to Damien?

"Foolish woman." Wandering Spirit grinned again. "Hawk didn't teach you very well, did he?"

The fire! It was a foolish idea. But she had been so cold. She glared at Wandering Spirit. He hadn't liked her in Big Bear's camp and most likely still didn't.

"Are you still War Chief?" She asked. "Will you take me to Hawk?"

Wandering Spirit shrugged, smiling. He pulled his mount

beside hers. *"Don' unnerstand."*

"Don't I know that so very well?" She muttered darkly. "Are we going to Hawk's place?"

Was she his prisoner? He hadn't tied her wrists and that gave her some hope.

"Maybe I'm gonna keep you." Wandering Spirit chuckled. "You gonna like me better than that coward."

Bobbie shuddered. She felt the blood drain from her face. She looked around and nearly laughed at her stupidity. Where could she run? Wandering Spirit knew these plains like they were his backyard. Damien said Wandering Spirit was a very honourable man. He knew she was Damien's wife. She chose to trust him. He was just trying to frighten her. She tilted her chin.

"Don't like that idea? Well Hawk always had a way with women..." Wandering Spirit shrugged. Reaching down, he grabbed Annabelle's reins. He kicked his horse into motion, riding ahead of her, leading Annabelle.

They rode all day, without speaking. With a sinking heart, Bobbie knew he wasn't taking her to Damien. They should have been there by now. It was dark when they rode into the town of Batoche.

"What are we doing here?" Bobbie pushed her horse forward to ride along side Wandering Spirit.

"I'm telling Gabriel about the soldiers." Wandering Spirit admitted. Then he grinned again. "And I'm bringing him a prisoner. I understand you're an important person."

"You're what?" Bobbie's words hissed through her teeth. "You can't take me prisoner."

"Be thankful I didn't kill you, Robin." Wandering Spirit's frame stiffened. "I thought about it. That damn Hawk. But I'm not really upset with him. Everyone can do as they chose. And I like you Robin. Even if you are white."

Stopping in front of a shabby shed, he pushed her off the horse and into a man's waiting arms. Saying something in Cree, she didn't understand Wandering Spirit waved and disappeared around the building.

"Come on." She couldn't see her guard's face. He was behind her and it was dark. He pushed against her back with what she assumed was a rifle. She stumbled to the door. Opening the door, he pushed her inside and slammed it closed. She heard the lock being fastened. Her face paled when she realized she was actually being held prisoner! Hopefully the parts of Wandering Spirit's conversation she thought she'd understood were something to the effect of not harming her. Or was it just wistful thinking?

"I want to see Gabriel. Take me to Gabriel at once or you'll be sorry." Banging on the door, she screamed out.

"It's no use." Someone spoke behind her in the darkness.

There was another prisoner? As her eyes adjusted to the dark, she saw there were at least a dozen people, dozing on the floor. A few sat up in confusion. She stumbled towards the voice. Then afraid she might accidentally step on one of the scattered forms, she sank down to the floor, near the door. Her heart was beating frantically.

"Where are we?" She whispered, hoping someone might answer.

"In Batoche." Someone said. "Who are you?"

"I'm Roberta – Larocque. I'm a reporter." She answered uneasily. Should she admit Damien was her husband? Were all the prisoners men? Would they harm her?

"I'm going back to sleep." She heard a man yawn and realized it was a way of telling her to be quiet. The others were obviously sleeping too.

Although she was weary herself, she couldn't sleep. How long would they keep her prisoner? Would Gabriel let her go to Damien? Or did he think, like Wandering Spirit, that Damien was a coward?

Sometime near dawn, she managed to doze. A piercing jab in her ribs caused her to straighten her tilted, sore back. Dim trickling light shone through an unadorned window on the other side of the room. She noticed haggard, unshaven faces staring at her with hollow, vacant eyes. From all directions she heard weak gasps of shock. She was the only female in the room. She shifted, pressing against the wall. Good heavens, they all looked desperate and capable of doing anything. Then she smiled grimly. They were just prisoners, like she was.

"Good morning, gentlemen."

"As empty-headed as ever, I see."

Yelping, her gaze jerked up to lock with Damien's inflexible expression. For long, dragging moments, she could only drink in the glorious sight of him. He was alive. Her nightmares during the night had included visions of Wandering Spirit torching Damien's ranch and murdering everyone.

"Come on."

Tilting his head arrogantly, Damien turned and walked out the door. Aching, she followed, breathing in the fresh, outside air thankfully. She nearly upset him as she slammed into his hard frame, just outside the wooden enclosure.

Steadying her with one hand, Damien reached around to close and lock the door. Heavenly delight made her trembling and weak. She was with Damien again! He looked so – angry? Clenching her eyes together, she shook her head. She didn't want another lecture from him. She wanted him to take her into her arms and love her. Slowly, her long lashes flickered upwards, begging him to understand.

"Couldn't you wait until I could come and get you?"

"No. I wanted you – right now!"

"Damn!"

In suave motion, Damien pulled her around to the side of the tiny house. Bobbie offered no resistance to his passionate assault. His lean body slammed her against the rough boards. With rough urgency, his lips invaded hers. Strong fingers dug into her scalp. His mouth devoured her.

She responded, twining her tongue with his. Seeing she was offering no resistance, his hands aggressively moved down to gather her wrinkled gown into his fists. He urgently slid the material up to her waist.

She sagged back against the wall, whimpering. Her legs felt like rubber. His adhering mouth continued to feast on hers. His hand reached between her thighs, nudging them to part. When his finger touched that delightful spot that drove her wild, she couldn't stop the scream from exploding. She was dying with pleasure and she welcomed it completely.

She felt Damien's tongue nearly plunge down her throat. She rotated against his straining torso. Yanking his mouth away, he snarled low in his throat.

"Do you know where we are, wildcat?"

Her nails dug into his back, cutting into the buckskin smoothness. She tried to bring him back. He sagged to his knees. Without his support, she slid down with him. Trembling, Damien flopped to his back.

For a few moments she sat in stunned confusion. Why had he stopped so suddenly? From the bulge she could see outlined against his tight pants, he wanted this as much as she did.

"Oh!" She felt the heat rising in her face.

It was morning. People were moving by on the street mere yards away. A cowbell clanked in the crisp sunshine. A rooster crowed nearby. Voices floated around them. Only a fine-laced budding shrub offered them any privacy. She yanked her skirts down over her knees.

Rolling over, Damien jumped to his feet. He stood, towering over her. Apprehensively, she tilted her neck to watch him. He still looked furious.

"You cost me a night's sleep, wildcat." He squatted down. "When Wandering Spirit told me, I nearly died. You're afraid of the dark, remember?"

"Wandering Spirit told you?" She shook her head. "But he called you a coward..."

"Even if he thought that... he's my brother." Damien's lips twisted. Maybe she shouldn't have told him? "But he knows – I've got a lot to lose. He has nothing."

"I've never seen him – smile so much." Bobbie agreed. Then she turned her gaze to the ground. "Damien – I just had to see you. How did you get here so fast? Wandering Spirit brought me here last night."

"I was on my way here – to talk to Gabriel." Damien

reached out to place his palms on her cheek, tilting her head. "You're lucky he didn't kill you. They killed over a dozen people in Frog Lake."

"He told me that." Bobbie tried to smile as she gazed into his mesmerizing eyes. "But he likes me."

"Oh, wildcat." Damien's eyes brimmed with amusement. He leaned down to kiss the tip of her nose. "Of course, he likes you – he thinks you're brave."

"And he called you a coward. I was scared maybe he…" Bobbie whispered in confusion. "He still talks to you?"

"Yes. It's the way of the People. No one has to fight. They will respect anyone for who they are. Did you really brave the wilderness all by yourself to come to me?" Damien grimaced, lowering his lashes. "Why?"

"Because I love you and I want to be with you." Bobbie's eyes lit with sincerity.

"It wasn't because your father gave Gilbert your office?" Damien asked. Standing, he pulled her up. "Let's go."

"You knew? The other night at the dance – you knew?" Bobbie stopped him. "You didn't say anything. Why?"

"I wanted you to make that decision, *mignonne*." Damien began moving again, pulling her along.

"Damien, that's about the nicest thing you've ever done." Bobbie whispered in awe. Damien had actually had the patience to wait for her. Yet he was always so reckless and impulsive.

"I plan on doing a lot more – nice – things to you." Damien grinned with lewd intent. "But let's get home first."

"Will Gabriel just let me go?" Bobbie took Damien's hand. Together they moved towards their tethered horses.

"Of course." Damien squeezed her hand. "You're my wife."

"He doesn't think you're a coward?" She asked apprehensively. She still wasn't sure what his reaction to that was. She untied Annabelle. Damien lifted her up to the saddle before she had a chance to mount. His hands tightened on her waist. His face was grim.

"Do you think I'm a coward?"

"Oh no!" Bobbie whispered, leaning down to stroke his taut

jaw. "I think you're about the smartest man I've ever met. I saw the soldiers. There are more than two thousand in Winnipeg, right now. How many *Metis* are there?"

"A little over three hundred." Damien grimaced, then turned to mount Attila. "But still..."

"Don't you even dare! Remember I won't let you!" Bobbie turned Annabelle in a south-westerly direction. "Please, let's just go home. I don't think Wandering Spirit really thinks you're a coward – Hawk. He let me live. He told you where I was."

"He told me something else, wildcat." Damien's voice sounded strained. He pulled Attila along side Annabelle.

"What?" Bobbie asked. They set their horses to a canter.

"He told me that a soldier knocked you out that night by Fort Walsh." Damien spoke slowly. "He told me that you were fighting him and demanding to stay with – me." Lifting his eyes to hers, she saw they were filled with sorrow and regret. "I'm sorry, so sorry, my little wildcat. You're right. I should have known. I'll spend the rest of my life showing you how sorry I am."

"No!" Bobbie's eyes filmed with tears as her last concern slipped away. "No – spend the rest of your life loving me – Hawk."

CHAPTER 28

Damien's house was overflowing with people when they arrived back in the tree-covered Eagle hills. Julian was waiting to take their puffing horses to the stable. Inside they were greeted by clamorous voices. Lisa flung herself into Damien's arms and had no intention of ever leaving them.

Bobbie's father began a lecture on her foolish trek and her mother sat on the sofa, wringing her hands. Gilbert, Marie and Pierre all stood by the window, smiling and shaking their heads. It was mass confusion.

"Wait!" Finally, Damien passed Lisa to Amelia. He put his arms around Bobbie, drawing her close. "We haven't had any sleep yet. We'll talk tomorrow. I just got my wife out of jail and we need some rest."

"Out of jail?" Myles bellowed. "They put her in jail. Those...'

Relax, Daddy." Bobbie interrupted, smiling up into Damien's teasing face. "I wasn't harmed."

"Are you hungry?" Eileen came in, both hands holding plates piled with fried chicken and freshly baked buns.

"Is there more? Do you need help?" Marie reached out to take the plates. "I'll help you."

"No! We're not hungry!" Damien eyes were blazing as he stared down into Bobbie's animated features. "We're going to bed."

"I want to straighten this out." Myles insisted, still holding Bobbie's arm. "Where did they put you?"

"For heavens sake, Myles." Surprising everyone, Amelia had a frown on her normally serene features. "Let them go to bed. They've been riding all day."

"Not to mention – all night." Damien murmured in Bobbie's ear. He straightened and winked at his mother-in-law. "Let's go, wildcat."

"I think that's the first time she's ever told Daddy what to do." Bobbie giggled at the astounded look on her father's face.

Damien manoeuvred her toward the fur-covered bed as soon as they entered their room. His lips played with his unique talent along hers. His fingers skilfully unfastened her gown.

"I love you, wildcat." He murmured against her lips. As her gown slipped to the floor, he reached up to caress her neck. His choker surrounded it proudly. She would never stop wearing it again. "And I'm glad you're wearing my necklace again."

"What did you think I'd done with it?" Bobbie whispered, rubbing her hands along his lean, welted back with awe.

"I knew – when I looked into your eyes – that you kept it." Damien murmured along her lips, touching her in all the exquisite places she loved. "That's when I believed you."

"You did?" Bobbie yanked his face back, holding it in her palms. She searched his fascinating face carefully. "We've wasted all this time – when you knew?"

"It was your choice, wildcat." Damien said simply. His eyes blazed with passion. Then he grinned wickedly. "Now be quiet. Maybe later – we can talk. Now – just let me love you – gentle – slow – like this…"

"Oh yes… And you know you can always do anything you want. I'm very open to any – new suggestions. It's your choice, my darling savage."

He growled low and deep in his throat. He pulled her down to the bed.

THE END

To order:
HAWK'S GIFT

Fill out order form and send with cheque or money order to:
Mary M. Forbes

#1 - 3 Cactus Crescent
Osoyoos, British Columbia V0H 1V1
Phone: (250) 495-4906
E-mail: marymforbes@hotmail.com

	QTY	EACH	TOTAL
Hawk's Gift		12.95	
Shipping & Handling (one book)			2.75
Shipping & Handling (up to 5 books)			5.50
TOTAL ENCLOSED			

****

To order:
HAWK'S GIFT

Fill out order form and send with cheque or money order to:
Mary M. Forbes

#1 – 3 Cactus Crescent
Osoyoos, British Columbia V0H 1T0
Phone: (250) 495-4906
E-mail: marymforbes@hotmail.com

	QTY	EACH	TOTAL
Hawk's Gift		12.95	
Shipping & Handling (one book)			2.75
Shipping & Handling (up to 5 books)			5.50
TOTAL ENCLOSED			

PLEASE SEND BOOKS ORDERED TO:

ame: _____

reet: _____

ty: _____

ovince/   Postal Code/
ate _____ Zip _____

•••

PLEASE SEND BOOKS ORDERED TO:

ame: _____

reet: _____

ity: _____

ovince/   Postal Code/
ate _____ Zip _____